# Of Soup, Love and Revolution

# Of Soup, Love and Revolution

A. P. S. Daniel

© A. P. S. Daniel, 2016

Published by Celeiros Press

A CIP catalogue record for this book is available from the British Library.

ISBN 978-0-9954684-0-5

Book layout and design by Clare Brayshaw

Original artwork by Sharon Snaylam

Prepared and printed by:

York Publishing Services Ltd
64 Hallfield Road
Layerthorpe
York YO31 7ZQ

Tel: 01904 431213

Website: www.yps-publishing.co.uk

For family and friends.
For all who care.
For one thousand gifts.
Thank you.

# I

**May, 1974**

There are times when life doesn't seem real anymore. There are moments when it doesn't make sense and there are instances of distinct incredulity. The world is viewed as if from inside a misty bubble. Sounds and voices become distant and muted. Life shifts into another position, another dimension, sometimes for a while, sometimes for ever. It will never return to what was known and understood.

Rebecca's life had changed. She felt as though she were cast adrift in a small rowing boat, no longer anchored to the shore. Her sense of belonging, her sense of being needed and loved, so important to her, shattered. She may have deluded herself, but she had believed that she was in love and that she was loved too. Then suddenly, when her life had appeared neatly in place, he left, one cold, mizzily March morning, never to look back, never to return.

She was not alone, though she felt it. There were constants in her life, but as her world fell into the deepest hole, and she was lost in hurt, she struggled to recognise any worth. He had stood by the door with a huge suitcase. He had said he loved her, but not enough. They both deserved better. There was no one else. That was the only explanation he would give. It wasn't true of course and the discovery only wounded her more. There had been someone else for quite some time and she had not known. Rebecca hadn't wanted better either, having felt quite happy. She had had everything she wanted. Now being single again didn't suit her. She felt his absence like a huge empty space. She felt profoundly unattractive and chose solitude.

When Rebecca finally set off on her journey, she did not expect to be confronted with an echo of her own experience and so the effect was more acutely felt. The image of the old Paris apartment held firm in her mind like a still photograph. At first glance, there were signs that someone had been there recently. Carol had left only a short while ago. She had slipped out to do some shopping, to meet a friend, somewhere not far away. The apartment was tidy. It was almost too tidy. Rebecca looked around. There was an empty mug and a plate left neatly on a little glass topped coffee table. A bright red jumper was draped over the arm of the sofa. A newspaper had been left open on the floor. Rebecca checked the date. It was the 27th April. As she stared at the open pages, she wondered if the date was significant and felt concerned with no reason. It had not been that long since someone had been there. She was sure. Apart from the old newspaper, was there anything really out of place? Yet, as Rebecca stood in the living room, the darkness of the street outside pressing into the room, she felt unnerved. Something was wrong. The atmosphere seemed strange and uncomfortable to her. It was only a feeling, she told herself, remnants of her own memories, nothing more. She sat down, quiet and still, thinking. She drew the newspaper towards her and looked through each article on the double page where it had been left open. It was a French newspaper, of course and her French was rusty. She understood a little of it and soon tired of trying. Lost in empty thoughts, she began to look around the room. As she did, she was drawn towards the walls. The expanse of white paintwork was a little greyed in the dim light cast from one pale lamp. It was the only light she had turned on in the apartment, the first she had seen as she entered the room. The curtains were partly closed. There was the hint again of the darkness outside. She went to the window to close the curtains fully. She was conscious that she was a stranger in the apartment and had no desire to be seen. It troubled her to feel quite so ill at ease. The noise of the city was barely perceptible. The light was subdued. She was alone in an unfamiliar place. It was natural to feel unsettled, she thought. However, as she turned away from the window, she noticed something which had escaped her conscious thought until that moment. Every picture in the room was turned to face the wall. Each image, each photograph, whatever the frame held, was obscured from view. Rebecca looked around and then, resisting a natural reluctance to intrude, she began to walk from room to room. She found the same in every room in the apartment. All of the pictures were turned to face the wall. Why would someone do that?

The apartment was decorated in its own very particular style. The design was minimal, but not overly so. Every piece of furniture, each object was carefully placed. There was a narrow use of colours; blues and greens, hints and flashes of brightness mixed with neutral shades against the white backdrop of the walls. The softer tones connected each room. The deliberate placing of each picture moved to face the wall jarred with the well-thought-through scheme of each room. It jarred with Rebecca too. A wave of disquiet continued to swell and break. More fragments of the past began to flood into her mind. She remembered the emptiness of a house, abandoned but only in part. A wardrobe with empty hangers, drawers sparse, clothing removed. Books toppled over on shelves where favourite volumes had once been placed. A bathroom which had been stripped of one person's belongings; toothbrush, shaving foam, deodorant, aftershave. A deep sadness overwhelmed her as she connected with the memories again. It was another space, another time, but the mood returned, a stark, cold reminiscence. Feelings which had been pushed away rushed back in again, though she tried to stop them. She had been battered by the betrayal. She had been wounded, cut down by the decisions and actions of someone she had loved. She was torn by circumstances she could not affect. It had seemed out of her control. She had been left trying to understand her part in it, for many months destructive thoughts sabotaging her chance of happiness. It was so long ago now, she reminded herself. This distress was present. She went to sit down on the sofa in the living room, needing to think, wanting to be calm once more. She brought herself back to the apartment and wondered if she should stay. It was not good for her to be there, but she had agreed to come. She knew that she needed to see the evening through. It was not practical to try to find somewhere else to stay at that time of night. She would be on her way again in the morning. Nowhere would feel comfortable for one night in a strange city.

She pulled her rucksack towards her and took out her notebook to check the train times for the next day. Paris was simply a necessary stop over. Rebecca was making a longer journey. She was on her way to a small town in the south of Portugal called Vila Real de Santo António. She knew of it, but she had only heard it described. She had never been there. Of course, it would have been easier to fly, but, as she had made plans, when making plans was nothing more than a distraction, the idea of an overland journey came to her. When her plans were much clearer, the thought had stayed fixed in her mind. Now she did not know anymore why it had seemed so important. She liked the idea of a long journey overland. It seemed romantic to her. Each mile would be made real, as she watched the scenery streak by, sometimes changing suddenly, others only gradually, imperceptibly. She would experience the feeling of having travelled, in the way earlier travellers had experienced the journey.

Many people finding themselves in Rebecca's position would have stayed with what was familiar to them. It was her first instinct. Some would have got stuck in the hurt for a long time. Others would have moved on with their lives much more quickly, it was true. Rebecca had needed time. For a while, there was nothing she could do except exist. When she tried to understand, nothing made sense. The hurt refused to go away. The weeks wore on and as they did, feelings of longing and loss turned slowly, with no real awareness on her part, into a kind of nostalgia. Nostalgia had always been an emotion which Rebecca felt deeply and now she became conscious of a returning fondness for people and places she had known long before. Nothing had ever really been forgotten. She found also in those reawakening thoughts and warmly tinted memories, a strength which she had forgotten she possessed. She had always been able to salvage something from a mess, to make some good out of difficulty. That strength had been absent, but now she pushed slowly and determinedly to find a way out, becoming more certain that this disappointment would not shape her. It came to her gradually. She was not running away. It would have been a natural reaction which many would have understood but it would have been pointless. No one could ever really run away, the old self tagging along, only place and scenery changing. The more she tried to find a way through her feelings, the more she drew from the past. She transferred memories of distant experiences, pulling them into the present, lifting her spirit, searching out ideas. So it was that as Rebecca came round from her sadness, she looked backwards and had found a different way ahead.

Still, sitting in that abandoned apartment, she felt very sad. She was hurting again and she had no desire to feel that anymore. She looked at her watch. It was late, but not too late. She could go out for an hour or two. She would have something to eat, make a phone call. Rebecca took a small handbag out of her rucksack and searched for a pen. She wrote a quick note on a page of her notebook, leaving it open and then left the apartment.

# II

When Rebecca visited the apartment in Paris, she was making her second journey to Portugal within a year. Until that particular year of her life, she had never been to Portugal. Deep in her past, she had a passion for the country, untrodden though it might have been. She was captivated, she had said, from the very first time she had heard Portuguese spoken. She was enchanted by a language whose sounds flowed like music to her, lyrical, emotional and mellifluous. She hadn't felt any inclination towards other languages, other than any her education demanded. A friend had once said to her that people only feel inclined to learn a language properly when they fall in love. Rebecca preferred not to admit to having had any such motivation. Whether she would admit it or not, it was true that her fascination came from a chance meeting. At the time, it had certainly felt like love. She was still young, not quite sixteen and on holiday with the family in Cornwall. On the very first day at dinner, they had met a Portuguese family who were staying at the same small hotel. She had never heard Portuguese spoken before and it appealed to her. That is what she told everyone, the ever practical, ever sensible Rebecca. She didn't want anyone else to know how she felt. It was obvious to others, though that it was the eldest son who was most appealing. He was an excellent teacher but his motivation was as transparent as hers. When the holiday ended, she had made him a promise that she would continue to learn. She would write to her new Portuguese friend. They would see each other soon.

They didn't. Young and impressionable, Rebecca missed him so much as those first weeks and months went by. She took solace in what she prided herself was a true understanding of the Portuguese word, 'saudades'. Hers was a longing with no real possibility of return. It was a secret first love, felt so strongly at the time. Studying the language was a way to hold on to some hope and as if to make up for the loss, she continued to study with quite some dedication. Time and distance, lives far apart, growing up, the friendship waned. For Rebecca, the fondness never did. It was something of a burden to a young woman with a sensitive and feeling spirit. Certainly no one else had seemed good enough in the years which followed. Perhaps the difficulty in letting go explained why Rebecca's love of the language never disappeared either. She continued to learn, to read and to listen whenever she could. It was a hobby, a challenge, interrupted every now and then as life brought its own distractions and then inevitably, she met someone who made her forget. By the time she returned to her memories of the holiday, it had been years since she had heard from Ricardo. The letters had stopped a long time before. There had been Christmas cards for a while. Rebecca couldn't remember who had stopped sending them first. When life made a shift and the hurt rushed in, she looked for something to do, anything which might occupy her mind and stop the noise. She didn't know why, but she picked up the old textbooks and began to connect again with a different longing.

Some plans come to us almost fully formed. Others evolve gradually and so it had been with Rebecca as she tried to move on. Unable to sleep one night, she turned the dial on the radio next to her bed, searching for something different to listen to. She felt irritated by the crackling noise, the broken sounds and silences. Distorted humming transformed into words, French, Spanish, German, Dutch. The radio waves didn't seem to reach from that small strip of land in the far west of Europe. She felt disappointed. She tried again and again moving through the frequencies, lying awkwardly in bed to stretch over to reach the dial. It was when fatigue was finally taking over and she needed to lie back down that she heard a voice. It was a man's voice, a deep bass. It was a stylised, affected radio voice, faint and intermittent at first. She moved the dial carefully, a fraction each time, hearing the voice pulling through the noise and then losing it again. She settled on a weak signal and listened for a while, trying to make out the words before she fell asleep. She woke some hours later to silence. Some evenings the voice was quite clear, others, almost imperceptible, the signal drifting and turning to white noise. She wasn't deterred. Each evening, she tried again.

The radio station was making world service broadcasts, programmes for Portuguese living abroad. The presenters encouraged listeners to write or ring, to get in touch. Rebecca wrote down the telephone number and thought she might ring, but then thought again. What would she say anyway? Each day, the weak signal continued to frustrate her. She strained to hear through crackling, fading sounds and pieced together the address of the radio station in Lisbon, a little at a time. Writing seemed much less daunting than picking up a phone. She wrote and posted a letter before she could think better of it as an idea. She was surprised when she had a reply, almost by return. The letter was friendly and encouraging. An English woman trying her best to learn the language of a country she had never visited had its own appeal. She began to receive a stream of packages; audio tapes of radio programmes, sent in case she had missed them. The sight of the postmark lifted her, as she returned from work to find one small parcel after another on the doormat. Her contact must have raised some interest because it wasn't long before she received another letter and the suggestion of a language exchange, an invitation to visit Portugal. It lifted her. It seemed like the first light after so long of feeling sad. It was something to do, rather than the nothing she felt and so she made the first journey, ready to drown her mood in another experience, another language.

Rebecca's contact was one of the administrators in the news office. Her name was Clara. French was her second language, she told Rebecca, but she wanted to improve her English. It would be far more useful to her at work. An exchange seemed the perfect solution for both of them. Rebecca took a flight to Lisbon on her first journey to Portugal. It was the September of 1973. She walked down the steps from the plane on a warm, sunny day in late summer. She had arranged to meet Clara at the radio station and arrived in the city on the airport bus. With a map in hand and her small rucksack on her back, she made her way uphill from the centre towards the radio station. Clara had said that she wanted to show her around and Rebecca, who had never been in a radio station anywhere in the world, felt quite excited to have the opportunity. When she arrived in reception, she asked for Clara and only a few minutes later, Clara burst through the door, smiling. She was exactly as Rebecca had imagined from her letters, chatty and enthusiastic. She didn't make any attempt to speak English and so Rebecca had to try her best to speak Portuguese from the beginning. She had to work hard to understand everything that Clara was saying, trying desperately to remember all she had learnt. The words came into her mind frustratingly slowly. Clara led her into the building and to the news room. She wanted to show her first of all where she worked.

'I like my job very much,' she explained, though it seemed obvious to Rebecca and she felt a pang that her own work did not make her feel the same.

She realised as Clara continued to talk that she did not know much about the country at all. She loved to read and knew something of the literature, of the art, the history, but not much at all of the present. She wasn't interested in politics. She found it difficult to follow. She hadn't given it much thought. There was a dictatorship, she knew that, but it didn't seem relevant to her. Tourists were encouraged and visitors seemed welcome. Clara began to talk about the news stories she was working on and as Rebecca listened, she wasn't sure how settled life in Portugal really was. Her impression of the country had been distorted. She had been listening to radio programmes about culture; music, history and literature and it had given her a rather idyllic perspective. These were difficult times. Rebecca felt a little unsettled but she was determined not to let anything affect her mood. She told herself not to worry. This was a big city and she wasn't used to them. It was natural to feel apprehensive. She reminded herself that Clara worked there. She lived there very happily. Rebecca wasn't going to be on her own.

Clara's tour took them into the basement and to a line of studios. The rooms all had large windows, each one allowing a view of the radio presenters and producers working on their radio programmes. Clara ignored the red 'on air' light and walked into one of the studios, standing inside the doorway. The presenter was clearly in the middle of a broadcast, but she didn't seem to care and no one seemed to mind. Rebecca hung back. The presenter beckoned both of them inside, motioning to them not to speak for a second. As she listened, she recognised his voice. It was the very first voice she had ever heard on the station, the deep bass tone of the practised DJ.

'Come in, come in. I've put a record on now, so we're alright for a couple of minutes,' he said, looking at Rebecca.

Clara introduced her to Bruno, a good friend, as well as a colleague, she said. Yes, Rebecca was sure now. She had heard his voice emerge through the white noise. Typical, she thought, a very confident guy and then was disarmed when his first question was to ask if she wanted to be interviewed on air when the record finished.

'It'll be really interesting for the listeners to hear an English woman talking about how she comes to want to speak Portuguese. My listeners will love it.'

Bruno was broadcasting to Africa, he explained. In a panic and looking to Clara for support, Rebecca declined, shaking her head, not wanting to speak in case her refusal in unsteady Portuguese was misunderstood.

'Another time, perhaps, we're heading out for something to eat soon.' Clara came to Rebecca's assistance.

'I'll be finished in twenty minutes. I'll come with you, I'm really hungry and I'd like to hear more about your friend.' He smiled and winked at Rebecca who smiled back nervously.

Rebecca checked a glance at Clara who seemed more than happy for him to come along. They left him to his programme and finished the tour of the radio station, arriving back where they had started in reception. Bruno turned up in the foyer, a little later than he had said, as seemed to be the way, Rebecca would learn. He was relaxed and in no hurry, despite having declared his hunger earlier. Clara had been chatting. She hadn't seemed to notice the time either. There was a small restaurant nearby which Clara and Bruno explained they knew well. Leaving the radio station, they made their way straight there crossing over the main road. As they walked into the restaurant, they exchanged greetings with the owner. It was almost as though they hadn't visited for weeks, though Rebecca picked up that they been for lunch the day before. She noted and liked the closeness. Clara ordered as they were sitting down and they didn't have long to wait before a large platter of Frango à piri-piri, pieces of barbecued chicken cooked with a chilli sauce arrived on the table. The chicken was served with chips, a small mound of rice and a mixed salad, fresh and crisp. The conversation flowed around Rebecca and from table to table. Every now and then, she was lost in words and sounds, not always understanding everything she heard. She was aware of feelings which were contradictory, her mind moving backwards and forwards between each thought. There she was, facing a month in a strange place with people she didn't know. Yet, everything seemed familiar to her on that very first afternoon in Portugal.

To be in Lisbon on her first visit to Portugal was, she would reflect later, the very best introduction to Portugal. Cities had never been her favourite places but this one was an exception. Clara was an excellent host. Rebecca's language skills improved quickly, mostly because Clara refused to speak any English. They visited some of the sights together. Exploring the city centre by the river, Clara showed her the two main squares and they wandered up and down the crisscross of streets, lined with elegant eighteenth century buildings. They climbed up past the cathedral to the castle with its wonderful views of the city. On the same day they travelled east along the river. Clara wanted Rebecca to see Belém. She led her from the tower and the Discoveries monument, perched on the river bank and on to the monastery. These were the city's famous icons which Rebecca had only seen in her guidebook. As she approached, each seemed unreal as though she were looking at a huge photograph. Clara's explanation flowed almost without a breath, as she pointed out the monastery's Manueline architecture and talked about the voyages of discovery. Rebecca was impressed and said so,

'You know such a lot.'

'No more than most people would. We're very proud of our heritage. We were once a great nation, you know. Shame it's such a long time ago,' she said laughing. 'Come on now. I'll introduce you to another great tradition. I think you're going to like it,' she added leading the way across the street and heading into a café whose décor was also of another time. A country fixed firmly in its past. In that little café, the Antiga Confeitaria de Belém, Rebecca had her first taste of a pastel de nata, the little custard tarts in their flaky pastry shells which were to become her favourites. Rebecca liked Lisbon. She found it strangely comfortable and staying with Clara, there were times when she almost forgot she was a visitor. Clara needed to work and wasn't always around. She made sure that Rebecca had something to do each day and more than not, someone to go with her.

Those observing Rebecca across the months of that year might have admired a strong woman who seemed determined not to let a breakup define the rest of her life. Rebecca recognised none of that. She had felt there was nothing left. She still struggled with a deep sadness. She had seen an opportunity to travel, nothing more, and even that had been a challenge. Andy had always been there for her. She had never been alone. Her naturally shy nature, which some mistook as loftiness, made a trial out of meeting new people. Now she felt even more self-conscious and awkward, unloved. However, once in Lisbon, it was different. She didn't want to hide away. She became lost instead in a place where no one knew her and absorbed in a language which allowed her to express her feelings as never before. She found a people who were kind, friendly; they had a courteous familiarity which suited her. Life wasn't easy for them, she was sure, but it had not defeated them. Rebecca's new friends encouraged her to return and long before the end of her stay, she knew she would. Here was somewhere she could be happy. Here was the chance to start again. Without much encouragement, she would have stayed but it was a holiday and she needed to get back to her work at the bank. By the time

Clara came over to visit her in England only a few weeks later, she had made her decision. Her days were routine, her job offered little chance of change; it was easy to leave. Clara had invited her back to Lisbon and Júlia had suggested she spend some time in the Algarve. Júlia, one of Clara's colleagues had joined the radio station much more recently. Rebecca and Júlia had a natural connection. Rebecca admired her. Júlia was determined to be a journalist. She had found work in Lisbon after she had finished university in Coimbra. She had had to leave home for the chance to follow her career and make some difficult decisions. She seemed so much braver than Rebecca had ever dared to be. However, there was another reason why Rebecca accepted her invitation with almost no need to consider. Júlia was from Vila Real de Santo António. Her family lived there. She went back as often as she could, she said. There it was, the town Rebecca had heard so much about, only a few kilometres from Castro Marim. She had never been but had so wanted to go there all those years before. Over the next months away from Portugal, Rebecca's desire to return became more and more compelling. Her certainty as to where she would go for her year abroad was almost complete.

# III

## 25th April, 1974

It began with music. The song was a sign to those who knew and were waiting. The radio played 'E depois do adeus', 'And after the good-byes'. A voice was heard across the airwaves just before eleven o'clock at night on the 24th April 1974. As everyone held their breath, an hour and a half later, 12.29am, another song, 'Grândola, vila morena' was sung by the songwriter, Zeca Alfonso. The long hoped for revolution began. The troops moved in as music continued to play. The presenter at the radio station was defiant. He ignored the bans and the censorship which for so many years had forbidden the songs he was playing. Announcement after announcement punctuated the broadcasts that day. The leaders of the armed forces wanted to avoid bloodshed. They called for calm, for citizens to stay at home and for the police not to resist. By half past seven in the morning, Captain Salgueiro Maia was standing in the Praço do Comércio, the main square by the river. He made a powerful show of strength, two hundred men gathered besides a battalion of tanks.

Clara had been at the radio station all her working life. It was a job which she loved. Across the years, others had questioned her lifestyle. Her independence was important to her. Her work was everything. Clara loved being at the centre of news, knowing so much. She loved her country and hated the poverty and hardship experienced by so many under the dictatorship. Hers was a country changed little in almost fifty years. People knew no other way of life. She had lived no other, but held firm that there was a better way. Clara had strong political views, but wasn't known to express them openly. Indeed, she quite purposefully kept them quiet. She made herself unobtrusive. She listened. She made little comment, other than would have appeared usual and simply got on with her job. Clara was not one of the many who had come to Lisbon escaping other lives, looking to break away from poverty. She was born in the city. Her family had lived there for at least three generations to her knowledge. She was single and saw herself as a truly liberated woman at a time when it was still seen as unusual, almost unacceptable. She had loved, but had always stepped away, not wanting to give up a cherished way of life. It would have been inevitable. She worked hard and had her own apartment in the city. It was a matter of pride, a demonstration of her self-reliance, not a necessity. Clara had inherited a small house in Sintra, a retreat from the city at weekends and in holidays. At work, she was friendly with colleagues, going out for lunch, occasionally for dinner, but never encroached on their lives at home. The only real closeness was with an old friend and two of her neighbours. She talked little about her own life. Some might have accused her of being a loner. Others described her as a little secretive, which raised some suspicions. None felt they knew her well, but Clara was liked. Colleagues found her amusing, always open to interesting ideas. She had spent time in France in her early twenties and took a keen interest in international affairs, as much as censorship would allow. It was no surprise when she volunteered to look after an English visitor.

In the months after Rebecca's first visit and more than any other time Clara could remember, the mood in the country was tense. She followed events closely. She felt both concern and hope, as resentment grew amongst officers in the army. It was not surprising there would be trouble. The government demanded more from the country and from a people already fully stretched. An enduring conflict in the African colonies, over ten years of useless struggle, was taking a huge toll. Few supported it. Most thought the wars unwinnable. More began to resist. Officers met in Obidos, north of the capital, to discuss how they could respond. They would strike against the government if they had to. Government ministers found out. They made no response. They were used to absolute power. They seemed unable to deal with the impertinence of challenge. More dared to say that the conflict must stop, seeing diplomacy as the only way to end the wars. The government continued as before, a mixture of resistance and inertia. Marcelo Caetano had taken over from an ailing dictator, Salazar, back in 1968. The changes he tried to make had satisfied few and challenge had bubbled up across the years. Finally, Caetano took action. He dismissed some of those resisting his authority, arresting officers and transferring others abroad. He tried to diffuse the opposition. Those like Clara who watched felt a mixture of excitement and fear that finally the country might be on the brink of real change.

The radio station was a natural target. Each day, there were rumours and reports of unrest and uprising. The threat was real and danger anticipated. March 16th had been a particularly tense day. When news came through that a large group of military personnel, as many as two hundred men from the garrison at Caldas da Rainha, had driven into Lisbon in armoured vehicles, everyone stopped and waited. The threat was over quickly. There was no violence to speak of and the men soon surrendered to troops who remained strongly loyal to the government.

Across all the years, there were those at the radio station who worked covertly for the resistance. If colleagues suspected, there was no acknowledgement. On the 25th April, 1974, it was a DJ at another station in the city who dared to lead the way. He played a well-known song, the agreed signal for the revolution. It was music which was forbidden but not forgotten. Despite the building fears, what happened on that particular day had not been anticipated, at least not by Clara. Unbeknown to others, she was close enough to the cause, but she had never been party to that kind of information. If she had been alerted to the fact that the challenge was imminent, she reflected afterwards that she might not have chosen to be at work that night. She had taken risks before, but they were calculated risks. The first she knew of the revolution, there was shouting, a huge commotion in another part of the building. Her instinct surprised and disappointed her. She hid beneath the large desk which had been her workspace for years. It seemed to her an obvious if not completely safe place to be at that moment. There she stayed, for what seemed a long time, her long dark hair pulled over her face, as if to protect her, until the commotion died down and she no longer felt the need to hide. So Clara, as brave as she had proved herself to be at times, was not so brave that night and spent at least part of what turned out to be an historic night, under a desk. For years afterwards, she told the story of how she had been there, right in the middle of the action. She was honest about her lack of courage, admitting it made her feel a little better.

Júlia wasn't working that night and she wasn't listening to the radio. She was fast asleep and when she did wake up, she was in a rush as usual, throwing on her clothes and heading out for work. She would stop at a café and get a coffee on the way. Like her, not everybody had heard the appeal to stay indoors. There were many others who had, but were too curious not to venture out. As she passed the local school on her way to the bus stop, she saw some parents with their children. They were talking to a couple of teachers at the school gate. For some reason, it didn't look to her like a normal school morning. Ever alert to a story, she crossed the road to go and see if there was a problem. The school was closed and one of the teachers, excited by the news of revolution, was explaining to the parents what he knew, which was very little. One of the parents mentioned the failed attempt at a coup by the troops in March and was dismissive of the teacher's insistence that this was revolution. Júlia wanted to understand more but any information they had seemed confused. If there was a revolution, no one seemed to know who was leading it. One of the mothers said she was going home and urged the others, including Júlia, to do the same, but Júlia was now keener than ever to get to the radio station. This was not a day she wanted to miss. The buses were not running, she was told. One of the teachers said he was heading into the centre to see what was happening and offered her a lift which she was pleased to accept. It wasn't easy to drive into the centre. The police were already diverting traffic away from the city. They got as close as they could and parked the car, deciding to make the rest of the journey on foot. On first view the morning, whilst a little quiet, seemed to be unfolding as any other normal day, but Júlia noticed that one of the banks was closed. It was unusual, now beyond the normal opening time. When they reached the centre of the city, they found the streets full of soldiers, huge tanks dominating even the tiniest of narrow streets, holding back the gathering crowds. Júlia tried to find out more but was met with the same confusion from everyone she asked. She decided to make her way to work and found the building surrounded by troops. She showed her identity card and was allowed in to work. The radio station was an important voice and one which the soldiers were there to protect.

Inside, Júlia found that none of the night staff had gone home. Even if they had felt they could, they didn't want to leave. She went to look for Clara to see what she knew. Full of the night's events and still nervous and excited, she explained what had happened. The dictatorship was disintegrating. Information was coming through that the Prime Minister, Caetano and President Tomás had sought sanctuary. News rolled in all morning, 'Golpe Militar', Military Coup; 'Amplo Movimento das Forças Armadas' 'Substantial Armed Forces Activity'. Clara explained that the radio station had been taken over in the early hours of the morning. They heard that the airport had fallen, then that General Spinola's troops were in the main square by the river. Apparently, tanks were also positioned on the opposite side of the river facing Lisbon. As the morning progressed, more troops joined the revolt and by lunch time, the General announced they were in full control. The PIDE, the feared secret police, were holding out. It was a worry. Troops had surrounded their headquarters. Some political prisoners were quickly released. In the afternoon, political groups started coming out in support of the coup. By the end of the afternoon, the Prime Minister had surrendered.

Leaders of the armed forces movement leading the coup continued to feed information through to the radio station. Like the television stations, they were asked to broadcast the message: 'We have liberated the people from a regime which has oppressed them for many years.' Other news came through quickly. The radio station continued to be a target for whichever faction was trying to seize power or wrestle it back. Júlia and Clara admitted to each other that they felt nervous. They heard that the PIDE was resisting the army, refusing to give in. That was the greatest threat. The crowds were angry. People had hated the PIDE for so long. The PIDE's officers were ruthless. They had wreaked fear across the country with arrests and torture for decades. If the coup was successful, they would not be shown any pity. News came that there was a crowd outside the offices of the PIDE, intent on setting fire to the building. Inside, officers were armed with machine guns. The crowds had nothing to fight with, only anger. Shots fired out from the windows. People fell to the ground. Five lay dying. Many others were wounded.

In the newsroom, radios were tuned into foreign stations to see what else was known. News at home was confused. As they listened to each report, nothing seemed any clearer. It was certain that no other country reporting the coup had any idea who was in charge either. The mood became calmer, but no one felt like leaving. In the lull of even the most intense of days, it is strange how quickly thoughts can turn to very basic needs. It was no different for Clara and Júlia that evening or for their colleagues, and so they went out in search of something to eat. They didn't need to go far. The kitchen wasn't supposed to be open but the owner of their favourite restaurant was pleased to see them. Some of the regulars had gathered there together and were anxious for news, no matter how limited. Clara and Júlia stayed a while telling them what they knew and returned to the station with supplies; sandwiches, roast chicken and cakes. No one slept that night. There was too much tension for anyone to be interested in trying to rest. The next morning, they decided to go into the centre of the city to see what was happening. Even early on, the streets were full of people. It was a stormy morning which only seemed to add to the mood. It was raining heavily. Lightening filled the sky and thunder cracked through the noise of the crowds. Tanks rumbled through the streets.

It was exciting to be in Lisbon. Júlia had had a phone call at work the night before from her parents who were concerned. They wanted her to go home. She understood, but at the same time, she felt irritated. She reassured them she was quite safe. She was protected by more soldiers than they could imagine, she told them. The next days were busy. She returned to her apartment for only a few hours at a time. She wanted to be at work. Neither Clara nor Júlia's work required them to be out in the city but when they could, they went out amongst the crowds. Reports came into the office that people were heading to the Chiado hunting out PIDE officers who they were sure lived in that area. It was close to the office and so they decided to go and see what was happening. Bruno who had finished broadcasting, grabbed his coat and went with them. They arrived to find huge crowds. This time, there were no celebrations, only fury. Only the presence of the army was stopping many of the PIDE from being lynched by the crowd. There was outrage, the anger of so many years bursting out. They weren't prepared to forgive or forget the beatings, the torture, the horrific violence, the humiliation. The crowd yelled. People screamed abuse and threats towards those they thought to be PIDE officers. A car was overturned, doused in petrol. Flames leapt into the air, any sense of control lost in the baying crowd.

'Let's get out of here,' Júlia yelled over the noise of the crowd. For once, she was really scared. She began to walk quickly away from the crowds. Clara and Bruno followed.

'Rebecca is coming over fairly soon. Do you think we should tell her to postpone her trip?' Júlia was talking fast as she continued to walk. She needed to close her mind on the scene, discuss something more mundane, more ordinary.

'She's coming over for a year and has been planning it ever since her last visit. I'm sure she must know about the situation and if she doesn't already, she will soon. It's been reported in Britain. She'll get in touch if she's concerned. She'll delay her journey if she feels she needs to. I don't think we should worry her. It could be very different by then. She's not coming for a month or so,' Clara reassured her, needing too to keep talking.

Rebecca avoided the news. It depressed her. It made her sad and she felt she had had enough upset. She connected strongly with the hurt when there was nothing she could do to help. So she had determined not to watch news reports, and for months she had done nothing more than check headlines. She didn't want to live in complete ignorance, but she did want to avoid the negativity. It was all too much and it was quite easy to ignore. She was busy making plans for her journey.

# IV

## 25th May, 1974

Rebecca may have made a decision not to watch much news, but it was hard to avoid the mood of her own country. It seemed that everywhere she turned, people were commenting on the recession, strikes, unemployment, and the threat from the IRA. At times, she was fearful of travelling anywhere and certainly avoided cities whenever she could. It troubled her but she was determined not to have anything get in the way of her journey. The revolution almost passed her by. Had she known much more, it might have concerned her. The little she did hear focussed on a peaceful coup. There were reports of red carnations, soldiers and citizens happy together, celebrating. The scenes appealed to the romantic view she had of the country. She felt sure that if there had been any real danger, Clara or Júlia would have told her.

There was a train station only a twenty minute walk from home and another on the outskirts of the Portuguese town where she was heading. Rebecca loved the idea that she could walk out of her house in England, get on the train at the local station, then keep travelling over land, until a thousand miles later, she would arrive in Vila Real de Santo António. She had booked the overnight train from Paris to Lisbon where she intended to stay for a couple of days. It was necessary to make a stopover in Paris on the way down, especially now she had agreed with Tom that she would stay at his sister's apartment in Paris overnight. Rebecca had known Tom ever since she was at school and had stayed in touch on and off across the years as part of a larger group of friends. Straight after university, they had worked in the same area and had seen quite a lot of each other for a while. They had always got on. Strange then that they seemed to lose touch so quickly, new lives bringing different distractions for each of them. Rebecca reflected that she had missed him. Tom was kind, unconventional; a little deep and quiet at times. Even when they were growing up, he had moved from one small crisis to another, from one love to another. It had always been the same. She hadn't thought about him for a while and she hadn't expected to see him. The last she had heard, he was living in the south of France.

Rebecca did not do weddings, which seemed to put her at odds with most people she knew. Still, it would have been her stated position if asked. She had never wanted to be the centre of attention in anything and certainly not a wedding. She had often wondered if there was something more fundamental in her feelings and that her resistance was not helpful to her happiness. Maybe she had never met the right person, even though she had been convinced she had. She loved other people's celebrations and to see other people happy. She would admit to being an incurable romantic, believing there was a soulmate out there for everyone, but often wondered why people could not be a bit more discerning, especially when she listened to the frequent complaints of married friends. Some women thought men were unfaithful, almost by nature. Despite her own disappointment, she refused to accept the stereotype. When a man fell for someone, he felt it deeply. People simply needed a bit more patience, but everyone around her seemed to be getting married, when she was so distinctly on her own. The problem with weddings was that they were a reminder of the hurt, of what she had lost.

When the invite had arrived, Rebecca hadn't been sure if she could make it to the wedding. She didn't know how she would feel. It was to be an informal affair though, in the late afternoon, nothing more than a reception, a party. There wasn't any excuse. Deborah and James were good friends. They had always been there for her. She needed to think more about others, put her issues aside. Anyway, this wasn't a wedding. Deborah and James were already married. Rebecca approved when others were critical. They had got married on holiday. This event was a celebration, a formal recognition of their marriage in front of friends and family. It was a party organised to appease aggrieved parents who did not understand why they had to get married in private. Rebecca loved it. It was romantic. She had already forgiven them for missing out on the opportunity of being a bridesmaid and having another big frock.

As Rebecca parked the car and walked up the driveway towards the front door, she was wondering who had lived in the house. It must have been someone rather grand, a country residence at some time, perhaps part of it still was. As she walked into a magnificent hallway, she noticed a long table displaying leaflets, a brief history of the house. Conscious of being on her own, it was tempting to have something to read. She felt awkward walking into a room of people, no one at her side anymore. She resisted her thoughts and walked on. She was later than she had planned. Nothing she had to wear seemed right and anyway, she had not wanted to be early. There was no one else in the hall, the room was full and people were already seated or chatting in groups. There was a baby grand in the corner at the front and someone was playing a song which didn't seem quite appropriate; 'Strangers in the Night'. Trust James to want to have some fun. He had wanted a party and anyway it was how they had met. The room made an impression. It was decked out with huge bunches of flowers, blooms in pinks of every shade. The handy work of James' mother, she loved a display. The chairs were laid out facing the front. As Rebecca sat down at the back, she noticed two old friends from university. She waved, smiled and mouthed 'hello', wondering if they had come together. She was curious. They had been fond of each other, although they had always insisted they were friends. Rebecca smiled. She felt that she was quite good at recognising when people should be together and was pleased she had been right. She looked around. Sitting at the back, it wasn't easy to tell, but she began to recognise more people she knew. It would be good to catch up after all.

It wasn't long before James, Deborah and their parents joined the guests. James took the lead, thanking everyone for coming and saying a few words about the ceremony that had already taken place. James and Deborah repeated their commitment to each other in front of friends and family. It was something both parents had wanted. There were smiles, laughter. There were some tears, despite the informality or perhaps because of it, but everyone relaxed as the only formal part of the day was out of the way and the celebration could get underway. It was a gorgeous late May day, a little breezy but the sun was shining. Rebecca could see a terrace through the window and what seemed to be miles of countryside stretching beyond the grounds of the house. She was drawn by the view to go outside as soon as guests began to get up from their seats. Even better, drinks were being served on the terrace. What a great idea to have the reception here. The guests could wander and relax while all the photographs were being taken. She had more time now to consider the house. It was a huge white Georgian building, with a long, wide driveway to the front and a fantastic aspect to the rear. It was elevated on a terrace above the main garden, with a small wood and acres of fields beyond. As she stared out across what seemed to be endless countryside, as far as she could see, glass in hand, she wasn't sure what exactly she was drinking, but it was very nice. It seemed just then to be the very thing she needed.

Lost in her own thoughts, she hadn't noticed him. She was vaguely aware of someone walking up the steep grassy embankment below the terrace and then he called her name. Those unexpected meetings are a real joy, connecting again with people with whom we have shared great memories and happy times. Those moments are a delight for the minutes before we come back to the present and know that time has moved on. Life is as it is now, different. He was back from the south of France, only for a couple of days for the wedding, he said and then quickly, his thoughts turned to Ana. It all seemed quite confusing, as Rebecca tried to follow his explanation, descriptions and fairly random thoughts. He had met her only four months ago when he was back in London for an exhibition. Six years younger than him, she was still very young, he knew, but the most gorgeous person inside and out that he had ever met. She was troubled. She needed him, he was sure and so a week later, he had followed her back to her home town and decided it was time for a move. Now he was living in the same town, but not with her, he insisted. He had rented some kind of garage. It had been converted into a small apartment with a mezzanine floor, giving space for a bed. It was in the middle of the town and not too far from where she lived. In a strange way, it all made sense, it was so very him. Trust Tom to need a muse for his art. His sister was an artist too, she remembered, as she listened. She would have preferred to have heard that he was happy and settled, she thought, but how honest was that? On her own again, she couldn't help but think that it would have been nice if she had been his long-lost love. It was no more than a fleeting thought. Friends was how she had always liked it. There had never been any suggestion that there would be anything else.

Rebecca and Tom were seated next to each other for the meal; large round tables, more pink. Prawn Cocktail, roast chicken and strawberry cheesecake. It was all very good and beautifully presented. Later she would make a note in her diary. When others were pouring out their thoughts and feelings in their diaries, Rebecca was always more reticent. She thought others might find her writing lacking, so ironically, she resorted to the ordinary, keeping her entries to the facts. It was over the meal, between a pause in his musings on Ana that Rebecca began to talk to Tom about her plans for the following week. She wasn't sure where she was going to stay in Paris. She knew that she needed to get on and book something. It was at that point that he showed the first real interest in her journey, actually in anything that she was saying.

'You're going to be in Paris, you need to stay in Paris?' he asked, now sitting forward, interested, and having had the confirmation, he continued, 'You could do me a real favour and it might work for you too. My parents are really concerned and have been going on all morning. They haven't heard from my sister for a while and that's really unusual. They want me to take the train back to the south of France and call in to see her, but I've already got a flight arranged and I really want to be back as soon as I can.

Also, the last thing Carol needs is to have me interfering, but if you need to stay somewhere, it's a great excuse. My parents would be so grateful. I'm sure there isn't a problem. She's been so busy, but they do worry and I would really appreciate you going to see her for me. You wouldn't need to worry about getting a hotel then, you can stay overnight. I'll let you have a key in case she's not there when you arrive.' He hardly drew breath, so keen to get Rebecca's help and agreement.

So it was decided, all very quickly. Rebecca was due to be setting off at the beginning of the following week and would check up on his sister, reporting back to him as soon as she had any news. Tom wrote down Carol's address for her there and then and Rebecca said she would call to see his parents and pick up his key to the apartment from them. Tom was going back the next morning. He seemed very happy for Rebecca to have the key without being sure when he would get it back, but he probably didn't think he would need it. He had other things on his mind and he was planning to stay in the south. Rebecca didn't know his sister very well. She couldn't even remember the last time she had seen her but it was only an overnight stop and although she had felt rather rushed into agreeing to call, she was happy to be able to help out, especially for his parents. They were such nice people. The more she had thought about it, the more she knew they would be worried.

As the day turned out, Rebecca found that she had really enjoyed the celebration, despite all her misgivings and prejudices. It was a chance to catch up with quite a few old friends. Everyone was in a great mood, the DJ played all the right music or so it seemed and the dance floor was full all night. Rebecca loved to dance. As the night played on, she was pleased that she had arranged to stay overnight, like quite a few of the guests. It was a good night and although it was one o'clock when she got to bed, she was up quite early the next morning. She had breakfast looking out onto the terrace. It was a bright, sunny morning. She would have been happy staying there, looking out across the countryside, feeling the warmth of the sun through the windows but she needed to get on. She said her goodbyes, agreed enthusiastically that she would be in touch, the usual promises, and told Tom that she would call in and get the key from his parents that evening.

It had been a while, probably a couple of years, since Rebecca had seen Tom's mother and father. As teenagers, they had spent a lot of time there. It was a large house, a house which was always busy with people, spacious, open and welcoming, and so it seemed the natural place for the friends to gather. Rebecca drove up through the right-hand side gateway of the long curved driveway which swept round in front of the house and back down onto the road again at the other side. She parked in front of the large garage, big enough for several cars, she remembered. The house was raised up in front of a long, wide garden which sloped down to the road where it was bordered by a high, sandstone wall, covered in moss and darkened with time. In all, the house was set in about half an acre of land, with a large landscaped garden to the rear, looking out beyond a gateway to woodland stretching towards the horizon. In the summertime, they had spent happy times together, chatting about all those issues which seem to occupy the teenage mind, matters seldom discussed with parents. Then, when they tired of talking, they would wander the pathways beyond the house and for the most part, they stayed out of trouble. That particular May evening, years later, Rebecca got out of the car feeling the strangeness of returning after a passage of time, remembering a life which seemed recent and distant, almost in equal measure. She felt a shyness sweep across her. Tom's parents had always been there in the background and they had meals together many times, but she had never been there on her own before. She walked up to the house and knocked on the large oak door. There was no bell, only a heavy round knocker and finding it hard to use, to get the correct level of loudness, she didn't know if anyone would hear her and so she stood there wondering how long was the right amount of time to wait before trying again, not too insistent as to seem impolite. She need not have been concerned. It wasn't long before she could hear movement in the house. The door was opened by Tom's mother, Ruth, beaming a huge smile and giving Rebecca an enormous hug. It was as easy as it always had been. Tom's mother seemed so pleased to see her. Rebecca noticed that as ever, Ruth was casually dressed. It was rarely formal in that household. Her hair was uncombed. She was wearing a loose, dark grey overall which was splashed with paint. She was an artist too, an amateur, but quite well known locally.

'Let me get rid of this old thing,' she said, taking off the overall and hanging it in the cloak room in the hallway.

'Come in, sit down, I'll make us something to drink. What do you want? Tea, coffee, something stronger?'

'Tea will be fine. I'm driving,' Rebecca replied.

'Tea it is then and that will go really well with the orange drizzle cake I made this afternoon.'

'Let's go into the sitting room. Tom's father is watching television but that won't disturb us. Come on, in you come.'

They walked across the wide hallway, with its wooden panelled walls, polished parquet flooring and dark wooden doors leading off into all the rooms on the ground floor, the kitchen and scullery, a dining room, a study that doubled as a music room and the sitting room. A large staircase turned in three sections leading up to the first of two further floors. Ruth led Rebecca into the sitting room through the door in the corner of the hallway next to the staircase. All now so familiar to her, the long sitting room stretched the width of the house. Tom's father who was sitting on the deep green draylon sofa looked up from the television, smiled and nodded.

'Lovely to see you. I'll leave you to it for a while. She's been really looking forward to your visit, ever since Tom said you'd call,' he said quietly and turned back to the programme he'd been watching.

Ruth and Rebecca went and sat out of the way on the window seat in the large bay window overlooking the back garden. It was still light and the low sun was brightening the house. Ruth seemed genuinely pleased to see her and her first questions were about Rebecca and what she was up to, but she was clearly worried about Carol and soon all thoughts of tea and orange drizzle cake were out of her mind and her conversation turned to her daughter.

'She's always been headstrong, had her own ideas. She wanted to get away from home as quickly as she could but in all the time she's spent now away from home, she's always kept in touch. It's so unlike her not to ring us at all.'

'She could be really busy at the moment. Wasn't she getting ready for an exhibition?' Rebecca asked, remembering what Tom had said.

'Yes, she's always busy with something but that wouldn't have stopped her getting in touch.'

Rebecca thought she'd try to change tack a little and asked,

'What about her boyfriend? Have you met him?' But it was the wrong thing to say.

'Never. I don't know why, but she didn't seem to want us to meet him. Every time we've been over, he's not been around and she came home alone last time she visited.'

Her husband who was still sitting quietly watching television, pretending not to listen, decided it was time to intervene and said gently,

'In fairness, dear, we've only been over twice and she's rarely home. We haven't really had the opportunity to meet him.'

'Maybe she wasn't yet ready to introduce him to you,' Rebecca suggested.

'She's been with him a long time now and seems very fond. He's Portuguese, you know. Other than that, I know very little about him. I'm so pleased you can call to see her and Tom tells me you can speak Portuguese, so you should get on.'

'I'm a bit rusty but I can get by,' Rebecca replied, but this, of course, had raised Rebecca's interest. She hadn't realised, what another strange coincidence. 'Do you know where he's from in Portugal?'

'Not really, he was at university there before he went to live in Paris but I can't remember which one, even if Carol did tell me,' Tom's mother replied, obviously not very interested in the boyfriend and unable to hide her irritation.

Better to go back to Carol, Rebecca thought. 'Tom mentioned that she's had other exhibitions. She seems to be doing well out there.'

'Yes, I think so. We were over for her first exhibition and she sold quite a few of her paintings. She seems to be getting commissions, but she does keep a little job going in an art supplies shop. She quite enjoys it. It's amazing how both Carol and Tom have decided to follow a career in art. You would have thought that my attempts would have discouraged them,' Ruth concluded modestly. She was really quite good.

She wasn't easily distracted and soon returned to her concerns about Carol's whereabouts. Her husband reminded her gently that he had heard her offer tea and cake when Rebecca arrived and asked if she wanted him to go and put the kettle on.

'Ah, right, of course. Sorry, Rebecca. No, I'll go and do it. Edward, you watch your programme. I like to keep busy.' And off she went to the kitchen.

Tom's father looked up again from the television. 'She's really worried and I can't seem to settle her down. She's not been out of touch long, but Ruth insists there must be something wrong. It's good that you can call and let us know what Carol is up to. I'm sure you can be subtle about it with Carol too. She hates us interfering with her life.'

Rebecca said that she would do her best and as they heard Ruth on her way back from the kitchen, they changed the subject to the programme on television and then all moved to sit on the sofas around the large square coffee table to drink tea, eat cake and with Tom's father's help, they kept the conversation fairly light and away from Carol.

Both of them came to the door to see Rebecca off, the goodbyes as warm as the welcome. Ruth gave Rebecca Tom's spare key to Carol's apartment and Rebecca said that she would keep in touch with Tom in the first instance and let him know what Carol was up to. His mum checked that she had his number in France. Rebecca tried to stay as upbeat as she could. She didn't know Carol very well but she seemed to be a fairly free spirit and was really settled in her life with her boyfriend in Paris from what Tom had said. It wouldn't have surprised Rebecca if she had gone off on holiday with him and had forgotten to let people know what she was up to. Rebecca told Ruth to try not to worry too much, then drove back down the driveway, looking in the rear view mirror and waving. Tom's parents were standing at the front of the house waving too, seemingly reluctant to go back inside. Rebecca turned out on to the road and made her way home to start to get ready for her journey.

# V

Back in the house, Rebecca made herself a quick meal. More accurately, she warmed up the macaroni cheese which Tom's mother had given her on her way out of the house. Rebecca was really touched to think that she had remembered it was her favourite meal when she used to visit, so thoughtful. Rebecca's tastes were no more sophisticated even now when she needed some comfort food and for some reason after her visit, she felt the need of a bit of comfort. Even after the tea and cake she'd had earlier, she was still hungry. She ate her supper in front of the television and washed up before going upstairs to her bedroom to see if she could make any more progress with the preparation for the journey. She was setting off early the next morning but she wasn't at all ready.

It was important to her way of thinking about this journey, which she had planned so carefully, that she travelled with the smallest bag possible. Travel light, as though she wasn't going very far at all, as though it appeared she was setting off for a day's walking and would be back soon. Somehow it helped her, the feeling that she could easily come back. There were many aspects of her life she could leave with no thought, but friends and family were another matter. They had encouraged her, though, knowing how much she needed something different and insisted they would be over to see her. She took a break and went to ring her parents, then made a drink before going back to her packing, feeling a little down. She would only be travelling for a couple of nights and didn't need much. The rest she would buy after she had arrived. It was to be a fresh start. No need for a big bag, nothing with her that might be a reminder. She continued without much conviction, annoyed at how long it was taking her to pack, messing around as usual, wondering if she had everything she needed, not sure what would be best to take. There were all the travel documents, then she needed something to distract her as she was travelling alone. Wasn't it enough to watch the scenery go by as she travelled through France and on through Spain and into Portugal? All those places she hadn't seen before? No, she had to have something with her to read. She didn't like travelling alone. The worst part of being a single traveller was mealtimes. When she gave it more thought, she knew that there were probably greater challenges to a woman travelling on her own, but that wasn't on her mind. It was those moments when it was obvious that there was no one else there with her that bothered her most wherever she was. Many people travelled alone. It didn't mean they were single, but she felt that people would know. It was better to have a book or a magazine to read than to stare into empty space, even though it meant having more to carry. She knew it was silly. Too self-conscious, too much self-obsession, she felt irritated with the way she was thinking. No one would be interested in her. The problem was that she thought it looked a little sad. The truth was that she missed being part of a couple. She missed Andy, despite the hurt and strangely it was in all those ordinary situations when she felt it most acutely.

Now on the evening before her journey, as she sat looking at everything scattered around her on the floor ready to be packed into her bag, a nagging thought came back into her mind. It was a thought which had been like a constant noise in the background over the last weeks, trying to hold her back, questioning her sense. She didn't know if she was doing the right thing. She worked hard to counter the negative thoughts. There was nothing to be lost from a year in another country and everything to gain. It was a skill to be able to speak another language and would give her other options when she returned. She hadn't enjoyed her job. It really was easy to leave that. Those close to her were supportive and looking forward to visiting her. Her mother had said that to her again on the phone that evening. If it didn't work out, she could always come back.

It must have been nearly two o'clock in the morning by the time she tried to get some sleep. She set the alarm for a quarter past five. That should be enough time because the bag was now packed, clothes for the journey laid out to the last piece of underwear, so that she wouldn't have to think what she was putting on, everything ready. She didn't sleep much at all, at least it was her impression that she registered each hour, heard the old clock in the hall, slowly and deliberately chiming the hour and the half hour. She didn't have any breakfast. She didn't feel hungry. More procrastination left her dashing around at the last minute, checking several times to see if the doors and windows were closed. She had done it before, left the door unlocked, sometimes all night. There had been one time when she had gone out and left the door wide open, not for a few minutes or for an hour, for the whole day. Too much on her mind. This time, everything seemed to be in order. She tried the front door again, feeling annoyed that she might miss the train with all the last minute checks.

It was not long after six in the morning, one of those fantastic bright, light May mornings, the birds still in full song. As she walked down to the station, checking her watch, she saw that she still had time for the slightly longer route that led along the single track lanes through the next village. She was reminded of how much she loved that time of year. Her own theory was that she was born in the summer and was, therefore, drawn to the light. Those natural connections with the world, with nature, place and people fascinated her. She felt she had her own natural connection to the summer, especially to those early days before the wetter months of July and August set in. The days seemed to have so many more possibilities at that time of year. Sleep, though necessary, didn't seem quite as important. She was feeling a little bleary eyed but not to worry, she could rest on the train at some point. Then a slight panic came over her, as she thought she might not have the key to the apartment in Paris. Of course she had it, she must have. As she rummaged through her bag, not easy as she walked quickly to the station, she felt annoyed that she had doubted it. It was in the section of her bag with all the valuables, passport, tickets, all the essentials. One final check of those too. It felt good finally to be setting out on a journey which she had planned for so long and it was such a great morning to start out. As she walked through the village, she noticed that there were more people about than she had expected, already on their way to work. She loved this little village. She loved being part of a small community where everyone knew each other. The bigger the place, the more impersonal. A nagging thought again as she wondered why if she liked living there so much, she was leaving it behind. It wasn't for ever. She turned her thoughts away from the annoying doubts. She knew they did nothing more than hold her back and put her in a bad mood. She turned her attention to the countryside around the village. She was so lucky to live in such a lovely spot and fortunate to have this opportunity and friends in another country. She was leaving for a while. It was only an interval and that was good. It was time for change and not simply of place.

When she had announced her plan of travelling by train, friends had a good time with all the jokes about British Rail, old trains, delays, strikes, would the trains be running? She would be fine if she could get to France, they said. Rebecca ignored the jokes. Her view of train travel was that it was glamourous, romantic and safe. She had probably watched too many old films, 'Brief Encounter', with Rachmaninov's Second Piano Concerto echoing in her mind. There was much talk of high speed trains but that was all in the future. Hers would be a journey which many others had taken across the decades at almost the same pace, be it steam or diesel. She was concerned that she would miss connections and get stuck at the ferry port or in the middle of London, but she tried to put such thoughts out of her mind. The train was on time, a few minutes after seven o'clock. There would be no problem making the connection. She hadn't really thought about the early morning commute. The train to York was busy, as was the train to London. As she hadn't booked a seat, she stood in the corridor by the door for quite some time until the first station on the way to London when a few people got off, dashing on their way to work. Not quite the glamorous train travel she had imagined. She felt tired and the time began to pass quickly as her thoughts wandered. Absent-mindedly, she watched the other people deep in their own morning thoughts, nose in a book or newspaper, chatting to others on the train, lost in thought or as she was, contemplating others. There was an irony. She liked to watch people, yet she was nervous of the scrutiny of others. She wondered where they were going, where their commute was taking them in London. For some reason, her thoughts took her to how many people there were in the world. She had no idea, but far more than she could ever understand as a number. They all had their own lives, families and friends. She was aware for a moment of how tiny a part of the world she really was, the smallest grain. For a few seconds, her feelings seemed ridiculous and quite insignificant.

Rebecca had not always been so timid or so self-conscious or obsessed with her own thoughts. She was naturally shy, it was true, but she worked around it. She was funny. People would always have described her as a happy, vibrant person. Circumstances can change people. People can change people. She didn't notice, though others did, as she became more subdued. It happened not by being with someone else who intentionally tried to change her, but by being with someone whose quiet nature invaded her. They weren't good for each other. He was right, but she didn't recognise it. The hurt was deep, because he had realised before she did. She had lost her confidence and brightness long before he walked away, though she hadn't noticed. She hated being on her own for the void it seemed to present, for the emptiness, without realising she had been isolated for too long. Now as she travelled south, she wondered what she was doing but knew she could only feel better by trying to start again. Nothing else had broken her mood better than being away in Portugal. Slowly and every now and then, she glimpsed the person she used to be and liked herself much better.

It had helped Rebecca to set out that morning knowing she now had another reason for the journey, at least for the first part of it. She had to go and check on Tom's sister, Carol. She always felt so much better when she had a purpose, when she could feel part of something, being able to help out. If there was a party, she wanted to be in the kitchen, to prepare the food, to make sure that everyone had a drink. It was all so much better to be involved rather than to be hanging around feeling self-conscious, wondering what to say. She began to think about Carol. Tom had said she was really happy living with her boyfriend in Paris. Rebecca felt a pang, a dip in her mood, as she wondered why she hadn't been able to be happy. It seemed to her that there had been too much loss. She knew it wasn't a fair position to take. Many people get hurt. She tried not to be hard on herself. When life turns the wrong way, it seems so acute and overwhelming. It rarely helps to know that people can be happy or that others are in a worse position. She had made her own decisions. She had given her relationship as little thought as she had accused others of doing. She had compromised and forgotten that she too needed more. Her thoughts were changing. She felt much stronger. With each mile she travelled, she was moving on. She felt a glimmer of her old optimism. She was sure she would know what real love looked like when she saw it but for now she had enough of such indulgence.

Rebecca lifted herself out of her wandering thoughts. As the train pulled into the station, she began to feel the heat of the city, the noise, the confusion and the oppression of the crowds, even as she looked through the window of the train. She had never lived in a city, hadn't even been to London before she was eighteen. City life appealed to many people but not to her. She reminded herself that she had chosen to visit another city, so she had better get used to it. She was only passing through this one. She didn't have too far to go. It was always busy. It was always hectic, such a mix of people, all unknown and she felt confused by it all, detached. She had passed through the station several times before but she had never really looked at it. It had been built in a grand age, intended to give an impression of greatness, importance, strength and permanency. There was the sense of service and security too, safe for the traveller, she thought, but it didn't feel that safe to her. In her mind, too many bad things had happened there or so she had heard, and it troubled her. There she was again, overthinking everything. Her disquiet made her hurry through the station. Standing by the main entrance, she felt a little wave of nervousness, the hugeness of London rising up in front of her, as she tried to get her bearings and remember how to get to Victoria Station. She checked her watch, wondering again if she had left enough time to make the connection. Of course she had. She didn't need to worry, she knew where the station was and how to get there. She needed to stay calm and focussed.

She was in plenty of time to catch the train to Dover. As she made her way, she congratulated herself on the idea of travelling light. It was great not to be dragging a heavy bag from one leg of the journey to the next. When she arrived at the station, she looked for the platform for the train to Dover, via Canterbury. She had chosen the route, because a friend had told her that it was the most scenic. The train wasn't too busy, so she quickly found a seat next to the window. She watched the miles going by, still feeling a little unsettled as the train made its way to the port but better with each mile. This time she had a ferry to catch and was trying to remember how to get from the train station to the port. Although she had travelled that way once before and remembered it as only a short walk, she couldn't picture it in her mind. It was fine. Many other people were making the same journey. It was a good connection and such a nice day to be near the sea. So as soon as she was on board, she found a spot on deck where she could sit and watch the journey go by. She knew that she would much prefer it from the busy, noisy inside and felt lucky to be crossing the Channel in such good weather. As the ferry moved away from the port, rolling gently towards France, she overheard a group talking about how the movement made them feel ill. She didn't feel that at all. The swell, the dips and rises seemed quite natural to her and the gentle movement of the ferry calmed her.

There were no delays and now she was keeping easily to her schedule, going straight from the ferry and catching the train to Paris. It occurred to her that, as she wasn't driving in Paris, she could have a glass of wine, celebrate arriving in France, without the delay her friends had insisted would be inevitable. It would start to make the journey feel a little bit more special. This is what she had planned, a long train journey, sleeping, eating and watching the world go by. Too much watching those old black and white films as a child, but now that she was in France, the journey was starting to feel much more glamorous, the way she had imagined. She became aware of feeling cold. She had spent too long on the deck of the ferry taking in the sea breeze. The good weather hadn't held its strength in the open sea. She was hungry too, so she started to make her way along to the restaurant car. As she reached the carriage, she paused, and seeing it fairly busy, she wondered if she should wait until she got to Paris. She could pick up a sandwich somewhere later. She urged herself through the door and to a vacant seat.

She felt the warmth return and her spirits lift as she sat in the dining car, the train travelling on through France. She stared out of the window. It seemed to her like the countryside which she had passed through on the way to Dover, not different at all. As field after field rushed by, she found her thoughts wandering again. There she was, a woman travelling on her own, thinking she would be noticed. Not at all. Theirs were fleeting thoughts like hers, another carriage full of people submerged in their own lives, noticing little else. She took out her book and started to read, or at least pretended. One would think that such preoccupation would lead her to be very aware of people around her but it was often quite the contrary.

'Are you travelling far? … Are you travelling far?' It wasn't until he asked the question for the second time that she realised someone was talking to her, trying to get her attention, a young man sitting at the table opposite.

French, she assumed at first, aware of an accent. It was not such a wild guess, as she was now in France. He certainly wasn't English, but she wasn't sure and didn't want to ask. His English was very good but there was something that didn't quite work with his accent. He was certainly not English. She always loved to hear a different accent, any accent, perhaps it was the musician in her. At that point, though, she was simply more concerned that a stranger was talking to her and her natural shyness was getting in the way. It was only later when she began to take more notice of him that she began to think she might be wrong. He had dark hair and his complexion was also quite dark, more southern European, she thought. She noticed his eyes, would always notice eyes, bright green, 'olhos verdes', very beautiful, the Portuguese would say.

'Are you travelling to Paris? Have you come far?' he asked. Rebecca decided it was better not to give too much away and kept her answers brief.

'Yes, I'm heading for Paris, I've travelled from the north of England,' she replied.

Maybe it was because she was a little reserved, but he began to talk about himself. People love to talk about themselves and she was happy to listen. She found it much easier and he didn't seem to mind her quietness. He had been working in London for a while, he told her, doing various jobs in bars and restaurants. He wanted to improve his English, have the experience of another country and give himself some time to know what he wanted to do. There was no rush, he said. As he talked, Rebecca tried to focus on what he was saying, but she found her mind wandering again. He was good-looking, a similar age to her she thought, perhaps a little older and once those thoughts were in her head, she felt that wave of shyness and a little embarrassment come over her again, so that instead of listening to what he was saying and getting involved in the conversation, she became more concerned about how she might be seeming to him and what he was thinking of her. He seemed not to notice, which was a relief and better still, his friendliness and easy nature soon had her forgetting her shyness.

It seemed obvious once he had asked. They were both wanting something to eat and they were both travelling alone, but she wouldn't have presumed to have said anything. It did seem silly that they were talking across the aisle and having asked if it was alright, he moved across to sit opposite her at the table. There it was again, those natural connections which she so loved, that synergy, those little coincidences in life that draw people together. Two people, two journeys made for different reasons but here for a while, together. She felt a strong connection, tried to dismiss it, not wanting it to get in the way. He joined her in a glass of wine. She felt as though she was being a bit indulgent having wine on the journey to

Paris. She wondered if he was being polite, but it was natural enough for him and even though it seemed quite early in the day to Rebecca to start drinking, she didn't object when he ordered a bottle of wine to go with the meal.

Maybe it was because he didn't think he would see Rebecca again. Maybe he was taking the opportunity to think aloud about his life in London, or he wanted to have someone to talk to, making the time pass more quickly. He continued to fill the journey with stories of the past months when he had been in England, the places he had visited, new friends he had made. In some ways, he was looking forward to a break in Paris and he had planned to be away for three weeks or so but he would be getting back to London sometime soon, because he loved the city and also because he felt that there was so much more of England he would like to see. In all the journey, he didn't really ask her any more questions about her plans, but she was happy to listen, to show interest and to keep herself to herself. The journey passed by quickly and he was still talking when the train's arrival in Paris was announced.

As the train pulled into the station and both of them began to look for their bags, getting ready to leave and moving towards the door, he said to her,

'Gosh, in all this time talking together, I haven't even asked you your name.'

'It's Rebecca,' she said.

'Very pleased to meet you. It's been a pleasure, Rebecca.'

And then as she was wondering if he would leave the train without telling her his name, he turned and said,

'My name is John, by the way, or I should say, it's João, but friends in London call me John. They don't seem to be able to pronounce João, so I let it go and became John.'

She was amazed at what she had just heard and a little annoyed that she hadn't picked it up, but he hadn't spoken at all about Portugal. Now it made sense, he wasn't French.

'You're Portuguese?' she said.

'Yes, I am. You got that from the name, I suppose? Not everyone would know that.'

'No, but I speak Portuguese, more or less. It's kind of a passion of mine.'

Now, she couldn't believe what she had said. How stupid must she have sounded? But he didn't seem to find it foolish, maybe he had missed the passion bit. She hoped so.

'Wow, it's not very often that you come across an English person who speaks Portuguese.'

'No, I don't get much chance to practise.'

'How long are you in Paris? We really must meet up,' he added as he rummaged around for a piece of paper and wrote down his name and number on the page of a notebook he had in his pocket, tearing it out and handing it to her. He looked enquiringly at her. I suppose he expected her to do the same but her mind was occupied with the thought that she was only going to be in Paris overnight and how would they have the opportunity to meet up?

'I'm not staying in Paris,' she said, then added. 'That's not strictly true, I'm here overnight checking up on a friend's sister.'

'You have my number, here. Give me a call if you get chance. I'm not sure what I'm doing myself yet and how long I'll be in Paris. Here, have my number in London too, just in case. You never know. '

She almost let the moment pass but changing what seemed to have been the habit of a lifetime, she didn't hold back.

'Here, let me give you my number in England.' And she quickly scribbled it down in the notebook he then passed to her, but I won't be there for some time. I'm on my way to Lisbon and from there to a little town in the Algarve, Vila Real de Santo António.'

'Oh, I see.' And he paused, as if there was something else to say that was significant. The moment passed. 'I must go. It's been a real pleasure talking to you. I really do hope we meet up again,' he said.

'Same here. You never know,' she said, deliberately echoing his earlier phrase. 'Até logo, see you soon,' she found herself saying in Portuguese and he responded in kind.

And with that they both got off the train, intent on the next stage of their journeys. Rebecca held back deliberately again. She was anxious to get on, but they had said their goodbyes. So for a while, she walked at a pace along the platform which was uncharacteristically slow in order to keep a reasonable distance from him. She couldn't help but notice that there was someone waiting for him, a friend, family, she wasn't sure but didn't like to watch in case he noticed. He turned and gave her one last wave seconds before he disappeared around the corner. Nice guy, she thought and then quickly her mind turned to Paris and she started to look for where she had put the address of the apartment. It was now pretty late.

# VI

João was indeed a handsome man, tall, slim with dark wavy hair and bright, deep green eyes. Some might have described him as charming. He was certainly very easy with people, relaxed and friendly in social situations but then he had been brought up in a family with a tradition of hospitality, people who loved to entertain, and in a house which always seemed full of people. He would not have described himself as charming and would have been uncomfortable with the thought that he was perceived as such. That might have suggested an arrogance which he would not have wanted to possess. He was certainly confident, at least to the outside world, a seemingly natural confidence. His small group of close friends loved his company. He was known to be a good friend, thoughtful, kind and above all, very funny. It would be wrong to suggest that he was without flaws. Like all human beings, he had attitudes that got in the way, and some would say, particularly of his own happiness. He was stubborn, head-strong and could be opinionated, especially where the family business and his part in it had been concerned. Despite his seeming openness, he could be quite reticent and deep at times.

He didn't understand why, but the thought that life was already planned out for him had felt suffocating and he had to get away. That is what he told himself but it was more complex. His apparent confidence belied hidden confusion and some regret. Life was tense. The colonial wars made unreasonable demands on young men and like so many others, he had no heart for the conflict. It wasn't a matter of courage. It was the principle he held, like so many of his generation, that it was simply wrong, irrelevant and a complete waste of lives. He persuaded his parents that time abroad would have many advantages and it would be good for him. It would be good for the business that he had experienced other ways of life and so they had acceded to his request. By the time he met Rebecca, his year had already extended and he felt happy, if not a little unfulfilled. He still wasn't sure what he really wanted. He had been drawn to Britain without really knowing why, but it was an obvious choice. London was busy, noisy and dirty. It was so different from the life he had known. He had found casual work, in the restaurants and bars of London and after the years he had studied, he was happy with work that didn't place any demand on him and allowed him to stay flexible, not tied down. The family had many business connections in Britain but he had resisted any introductions, wanting to make his own way or at least preferring to merge into the background for a while. No one amongst his friends in London had ever questioned how he managed to afford the rent on the apartment. The truth was that it belonged to a close family friend. His independence had its limits. He didn't talk much about his life in Portugal and no one asked. Now, he appeared to those around him to be quite settled. There were times when he felt his past life was completely irrelevant, that London or at least somewhere else in Britain could be home, that it was where he belonged. He kept the rest of his life fairly separate, but every so often amongst family friends and acquaintances, out for a meal in the Restaurant Caravela in Knightsbridge, perhaps, a deep wave of 'saudades,' of longing, would engulf him and for a while he would long for home. He had never quite got used to the cold, grey days in England. Days which could be grey not only of winter. He had felt the weight of those dark days, certainly through that most recent winter and finding work had not always been easy. Times were difficult for everyone; unemployment, strikes and a country less safe than he had imagined. Portugal had its problems and restrictions. Britain, despite its own difficulties, afforded him more freedom and that remained very attractive to him.

As he got off the train in Paris, peering through the crowds, looking out for his cousin, he was thinking about Rebecca. For a brief moment, he had an overwhelming feeling that he should go back to her, make sure he could see her again. It so surprised him that he pushed back at the thought and almost resisted looking back even for that one last glance. His cousin was there to meet him on the platform and they walked along together before unable to resist any longer, he turned and looked at her again, one last time.

It wasn't long before he was in a car heading out to the suburbs. José was a cousin who had settled in Paris, having moved to study, but also, like many other of his compatriots, to avoid being drafted into the army, sharing strong views on the matter with João. The two families had been very close when the children were growing up and they were soon talking easily with each other, catching up, filling in the gaps. João didn't know why he had decided to stop off in Paris. It was good to catch up with José. It was good to break the journey, but it was nothing more than procrastination. He had felt the pressure of being expected home and so he had decided to stay a night, maybe two, in Paris before carrying on his journey. He hadn't mentioned to Rebecca that he was heading home, naturally avoiding the subject. Come to think of it, he hadn't said anything either about Vila Real de Santo António, a place he knew well. He didn't know why. He was always very happy to talk to people, but his openness was no deeper than the surface, never wanting to give too much away, not wanting to get too close. He had felt very easy with Rebecca. In fact, he had felt a strong connection, but it was a casual meeting.

They went back to José's apartment but only to drop off João's bag. They had decided to go out to get something to eat. Much of the conversation that evening was about José's life in Paris and João's in London, comparing notes on each city, but inevitably, reminiscing about life back in Portugal. It wasn't long before José was talking about the political situation at home and speculating as to how it might affect their families. João had been happy to leave all of that behind. He listened and realised how very successfully he had put it out of his mind. As José continued to talk about news from home, about the revolution, the concerns of business people, the many talking about leaving Portugal, João became uneasy. In Britain, there hadn't been much reported. The revolution had seemed calm. No one at home had raised any concerns. João hoped that the coup would bring real change and freedom, an end to the wars, but in all the uncertainty, he had been happy to be away. Now he wasn't sure.

'My father said there were some business matters that he needed to talk to me about. Have your parents said anything about how things are on the estate?' João asked.

'I think they're fine as it is. Nothing is certain. Nobody knows who exactly is in charge. The communists are a strong influence and that could lead to a very different Portugal from the old regime,' José explained what he knew.

'I had picked up that things were a bit confused but I hadn't appreciated how tense it is,' João said, with a growing feeling of guilt which he couldn't quite explain. When his mother had encouraged him to come home for a holiday, there was part of João that was sure his father was behind it. He thought that it was a ruse to get him back home. His father had never been completely happy about him going to London, or was it the fact he had stayed? His son's place was with the business, but he was also realistic that life in Portugal did not always bring those free choices, not even to the privileged.

'My father is realistic, but in his heart, he wants me home to continue the family business, as it has been for ever. He's always been unnerved by my lack of certainty. He doesn't understand why I might want something different for my life,' João tried to explain to his cousin.

'I get that, but I'm not sure it's quite as simple. There might be some big changes coming his way.' There was a certain gravity in José's voice which was increasing João's anxiety, although he didn't saying anything.

'How long are you planning to stay in Paris before heading home?' José then asked.

João had been vague about how long he would stay in Paris when he had spoken to José before he set off and José had been quite easy about it.

Now he was pleased he had been quite vague. He needed to get back and see for himself and he didn't want to let on to José that he was feeling that way. He was also remembering that Rebecca was travelling on to Portugal and other thoughts started to build in his mind.

'I thought I would break up the journey and catch up with you before getting back. I'll stay overnight with you, if that's ok, and then get back into the city in time to catch the night train to Oporto tomorrow lunchtime. I'll need to go to the station fairly early in the morning to book a ticket, but it should be alright.' João was thinking it through only as he was speaking.

'Up to you. You can stay at my place as long as you want, but you haven't been back in a while, so I can see you'll want to get on.'

'Yes, thanks for the offer, but they're expecting me, so I'll let them know I'm on my way once I'm sure which train I'll be taking.' On this one, João was now clear.

# VII

It had been a long day. Already late in the evening, Rebecca was keen to find her way to the apartment and was wishing now that she had thought it through a bit better, getting some more detailed directions from Tom. She realised that she could have asked João also. Although she didn't know how familiar he was with Paris, she wondered why she hadn't taken the opportunity when it was there. She had been happy to listen to him. She headed towards the ticket office which wasn't busy, thinking she might find someone friendly who wouldn't mind giving her some directions. Her spoken French was far from good, but she managed to make herself understood and not to assume that everyone else could speak English. She made her best attempt at French and the ticket man was really helpful, drawing a little map. As she walked away, studying the route, it looked fairly complicated and she started to feel tense that it was late, that she still might get lost. She walked towards the exit and spotted the taxi rank. She wasn't sure how safe that option would be on her own, but surely the taxis at the station were fine and it seemed better than wandering the streets of Paris. She showed the address to the taxi driver and soon they were travelling through the city. It was almost dark now. She couldn't recognise anything and told herself to sit back and trust the taxi driver. He was quiet and that suited her. She never wanted to give the impression that she was unfriendly, but sometimes it seemed like too much effort to make small talk, especially when the language was a struggle. She was now feeling tired, preferring to lose herself in her own thoughts. As they turned a corner, she saw Montmartre. She had forgotten how magnificent it was and even more so lit up, piercing through the darkening night sky.

'Not far now,' the taxi driver advised. Of course she thought, it was no surprise that Tom's sister would choose to live in this part of Paris, under the gaze of Montmartre and amongst so many artists.

Rebecca paid the driver and got out of the taxi, walking towards the old wooden door which he had pointed out to her as she said goodbye. The building looked as though it had once been a single house, but now the panel of buzzers at the side of the door gave away that it had been divided into apartments. Carol's name was there, along with another name, at the side of the button which indicated the second floor apartment. She tried the buzzer. Carol might be at home. She could have been keeping a low profile with the family, it didn't mean she wasn't there. Nothing. Rebecca tried again and waited a while, but nothing, no reply. So when she felt sure there was no one in, she slowly turned the key in the lock of the outer door. She tried to make as little noise as possible, not to draw attention to herself and when the door opened, she walked into a wide, dimly lit entrance hall. She looked to see if there was a lift. She always preferred to use the stairs, no matter how many floors, but she was curious. No lift, no matter, she climbed the steep stairs and came to the door of the apartment on the second floor. Still not completely convinced that the apartment was empty, she knocked and waited quite a while, then knocked and waited a second time before gently unlocking and opening the door.

'Hi, are you there, Carol? It's Rebecca, Tom's friend.' Nothing.

It was clear that Carol was not around, but Rebecca felt distinctly uncomfortable being in someone else's apartment when they weren't there. She wondered how Carol would feel if by chance she came back later to find her in the apartment but it was late to be looking for a hotel. Carol might not be too far away but the longer Rebecca was there, the more she felt unsettled. Once she had noticed the strange positioning of all the pictures, and not one or two, but all of them, in every room, she was sure that there was something very wrong. It was a feeling which connected so deeply with her own experience, but it felt so particularly strange. She looked around the apartment again, one more time into every room, listening out all the time, not to miss the key turning in the door and then went to sit quietly on the sofa. It was late, but she needed to get out, so she decided to see if there was a phone nearby where she might be able to get hold of Tom. She could ring home, too. She took out her small handbag, wrote a quick note on a piece of paper, which she left on top of her rucksack just inside the entrance to the apartment and then locked the door, walking quietly back down the two flights of stairs, not wanting to attract the attention of any neighbours, and then out onto the street. There was a little square only a few meters away and fortunately, a pay phone in one corner. She didn't have much change but managed to get through to him. He insisted that she stay. He was concerned to hear that his sister wasn't there, but he suggested that she could be out for the evening. Rebecca felt sure that he had assumed there was some reason why she wanted to keep a low profile from her parents, if not from anyone else. They had never been completely comfortable with the idea of her living in Paris and hadn't been happy with the relationship, especially never having met the man who she had lived with for what must have been at least five years now, Tom said. Rebecca didn't tell Tom how she had found the pictures in the apartment and how strange it had appeared to her. Maybe she was making too much of it. He seemed worried enough and like him, she still hoped she would find a simple explanation. There was something wrong, but Rebecca wasn't convinced enough to draw any firm conclusion that something bad had happened. If she told Tom, what would it achieve? He asked her if she would contact some of Carol's friends and see if they had heard from her or if they had any idea as to where she might be. Rebecca wasn't sure how she could do that, but said she would see if she could ask Carol's neighbours. She might be able to speak to them in the morning. Her disquiet returned and for a brief second, she thought to suggest that he got in touch with the police. Something held her back, as she imagined the conversation – we haven't heard from her and she seems to have left the apartment – not enough as it stood for them to get involved. She said that she would keep in touch, that she would ring him the next day if she found out anything significant and if not, she would ring when she arrived in Portugal. She assured him that she would do whatever she could to help. She made a brief call home with the last of her change and then went to a café across the square, not wanting to spend longer than she needed to in the apartment. The café was still open. There were a couple of other people inside having a drink. Rebecca was pleased that she wasn't the only person on her own late at night. She had something to eat, stretching it out as long as she could and then wandered back to the apartment when she felt that she couldn't put it off any longer. It occurred to her that if by any chance Carol had just been out for the evening, she might be back by now. She rang the buzzer again and once inside and up the stairs, knocked on the door of the second floor apartment and waited for a little while before turning the key and going in. No one there, nothing. Carol hadn't returned.

As Rebecca was getting ready for bed, she was drawn again towards the picture frames all turned to face the wall, curious to know what those images might be that had to be hidden from view. As if still not convinced that someone might come in at any moment, she stood and waited quietly for a while and then she looked at each one, lifting and then turning them long enough to get a glimpse of each image before carefully placing them back in position. One or two were prints. Rebecca didn't recognise the artists, but others looked as though they were original paintings. She guessed that they might be Carol's own work, but it was the photographs that she found most interesting and although there were several, it was one of them in particular that she found herself studying. It was a picture of Carol sitting with a man on the steps of Montmartre, looking really happy. In fact both of them looked so happy. She had remembered his name. Tom had said that he was called Tó Zé. She assumed it must be him. He was strikingly good-looking, deep brown eyes, dark hair, which was a little shaggy, but somehow, very attractive. So that was Tó Zé. The family knew very little about him. She wasn't even sure that Tom had met him. Rebecca then looked again at the other photographs and in everyone, they were looking happy, comfortable in each other's company. Rebecca felt cheered as she looked at those moments, capturing what appeared to be really good times. If the family had seen any of the photographs of the two of them together, they must have been reassured, at least, that they were happy together. She wondered why Carol had been so secretive about Tó Zé.

The next day, Rebecca woke early and packed the few things she had taken out for the night back into her rucksack. She was hungry and ready for breakfast, or at least something to put her on and now she felt anxious to leave the apartment and continue her journey. However, a thought occurred to her. Perhaps there was more the apartment could tell her. She went into the kitchen and began to open the cupboards. They contained a few pans, some basic crockery and cutlery, but as she opened each cupboard, no food, nothing, not even a few jars or tins, empty. As if still not sure that Carol hadn't come back during the night, she crept around and knocked quietly on the door to Carol's bedroom before slowly opening it and going in. She was intruding, she knew, but she felt compelled to look. Carefully, she opened the wardrobe, trying not to make any sound. Nothing. It was completely empty, and then each drawer of the chest of drawers at the other side of the room. Nothing. Every item had been removed. Perhaps they were moving. Strange then that the newspaper had been left open and the jumper. Was that a last minute oversight? It must have been. She had seen enough and needed to get away. She was mixing up too many of her own memories and it wasn't helping. She made one last check of the apartment to make sure that she had left everything exactly as she found it and then locked up. She went back to the little café in the square and ordered a large coffee and a croissant, thinking that was the thing to do for breakfast when in France and not really knowing what other options there might be. While she was eating, she remembered that she had said to Tom she would try to have a word with Carol's neighbours before she left and so after a while, once she thought that it was time people would be up and about, she crossed back to the apartment to see what she could find out before she left.

Rebecca was booked on the southbound train to Lisbon. It was due to leave Paris around lunchtime and would take her overnight across the Spanish border into Portugal, calling early the next morning in Oporto before travelling on to Lisbon. This time, she had been sensible and booked a couchette. She had tried to sleep on too many trains as a student. Now she wanted a little more luxury and a relaxing journey. She had also treated herself to dinner, despite still feeling reticent about dining on her own. This year was about challenging herself and all of those silly preoccupations which got in the way of her feeling happy. A sandwich would not do and she was reminded that a visit to the restaurant car had made for an interesting journey to Paris.

Rebecca arrived at the station and having got her bearings, walked slowly down the platform. She was early. The train was already there at the platform which made her quicken her step for a moment, until as she approached, she could see that the doors were still closed, staff getting the train ready for the overnight journey. As she began to look for a seat on the platform where she could sit and wait, she heard a voice.

'So you're stalking me now are you, Rebecca?' She turned around and was astonished to see João.

'João? What are you doing here? I thought you were staying in Paris.'

'That was the plan. I was hoping to have some time with my cousin in Paris but I have to go home. Something's come up,' he gave by way of an explanation.

'Are you going to Lisbon?' Rebecca asked, thinking it was obvious he must be going now to Portugal.

'No, only as far as Oporto and then I've another train to catch from there. I thought you'd be on this train.'

'OK, I see. So actually, you're the one following me.' She laughed and although she had been surprised to see him, she was also really pleased to meet him again.

'It's always good to have some company on a long journey and the food's quite good on this train. I assume you'll be needing dinner again.'

'You seem to have thought it all through. I have actually booked a table and yes, it would be nice to have company, always better than eating alone.' Rebecca tried not to sound too enthusiastic. He was being friendly, nothing more, she was sure.

The doors then opened and they got on the train, managing to find seats together. In one way, it seemed strange to see João so soon again, in fact, to have seen him again at all, but in another, it felt very natural, as though they were old friends who had planned to meet up. It was different this time, though. Gone was the endless chatter about himself and what he was up to. He seemed less inclined to talk about home or his reasons for having to go back there, changing his plans, as far as Rebecca had understood it. The conversation turned to Rebecca's brief stay in Paris.

'So you've no idea where his sister might be,' João said when she had finished.

'No, I caught up with a couple of her neighbours this morning. I don't know whether it was my less than adequate French or simply that they all prefer to keep themselves to themselves, but I didn't find much out, except that they didn't seem to have seen her for a little while. One of them said she hadn't seen either Carol or Tó Zé in recent times and she had assumed that they were on holiday.'

'That seems like the most plausible explanation,' João commented.

'I don't know why she wouldn't have mentioned it to someone at home. The family is certainly worried.' Rebecca was pensive. She was still wondering how much she would say to Tom when she rang.

'Were all of the pictures turned towards the wall?' João then asked, as curious as Rebecca had been.

'Yes, all of them, in every room. It felt so strange to me. I was glad to get out of there and not only because of that. It would have seemed a bit awkward if Carol had returned, not knowing that someone was staying in her apartment. Her parents thought it was fine, but I wasn't sure how I would feel if I were her. We're not close. I know her brother. It felt like an intrusion, but I didn't like the feel of the place.'

'It was probably the fact that you were staying on your own in a strange city,' João suggested.

'Her boyfriend was Portuguese too. Perhaps you know him.' Rebecca realised that it was a daft thing to say almost before she had finished saying it, but it was too late.

'Portugal's a small country, is that it? You think we're all related?' He seemed a little bit touchy or did he find it funny? Rebecca wasn't sure, she didn't want to upset him. She liked him.

'No, I didn't mean that.' She did feel a bit stupid now. She wasn't thinking that at all. It seemed like a strange coincidence to her that she had come across two Portuguese men in Paris. She tried to retrieve some ground explaining as much to João. He seemed to understand her point and went on to say,

'There are a lot of Portuguese in Paris these days and have been for a long time. Many have come across the years looking for work, when there's been little in Portugal. Quite a few students came to study, others needed to get away. Many Portuguese feel they've good reason to leave Portugal. It has been hard for people to make a living, especially in the countryside and it's also been a difficult place to be for anyone with any ideas at odds with Salazar.'

Rebecca still didn't feel particularly knowledgeable about the politics and was interested to hear more of his views and opinions, but he seemed irritated by the subject and soon turned the conversation away. She didn't know anything else about Tó Zé that might make a connection and still feeling daft for seeming to suggest that all the Portuguese people abroad must know each other, she was happy to talk about other things.

'What are your plans, Rebecca?' he asked a direct question.

'I'm calling to see friends in Lisbon for a day or so, I'm not quite sure exactly how long but I'm planning to head to the Algarve. I have this idea that I'll spend a year in Portugal, really to improve my language skills.'

That was as much as she wanted to offer as an opening. It seemed strange now talking about her plans and as she didn't really have much idea what she was going to do, she was hoping that he wouldn't ask too many awkward questions.

'I think you've got a good grasp of the language as it is,' João complimented her.

'It's kind of you to say, but I know how much effort it takes and I want to be fluent. When no one can tell I'm English, I'll have achieved what I set out to do,' Rebecca said.

'I think most people would find your accent endearing. I wouldn't worry about it. Where are you heading for in the Algarve?' João was a little more than curious. Rebecca may have forgotten that she had mentioned it as they were leaving the train in Paris, but João hadn't. He wanted to be sure.

'I have it in mind to stay in a little town on the Spanish border called Vila Real de Santo António. I have a little bit of an old connection with it and then, a coincidence, a friend of mine who I met first in Lisbon, where she works now, is from the town and invited me to go with her and stay at her parents' house for a while, until I know what I'm doing. Do you know it?' Rebecca asked.

'Yes, I do. I'm quite familiar with it.' So he had remembered correctly, João thought as he answered her.

'How do you know it?' Rebecca was now curious.

'I spent time in that area in the summers when I was growing up.' He offered no more and quickly went on to ask, 'So why that town, what's the old connection?'

'Oh, it's a long story. I'm kind of acquainted with a town nearby, Castro Marim, and several years ago, I heard so much about that area and about Vila Real. It's always been in the back of my mind to go there.' Rebecca was now the one being deliberately vague.

'Sounds interesting. Tell me more,' João said.

'I think the dining car will be open now. I've booked a table. Are you ready for something to eat?' Rebecca asked changing the subject. If she told him, he would think she was mad.

'That's a good idea. After you,' João said getting up and allowing Rebecca to lead the way to the restaurant car.

The food was as good as João had assured her it would be, helped no doubt by the addition of a nice bottle of wine. They talked and talked, staying in the restaurant car while the waiters cleared up around them and until it was obvious it was closing and they must leave. João had a seat but hadn't booked a couchette. Neither of them seemed to want to give in to the night. They made their way down the corridor to where Rebecca was staying and stood outside chatting. João, concerned that Rebecca might want to rest commented that he was keeping her up but he didn't want to leave, he didn't know why, and nor did Rebecca. She was tired but she ignored it and they talked through the night, moving back to the restaurant car for a coffee as soon as it opened again. It was close to the time, in the early morning, when the train would call at Oporto station.

# VIII

João got off the train in Oporto feeling a little tired but good. He was really pleased that he had managed to see Rebecca again. It had been on his mind to see if there was a chance he could get the same train, a distraction from everything else that was going on. He liked Rebecca, enjoyed her company and her humour, which very much resonated with his. He really didn't know why he hadn't told her more and began to entertain thoughts of how he would see her again, even though he hadn't made any suggestions to her. His excuse was that he didn't know what he would be doing and how long he would be staying. As he walked along the platform, something Rebecca had said to him the night before came back to him. She said that the very first time she arrived in Portugal, she had an overwhelming feeling of belonging, of having been there before, strong and quite inexplicable. It had never left her and she felt it each time she returned. How strange that they should both have strong feelings for another country. It was a fleeting thought, he needed to get on. Now in high spirits, he was surprised to feel a wave of pleasure at being back in Oporto again and he began to observe his surroundings with the attentive eye that comes from time away. Despite its familiarity, the magnificence of the old station building with its ornate tiles didn't escape him. He felt connected and proud of his country, deep feelings which had almost been forgotten in his absence. He stopped and looked up at the walls of the station which were lavishly decorated with huge pictures in tiles, most in blue and white, others brightly coloured. Moorish influences distinct in the designs around each picture, images depicting the arrival of the railway, a steam train pothering smoke, speeding towards the city, juxtaposed against a pastoral scene, workers in the surrounding fields, marvelling at the arrival of the train. However, João's favourite had always been the picture depicting the wedding procession of King João and his bride, Eleanor of Lancaster, passing through the city gates, rose petals strewn at their feet. Perhaps originally, as a child, he had been attracted to the picture because he shared his name with the king, but that morning, he was aware of a more particular significance, the Treaty of Windsor in 1386, a marriage and the coming together of two nations, Portugal and England, the longest alliance in history.

João looked around for his brother. His mother had said that he was in Oporto on business and as he was due to return the next day, she would contact him. She thought it would be good for them to travel back together. It was very early, though, and João was not sure he would be there. Sure enough, he was, deep in thought, leaning against the wall at the side of the newsstand under the old clock near the entrance. That particular spot had always been their meeting place at the station, the most obvious place. João and his brother, Pedro, were so alike. There was no mistaking the fact that they were brothers. Close in age, there was less than two years between them. They had occasionally been mistaken for twins, but though they were close in appearance and in their fondness for each other, that was where the similarities ended. Pedro was quiet, happy with his own company, content to be part of the family business, working on the estate. He had married young and his wife, Céu was expecting their first child. João was fond of Céu. He had known her almost as long as Pedro had and he had always felt she was good for Pedro, brought him out of his shell.

Pedro looked up, sensing his brother walking towards him. They beamed huge smiles at each other and shook hands, nothing said about absence. At that moment, no time had passed at all. João's thoughts turned then to the onward journey. Sometimes Pedro would drive to Oporto, but he had stayed overnight with a friend and thought it would be easier to get to the city by train.

'Have you got the tickets?' João asked.

'Yes, we've got a while before we need to be on the platform. Shall we get a coffee?' Pedro suggested

They walked out of the station to the nearest café and both ordered a 'bica', a small expresso coffee and 'torradas', thick slices of hot toast oozing with butter. Until then, João hadn't realised quite how much he had missed the tastes of home. When the waitress passed by again, he ordered two little cakes to take with them for the journey, toucinhos de céu, 'bacon from heaven' as they were called, rich with almond and cinnamon.

'How are things then at home? How's Céu doing?' João asked.

'She's really good and looking forward to the birth, although there's a little while to go, but it can't come fast enough for both of us now.'

João felt a pang of something almost approaching guilt that he hadn't been planning to be around for the birth, but there was a little disappointment too that he would be missing out. He had planned to go back to London. For some reason, the conversation he'd had with his cousin came back into his mind and he felt unsettled.

'I was intending to come back for a holiday but mother was becoming quite insistent. Is there anything I should know about?' João asked.

'Don't ask me about it, you're your own person and I prefer not to get involved. I hear enough about it as it is.' But he didn't stop at that, having been asked. 'You know that mother and father have mixed feelings about you living in London. They don't really like it. They know there are advantages, but there's so much to be done here and it's your heritage. It was alright at the beginning when they thought you would stay away for a while, but everything is so uncertain and even more so in recent days. They're worried that you may want to settle there. They are really unhappy about it.'

'They don't say much to me,' João commented, trying to suggest that Pedro was making more of it than there was.

'They wouldn't, would they? They're worried as always that it would only make you more determined. I'm the one who has to listen to it,' Pedro said, obviously irritated by the subject.

'I'm sorry about that. It isn't your issue.' João genuinely didn't want his brother to have to be bothered by it.

'No, it shouldn't be.' Pedro did feel annoyed, his mother particularly was concerned and talked with him often, as though he could influence his brother.

'I haven't made any decisions yet. I like it over there and I've a great group of friends. Mind you, I'm not going to tell mother and father I haven't made a firm decision. They'll start making assumptions about me coming back and mother will start to plan out my entire life. There's a lot to think about. It's complicated.'

'You are the eldest son. It's all going to fall to you one day and father is keen to slow down and enjoy life a bit more aside from the business,' Pedro commented.

'What century are you living in? Eldest son? Surely it doesn't work like that anymore and we've always been treated equally,' João said, trying to reassure his brother. 'There's room for all of us in the business if that's what we want.'

'I'm just saying, that's where the thinking is.' Pedro was obviously feeling insecure and João wasn't sure why.

'It's a time for change, in more ways than one.' João made his last comment on the subject and called the waitress over to pay the bill.

Half an hour later and the brothers were on their way home along one of the most beautiful train routes in Portugal, the Linha do Douro. For a while, they didn't speak, deep in their own thoughts. The train passed through stunning scenery, following alongside the banks of the majestic Douro River, a bright blue morning sky casting a deep blue hue onto the river, as it wound its way through lush green rolling hills scattered with small settlements and then travelled on through steeply terraced hillsides. On each side of the river, the hills were covered in bright green vines producing grapes of all varieties, not only for the port wine which João's family had produced for centuries, but also other great wines of the region. Pedro never tired of this scene and knew much about the different grape varieties growing on that land, mentioning each one, not for the first time, to his brother: Touriga National, Touriga Franca, Tinta Barroca. As Pedro talked, João's mind began to wander to the generations of people who had lived there and worked the land, honed the giant stepped terraces out of the solid hillsides, tended the vines and harvested their grapes. The train travelled on through a dramatic backdrop of steep rocky outcrops, cutting its way through dark tunnels along the side of the river until it reached the station at Pinhão, the brothers' destination.

João was home. He felt that very strongly, and no less so than in Oporto did these scenes of home assume a freshness, the observation and attention of a visitor. São Bento Station in Oporto was impressive, but João thought that Pinhão's railway station must be the most beautiful in the whole of Portugal. Its exterior walls were decorated with tiled panels, each one depicting an aspect of the port wine trade. This was the life which he felt he had left behind and ironically, was now impressing itself on him again. As he stared back at the station building, he saw, as if for the first time, the two panels of the Cachão da Valeira and the iron bridge of Ferradosa. Those actual scenes of his homeland were now lost, the pictures the only reminder that they were once part of the landscape.

They were heading for the family's estate on the banks of the River Douro. A Land Rover was parked outside the station and leaning against it, taking in the sunshine, was Jorge. He was waiting to collect the brothers and drive them home. Jorge had worked all his life for the estate and the brothers had grown up with him. They had always known that he was their father's most trusted man, dependable in every way and entrusted with any errand which involved his children. Jorge had always been very fond of João, though he did his best to hide it.

'Who's this you've brought with you, Pedro? Ah, João, about time you made us a visit,' he teased, confident in his familiarity, as he climbed back into the Land Rover.

They travelled from the station through the town and out into the countryside, driving along the dirt track roads which wound through the landscape of terraced vines and chatting as they went. Nobody could fail to be impressed by the spectacular scenery, steep hillsides rolling down to meet the river. This was a very special landscape in an area protected by mountains with its very own climate. It was warmer and drier than the surrounding areas. Its rich, dark lava soils gave such excellent conditions to grow the grapes, purple and ruby clusters, which ripened in the sun. The land produced a myriad of port and fruity wines with rich and distinct flavours.

João had left behind a life that many would envy. He was the elder son of the most recent head of a port wine dynasty. The business had been established by his great, great grandfather and had remained solidly in the family, a Portuguese family amongst the many British who had taken advantage of the area, becoming rich on the port trade. João had never told his friends in London about the family business and the estate. It had never come up and he saw no reason to talk about it. He preferred that others didn't make assumptions about him. He wanted to be himself without any preconceptions. As the Land Rover turned the last corner and the driveway came into view, João felt another faint pang. A part of him had missed this land, and though deep down he knew it to be the case, these were feelings he suppressed. His reasons for leaving Portugal had been more confused than he liked to admit.

His mother must have been listening out for the car, because she was standing at the front of the house looking down the driveway as they arrived. Maria João was an elegant, good-looking woman, though she showed little awareness of her effect. She was as happy helping out on the estate as she was receiving some of the grand guests the business attracted to the estate. She loved her children dearly and equally, despite their differences, and though she tried not to show it too much to him and she tried her best to understand, she was very unhappy that João was so far away and was showing no sign of being interested in returning. It had been eighteen months since his last visit. He hadn't been back either at

Christmas or at Easter. As João got out of the car, she walked towards him with open arms and gave him a hug, not wanting to let go.

'Welcome home. It's been so long,' she said.

'Not that long, mother.' João tried to play it down.

'Not that long, it must be two years,' his mother insisted.

'Now you're exaggerating, it can't be more than a year.' João couldn't resist pushing back.

'Eighteen months,' Pedro muttered, as he pulled João's bag out of the boot of the car.

Walking back into the house seemed strange. Everything was so familiar but somehow distant. It was a beautiful, elegant house; he saw that now. Here was his family home, the manor house, its chapel, the magnificent adega, its wine cellars, offices and dormitories for the harvest workers. The welcome out of the way and wanting to extricate himself from any further reference to how long he had been away, João took his bag up to his old room. It was the same. Nothing had changed. He quickly had a shower and changed his clothes, refreshing himself from the journey. He realised that he was now pretty hungry and was pleased to hear his mother calling him and his brother for lunch.

'Where's father?' he asked as he sat down to eat.

'Estate business. He's gone into town but he'll be back this evening and your grandparents are joining us all later for dinner,' his mother replied.

'What's the occasion?' João said, knowing it would irritate his mother.

'Does there need to be an occasion? We often dine together, as you know and having you home after nearly two years, I think that can count as an occasion.' His mother changed the subject away from the evening meal and then, as they ate lunch, asked what seemed to be a continuous stream of questions about João's life in London.

João was feeling a little overwhelmed. He was not at all easy with the situation and he was annoyed with himself for the way he was responding to all the questions. After all, they were to be expected. It seemed like too much to go through almost as soon as he had set foot in the house. He decided to get out and go for a walk, making an excuse that he wanted to have a look at the old place and see what had changed. He was careful not to say that he had missed it, not wanting to give anything away, but he was now looking forward to seeing it again. In his mind, away from home, when he thought about the estate, he remembered it as remote, inaccessible, far from any sense of life, but on that warm sunny afternoon, he found a calmness in the remote location and the grand buildings, some of which had stood for centuries. For him as he grew up, life on the estate had seemed slow and far too leisurely. There was little to do in winter months, then pruning, maintenance and repairs, trellising, training and shoot management until harvest. After that, all there was to do was to wait, so much waiting for the wine to mature, watching the estate's experts tasting at each stage, blending the wine. As he grew older, he had never shown enough interest, he thought, although he had as a child. He remembered summers that were hot and dry, cold severe winters and the inconvenience of the climate. He had not always appreciated at the time what a special region it was, how important its climate and rich soils were to the success of their business. This had been their land for so long, such ideal conditions for making excellent wine. He was proud, though, that his family's estate produced wines of the highest quality and could boast vintage ports year on year.

Beyond the immediate buildings of the estate, he could see the terraces and some of the old vineyards. This was the time of year when the fruit would be setting. Work would be needed to maintain the vines and the trellises. The terraces were supported by dry stone walls, built by hand on the steep hillsides. It was such hard labour, much of which had been carried out many years ago. The vineyards were almost empty of people that late afternoon, but when the time came to gather the grapes from the vines which teetered on these high hillsides, there would be many grape pickers, usually women and girls scattered across the steep slopes, the grapes carried down the hillsides in huge wicker baskets. On the estate, the grapes were still trodden by men with bare feet. His father was adamant that this was the only way to get the important depth of colour for the port wine. João remembered the grapes in large open tanks trodden to the sound of the accordion, the music getting faster and faster, and how when night fell the grape pickers would return from the slopes to watch the grapes being trodden. Those were great days, he thought.

As João wandered through the estate, he continued deep in thought. He wasn't naive nor had he been completely ignoring the events taking place in his country while he had been away from home, though he had tried his best. Somehow, he didn't expect that it would be a danger to his family, away from the city. After all, the business had seen many changes. It had stayed firm and relatively unchanged through difficulties before, over many, many years and under many regimes. Wine has been made in his area for two thousand years. His family had made wine for centuries. They had survived other threats. In the last century, they had even survived the Phylloxera blight, adapting and changing whilst others watched their vines wither, starved of water and nutrients, as the insects fed on the vines' roots. His family had supplied the tables of the wealthy with vintage port until the 1930s when times became hard across the whole of the western world and after the Second World War, when port became less fashionable. They had responded with their usual resolve and had made changes to the business which kept it strong and thriving. Their name and reputation was paramount and they relied on the quality of their wine, but above all, they had been determined to stay as a family business. His cousin in Paris had taken a pessimistic view which had unnerved João. He felt that the revolution posed a problem for all businesses and the uncertainty would inevitably lead to many business men and bankers leaving the country, heading to Brazil or other countries to wait and see what would happen. The biggest concern would be that investment might come to a halt, but João felt certain that his father would make sure that the daily routines continued and that he would find a way through any problems. He was an optimist and strong minded. He had always found a way through the problems. He would again.

It is natural to all of us that when we feel something pressing, we push back. It is natural to feel that there must always be something better elsewhere. Sometimes too, we resist the strong draw of a place, of our past.

These were not feelings of which João was consciously aware. He loved this place. He knew it and it annoyed him when he felt it wouldn't let go. It was that deep sense of belonging, a connection with centuries of living and being, of people's lives entwined with place and commitment to land. Simplicity and timelessness, so hard to resist even in someone who had such a strong desire to break free and to be different, to make his own way.

The next morning, feeling again the need to get out of the house, he walked, without any sense of where he was heading, through the grounds and down towards the estate's offices. As he passed, the morning sun was reflecting on the windows and obscuring any view through the windows and into the building. He sensed movement, a face, a gesture and turned towards it. There was someone there and as he moved closer, the image became clearer, until there she was, Ana Rita. Naturally and instinctively he waved at her and saw her move away from the window. Moments later she came out through the door to the side. Still so pretty, João thought, petite, her long, dark wavy hair shining in the sunshine and that impression of vulnerability, which wasn't real, but which had always made him feel so protective towards her.

'João! How are you doing? I'd heard you were here.' She was, as she ever was, smiling, open, welcoming, straight away wanting to know how things were and what he'd been up to in London.

João was a little dismissive. He had had enough over the last day or so of describing his fascination with another place. Maybe he had talked himself out for a while, but here, he had been caught off guard a little. He hadn't expected to see her and he was unnerved, wondering how she would be.

'Still working here, then?' He said, but it seemed obvious and he hadn't thought to ask his parents.

'Of course. Where else would I be?' The best view from an office window anyone can get,' Ana Rita replied enthusiastically.

'Right, I remember. How many times have you said that? I'm sure you say it to try to convince yourself,' João teased her, but she wasn't impressed. Ana Rita came straight back at him.

'And how many times have I told you that we're not all the same and you shouldn't make assumptions about other people just because you can't see the point of something.'

Then it appeared that no time at all had passed. They were back to the same familiar banter. There was no need for politeness and reserve, but he hadn't missed the hint of annoyance in her voice either. It wasn't really the same and understandably, it was going to be tense. What else did he expect?

'What time do you have a break? We could go and get a coffee. Catch up a bit more. I'd like to talk to you but I need to get back for breakfast. They might be wondering where I am and as you know, I'll be expected for breakfast. We have to stick to the old routines.' João tried to keep the mood light.

'Routines are alright, João.' Ana Rita wasn't prepared to let him get away with anything, but she was annoyed with herself too for letting her tension show.

João tried hard to be as natural as possible, but it probably wasn't very helpful to act as though nothing had happened and it was time to face up to this one, so he was pleased when Ana Rita accepted the invitation for coffee.

The fact was, Ana Rita had agreed to have coffee with him without thinking, a reflex reaction. She hadn't expected to see him that morning or that he might suggest they talked. She had thought that he would keep some distance and so she had not been prepared. She returned to the office as João went back in the direction of the house and now she was feeling more than slightly irritated. She had a lot to do, had planned to work through her breaks today and was happy to do so. Still, João might change his mind before then. She had never found him particularly reliable about arrangements and once he got back to the house, he might have second thoughts. He was probably only being polite, caught off-guard as much as she had been. So she got on, sinking into the paperwork which was strewn randomly across her desk, but which was ordered in her mind at least.

The morning passed quickly and as the hours wore on, Ana Rita thought she had probably been right, he wouldn't be back today, but sure enough, as lunchtime approached, there he was. João had always been able to talk to Ana Rita. It had been an important part of the relationship for him. She was so consistent. She had always helped him make sense of his thoughts and feelings, even in the most difficult of times. It didn't really occur to him that he shouldn't have that expectation of her now. It was the way it had always been. As the morning had worn on, his resolve to face up to Ana Rita began to wane and as they sat down in the café, it dissolved. He turned his mind to other thoughts, keen now to know if she had a view about how the business was going and whether there were any obvious threats. He was sure he could learn more from her than from the family. It would be a much easier topic, he thought and convinced himself that this was neither the time nor the place to have that other conversation.

'Since I've been back, several people have suggested that the new regime, whatever that turns out to be, could be a serious concern for the estate. What do you think?' João had waited until the coffee had arrived to ask Ana Rita.

It wasn't the first thing she thought he would say. She had been given the impression that he wanted to talk about their relationship. Ana Rita was determined this time not to show her irritation, but she wasn't sure if it would be possible.

'You should know, João, as much as anyone else and especially as someone who wanted to break free, that this country has needed to change. So many restrictions, so much fear, the conflict in the colonies, people leaving in huge numbers, families disjointed, trying to make it work. Not only that, the country has been drained of anyone with ideas and of the people who would challenge. You wanted to get away.'

'Yes, I know. It was complicated.' João felt defensive.

'You could say that. Whatever you might think, João, and sometimes you don't think, out here in this part of the country, on this estate, to a great extent, you've all been able to get on with your own lives and not feel quite the same effect that others feel. Your family have been here for ever.

You have connections not only here but in Britain too. You're privileged and not at all as restricted as you feel and certainly nowhere near the restrictions that others had in this country.'

Ana Rita's frustrations were beginning to show and she wondered why he could never be satisfied with a way of life that had so many advantages. As past irritations began to rise up in her, she stopped short of any other comment.

'It's time I got back.' As she picked up her bag and moved towards the counter, João got up and followed her.

'Let me get this,' he insisted.

He paid and they left the café. Ana Rita was keen to get back and so they returned more quickly than they had walked down to the café earlier. They said little, both occupied with their own thoughts.

João knew she was right. Sometimes he couldn't make much sense of himself and why he hadn't been happy to stay. It seemed to suit his brother and he admired him for that, so much more simple. It wasn't the first time that he had lived away from home, though, and so it had never been a case of staying, more of whether he returned. Being away from home had changed his views, mostly in a good way. Wasn't that what it was supposed to do, that was part of going away, to learn, to experience, to question, to bring back new ideas, keep the business refreshed? The success of the family business hadn't been built by people who were isolated, who stayed, who didn't question. They had grown, changed, reacted and adapted and he felt strongly that this would be the case again, despite the concerns.

João had been avoiding a conversation with his father too. After speaking with Ana Rita, he was annoyed for not facing up to all those unresolved issues. He had had an opportunity to talk things through with Ana Rita, but instead he had talked about his problems again. He went back to the house looking for his father and was told that he was out in the vineyards, some way from the house, so João borrowed the Land Rover and headed out to meet him.

When he arrived, his father was chatting with one of the workers, inspecting the vines. João greeted them both, easily and naturally joining in with their conversation. Once he was alone with his father, he decided to address his concern about the business directly and see if he could get a better idea what his father really thought both about the current situation and about him staying away. He needed a way in, so he asked him first about his views on the political situation.

'How do you really think we'll be affected out here?' João asked.

'It's hard to tell, son, but what I do anticipate is that it will become more difficult to keep the investment going in the business. Some of the big bankers are feeling under threat and have decided that it's best not to stay. Quite a few have already gone to Brazil and there's no telling if they'll return,' his father explained.

'You're not thinking of joining them?' João asked, not really serious.

His father resisted a comment about people who abandon their country, realising that it really wouldn't help and he was pleased that João had at least found him out to talk about the estate.

'I don't know how things will work out, but this isn't the kind of business you can leave. We're caretakers of this land and it needs constant tending, not only that, many people rely on us for their livelihood. We've been here as a family for centuries. There have been plenty of difficult times and we've always survived. This does feel different, though.'

It wasn't like his father to express concerns, although João had asked, but it had made him feel more concerned. He had expected to have a lecture about his family responsibilities, facing up to the current situation, the pressing issue of the draft, whether it was right to stay away and so on. He had expected to have to defend again some of his own decisions, for the old arguments to surface, but nothing of the sort. João had anticipated a fight and it wasn't there. He had thought that returning home would only convince him that he needed to be away. Now he felt confused, and that morning too, rather than finding it difficult, it had been good to see Ana Rita again. He left his father saying that he had said he would spend some time with his mother that afternoon and needed to get back. It was true that when he had set out to see his father, he had said to his mother that he would be back and would go into town with her. He wanted to go for the drive and he knew that his mother would appreciate the company.

Spending the rest of the afternoon with his mother didn't help much either. She had obviously decided to take a different approach with him and avoided completely any difficult subject. He enjoyed being with her. He had missed her and now he felt even more confused. That evening, he decided he would get in touch with one of his friends, Rui, who he knew would help him think it through. He was sensitive and dependable and he was a great friend. So after dinner, he gave him a ring. Even though João said he wasn't sure how long he was staying in Portugal and didn't think he had the time, Rui insisted that they should see each other and asked him to go and stay for a few days. In the end, João didn't give it too much thought. It was tempting for various reasons and so it was agreed, he would travel down to the Algarve. As he might have expected, his mother was not very pleased, but she accepted it more easily than he had imagined as he put down the phone before going to find her. As he tried to explain why he wanted to go, it occurred to her that connecting with his old friends might help João to feel differently and so she made no more comment.

# IX

As Ana Rita made her way home that evening, she was aware that she was feeling less content than usual. She knew that it was João. It was all his doing again, she thought. Ana Rita loved her family and she loved home. Life was changing for her too. Normally she wouldn't be thinking or worrying too much about the fact that she was still living in the family house. It was true that most of her friends were either married or like João had left to make a life somewhere else, but it hadn't bothered her. However, this evening, it was all that she seemed to have on her mind. They were a traditional family and it was usual for families to live together under one roof. Quite a few of her friends had headed off to work in Oporto and seemed happy living in what to her was a very different world. Some friends had gone abroad, places she knew very little about. Those were the friends she heard little of now. They were rarely in touch. News came so infrequently. As she approached the house, she could smell dinner and as is the case when that most basic of senses is aroused, she began to feel better in anticipation of sharing one of her mother's splendid meals around the table with family. She remembered too that her sister and husband were joining them. Her mother was a great cook, ingredients were abundant and excellent. Fresh food was so much part of their life. To eat well came first, even if it meant that a large part of their income was spent on food. When she entered the kitchen, her mother was checking the taste of a huge pot of 'Feijoada à portuguesa', a pork and bean stew. She had her own special recipe that she insisted was a secret recipe. It was delicious and one of Ana Rita's favourite dishes. It being almost dinner time, her mother was frying bread in a large round heavy pan. It had been seasoned to perfection and would be ready soon, so tasty, especially when dipped in the stew's rich gravy. Ana Rita noticed that her mother had excelled herself that evening, making 'Pudim do Abade de Priscos' for dessert. It was an egg pudding, very sweet, made with lemon and cinnamon. Strangely too, as it was a sweet pudding, there was a little bacon in the recipe, giving it an unusual and quite special flavour. It had been her brother-in-law's birthday, she remembered and it was his favourite.

Ana Rita was very like her mother, in many ways, but of the two daughters, she was most like her in looks, as was often commented. Ana Rita loved and admired her mother greatly, but quietly, she wanted to be different. Her mother was strong, held the family together and her faith was very important to her. Ana Rita was steeped in that way of thinking too but she was determined not to be dominated by it and didn't like what she saw to be the claustrophobic and superstitious ways of some aspects of daily life. She also felt frequently irritated by the way in which the local priest always seemed to have a view and an influence. Maybe that was unfair. He was a good man.

'How was your day?' Her mother asked as she walked through the door.

'Rather like most other days at the moment. There's a lot on and a lot to get through. I've been pretty busy,' Ana Rita replied.

'Not so busy to have missed an hour or so having coffee with João, I hear.' Her mother was never one to keep her thoughts to herself.

'Is there nothing that escapes you? How did you hear about that? It was nothing much,' Ana Rita said defensively. She knew that her mother would have a view about it.

'Never you mind. I have my ways of knowing.' She was standing by the stove and had continued to make herself busy while she was chatting with Ana Rita, but at this point, she paused and turned to say,

'I'll never understood how you let that one go. Such a lovely young man he was and it was all there in front of you.'

'Oh, mother, not that one again and why whenever it comes up do you always make me feel that it was all my fault?' Ana Rita had always felt upset with the way her mother had blamed her. She hadn't been able to do anything about it.

'Sometimes we have to try a bit harder when things get difficult, not give up at the first hurdle,' her mother commented.

'Please, mother, Anita and Lauro will be here soon and I don't want to spend all evening talking about my past. I've moved on and there are a lot more interesting things going on at the moment,' Ana Rita appealed to her mother. She wasn't about to admit it to her, but it had been a hard enough day as it was meeting João again. She went upstairs to get changed, but also to get away from the conversation. It wasn't long before she could hear other voices in the kitchen. Her sister must have arrived.

The estate was an important part of their lives and Lauro was also employed by João's father. It hadn't escaped him that João was on a visit, but he knew better than to mention it; he had been reminded by Anita to be careful what he said before they left home. He was more interested in the state of the business and primarily, having work and staying employed. Ana Rita worked in the office and often knew a lot more about what was going on.

'Some of the men were saying that things are getting tense at the estate. Work seems to be winding down a bit and we're not getting deliveries of all the provisions that we need. Is there a problem? Have you heard anything?' He asked Ana Rita.

'I don't think I know anything more than anyone else. You, as much as the next person, Lauro, have wanted change. Now it's here, everyone seems to be afraid of it and perhaps rightly so.' She didn't know why everyone thought she would have the answers and she was aware that she was almost rerunning part of the conversation that she had been having with João earlier in the day. She stopped herself short of commenting. These were difficult times, but although she understood why everyone would be concerned, as there were so many uncertainties, she could only feel that it would lead to much better times. She didn't share the same worries. It could have been that it was the end of a long day for everyone, or the lure of the good food, but soon the family was all gathered at the table, enjoying dinner and talking about much more mundane matters. Ana Rita was pleased that the conversation didn't return to her meeting with João and relaxed into the evening.

Ana Rita woke the next morning feeling much better for a good night's sleep. Meeting João yesterday had unnerved her. She hadn't expected to see him and for some reason, she had found herself plunged back almost two years. It was as though nothing had happened in between and although she thought she had done a pretty good job of keeping it to herself, all the old hurt had rushed back in. She had moved on, put João behind her. She had met someone new, a friend of a friend in Oporto and although it was all fairly recent and not easy given the distance, she was happy. She hadn't mentioned anything to the family. She wanted space from all the questions and expectations; her mother would certainly interfere. So far, it had been fairly easy to hide the relationship from her family because it wasn't unusual for her to spend weekends with friends in Oporto. She didn't feel tempted to look for work there. It was too early to contemplate it and she didn't want to leave home. Her mother knew that and so had been happy for her to keep in touch with friends. However, Ana Rita was going to see him that weekend and realised how much she was looking forward to it, especially after her meeting with João. She really needed to see Anselmo. Ana Rita could have mentioned him to João and wondered why she hadn't. Surely it would have made her feel better to let him know that she had moved on and there was someone else in her life, but she had more concern to keep it quiet from her family for a while longer than to score points with João. With the perspective of a new day, she was pleased that she hadn't told him. She didn't like to think she had any regrets about her relationship with João and part of her was quite realistic. Those first long relationships didn't always work out, but João had got it wrong and she had been very hurt. In her view, he had run away from her. That was his way of ending the relationship, abandonment. They had grown up together and knew each other intimately. She didn't know why they hadn't been able to work it out or at least avoid so much hurt, the rejection, the embarrassment. What she had hated most was losing his friendship, being cut off as though all those years growing up together had meant nothing and there he was yesterday, acting as if nothing had happened.

Part way through the morning, Maria João called in at the office. João had mentioned that he had seen Ana Rita and she was almost as keen as Ana Rita's own mother to encourage the two of them to be friends. Her motive, of course, was for João to have another reason to feel connected with home, rather than to approve the relationship. She didn't know exactly what she would say to her and didn't want to make it too obvious. While she continued to convince herself that João's trip to the Algarve might be helpful in making him realise what he was missing in Portugal, being reminded of what he had given up in leaving Ana Rita might also help to sway his decision. She wondered what Ana Rita was thinking and as she found her alone in the office, it seemed a good opportunity to try to find out.

'João said you met for lunch yesterday. I was really pleased he came to speak with you,' Maria João offered as an opening.

'It was nice to see him. I don't think he was looking for me, though. He seemed fairly surprised to see me still working here. I'm not sure why. He was out for a walk before breakfast and I was here early,' Ana Rita replied.

For a second or two, Maria João wasn't sure what to say next and there was a slightly awkward pause, as Ana Rita didn't seem to have anything more to say about the meeting.

'He's going to the Algarve for a few days to catch up with Rui.' Maria João tried to make it sound as ordinary as possible. She didn't want to admit either to the disappointment or to the fact that it had been a surprise to her, so soon after he had arrived.

'Running off again.' Ana Rita was annoyed as soon as she had said it.

'Oh, I don't think so. It's good for him to catch up with old friends.' Ana Rita's jibe had not escaped Maria João. Her instinct was to defend him, but Ana Rita was right.

'He was wrong to go away and leave you like he did. I'm sorry, Ana Rita. I do hope he can make amends,' Maria João said quietly, showing genuine concern.

Now Maria João made no attempt to defend João, quite the opposite and Ana Rita was surprised. In all the time she had known her, she had always defended her boys, even when others might argue that their behaviour had been indefensible. Ana Rita was disarmed for the second time in two days.

'Thank you. I really appreciate you saying that,' Ana Rita said instinctively.

Maria João realising she had let her guard down a little now found a reason to hurry along.

'That's ok. I know it was difficult,' she said and added, 'I'd better get on. I said I'd give him a lift to Oporto to help him on his way. It's a long journey for him, but I thought I could combine it with a visit to see my sister-in-law, Emília. You know João's aunt, of course.'

Ana Rita was distracted for the rest of the day with memories of the past. She and João had grown up together, played together. From very early on, the strong bond between them was noticed by everyone. They were inseparable as children and despite their different backgrounds and positions at the estate, no one ever discouraged their friendship. It was the sweetest thing. As João grew into a teenager, his reliance on Ana Rita worried his mother and she tried to encourage him to other friendships and other girlfriends.

'You'll never know who the right girl is for you, if you don't spend more time with others.' It was a sentiment that João often heard his mother express and he would laugh about it with Ana Rita, insisting that his mother simply didn't know him. They were soulmates, weren't they? Every day, every occasion, every festival and celebration, from being very small, they would be there together. They loved to dance and knew all the traditional folk dances. They danced so gracefully and were much admired as a couple.

It was always expected that João would eventually take his place at the head of the family estate. There was nothing as he grew up to suggest any different. He had loved that land from a very early age. He had spent his free time with his father and trusted workers on the estate, learning about the land, something that in more recent times, he pretended he had forgotten and not without some truth. There was now much he couldn't remember. As a small child, visitors would be amused by a little boy who could tell them all about the grape varieties, the vines that were planted on the acres of terraces surrounding the family estate, the grape harvest and how port was made. Ana Rita shared his enthusiasm for the land and was often there by his side. Nevertheless, his mother, as carefully as she could, continued to encourage other friendships. Ana Rita was a lovely young girl, but in so many ways her experiences were different from João's and she felt that gap would only become more distinct with time.

The time came for João to go to university. His father had attended Coimbra University and so it was the obvious choice. No other was considered. Education was important to the family and they saw the experience, not as necessary for his career, but as cultured; learning for learning's sake and a chance to make other connections, new friends. Ana Rita had stayed at home while he was at university. There was never any opportunity for anything else, but she was a bright young woman and learned easily and quickly. By the time she was sixteen, she was helping out in the estate office and it wasn't long before her attention to detail and understanding of the work made her quite indispensable. She had never had any other job and saw no reason to want to leave the place where she had grown up and that was to her so special. João's open nature meant that he quickly made friends at university and his mother delighted in hearing about his friends and his time in Coimbra. However, the hope that he would drift naturally and gently away from his reliance on Ana Rita faded across time, as on each return from university, the bond only seemed to strengthen and the relationship continued and flourished. Ana Rita didn't like being away from him, and at times felt both outside his life and also intensely jealous, as she heard him talk about his friends, amongst them women.

Ana Rita remembered one particular time and wondered if despite all the certainty João expressed and the assurances he made, if it had been a turning point. João had friends over for the weekend and Ana Rita was feeling left out. It had caused tension and strained words between them. Ana Rita and João's friendship had never been one-sided, no one individual dominating the other. They both had strong ideas and views and there were many times when they disagreed with each other about something but never fundamentally with each other's attitudes until that day. It was inevitable that being away from each other would bring its difficulties and it seemed that they quickly forgave each other. The relationship continued, more or less, as before but João knew that their relationship had changed while he was in Coimbra and it troubled him. Ana Rita was important to him. He couldn't imagine her not being part of his life and he didn't want to lose her.

Impulsive might not have been a word that many would have used in connection with João. On the day he returned for the last time from university, having completed his degree, he was in high spirits. It was a real mixture of elation, feeling that the world was open before him and this was where his future began, but also of a loss. His time in Coimbra was over and his good mood seemed to be set against the backdrop of a kind of silence; mixed feelings that didn't make sense. He felt it was a time for decisions. He shrugged off the feelings. It would become clear, he assured himself. He went upstairs, threw his bags in his room and went out to find Ana Rita. She had been expecting him all day and was bursting to see him by the time he arrived.

'So, here you are. All finished. How does it feel?' She asked him, throwing her arms around him.

'It feels great and it feels good to be back,' he said. 'I've been thinking. Let's get a picnic, go for a walk and find somewhere to eat. It's a lovely evening.'

João had raided the pantry. He brought bread, goat's cheese, huge ripe red tomatoes and 'presunto', cured ham, and some little 'queijadas', sweet egg tarts. They talked about his feelings on leaving university, what he might do, discussed work at the estate, the preparations for the harvest later in the year and drank a bottle of red wine with the picnic, happy to be together. João wasn't sure when he looked back how much he had been influenced by the strong emotions that he had felt that day, an important stage of his life now at an end. It could have been the wine, or an outstanding sunset streaking the hillsides with deep orange light, but as the sun began to fall behind the rolling hills in front of them, João turned to Ana Rita and said,

'We've been together for ever, I can't imagine us not being together. I don't know what I'll be doing next, but I know that I want you with me.' He paused, looking at her intensely. 'Will you marry me?'

Ana Rita was stunned, only for a second, but there was no doubt in her mind.

'I can't think of anything I would want more,' she said and that evening as the sun went down, they drank wine and made plans.

João's mother's reaction was predictable, but she knew her son enough to know that any resistance would only make him more determined.

Soon everyone knew. Ana Rita's family was delighted. Most people felt it was a great match and had been inevitable, although there were others who were cynical, feeling the differences in background were too great.

The plans for the wedding were fully underway when João announced to the family that he was leaving and few understood his decision. He needed time away, he said, on his own.

# X

**28<sup>th</sup> May to 1<sup>st</sup> June, 1974**

Rebecca watched João walk along the platform until he was out of sight, the early morning light giving a hazy, low glow, almost as though he was walking into the mist. She felt sorry to see him go and wished he had been travelling to Lisbon. She liked him. She had really enjoyed his company, but although they had checked contact numbers again before he left, there was something a little distant about him this time which made her wonder if they would ever meet up again. After all, he was from the north and though she was fairly sure he knew a lot more about Vila Real de Santo António than he had given away last night, it was a long way south. She didn't hold out much hope of seeing him again while she was in Portugal. If he had been keen, she felt he would have at least made a suggestion but he hadn't. She had planned to stay for a year, so there was a faint possibility she would see him. If not, by the time she was back in England, he would probably have returned to Portugal. That seemed to be how it was for Rebecca. Timing was everything. It didn't seem to be working in her favour and so she thought that she had better try to put this meeting down to experience. It had been great to have his company, but probably they were destined to be two of those passing ships, as the worn cliché went. The journey to Lisbon seemed long, although without any of the stops of the regional trains, it was only a couple of hours. Rebecca spent most of it staring out of the window, alone with her thoughts.

Occasionally she wandered out into the corridor to stand by the open window, where they had stood together through the night. She went over the conversations they'd had. She was tired and now she wished that she hadn't wasted her couchette and the chance of a good sleep.

As the train drew nearer to Lisbon, fields, single houses, farmsteads and small settlements gave way to more densely packed apartment buildings, as the city drifted more and more quickly towards her. It was a bright, sunny morning as she emerged from Santa Apolónia station, nestled alongside the river with the hills of the Alfama in the background. It was a splendid building, grand, neoclassical. It reminded her more of a classy hotel or a government building than a station. As she walked into the sunshine, she looked back to check the time on the clock set high at the top of the building. The sky was of that deep, incomparable blue which was so characteristic in her mind of the Portugal she loved. A few light wispy clouds were streaked across the horizon, no threat at all of rain. She felt an immediate lift and stood for a minute to admire the scene. In front of her, the red tiled roofs of the buildings were said to be spread over seven hills, as the city rose from the edge of the river, houses set in terraces. As she still had time and the advantage of a small rucksack, light to carry, she began to walk towards the centre of the city and along the streets running parallel to the river, down the Rua da Alfândega and into the Praça do Comércio. She walked into the middle of the huge square, pausing and turning around to look at the buildings on three sides, pastel stonework, yellow painted façades and shady arcades, the balcony where Clara had explained the first Portuguese Republic had been declared and the grand archway which led back into the city. She knew where she was going, making her way alongside the busy road and the Avenida da India which led to Belém. She could have taken a tram, but even as far as it was, she felt she needed the walk to clear her head. It was all now very familiar to her. Her route took her past the imposing Salazar Bridge suspended above the wide river mouth, its structure mimicking the Golden Gate Bridge. She wanted to see again those icons of Lisbon, the Cristo Rei, the tall statue of Christ with arms outstretched standing high on the south bank of the river, a hint of Brazil, the Belém tower, the monastery and the monument. She had also promised herself a pastel de nata when she arrived and as she wanted the best, was heading back to the café in Belém. They said the recipe was a secret. All she knew was that the custard tarts were delicious and though other cafés made a good imitation, she wanted the original. It felt like stepping back in time, walking into the old café with its blue and white wall tiles and red tiled floor. She might even have to buy a few to take away, wrapped so beautifully in their white and blue cardboard pouches.

Rebecca had never intended to go straight on to the south of Portugal that day, even though it were possible. She had planned on having a couple of days in the city to take in some of the sights again and to meet up with her Portuguese friends from the radio station. Rebecca was looking forward to catching up with Júlia now that she had taken her up her invitation to stay with her family in Vila Real de Santo António, but that would need to wait a couple of days. She had arranged with Clara that she would meet her and Bruno at the radio station around lunchtime, and then after lunch decide what to do for the rest of the day until Clara finished work. She had enjoyed the walk to Belém, had felt the lure of a custard tart quite justified, but had forgotten quite how far it was to Belém. She decided to get the tram back to the Praça do Comércio. It wasn't too far from there up to the radio station. As soon as Rebecca arrived, Clara and Bruno led the way to the restaurant nearby, ordering food and drinks as they sat down. The conversation soon turned to news and the revolution. Rebecca admitted that she hadn't heard very much at all back at home and Clara was surprised. As Rebecca listened, she reflected that if she had known more, she might have been reluctant to travel, but felt safe enough now she was in Lisbon and was interested to hear more. Her attention deepened when Clara and Bruno began to talk about friends who had been out of the country for years and were now returning. She wondered what João's reasons for coming back might be and if there was more to his decision than she had assumed and then her mind turned to Tó Zé, missing from Paris. She knew nothing about him and very little about his reasons for living in Paris. Tom had said he had gone there to study at the university. Her thoughts moved to Carol. Probably she had expected more news of the revolution in Britain and thought her parents would be unhappy if they had known she was travelling to Portugal for a holiday. Perhaps both Carol and Tó Zé were in Portugal.

The conversation turned to Rebecca's plans and her journey to the Algarve. They were interested in her decision to travel overland. She decided to avoid telling them about João. She didn't know why. She chose instead to talk about her brief visit to Paris and the overnight stay. It turned out that Clara had spent quite some time in Paris and knew that particular area. She had friends there, she said, and her French was much better than her English, having learned it at school and studied French at university. She was particularly interested to hear that Carol had a Portuguese boyfriend and asked Rebecca quite a few questions that she couldn't answer, knowing so little about Tó Zé, his time in Paris or his relationship with Carol. Clara felt sure if she didn't know him, then someone she knew would. It was a different reaction from the one she'd had from João when she had felt so embarrassed suggesting he might know him. Despite Clara's interest and questioning, Rebecca couldn't give her much more. She knew his first name and she had seen a photograph, but no more than that. They agreed that Carol's disappearance was quite worrying, particularly as she had said nothing to anyone and the apartment had been left so strangely. Clara said that there were different reasons why the Portuguese had settled in Paris. Most left Portugal for work, but some had needed to get away. She asked Rebecca if she could get some more detail from Tom. Tracking down Tó Zé must surely give some answers as to where Carol was.

Rebecca's friends in Lisbon seemed disappointed that she was only planning to stay a couple of nights, but Rebecca insisted she would keep in touch and would return to spend more time in Lisbon while she was over in Portugal. There was so much more she wanted to see, particularly a little further afield, outside the city, but she needed to find out if it were possible to get settled in the south first. Júlia, whose family she was staying with in Vila Real de Santo António, had already travelled south ahead of Rebecca.

Clara and Bruno went back to work for the afternoon. Rebecca walked with them to the radio station, so that she could leave her little rucksack with Clara and then she went down towards the centre of the city to do a little window shopping in the Rua Augusta and the Rua da Prata. She would need some new clothes. She looked around, tried on a few things, but felt it could wait. She wasn't sure what the weather would be like in the Algarve and just how warm. She returned at the end of the day to meet Clara. They made their way through the rush hour back to Clara's apartment in Lumiar for dinner at home and to watch the latest of the telenovelas which had Clara hooked.

Rebecca got up the next morning wondering why she had decided to stay a couple of nights in Lisbon. Now she was in Portugal, she felt anxious to get to the end of her journey, but she had planned her day in Lisbon before she left home and she was determined to enjoy it. She travelled into the city with Clara, so had an early start. She had thought she would explore the Alfama, so when she left Clara, she headed towards the old cathedral and then along the Rua do Limoeiro before cutting up to the castle, through the narrow cobbled streets of Santa Cruz, past houses with peeling paint and potted plants, with washing hanging from nearly every balcony and window sill. At one of the windows, there was a young man playing his guitar and singing badly, she thought, but he seemed confident enough. Rebecca was a little disappointed to hear him singing in English and as she approached, he came to the end of his song and spoke to her in English too. How bizarre, she thought. She had been to the castle before, but she wanted to see again the marvellous view of the city and the river from that high point and so she made her way to the wide open terrace. The view was as breath-taking as it had been the first time she had seen it. Such was her contrary nature, that instead of wondering why she was staying another night in Lisbon, as she had less than a couple of hours before, she was now wondering why she was travelling any further. Surely there would be more opportunities in the city than in a small town, which she had never been to and knew so little about. She knew her route through the city, more or less, and made her way down the Rua de São Tomé searching for the square, the Largo das Portas do Sol. She was hungry now and had remembered a little café with tables outside which looked over the whole of the Alfama to the river beyond. Breakfast was her usual galão, a milky coffee and toast, smothered on each side with hot butter. Gone was her usual dislike of eating alone. She was transfixed by the view and warmed by the morning sunshine, giving the fact she was on her own no further thought, simply enjoying being there. As if she couldn't get enough of the view, when she had finished her coffee, she walked the short distance to another terrace, the Miradouro de Santa Luzia by the church to appreciate that particular aspect of the Alfama and the river. The pergola, festooned with bougainvillea gave some welcome shade. Rebecca was drawn to the tiled panels on the south-facing wall and especially the one of the main square, the Praça do Comércio, caught in time, as it was long ago before it was changed forever, and destroyed in the 1755 earthquake. From that vantage point, she could see exactly where she was heading next, Santa Engrácia church with its large dome dominating the skyline. She made her way down the steep alleyways between the tightly packed houses and unexpectedly, came across a fish market. It would have been far busier first thing in the morning, but was now winding up. She took a little time to look around. Such a variety of fish, which she would never see at home and no real smell of fish, only a hint of salt and the sea. The route to the church had seemed clear as she had viewed it from the terrace, but as she descended, her path became less obvious. She twisted her way through the streets, not always sure she was going the right way until eventually, she came across the church. The inside was no less impressive than the view from the terrace, a huge open space, beautifully coloured tiles spread out under the dome. She wanted to see the cenotaphs of Vasco da Gama, Alfonso de Albuquerque, Henry the Navigator and Luís Vaz de Camões. It was those great travellers and discoverers who drew her to the church. The Portuguese were so proud of the discoveries and she wanted to know and understand more. She didn't think about stopping for lunch. Her next intention was to find the tile museum in the cloisters of the Madre de Deus convent, some distance further on. She loved all the beautiful tiles which decorated so many buildings throughout the country and Clara had told her that the museum was a 'must see'. She wasn't disappointed. The history, tile making, all explained, rooms arranged in order from Moorish tiles through to the 20th Century, and the church of Madre Deus was impressive with its elaborate decoration and extravagant Rococo altar. She was engrossed, lost for a while and as she began to make her way outside was astonished to realise that it was closing time, six o'clock. Clara would be wondering what had happened to her.

When she arrived back at the radio station, Clara had left for the day, leaving a message that they had been invited for dinner at her neighbour's house at half past seven. As Clara had several things to do that evening, she thought she had better go ahead. The message also left instructions on how to get there, just in case Rebecca had forgotten where to catch the bus, but Clara needn't have worried. Rebecca picked up some flowers on her way back to take with her and arrived almost as dinner was being served, apologising for her lateness. She had completely lost track of time. Clara was quite easy about it. She was pleased that she had got back. It was a great evening, fabulous home cooking and as always, so much of it. Clara's neighbour, Dona Isaura was a great cook and loved to have company. She had prepared a three course meal. The soup was almost a meal in itself, 'Sopa de Tomate com Ovo e Pão', a thick tomato soup flavoured with garlic, paprika and parsley, poured into the bowl over a slice of bread and served with a poached egg garnishing the soup. The meal was savoured, not rushed. As it happened, Dona Isaura had been to the same fish market that Rebecca had seen that morning, although she had been there much earlier. For the main course, she had prepared 'Caldeirada à Fragateira', a rich fish stew which must have contained at least half a dozen different kinds of fish. It was garnished with fresh coriander, which had been Rebecca's favourite herb ever since her first visit to Portugal when Clara had pan fried some chouriço with lemon. Clara had finished the dish with coriander and served it with newly baked bread. It had been delicious, as was the fish stew. Pudding was a 'Tarte de Macã', a pastry tart made with Reineta apples in custard, a kind of crème patisserie. Dona Isaura served it with cream. It was fabulous. The wine flowed all evening. Rebecca had to try hard to concentrate. Her Portuguese was improving, but late at night after a big meal, she faded in and out of the conversation. The discussion turned to politics and the confusion everyone was feeling about who was really in charge and whether the new government would be any good or indeed, if it would last. It seemed that everyone was interested in politics, so unlike home. Rebecca was enjoying the company and for the second time that day, she began to wonder if she was doing the right thing heading south. She could always come back, she reminded herself, although what exactly Clara might think about that, she wasn't sure and considering the unrest, it was better to be out of the city.

The following morning, Rebecca again got up at the same time as Clara and travelled into the city with her as she went to work. She said goodbye and promised to be in touch when she had a permanent address and also if she found out anything more about Tó Zé. Clara was still keen to see if she could help. Rebecca had left plenty of time for this last leg of the journey, so she called into a café for coffee and toast one last time before she left Lisbon, although she was still feeling full from the meal the night before. She then made her way to catch the ferry at the terminal, the Cais do Sodre near the Praça do Comércio. She needed to cross the river and then take the train from Barreiro station to Faro in the Algarve. The ferry gave her a magnificent view of the grand square on the river bank and the city rising beyond. It held her gaze, as the ferry pulled away and provoked a genuine sadness in leaving. She wondered if the discoverers had felt the same or were simply eager to travel. This was the first time that Rebecca had made the journey and she wanted the very best view. The train was heading almost directly south, so she found a seat on the right hand side of the carriage hoping to get a glimpse of the sea whenever she could on the journey. It made its way first of all to Setúbal, an industrial port town, but with views across the estuary and out to sea. It travelled on past the town of Alcácer do Sal, before heading inland through the western Alentejo with its rolling hills. Cork trees were scattered across the landscape, some with newly peeled bark, revealing bright orange beneath.

It would soon fade to rusty red. Olive and fig trees with their white and green leaves, fragrant pine trees, and whitewashed houses in tiny villages rushed past the window, until finally the train travelled through Tunes and on to Faro by the sea again.

When Rebecca arrived in Faro, she had a little time to spare before she needed to catch the train for the final leg of her journey. She had told Júlia that she would aim to arrive in Vila Real de Santo António early evening. She checked her watch, double checked the time of the train that she thought would be the best one to catch, then went out of the station to have a look at the city. She crossed the little square outside the station and turned right. She didn't have a great sense of direction but this time was heading the right way. She hadn't realised how close the railway station was to the harbour and the old part of the city and was pleased, as it meant she would have time to explore a little. She had read that the city had been badly damaged in the same earthquake which had destroyed so much of Lisbon in the eighteenth century, so many of the buildings dated from after that time, but part of the ancient city walls were still standing. She walked through a little garden and under the 'Arco da Vila', the archway leading into the old city, and headed for the cathedral. The musician in her was interested in having a look at the organ which she knew had been played by many of the world's greatest organists, an imposing size and decorated with Chinese motifs. She was sorry that no one was there playing it. She had hoped to hear some of its stranger sounds, like the echoing horn and the nightingale's song; another day she thought and then feeling hungry, she made her way back towards the harbour and found a little café. As it seemed a little late in the day for coffee, she ordered a small beer along with a 'tosta mista', a toasted sandwich with ham and cheese and treated herself to yet another pastel de nata, which she thought didn't taste quite so good accompanied by the beer. It was a sunny day with hardly any breeze and warm enough to sit outside the café watching the boats go in and out of the harbour. She felt calm and content, and then was surprised by a thought that she would love to tell João all about her day, share it with him. She urged herself not to feel an attachment to someone she had little chance of seeing again.

The final part of the journey was a little over an hour. It impressed her more than any other section of the journey. As the train headed east following the coastline, it gave wonderful views of the sea. It wasn't long before the train reached Tavira and travelled over the high bridge where she could look back over what seemed to be a very pretty town. She made a note to come back and explore. Not far now; it had been a long journey and home seemed so far away, both in time and in distance. Finally, the train moved slowly into Vila Real de Santo António, the end of the line. There was no chance that she would miss her stop. She picked up her bag and looked in the front pocket for the address and directions which Júlia had sent in her last letter. Júlia had said that she would meet her at the train station, but as Rebecca wasn't sure which train she would get, she had insisted that she made her own way to the house. Only three other people got off the train, although quite a few were waiting for the return journey to Faro. She followed the others out of the station, assuming they would be heading into the centre of town or at least in that direction. She continued walking straight ahead until she could see the quayside on her left and then she made her way towards the river. Júlia had told her to look out for the grand Hotel Guadiana on the river side. There it was, an imposing building, which Júlia had said had been built in the 1920s, much later in date than the building where Júlia's family had their house. The hotel looked as though it had passed its grandest days, built, she had said, for the wealthy visiting merchants involved in a once thriving canning industry. As Rebecca walked by, she glanced into the reception area, with its ornate tiles and polished wooden desk. That part of the hotel looked as if it were unchanged since those early days. She paused a while and looked up at the large picture windows, each with a view out onto the river. Across the way, she could see the Spanish sister town of Ayamonte. It was a short ferry ride away. She began to feel the weariness of a long journey catching up with her and now she was so close, was feeling nervous at the thought of meeting new people, wondering if she was imposing on the family. She was wishing that she had booked a couple of nights in the hotel. She would try to find somewhere to stay as soon as she could, she thought and then, seconds later, realised that she was already outside Júlia's house. She checked the address one last time and then tentatively pressed the button which rang a loud door bell. Within moments, Júlia appeared at the door.

'Hi, come in. It's great to see you. Come and meet my parents. How was your journey?' Júlia greeted Rebecca enthusiastically.

Rebecca needn't have worried. As she was introduced to Júlia's parents, she felt welcome and comfortable straight away.

'We're about to have dinner. Have you eaten?' Júlia's mother asked.

Rebecca then realised that she hadn't eaten a lot all day, other than the toasted sandwich. It could have been the marvellous smells of cooking which had greeted her as she entered the house, but she suddenly felt very hungry. 'Dinner would be great.'

They sat down to a delicious three course meal. Júlia's family had staff, which surprised Rebecca. Júlia had never mentioned it, but there was no reason why she should. There was bread, also cheese and olives on the table. The meal began with 'Sopa de Ameijoas', a soup made with rice and cockles which Júlia explained were fresh from the beach nearby that morning. Rebecca had never eaten cockles and was a little unsure, but tried not to show it. As it turned out, she found the soup delicious. It was followed by tuna steak, cooked with garlic, onions, parsley and lemon, served with sautéed potatoes. Rebecca felt she had been eating huge meals ever since she had arrived in Portugal and after another, was pleased when fresh fruit was served for dessert. There was, as ever, plenty of wine with the meal and Rebecca soon felt completely relaxed. They wanted to hear about her journey and her plans. She had to admit to them that they were a little vague, other than that she wanted to spend time in the country improving her language skills. She wanted to find somewhere to live and some work, although she could manage for a while if it proved hard to find work.

After dinner, Júlia showed her to the guest room and Rebecca, feeling quite tired, got ready for bed and slept through until the brightness of a sunny morning woke her. She got up, had a shower and then went down for breakfast before going out for a walk along the river with Júlia. The sun was now quite high in the sky which was a brilliant bright blue without a cloud. The river reflecting its brightness moved slowly towards the sea, the deepest blue. A small fishing boat was heading out to sea followed slowly and gracefully by a yacht. Rebecca felt she could watch the river for ever. When they reached the river mouth, they paused for a while to enjoy the view disappearing into the horizon and then walked back the same way along the river and beyond Júlia's house, so that Rebecca could see the rest of the buildings standing along the river front. She noticed another grand house at the side of the hotel which she had walked straight by the evening before. It was painted in bright yellow with large open verandas and pan tiles decorating each roof section. Rebecca loved the house and as she stood there, saying as much to Júlia, she felt different. She felt lifted. She could change, could live differently and she could start again. Could it have been as simple as a change of scenery? No, it was never that easy, but it was a start.

'What a fantastic house,' Rebecca said, looking up at it.

'Yes, it's quite magnificent. The family who lived there originally was important in the fish canning industry and also played a large part in the construction of Hotel Guadiana,' Júlia explained.

'Who lives there now?' Rebecca asked.

'Actually, the family who live there now are good friends of ours. They've had the house for several years. I'm sure you'll have the opportunity to meet them while you're here; we often go over for dinner.'

As they walked along, Rebecca told Júlia about her stay in Paris and thought that she should get in touch with Tom. There was a little time in hand before lunch, so although Júlia tried to insist that Rebecca rang from the house, she decided to go along to the telephone exchange to see if she could contact him and see what he could tell her about Tó Zé and his sister's time in Paris. She didn't know if she would be able to get hold of him, but sure enough, he answered the phone almost straight away. He had been hoping for news of his sister and was disappointed not to hear her voice. He was, though, pleased to hear that Rebecca had been asking around and was happy to continue to help. He said he was fairly sure that Tó Zé had been at university in Portugal before going to Paris.

'Can you remember which one?' Rebecca asked.

'I might know the place if you said it,' Tom suggested.

'Was it in Lisbon?...Oporto?...Coimbra?...'

'That's it, Coimbra.' Tom sounded fairly sure.

'I could do with more to go on. Do you know his full name?'

'António José (shortened to Tó Zé) Gonçalves da Silva, I'm fairly sure.'

Noting down the name, Rebecca told Tom that she would continue to see what she could do and would be in touch in a couple of days to see if he had heard anymore. She said that she had heard that many Portuguese nationals had returned after the revolution and put her theory to him that Carol could have travelled to be with him, not saying anything, because she thought they might worry. Tom seemed to take some comfort in the idea, but as Rebecca walked away, she had the image of the apartment in her mind again. It didn't look as though the two of them had set off on holiday.

# XI

**5ᵗʰ – 8ᵗʰ June, 1974**

João had promised himself no more than a month in Portugal before getting back to London. He was feeling a little guilty now that he had decided to spend some of that time visiting friends, but it would be good to see Rui and he was sure it would help him think things through. He had tried to make things better with his parents by offering to meet some business acquaintances while he was there. It seemed to appease his father. He decided he would take the train. It would give him time to think and it was quite a long time since he had made the journey south. As a family, they had usually travelled there for the summer holidays by car, so it would be different. He did take up his mother's offer of a lift as far as Oporto, especially as she seemed keen to visit his aunt. She dropped him off outside the station and he caught the train to Lisbon, spending much of the journey gazing out of the window, surprised at how quickly the time seemed to pass. It didn't escape him that his new friend Rebecca had done the same journey only about a week before, both of them with the same destination. He wondered if she would have arrived by now or had stayed longer in Lisbon. He hadn't mentioned the possibility of seeing her. He hadn't intended to be visiting, but he knew that knowing she might be there had swayed him to say yes to Rui's invitation.

João would have liked to have stopped for a couple of hours in Lisbon on his way down, but the journey would take the best part of the day and he didn't have time. He took the ferry to Barreiro and then the train to Faro, exactly the same route as Rebecca. His mother had made sure he had plenty of food for the journey, but when he got to Faro, with a little time before his last connection, he walked out of the station and across the square to get himself a beer at the café opposite. Half an hour later, he was on his way again and pleased to be getting nearer to Vila Real de António.

His friend Rui was there to meet him at the station, friends from being very young, João couldn't remember their first meeting. The families had made friends when João's parents had taken the children to the Algarve for the summer. Most summers over the years had included a trip to the south and João had spent many happy times on holiday, sometimes staying with Rui and his family. When they had finished school, in two distant places, Rui and João had chosen to go to the same university and follow the same course. Over the years, they had grown close and studying together appealed. Rui was an only son with three sisters, older and younger. He had been disappointed when João left for London, but João had confided in him and he understood his decision more than anyone else. The two friends had kept in touch with regular letters, but Rui had really missed his old friend.

Rui's family was in business, but it was a business honed from the sea and not from the land. His family business, like João's, had been established by earlier generations, although not with quite so long a history. The business had grown out of the fish canning industry in the previous century, but while they continued to have strong connections with elements of the original business, the family had diversified and made other investments. Rui too had been under pressure to stay with the family business. It was something they had often talked about and especially through university, but unlike João, Rui had been happy to take up a position in the end.

João and Rui walked out through the small station building and turned left towards the river, walking with the old canning factory buildings on their right hand side, the lights of Ayamonte beginning to shine across the river. The grand house was less than a ten-minute walk, sitting right on the riverside in front of the small port. A couple of fishing boats were heading noisily down river and out to sea for a night's fishing. The last ferry crossing of the day was about to leave. João had almost forgotten how much he loved the town. The late spring temperatures hadn't yet stabilised into the constant, guaranteed warmth of the summer months, but it had been a sunny day, some of the heat retained into the evening. A light breeze was crossing the coastline and travelling up the river, the same breeze which could bring a certain freshness even on the warmest of days.

Rui's mother had made sure the room where he had stayed so many times was ready for him. It was good to be back. He wanted to hear what Rui had been up to and so they talked late into the night. Even so, they arranged to be up early to go for a run the next morning and take a swim in the sea before the sun was really high. They ran along the riverside before following a wandering pathway through the scrub and woodland which edged the coastline. For the first time in days, as João sat on the beach drying out gently in the morning sunshine, he felt free and content, all the issues that had been filling his head, forgotten for a while. It was Rui who brought up the subject of London again, always curious and never quite accepting that João would want to stay for ever.

'Do you think you'll stay over there then?' Rui asked.

'That seems to be the question that everyone's asking me at the moment,' João replied, sitting up now and staring out to sea.

'It seems that lots of people are making the decision to return hoping that life will change. I'm sure once it settles down, there will be so many more opportunities. It's not an easy time, though, my father seems quite worried about it,' Rui said.

'I know what you mean. My father has similar concerns. Part of me feels that I should come back and face the responsibilities I have, but I'm enjoying London and don't see much reason to return as things are. I can't see the government changing their position on conscription any time soon. I don't think life can be free here. It's different in London,' João felt Rui would understand.

'The way I look at it, most of us think that we've a plan and we're making decisions in some kind of a logical, rational way, but when it comes down to it, it's often chance happenings, unplanned events that make for real changes,' Rui said, surprised at his own thoughts.

'Too much thinking, Rui. I could do with breakfast. What about you?' João asked, trying to change the subject.

For the first time since he had arrived in the town, as they walked back along the river, not needing to say much to each other, João couldn't get Rebecca out of his mind. Finally, he broke into the quietness.

'I had an interesting journey to Paris. I met an English woman on the train. We spent the journey together, had a meal, chatted all the way.' João thought he would confide a little in Rui.

'It's been a while, hasn't it? Is there anyone in London?' Rui asked.

'No one in particular. There's a good social scene and I've a great bunch of friends, good people, men and women, but no one I'd call a girlfriend. I needed a break after everything that went on with Ana Rita. I made a mess and I haven't really trusted myself since.' João admitted to Rui what he wouldn't easily say to anyone else.

'She was staying in Paris for one night, that's all, so although we exchanged contacts, I didn't think I'd see her again. She's from the north of England and planned to stay in Portugal for quite some time, so I felt it was unlikely I'd catch up with her back in England, either. I changed my mind, though, about how long I'd stay in Paris, deciding I'd better get back home and managed to get on the same overnight train to Oporto. She was on her way here,' João explained.

'Hang on. Instead of staying with your cousin in Paris, you followed this woman down to Oporto and now you say she's here. What's going on? Sounds as though you're fairly interested in her. Tell me more.' Rui was interested too now.

'It's not quite as you seem to be suggesting. I met her, got on with her and when my plans had to change, I was happy to get to know her a bit better. That's all.' João tried to play it down.

'Why was she coming here?' Rui asked.

'I've no idea. I assumed to visit someone,' João said.

'You mean you didn't ask her. Where's she staying do you think? She could be in the hotel next door,' Rui suggested.

'No idea either. I have her contact address in England. I wasn't sure of my plans. No, I didn't ask or at least if I did, I can't remember. Something about friends, not sure.' João could see why it might seem a bit strange to Rui. He was usually more inquisitive.

'It's a small town, but that's no guarantee that you'd bump into her while you're here. I'll ask around if you want. There are a fair number of English visitors along the coast, but they don't tend to stay in the town.' Rui was now keen to track her down.

'No, it's ok. I've got other things to do while I'm here. I probably won't have time,' João insisted, but neither he, nor Rui understood why he was reticent.

Before leaving home, João's father had made the phone calls and had arranged for João to join a couple of his business contacts and their wives for dinner the next evening. Rui and his parents were going along too, friends and business associates. It was simply a good opportunity to do some networking and his father was keen that João had the opportunity to represent the business. Everyone met at the house first for drinks and then the group moved only the short distance to the restaurant in the Hotel Guadiana next door. It was true that João hadn't attended a business dinner for quite some time, but both João and Rui had grown up used to such occasions. The evening was convivial and easy going. João wasn't amongst strangers; two of the couples, including Rui's parents, were family friends. There was another couple who he had met once before. It wasn't that long before the conversation came around to João and London. For a moment, he felt tense that the spotlight was on him again, but he soon realised that with all their different overseas connections, it was quite natural to be showing interest. They hadn't been primed by his father, who was a fairly private person when it came to his thoughts and concerns. He wouldn't have spoken about his son with either his friends or his business contacts. However, João hadn't anticipated that there was another reason why there might be an interest.

'We have an English woman staying with us at the moment. She's called Rebecca. She's from the north of the country, not far from the city of York. It's a lovely city. Most of our associates are in London, so it's been interesting to meet someone from another part of the country.'

João had noticed Rui's reaction and shot a look in his direction, wondering if he would give anything away. It was one of those moments when you feel you have to make a quick decision about whether to acknowledge an interest or let it play through for a while. Make the wrong decision and people might wonder why you didn't say anything straight away, jump in and lose the opportunity to find out a bit more and João was now more than curious.

Rui was there before him. For a second, João didn't know which way Rui would take it, but his natural curious nature made him ask more questions about Rebecca rather than giving away that his old friend probably knew her and had followed her all the way from Paris, as it seemed to him. The conversation continued about Rebecca and her stay in the town long enough to give João time to think and to declare his hand.

'I travelled down by train to Oporto with an English woman called Rebecca and she was on her way to the south,' João said.

As might be imagined, this was quite an interesting turn in the conversation and attention was back firmly on João, on amazing coincidences, on the nature of it being such a small world and so on. Descriptions of Rebecca were exchanged and it was decided that it must be one and the same person. João and Rui were invited around for dinner the next day. João felt a little awkward, but thought it was probably all quite natural. He shouldn't worry what Rebecca might think.

The meal over, people made their way back home, but João and Rui decided to go to a bar in the town, not quite ready to turn in for the day.

'So she's staying with Júlia then,' Rui commented once they had ordered their drinks. 'That is a bit of a coincidence.'

'Didn't Júlia say anything?' João asked.

'I haven't seen Júlia for a little while. She's been working up in Lisbon and as far as I know she feels fairly settled there. She's been there for about eighteen months now.'

'What is she doing there? I can't remember her talking about working in Lisbon.'

'She was keen to get into journalism and she's been working for one of the radio stations, the one that does all the overseas broadcasting,' Rui told him.

'So I take it that you're no longer seeing Júlia, then. You didn't say anything,' João offered wondering if he was on difficult ground.

'Júlia and I are good friends. Always have been and always will be, I should hope. As far as anything else is concerned, we've drifted apart recently. Other things have become more important. I get up to Lisbon at times but most of my work can be done here or from the office in Faro. She's got her own life up there.' Rui tried to be matter of fact, but João wasn't convinced.

They walked back to the house through the grid system of narrow streets, and as it happened passed by the headquarters of the local communist party, proudly displaying triumphant slogans and celebrating the revolution.

'I can't help but wonder what there is to come. It all seems a bit of a mess at the moment but the sense of freedom has certainly been long awaited,' João said.

'Júlia will have quite a bit to say about all of it. She always was very interested and she may have seen some of it first-hand. It will be good to catch up with her. I've been worried about her.' Rui was keener to see her than he was admitting.

Rebecca had travelled down to Vila Real de Santo António shortly after Júlia had made her way south to spend a few days with her parents. Júlia had wanted to reassure them that she was perfectly safe working in Lisbon. Rebecca hadn't planned exactly where she was going to stay long-term, because she wanted to have a look at the town before she committed to anything. She hadn't thought it would be too difficult to get accommodation. When Júlia insisted that Rebecca stay with her family, it wasn't a purely altruistic move. She thought it would be good to have someone else at home. Her parents loved visitors and an English visitor was a novelty.

Carol's disappearance had left Rebecca troubled, even though she tried to convince herself that there was a simple explanation. Carol's parents were worried. Rebecca's visit to Paris hadn't made things any clearer. If anything, it had raised more concerns. It had been a couple of days since Rebecca had spoken to Tom, so she decided to ring again to see if there was any news and if not, if he had found out anything else about Tó Zé. His mother hadn't been able to settle. Unable to wait any longer, she had gone over to Paris. With still no sign of Carol, she had contacted the French police, but they seemed slow to show any concern. She had spoken with a friend of Carol who had said Carol hadn't given any suggestion she was going away. Carol had mentioned, though, that Tó Zé was visiting family in Portugal for the first time in years. Another friend had mentioned the name of the place in Portugal and although it didn't appear to be quite as straight forward, given the way the apartment had been left, Tom's mother was trying to hold onto the hope that Carol had decided to join him. Maybe Tó Zé had decided to stay in Portugal for longer. It was strange that Carol hadn't told friends she was going, but perhaps she hadn't had the chance. Apparently, Tom's mother was quite distressed. He was going to join her in Paris, but asked Rebecca if there was any possibility of her helping out again. Rebecca was feeling dreadful. If she had said more about the way she had found the apartment, his mother might have been more prepared, but she had been convinced there was a simple explanation. She had felt she was reading more into it because of her own mood. Carol would be in touch soon, she had hoped and at the time, she hadn't wanted to cause any unnecessary upset.

'What did you say his name was?' Rebecca asked. She had written it down, but hadn't committed it to memory.

'Antonio José Gonçalves da Silva,' Tom reminded her.

'And what else do you know about him?' Rebecca asked.

'I mentioned before that he was at university in Coimbra. We think that he left Portugal around 1969 and relocated to Paris to carry on his studies,' Tom said.

'Coimbra's a pretty big city and that was five years ago. Most people travel to go to university. It's unlikely that he was from the city originally.' Rebecca was thinking aloud.

'Carol's friend, Claudette asked a couple of Tó Zé's acquaintances in Paris, some guys that she didn't know very well, but had met briefly at a preview. They said that he was from a village some distance east of Coimbra, but not as far across as places such as Fundão. The names mean nothing to me. I've had to look at a map. There is also some connection with a village much nearer to Coimbra, but I'll have to find out what it's called.'

'It would be a start. Let me write down the details. I'm in the far south of the country and these places are much further north, but leave it with me,' she said, saying she would be in touch again soon.

Rebecca walked away from the phone booth wondering why she hadn't been clearer about how difficult it could be for her to help. She really hadn't thought it through. She didn't know what she could do, but couldn't walk away from it. When she got back to the house, she talked it through. Júlia wondered if Tó Zé had been in Coimbra at the same time as she had been there or at least if there was anyone she knew who might remember him. They had a quick look at a map so that Rebecca could get an idea of the geography of it all, but they didn't have long to consider it, as they needed to get ready. Júlia's mother had announced that she'd invited two nice young men over for dinner for them. She took great delight, at first, in being secretive about who it was, but eventually gave in to Júlia's insistence. Of course, the names didn't mean much to Rebecca, fairly common names, but they didn't pass her by without the thought that here was another João. Júlia's mother decided that she wouldn't mention that it appeared that Rebecca and João might have met. It would be nice to see the surprise and the reaction. She could explain later.

'Who are these two, then?' Rebecca asked, as they were getting ready.

'I was at university with both of them. Rui is an old friend. In fact, he was more than a friend at one time, but we drifted apart. I started to spend so much time in Lisbon and now since I have been working at the radio station, we've seen very little of each other,' Júlia explained.

'Is it going to be difficult for you?' Rebecca wondered if it might be awkward, but Júlia seemed quite relaxed.

'No, it'll be good to catch up with him again. I could do without my mother trying to manoeuvre us together whenever she can, but it's no problem.'

It was a lovely warm evening and once they were ready, they decided it would be good to get some air and set off to walk along the side of the river, down towards the river mouth. Once they had walked as far as the river would allow, they found a bench and sat looking out to sea, chatting until the sun began to fall behind the town and the pale blue sky became tinted with streaks of deep orange. A pale salmon pink light was reflected across the surface of the river. Happy to sit for a while, they hadn't quite realised the time and when they arrived back at the house, they could hear voices. The guests had already arrived. They walked into the sitting room. Júlia went straight over to kiss both Rui and then João, and then to turn and introduce Rebecca, who by then was looking somewhat astonished.

'João!' she said, not able to hide the surprise.

'Hi, Rebecca,' João replied and walked over to kiss her, on each cheek. She would have loved it whoever it was, such a charming courtesy which she was getting used to, but this was João.

Júlia was as surprised as Rebecca had been. 'You two know each other?'

Júlia's mother looked on with a smile, 'Yes, quite a coincidence, don't you think?' her mother said and the connection between the two of them didn't go unnoticed either.

It was a great evening. Rebecca surprised herself at how quickly she relaxed. The thought did occur to her that it was strange João hadn't mentioned quite how well he knew Vila Real when Rebecca had talked about it on their journey. She told herself not to over-analyse it. As the meal drew to a close, Júlia brought up the subject of Tó Zé and Carol, and of Rebecca agreeing to head off on what both of them thought could easily be a wild goose chase across Portugal. João, of course, knew something of Rebecca's concerns. Júlia was becoming increasingly interested in it as a story, especially given the context of the revolution and other returning exiles. She felt sure that if Tó Zé had left Paris, he would be in the country by now.

'I'll be heading back up north in a few days if you want a bit of company part of the way,' João ventured, and realising there was a chance that Rebecca might begin to find his willingness to join her on her journeys across Portugal a bit of an unwelcome intrusion, he added. 'I'm not trying to follow you around Portugal, unless you're beginning to worry.'

Rebecca had enjoyed his company and had loved spending time with him again that evening, she wasn't concerned at all, simply pleased that he had offered, as she had no idea what she was going to do. She tried not to sound too keen. 'I'll see what I decide to do; not sure I'm going anywhere yet but, as ever, it would be good to have company, at least part of the way. I don't know the area at all. It would be easier if it had been Lisbon.'

The four of them spent the next day together. They walked to the beach, took a picnic with them and even though the water was still fairly cold, they had spent almost as much time in the water as out. Júlia had been in touch with Clara first thing in the morning, letting her know what else they knew about Tó Zé. Clara said she would see what she could find out. Rebecca had been in touch with Tom again and had agreed that she would take a trip to Foz de Caneiro, the village which Tom believed Tó Zé was from originally. It wasn't too far from Coimbra.

'I've never been to Coimbra. I did meet up with some musicians over in England who were from Coimbra and I've had it in mind to visit the city ever since.' Rebecca was now certain that she had to go and explained what she thought she might do as they all tucked into the picnic.

'When are you heading off?' João asked.

'I'll take the train, so I'll have to have a look at the journey times, but probably tomorrow or the day after if I can't get a ticket for tomorrow,' Rebecca said.

When they got back into town, Rebecca left the others and went to check out the times of trains and firm up plans for her journey. João hadn't said anything again about joining her. Maybe he had thought better of it. Rebecca felt a little disappointed. She was enjoying his company more and more and she would have liked someone to travel with, at least for part of the journey. She realised, though, that he probably wasn't ready to go home yet and she couldn't delay any longer. Rebecca and Júlia had arranged to meet Rui and João for a drink that evening. Rebecca was pleased at least to have the opportunity to see João again before she left. She was fairly sure that he would have returned home by the time she got back to the south. She was thinking about how she might suggest they kept in touch without seeming too pushy or without them both being so vague again that it never happened. Rui and João were already at the café when Rebecca and Júlia arrived.

'Are you all set for tomorrow, then?' Rui asked Rebecca.

'More or less. I haven't got my ticket booked so I'm hoping that won't be a problem. I wanted to be flexible in case Tom has some more news,' she said.

'That's good,' he then said, and for a second or two, Rebecca wondered what was good about her going away. He continued,

'How about we come with you, Rebecca? Júlia, you could come too. It would be fun, a weekend in Coimbra, a bit of a nostalgic trip.' Rui, it appeared had worked it all out. 'My mother says I can have the car.'

Rebecca quickly warmed to the idea. It was always better to travel with others and it would be good to be with people who knew the city. It would also be good to have others there to get a view about anything she might or might not find out. She would have been happy to tag along with Rui and João but liked the idea that Júlia would join them too.

'What do you think, Júlia?' She asked.

'I'm not sure. It's a bit sudden,' she said but there was a story in it and it took only a few moments thought.

Rui got in first, though and teased her. 'What's this? Lost your spontaneity?' Can't see a good story? I thought it was me who always had to weigh up all the options before making a decision.' He knew that would be enough to push her. The possibility of spending time with Júlia was his motivation for going, though again, he wouldn't be admitting it.

'Go on, then. My parents have friends over this weekend. They're not going to miss me for a couple of days.' She also knew that any plan which involved Rui would be well received by her mother. On the one hand that was a bit irritating, on the other, it would mean that announcing she was away for the weekend wouldn't be a problem.

It was decided very quickly, without much more thought. They didn't stay out late, all of them wanting to get back and make arrangements for the following day. Rui and João agreed they should get an early start and that they would pick up Rebecca and Júlia at eight o'clock the next morning.

# XII

## 26th April, 1974

Tó Zé's decision to make the journey seemed unusual in two ways. In all the time that Carol had known him, he had never expressed any wish to go home, although she felt that he must miss home. Also, this was a sudden decision, made the day before, completely unexpectedly. Ever since they had first met, they had been so close, spending almost all of their spare time together, evenings with friends, weekends away. They hadn't known each other long before they decided to live with each other. It wasn't that they were inseparable. Both of them had their own interests and routines, their work, but Carol felt the relationship was open, honest. She trusted him completely and in a way that seemed natural and not intrusive. When they were apart, she always knew where he was. She didn't ask, he seemed always to want her to know.

Tó Zé packed only a small rucksack for his journey. He didn't think he would be away longer than a week. Ten days he had told himself with little conviction. He only really needed a couple of changes of clothes. It was very much the way he liked to travel. He hadn't asked Carol to go with him. It would have been difficult to ask for the time off work at such short notice, but she felt a little irritated that he hadn't asked. It was family business, he had told her, and she would only be bored. There would be other times when she would be able to visit. Carol wanted to go with him to the station and wait to see him off on the train. He resisted, didn't want to make a big deal of his journey and instead persuaded her to meet him for lunch at a café not far from the station. It felt tense. Carol clearly wasn't happy, but Tó Zé chose to ignore any hints of annoyance and kept the conversation as far away from his journey as he could.

'How are the plans going for the exhibition?' he asked, as they ordered lunch. 'Have you got everything ready?'

'I'm not the main exhibitor, you know. It's an exhibition space for the duration of the show. I'm one of five new artists who have been given space, nothing more,' Carol answered, but she didn't really want to talk about it. She was irritated now. It was fairly obvious that he would miss the private viewing and she would have to go alone, so why pretend to be interested?

'Still that's great to have the space. It's a fairly high profile exhibition and it's bound to get you some recognition,' he said enthusiastically.

Carol wasn't easily drawn, nor did she feel at this moment inclined to share his enthusiasm.

'We'll see,' she said in a fairly dull tone.

Tó Zé had always been such a supporter of hers, encouraged her. It seemed a bit churlish to be pushing back, but she wasn't in the mood.

Tó Zé made another of what were in the end several attempts to change the direction of the conversation over lunch, trying to keep the conversation going.

'Have you heard from your brother recently? I thought you said he might come over for a visit.'

'The last I heard, he was pursuing some new girlfriend half way across Europe,' Carol said, now transferring her irritation to her brother.

Carol's mood wasn't for changing and Tó Zé felt a certain relief when she announced that she had better get back to work. Carol had had one or two part time jobs in the time they had been together. It was the only way to pay the bills. Although she did sell some of her paintings, it wasn't enough to keep the steady income that was needed to maintain their life in Paris. She enjoyed the job in the art shop, though, and didn't want to upset the owner by being late after lunch. It was a good excuse to get away.

The café was on a small square amongst other shops and cafés, shop fronts and awnings displaying brightly coloured signage, advertising each business. An artist had set up an easel, finding the immediate vicinity and the city scape worthy of record and interpretation. At times over lunch, Tó Zé had been pleased of the distraction, both of the busy Paris square and of the artist to take his mind away from the sporadic silences in between stilted, difficult conversation. The sun was shining as they paid and left the café. Tó Zé crossed over the street to a newsstand, strewn with magazines, newspapers and books.

'I'll get a paper for the journey. Wait a moment,' he said.

Carol waited patiently by the café. She couldn't be bothered to follow him over to the newsstand now and was keen to get back to work. If he was going, he might as well get on with it, was where her thinking had settled. Tó Zé came back over, newspaper in hand and gave her a hug and kissed her.

'See you soon,' he said.

'OK, give me a ring when you get there,' she said.

She felt anxious now, didn't want him to leave and didn't know why. Tó Zé gently pulled away, smiled and headed towards the station. Carol stood and watched him until he was out of sight. He walked through the entrance of the station and then as she lost sight of him, she turned back towards work, realising the time, nearly opening time. She speeded up. She didn't want to be late.

By closing time that evening, Carol was in a much better mood. The shop had been busy, and she always liked to keep occupied. She'd been able to help out a young student who was wanting advice choosing the right materials for a project he had at college. A close friend, who also had a space in the exhibition had called by to ask if she wanted to go out for something to eat later after they'd finished the final setting up for the preview. Things weren't as bad as she thought. It would be the longest time they'd been apart, other than when she went home for Christmas, but she was busy. The time would soon pass and now she had plans for the evening. She would have to focus on work and the exhibition for the next few days. Her life was pretty interesting whether or not Tó Zé was around. She began to feel a little annoyed that she hadn't been more upbeat and enthusiastic about Tó Zé's trip. It wouldn't have hurt to have wished him a good journey, to have told him she would miss him, to have shown more interest. Now she felt she would have preferred him to have seen her in a good mood. She would have liked to have given the impression she was pleased for him to go. It might have made him hurry back a bit more quickly. Still, it was done now. She would have to work on being a bit cooler when he got back.

She went home from work, got in the shower. She changed, choosing a pair of jeans and a bottle green silk top which she loved to wear as much for its feel as for the way it looked. She was conscious that she needed to lift her spirits and happy that she was doing something about it. When she arrived at the gallery, her friend Claudette was already there. She didn't have anything else to take over to the gallery; Tó Zé had helped her with that the other evening. All that was left to do was to make the final decisions about how the paintings would be displayed. A couple of hours and everything was ready. Carol and Claudette left for a nearby restaurant. It was a warm evening for the time of year. The restaurant was busy and they were soon joined by other friends, a regular meeting place on the way back from work. Carol ordered braised lamb, a kind of cassoulet with butterbeans and garlic sausage and a glass of red wine, tucking in when it arrived, realising that she was hungry. She had rather picked at lunch, she remembered. Then, still not completely satisfied, she treated herself to a pain perdu with warm raspberries. She went home that evening, feeling much better for having had a good meal and, warmed by a second glass of the red wine and good company. She was soon sleeping soundly.

Carol had been preparing her work for the exhibition for quite some time and it was, as Tó Zé had said, an important event for her. She thought that she might feel nervous but when it came to it, she was swept along in the atmosphere and had too much to think about than to worry. There was a fairly extensive guest list. All the important and influential artists and gallery owners on the scene had been invited, along with a select number of guests that each of the newer exhibitors had been allowed to invite. It was a good evening. Carol made the most of it, circulating and networking. At the end of the evening, when the room had begun to empty a little, Carol made her way over to a group of friends across the far side of the gallery. As she walked over, pausing occasionally to exchange words, thanking people for coming as they were making their way to leave, she noticed three men who weren't usually part of the group. One of them she recognised as a friend, an acquaintance of Tó Zé. He was someone they had bumped into one evening. Tó Zé had mentioned that he attended one of the evening classes he took. The other two she didn't recognise at all. That was not unusual, of course; there had been a lot of people at the gallery that evening who she didn't know. Claudette also was standing with the group, along with another friend, Marie. As she drew near, she overheard a snippet of the conversation.

'Do you think there'll be a problem?' one of them asked. 'Can't say,' came the reply. It was innocuous enough, but for some reason, Carol stopped herself from asking the obvious question about what might be a problem. That would have been rude. She hadn't been introduced and would have been breaking into the conversation. She was curious, though, feeling relief at the end of the evening and with the encouragement of a glass of champagne, she was tempted to ask.

'What problem?' the question stayed firmly in her own mind, unasked. She didn't know why it jarred. The situation felt uncomfortable and as if to confirm her thinking that something was wrong, she was sure the conversation changed quite distinctly as soon as she joined the group.

Carol and Claudette lived in apartments quite close by each other and so made their way home together. Both of them were still feeling quite happy. It had been a really successful preview for the gallery and for all involved. They were pleased to have the walk home in the fresh night air as a way of settling down after the intense emotion and pressure of the evening. Most of the conversation was about the exhibition, who had been there, who knew who, had anyone sold anything? It was strange that a fairly insignificant question would linger in Carol's thinking and as they approached home, she moved the conversation back to the group of friends.

'I didn't recognise everyone in the group that you were standing with when I came across at the end. Who were those three guys?' She asked.

'I didn't know two of them. Never even seen them around, I have to say, but they seemed to be with Marie's boyfriend,' Claudette said.

'He's fairly new, isn't he?' Carol was curious as she hadn't seen him around much.

'Yes, fairly recent, but I think they've known each other for quite some time. You'll be able to compare notes, or she can get some tips from you,' she said.

'What do you mean?' Carol asked.

'He's Portuguese. He's called Luís. He said that he was a friend of Tó Zé. He certainly seemed to know him quite well.'

'I don't think so,' Carol responded, a little indignant. She had certainly never met him before.

Whether it was the way Carol had reacted or simply that it was the end of a long evening and Claudette was getting close to her apartment, Carol's comment brought the conversation to a halt. They said they would be in touch soon and Carol walked the short distance home.

As she was getting ready for bed, her thoughts lingered firmly on Claudette's last statements. So the boyfriend was Portuguese and so were both of the others he was with. She didn't know Marie's boyfriend. She knew one of the others and then only vaguely. She was sure of that. There was quite a large Portuguese population in Paris. She knew that too and Tó Zé didn't have a lot to do with them in general, other than his evening classes. Maybe that was the explanation. Carol and Tó Zé had a fairly mixed group of friends, as might be expected from two foreigners in Paris. It seemed strange that she had never met or even seen this guy who Claudette was now suggesting was a friend of Tó Zé. Despite the glass of champagne, perhaps because of the excitement of the evening, Carol didn't sleep at all soundly that night. Her thoughts wandered back to the three young men, to the comment she had overheard and to how quickly the conversation had changed.

To most of her friends and her colleagues in the shop where she worked, there wouldn't have seemed anything of particular note about Carol's behaviour over the following days. There was nothing outwardly different. She carried on as usual. She went to work. She went home each evening at the usual time, sometimes joined friends at the nearby restaurant for lunch or dinner. She called by the gallery a couple of times to see how the paintings had been received and whether or not she had managed to sell any of them. She had in fact and was delighted. She had sold paintings before, but this was more significant. It was a much better opportunity to get her work known. However, the phone call which Carol had asked for and had expected when Tó Zé arrived in Portugal did not come. She didn't know how easy it was to make a phone call, but she was sure there would be a public phone, even if there wasn't one at home. The silence was so unlike him. As the days went by, she began to be more concerned and to feel more and more distressed. Her first thoughts were that he must have had an accident. She knew it was unlikely. She tried to steady her thoughts.

Why Carol had not shared her plans with friends was something which occupied many of their minds when Carol went missing. When Carol's mother spoke with them, there was nothing they could say to help or to give any indication as to where she might be. They simply did not know.

# XIII

**Friday 7<sup>th</sup> June, 1974**

It was going to be a long journey. It would be at least four hours, probably nearer five, something which hadn't troubled them the night before. They had been focussed on the idea of a weekend away in Coimbra. Once Rebecca and Júlia were in the car, Rui suggested that the quickest route would be to travel along the coast and head north, as the train would, at Tunes. They could make the first stop around Alcácer after a couple of hours driving. Lunch could be somewhere in the Almeirim area or even better, if they were happy to go a little further, in Tomar. He said it was a place which Rebecca should see, if only for a quick visit this time.

'We'll stop for some lunch in Tomar, then, if we can wait that long and if that's alright with everyone. Let me know if you'd like a break anywhere else. It's quite a drive, but we can take the day. It would be good to get on, but as I say, we could do with a coffee at some point before that.' Rui and João said they would share the driving if Rui got tired, but he loved driving.

To begin with, the conversation was animated, ideas for the weekend, anecdotes about their time in Coimbra. An hour or so into the journey, they all felt settled enough in the company to sink into their own thoughts. When Rui spotted a possible pause for a coffee, everyone seemed to be ready to stop.

Sitting outside the café, Rebecca noticed a phone booth in the little square by the church across the road.

'I think I'll see if I can get hold of Tom. He may already have news of Carol and then we can get on with the weekend,' she said getting up, always hopeful of news.

'I'm sure the family will be relieved when she turns up, so I hope for their sake, she's already surfaced. Don't worry about us. We've followed you here and we're happy to help out,' Júlia reassured her.

Rebecca got straight through to Tom. She began to think that he must be waiting for her calls, not wanting to go out in case there was news. He confirmed that nothing had changed, even before she asked the question.

'No, no news at all,' Tom said, he sounded rather despondent. 'But Claudette has been back in touch. I'm sure now of the name of the village. Where are you?'

Rebecca explained what she was doing. Tom was relieved that someone was close to where Carol might be. He was sure she must have joined Tó Zé.

'It will be tomorrow at the earliest before we can drive out to the village. I'll ring you as soon as I've been there,' Rebecca said.

'Give her a piece of my mind when you see her,' Tom said, now feeling more lifted.

'Will do. Speak soon.' Rebecca finished the phone call and walked back across the road. She really hoped Carol was there at the village.

They continued their journey, crossing the river, the Tejo, south of Golegã, Rui explaining as they passed the town,

'We're not far from Tomar now, only half an hour or so. If we were here in November, Golegã would be heaving with people. There's a really famous horse fair here. Worth seeing if you like horses.'

'Humm...,' was the best Júlia could manage on behalf of all of them, 'let's get on to Tomar before we miss lunch.'

As they approached Tomar, Rui explained that he would need to take a little detour, although they would still be heading north. He felt sure it was a town Rebecca would like and as they were so close, it was a shame not to have a look. They drove into the old historic centre of the town and parked. Rui led them through the narrow streets, heading for the main street. At the end of that road, high on the hill, the castle and convent looked down over the town. Rebecca was fascinated. She hadn't known what to expect, but this town was beautiful and she felt so lucky to be there with friends who were so familiar with the place. Rui was heading for the main town square, the Praça da República, because he wanted to show Rebecca the gothic church and clock tower. Júlia was keen too that Rebecca should appreciate the town, but she was also conscious that they hadn't had much to eat.

'Don't you think we should get something to eat, Rui?'

'That's where I'm going. There's a place near the river, by the old bridge, but we have to go this way, so I thought Rebecca might like a quick view of the square and the church.'

Hungry as they were, they decided to have a snack and save themselves for dinner in Coimbra. Rui and João had the idea over lunch that they should go down to the river and see if they could hire a boat. They spent the afternoon literally messing around on the river, concerns about Carol set aside for a while.

From Tomar, the journey to Coimbra was not much more than an hour. The city emerged in front of them. Its grey and pink buildings rose from the banks of the River Mondego in a huddle of red clay tiled roofs. The grand, majestic university buildings rose above all, dominating the very highest point of the city. Júlia's mother had rung ahead of them that morning. She had booked two twin rooms at the Astoria Hotel which looked on to the river and was convenient for the city. Rebecca had to smile. It was one way of ensuring they kept a sense of decorum. They booked into the hotel. Each pair then took a little time unpacking, resting and getting ready to go out for dinner.

Rui and João had told Rebecca and Júlia to be ready for seven o'clock. They knew exactly where they wanted to have dinner and thought that it might get busy. The restaurant wasn't far at all from the hotel, hidden away down a narrow side street in a little alley. They ordered and shared a large platter of 'Lombo de porco', pork loin, marinated with garlic and white wine and cooked with red peppers. It came with chips, rice and a salad of lettuce, tomatoes, onions and olives. They chose a bottle of white wine. None of them could eat a pudding by the time it came to the decision. As the meal came to a close, Júlia announced she was really tired after the journey. She wanted to go back to get some sleep, so that she could make the best of the next day.

'I'll walk back with you,' Rui suggested. 'You forget how far it is,' he joked. Júlia put up no objection.

Rebecca didn't see either of them as people who were concerned about how much sleep they got. It certainly was no further than a couple of minutes to walk. She had seen the closeness between the two of them through the day and thought maybe they wanted a little time together.

'Do you fancy a walk, Rebecca?' João asked. 'It's a beautiful city at night and I don't think I could sleep if I tried. I've eaten too much.'

'Yes, that would be good.' Rebecca wondered if she had answered too quickly, sounding a bit too keen and then remembered she was sharing a room with Júlia. 'I won't disturb you too much if I come back later, will I?'

'I doubt it and I'm sure you won't be banging around and putting all the lights on.'

'No, I'll be as quiet as a church mouse as we say in England,' Rebecca said as Júlia and Rui got up to leave, exchanging kisses, Rui and João shaking hands. Rebecca was sure that these courtesies would always feel special to her. She would never tire of them. She loved the closeness and it was so un-English.

'I love this city at night. Are you sure you're alright for a walk? It will take a little while. I thought we could wander further into the city and then climb up towards the university. We should be able to get a good view of the whole of the city from higher up than we are at the moment. We're too near the river. I know a great viewing point.' João took Rebecca's hand as she got up. Again, that ripple of pleasure. There was more contact. It was so much more tactile and somehow more gracious. It suited her.

They headed down the Adro de Cima and up some steps. João explained that they were called the Escadas de São Bartolomeu. They crossed the road, the Rua Ferreira Borges to the Arco de Almedina, the twelfth century archway which was the gateway to the city, and then went up another set of steps passing the Torre de Anto. João said the tower had been the workshop of the famous sculptor, Jean de Rouen in the sixteenth century. He was keen to tell her all about the area and to show her the houses that lined the steep narrow streets. It was where he had spent his student years. Finally, they made their way past the old cathedral to the square where the new cathedral stood, then up towards the old university.

'This is it. It's a great view, don't you think?' João was enthusiastic.

'Can you see the old and new convents of Santa Clara across the river? They're worth a visit.' João was pointing into the distance.

'No, where exactly are you looking?' Rebecca asked, straining to see what he was pointing at.

João drew close behind her. He took her hand and used it to guide her gently in the right direction. She felt her heart beat increase as he touched her.

'Yes, I see it. Coimbra is very special at night, I can see why you like this city.' Rebecca tried to appear as calm as she could, but she wasn't calm at all.

João didn't let go of her. Still standing behind her, he drew her to him, putting his arms gently around her waist. Rebecca hadn't expected him to want to be so close. She was surprised but happy and didn't pull away. Looking back, she wasn't sure how long they stood there together looking at the city. She would have been content to stay there all night, she knew that. Years later, it would remain one of her most special memories, a treasured moment.

When they had booked into the hotel, the receptionist had said that breakfast was from eight o'clock. They had agreed the night before that they would get up early so that they could make the best of the day. Rui had been teasing João since they had both woken up.

'How long were you out, then? I didn't hear you coming back in. Must have been three or four in the morning, I reckon. You really like her then? Is there anything you'd like to tell me?'

João offered very little. If he had been prepared to talk about it, he would have had to admit that he was feeling a little confused about his feelings. He tried to keep his comments light.

'Yes, I like Rebecca. She's great, there's something different about her, but we've only just met.'

'She's English. That's different,' Rui said making an obvious observation.

'Yes, that's not what I meant.'

João was unusually quiet and Rui, realising he wasn't going to get much more out of him, checked the time and said,

'Let's get down to breakfast. I had enough to eat last night but I've woken up really hungry. Let's hope it's a good breakfast.'

Breakfast did not disappoint. There was a huge buffet of freshly baked rolls and pastries, cheese, ham, fruit and yoghurt, with fresh orange juice and strong black coffee. As they were eating, they made plans for the day.

'You don't have to come with me, if there are things that you can do in Coimbra. I can get a taxi and hopefully be back fairly quickly,' Rebecca suggested.

'Don't be silly. We've come this far and a drive out would be fun. We can take in some other places along the way or a bit further afield if we want to explore. I've had a look at the map and it's not too far.' João was straight in. He wanted to spend the day with Rebecca but as soon as he said it, he realised that he wasn't the one who had the car. He needn't have worried. Rui was happy to do the trip.

'Yes, we'll all come along. It's part of the reason we're here. What do you think Júlia?' he asked turning towards her. 'You're still keen to get to the bottom of this too, I take it.'

'Yes, I hadn't expected to do anything else this morning. I thought that's why we were up early. We can be flexible and as you say, once we've found Carol and Tó Zé, we could do a bit of touring around. We didn't have a car very often when we were up here as students, so it will be good to have a bit of a look around.'

So it was easily decided. Rebecca felt better that they could make a day of it. They went back to the rooms to get what they needed for a day out and were soon ready to go.

They set out along the N110 main road taking a route alongside the river Mondego. They headed towards the town of Penacova, passing through pine woods, maize fields and orange groves. João noticing some of the strips of sandy beach on the river bank suggested they might stop for a swim on the way back if they had time.

'I haven't brought my costume with me. I hadn't factored swimming into a weekend in Coimbra,' Júlia said.

'Never stopped you before,' Rui said, smiling.

'We'll see. Is it much further?' Júlia asked changing the subject.

'Only a few kilometres, we should be there soon,' Rui replied.

They continued along the road, as the banks rose more steeply from the river. Ridges of granite jutted out of the landscape, olive groves on either side of the road. Rebecca hadn't given the village much thought but as it came into view, she was impressed. The tiny village of Foz de Caneiro was pressed into the steep slopes of the landscape, the houses rising in tiers from the river.

'Wow, that's stunning. I didn't expect that,' she said. 'It looks pretty tiny. It shouldn't be too hard to find someone here.'

'Let's park and see if there's a little café,' Rui suggested.

There was. They ordered coffees and went to sit outside. The café owner seemed particularly grumpy. For a while, Rebecca felt reluctant to ask, but once she had been fortified with what was a rather delicious 'galão', she plucked up courage to go back into the bar, leaving her friends enjoying the sunny morning.

'We're looking for a friend of ours.' Rebecca gave his full name but nothing else. She reckoned that in such a small village it wouldn't be necessary to give any other information as an opening.

'Are you indeed?' was the café owner's response.

Rebecca wasn't sure where to take it, as that hadn't been at all helpful. There was an awkward pause.

'You speak Portuguese,' was his next offering.

'Yes, I do. It needs a bit of work, but I get by most of the time,' Rebecca replied.

'Unusual. You're English.' It was an easy guess Rebecca was thinking but it wasn't getting her anywhere.

'Yes, I am,' she said, trying not to show her frustration.

'Someone must have put us on the tourist map. That would be good, business is very slow. I could do with a bit more passing trade,' he said, clearly not interested in Rebecca's original question. 'You're the second English woman to visit recently.'

The conversation wasn't getting anywhere. Rebecca didn't know what to say, so she paid the bill and went back outside to speak with the others. It would give her time to think and she could get a view as to what to do next. She was going over the conversation with her friends when a man came out of the café and walked over to them.

'He's a grumpy one, that one, and he wonders why trade isn't better. Did I hear you say you were looking for Tó Zé?' he asked.

'Yes, do you know him? He's from here, isn't he?' Rebecca asked.

'No, but he is the café owner's nephew. There was a woman here not so long ago asking for him. I can't remember exactly when.' He offered a vague description.

'Could that be Carol?' João asked.

'Yes, certainly it could be,' Rebecca said. 'But it could as easily not be her. It's hard to say.'

The villager continued, 'She was a bit distressed by all accounts, according to Martim in the café. She didn't stay long. She was in a taxi and the meter was running. I don't suppose Martim gave much away. That's his nature, but I don't know.'

'The woman you describe could be the person we're looking for. You don't have any idea where she'd come from, do you? Did she say where she was heading?' Rebecca asked.

'I've no idea,' he said and it seemed to Rebecca as though they might have reached a dead end.

They began to discuss what they might do next. They were still wondering if there was any trail that they could follow, when the man who had continued to listen in, offered a little more information.

'Tó Zé has been out of the country for quite some time, but originally he was from a village quite some way east of here, Janeiro de Cima, not that easy to get to but you've got a car, I see.'

João thanked him. It was at least something to go on. Rui took out a piece of scrap paper from his pocket and wrote down the number of the hotel and his home telephone number.

'It's fairly important that we find the woman you describe. It seems to be the person we're looking for and her family is very concerned about her. I'd be really grateful if you could contact one of these numbers if there's anything you remember that you think could help. Her name is Carol. She's a long way from home and unlike our friend here, she doesn't speak the language, as far as we know.'

'I'm not sure what I can do but yes, I'll be in touch if there's anything else and if by any chance she comes this way again, I'll ring and I'll let her know you've been,' he said, wanting to help if he could, but not sure that there was anything else he was prepared to disclose to a group of strangers.

Rebecca was wondering what to do.

'At least I can call Tom and tell him Carol is probably here in Portugal. If it is Carol, she's clearly not with Tó Zé. I don't know whether it will make it better or worse. Where is the village exactly? How far is it?' she asked.

Rui said he would have to look at a map. He had never heard of the village but the villager had been clear that it was some fair drive from where they were. With that information, Rebecca really wasn't sure what to do. She was still hoping that Carol would get back in touch with home soon.

'I need to think about what to do next and get back in touch with Tom,' she said to the others. 'There's no point in doing anything else until I've checked with him. Let's enjoy the day.'

'Are you sure?' João asked, concerned.

'Yes, I'm sure,' she said.

'Come on,' said Rui, 'We're not far from Penacova. Let's have a look and see if we can get some lunch.' And with that they got back in the car and headed to the town. Penacova turned out to be a good place to spend some time and to have lunch. It was a pretty town set high above the Mondego River. They headed for the town square in search of another café.

'A toasted sandwich and a beer will do me,' João suggested and they agreed that would do after eating plenty at breakfast. There was a balcony forming one side of the town square giving spectacular views across the countryside from the town's elevated position. They found a café close by.

'It was worth calling in the town if only for that view,' Rebecca commented and they all agreed. The church, they were told was seventeenth century and after lunch, they decided it was worth a visit before they moved on. They went back to the car a little later to have a look at the map and found the village they were looking for. It was a long way.

'I think it's probably too far for today,' Rui concluded.

'It's ok,' Rebecca said. 'I'm quite settled to the fact that I can do nothing about it today.'

Rui suggested that they drove North West to the forest of Buçaco. It was amazing, he told them. It was an area of more than a thousand acres of forest with a huge variety of trees. Many of the species had been brought back from all over the world by the great discoverers, he explained. The road from Penacova to Buçaco took them through beautiful scenery. Rebecca found the forest enchanting. Seeing the size of it, she was sure that it needed much more time than an afternoon visit. Rui knew exactly what he wanted them to see so that he could prove his point; it was a magical place. They entered the forest at the Porta da Cruz Alta, the gateway to the high cross and went first to Cruz Alta, the highest point of the forest where they could see the palace and across the whole of the forest. It was a clear day. There were fantastic views stretching to Coimbra and along the Mondego valley, as far as the sea in one direction and to the mountains of the Serra de Caramulo in another. In the distance, they could see the mountains of the Serra da Estrela. It was amazing. The group of friends fell silent for quite a few moments. They stayed a while before Rui suggested he would guide them down pathways winding through the forest to one of the Baroque chapels. He wanted to show them the Stations of the Cross with the life-size terracotta figures of Christ and his disciples. He didn't stop. He took them further into the forest to see the Buçaco cedar, a huge, ancient tree which he said had been planted in 1644. He then guided them to another gateway and took great delight in telling Rebecca and Júlia that the papal bulls which decorated it were there forbidding women to enter the forest. It was a bit late, Rebecca commented. Finally, Rui took them to the Cold Fountain to see water cascading down the steep steps from a cave in the mountain. At the bottom, the water flowed finally into a pool lined with magnolias and hydrangeas. Beautiful, Rebecca thought.

There was so much to explore but they didn't have a lot of time. They made their way back along the woodland pathways to the car. On the way back, Rui and Júlia were deep in conversation. Feeling instinctively that they needed some space, João and Rebecca walked a little more quickly ahead of them. It was João now who did most of the talking. He spoke about the forest. He had seemed rather distant all day and certainly in the afternoon. He was not at all tactile. There was none of the close affection that he had shown her the night before. Rebecca tried to put it down to shyness in front of the others. Perhaps it wasn't considered appropriate in the public view of daytime. She couldn't help but feel a little hurt. She longed for him to take her by the hand. They reached the high point a good five minutes before Rui and Júlia. She wanted him to hold her while she looked at the view, as he had done the night before, but he stood apart from her. When Rui and Júlia caught them up, he led the way back to the car.

'Now we've come this far north, I think it might be quicker to carry on towards Luso, the spa town and then take a circular route via Mealhada back to Coimbra. The road will be better. We can have a quick look at Luso too if we've time,' Rui suggested.

'You're driving, so you decide,' Júlia said and the others agreed. Rebecca was happy to go along with whatever the others wanted to do. She was having a lovely day and told them so. It was marred a little, though, by her concern for Carol and also, by João's distance. She kept those thoughts close.

They did call in briefly to see the town. It was quite busy with visitors taking in the waters from the St John Spring. They found a charming art nouveau tea room and stopped for a drink before making the rest of the drive back to Coimbra.

That evening, Rui and João decided that they would like to revisit a favourite place. It was a restaurant they had frequented as students. Having got changed, they met in the hotel foyer. They made their way along the riverside to the restaurant which nestled at the foot of a steep set of steps. Rui explained that he had always liked the place. There was a good mix of people, some students, but also people from the town. It was a great place to meet and to talk, to discuss the big issues of the day. He explained to Rebecca that by the time they had been students in Coimbra, the dictator, Salazar was failing. It had been easier to discuss politics more openly. The secret police had always found it difficult to recruit amongst students. In that particular bar, any unwanted visitors would be easily identified.

Inside the restaurant, the walls were painted a stark white. The décor was basic, the room furnished with plain wooden tables and chairs. When they arrived, it was already quite busy. Waiters in short white aprons moved between the tables taking people's orders. Rebecca was struck, and not for the first time, as to how few women were there. Portugal was a very different place for women. There were social restrictions. It still felt very much as though women had a place. She had heard a quote once which she thought she remembered as being attributed to Salazar, 'Homem praça, mulher casa', (literally men in the town square, women in the house), clearly emphasising that it was not alright for women to be out and about. They had their place in the home. It was already quite different for women in Britain. Rebecca didn't feel restricted. She had always been careful in the places she chose to go. She had always let her parents know where she was, who she was with and how she was getting back. She had seen that as sensible and courteous rather than giving her any sense that she couldn't go where she wanted. She had travelled abroad on her own, of course, and her parents hadn't discouraged her at all. Here, one of the attitudes which most irritated her was the way that some men would openly stare, whistle or comment as a woman walked by. She knew they were married and what made it worse was that sometimes these gestures were made in front of their wives. It was clearly different for some women. Júlia and Clara didn't seem restricted. Perhaps that was their background. Maybe they had already established their independence, having gone to university. It would be different living in a big city, where surely attitudes would change first. She felt rather conscious that there was interest in her and Júlia as they moved towards their table. Rui had said she looked different, distinctly English, whatever that meant. As they sat down, he was talking enthusiastically about the food which he said was simple but delicious.

'Can I order for us?' he asked. 'We can get a big platter and share like we did last night.'

'Fine by me,' João replied. He was pretty sure he knew what Rui would go for. He ordered it nearly every time he was here.

'I don't mind,' Júlia said, 'You go ahead. I'm happy for someone to make the decision for me.'

'Yes, go ahead, there are dishes on the menu that I've never tried, so it will be a new experience for me whatever we have,' Rebecca added and with that Rui ordered. The wine came to the table in an earthenware jug. Rui poured a glass for everyone and they began to relax after what had been a busy day.

'Have you thought what you might do next, Rebecca?' Rui asked.

'It's been on my mind on and off all day,' she now admitted. 'I think I should try to ring Tom, as he knows I was going to the village today but I've so little to tell him, other than it isn't where Tó Zé comes from. How far did you say you thought the other village was?' Rebecca felt she'd come this far and she now had a clear lead on Tó Zé. The man who had spoken with them knew Tó Zé. She was sure the information he had given was accurate and so this time, she would find him.

'It's hard to say without looking at the map. Some of the roads will be fairly slow going, especially the last part of the journey, but it's possible to make the trip within the day. We can go tomorrow. We still have another full day before I've got to be back,' Rui said.

'It's a lot of driving when you've the journey home the next day.' Rebecca was concerned that she was asking too much for them all to travel across the country. As they were talking, she knew she had to go. She didn't know how she would get there on her own. She was wondering what João was thinking. He was very quiet again, like he had been during the day on and off, much more distant than the night before. Perhaps she was reading too much into it, but it felt strange.

'I like driving,' Rui said, and turning to João and Júlia, he went on. 'If you two would like a more leisurely day, more time in Coimbra before we go back, I can take Rebecca.'

Rui was fairly sure that João wouldn't want to stay and saw him check with Júlia. No matter what the draw to Rebecca, Rui knew that João wouldn't leave Júlia in the city on her own if she didn't want to go.

'It's an area that I've never been to before, so I'm more than happy to take another trip out and as ever, you know I'm interested to try to solve this one. We can have a look tonight when we get back and see what there is worth visiting in that area too. I can't imagine you would want to stay for long when you find Carol, would you, Rebecca?' Júlia said.

'No, probably not, so long as she's ok. I don't know Carol very well. I'm only doing this for Tom… and for his parents…'

Rui had noticed the slightest of reactions from João, as though he were about to ask something or make a comment, but João stopped himself. Rui reflected that they knew very little about their new English friend.

'Ah, here it comes!' Rui beamed and eagerly made way in the middle of the table for the large platter that the waiter was carrying towards them.

It was a huge plate of grilled steak with four fried eggs, served on a bed of sautéed potatoes with little stacks of rice, crisp lettuce leaves and olives. It had always surprised Rebecca that meat dishes were accompanied by both potatoes and rice. It could be a way of bulking up the meat, although there was plenty for everyone here. They tucked in and complimented Rui on his choice. Rebecca ordered chocolate mousse for dessert. It was one of her favourites and this one was divine. As the meal progressed, Rui started to talk about other times when they had been to the restaurant as students. They had had strong views like many students, he explained to Rebecca and they had discussed them openly. The tables in the restaurant were close together and as the meal progressed, seats nearby were filled. The room became noisy and animated with conversation, the volume rising as people lifted their voices to be heard. Rebecca became aware of the conversations around her, only snippets, fading in and out. She caught the odd phrase. With so much to listen to, this was when she felt her language skills most challenged. Sometimes nothing of what she heard seemed to make sense, other than the occasional word. She could tell though that the heated discussion next to them was about the revolution and the recent change of government. Gradually the others were drawn to the conversation. Naturally and without any appearance of intrusion, they had joined the discussion that was ongoing next to them. Rebecca now feeling a little tired with all the activity of the day, the delicious food and the wine, found it harder and harder to concentrate but she was interested. This was an aspect of life there that as a visitor, she knew little of. She wanted to understand. She wanted to know more. On the way back to the hotel, she spoke with the others, checking and clarifying some of the ideas that she had picked up on.

'We heard very little about the situation over in Britain. So it was a peaceful revolution, then?' She asked.

'In the end, yes, but there had been a push for change for a long time. Many at the university were politically active and some pretty radical. There were protests and there was always a backlash. It could be quite scary at times,' Rui said.

'Were you involved?' Rebecca wasn't sure if it was too direct a question, but there it was.

'It depends what you mean about being involved. It was hard not to be as a student. Many of us had strong views. We found every way we could to protest, not only joining in the big protests you might have heard of. We boycotted exams, wore jeans, grew beards. That was the men!' He laughed, but he was becoming more intense as he spoke. 'There was the constant threat of the PIDE. They did horrible things if they suspected any of us. None of us liked the way we had to live. We felt we were missing so much. A lot of music was banned, like the Beatles. If we managed to see a film, it would be heavily censored – they cut the kiss out of Casablanca, for goodness sake! With the way the government thought, it was hard to see a future. We were studying hard but all there was in front of us was war. So many didn't come back and it isn't finished now, not even after the revolution. Quite a number of students decided it was better to get out. Some of them had to leave for their own safety and continued studying abroad, especially after the situation became tense in the late sixties. I really hope it can change now.'

Rebecca noticed that João had gone very quiet but she was thinking about Tó Zé.

'Do you think Tó Zé was involved?' Rebecca had the impression that Tó Zé had made a choice to live, study and then work in France. It was how Tom had described it but hearing the conversations that evening and knowing more about it, she began to doubt it.

'I'm pretty sure,' João said, 'It wasn't that easy to get out of the country at the time. It would be a fair guess that he had been involved and used contacts to get to France.'

It was a side of Tó Zé that Rebecca had not contemplated before. She had not been aware enough of the politics.

# XIV

The next morning they met for breakfast at half past eight. Despite having quite a long journey ahead of them, they'd had a late night and wanted a more leisurely start to the day. A strong smell of coffee and freshly baked rolls wafted out of the kitchen behind the small dining room. Rebecca tucked in to honey-soaked warm rolls, freshly squeezed orange juice and coffee.

The sun was shining, the sky a pale but bright blue, cloudless, as they got into the car.

'Ok, so we'll go straight there and then when we've checked out the village and spoken with Tó Zé, we can see what time it is and what else we might be able to do with the day. Is that the plan? Everyone ok with that?' Rui checked before turning the key in the ignition.

'Yes, that sounds good. Let's get on.' Rebecca replied for all of them and with that they headed south out of Coimbra on the N17 towards Góis through pine forests and small villages, and then south on the N112, until they reached Pampilhosa da Serra around an hour and a half later. Rui was right; the road wound along the edge of the mountain range, twisting and turning. Twenty kilometres or so south of Pampilhosa, they crossed the river Zêzere and then turned off the main road towards the village.

Janeiro de Cima was situated on the bank of the river Zêzere, surrounded by agricultural land. No white-washed houses and red tiled roofs here, the houses were built with stonework open to the elements, from local schist and large stones lifted from the river, held together with clay. The windows were small, Rebecca assumed to keep the houses cool in summer and warm in winter. Steep steps led up to the living quarters of each house.

Rui parked the car and asked the others, 'Shall we try and see if there's a café or bar again? We found it fairly easy to get information that way yesterday and it's usually a good starting point.'

They walked through the village towards the church through narrow, twisting streets. The houses were tightly packed with some of the passageways between the houses no more than an arm's width apart. Eventually, they found a tiny café.

'Do you want me to ask this time?' João asked. 'If the guy is as closed as yesterday, he might be less suspicious talking to me.'

Rebecca was happy for him to ask. 'Yes, go on then.' They ordered coffees again and sat outside while João spoke with the guy behind the bar.

When he came out, Rebecca was keen to hear what he had found out. 'Are they here? Does he know Tó Zé?'

'Yes to the second question. No, unfortunately to the first.' João replied.

'What do you mean?' Rebecca had expected him to be there. If he had returned to Portugal, where else would he be going except to visit family.

'This is Tó Zé's home village but the guy in the café, Tino he's called, said he hasn't been home for years and as far as he knows the family hasn't had news for quite some time. He gave me directions to the house. I'm not sure it would be a good idea to speak with the family if nobody has heard anything.'

'It's not great news for Tom. Each day I keep thinking that Carol will be in touch with home and all this will get sorted out. If we don't call at the house to speak to Tó Zé's family, did you manage to get the address, so that I could be in touch with them later, if I needed to?' Rebecca asked.

'Yes, I have the address. I've taken the phone number of the café and left contact numbers there. I suggested that he didn't mention to the family that we had asked, in case there's a problem. Of course, I don't know what he'll do. He did say that someone else had been asking about Tó Zé.'

'Who was that?' Rebecca thought straight away that it must be Carol.

'He didn't know and I didn't like to ask much but from what he said, it could be the same woman as the other guy described yesterday.' João explained also that the woman had arrived by taxi, but that was the only information he had.

'I don't know what to do now.' Rebecca was pensive and began to feel a little anxious.

'At least you know that Carol is very likely in Portugal and that she's looking for Tó Zé.' Rui could see Rebecca was concerned and was trying to be positive. 'Nothing terrible has happened to her.'

'If it is Carol, then she was fine not too long ago.' Júlia was speaking her thoughts aloud and as soon as she said it, realised it wasn't a helpful comment for Rebecca. 'I'm sure she's alright,' she added quickly, trying to retrieve the comment.

'I think we should go.' Rebecca now felt a strong urge to get away, put as many miles as possible between herself and the problem. She really didn't know what she could tell Tom. There was so little to go on.

'Don't you think you should speak with the family while you've got a chance? You've come a long way.' Rui didn't feel like giving up that quickly.

'I don't want to make worse a situation which I don't understand by suggesting to Tó Zé's family that there might be some problem, not when as the man in the café said, they hadn't heard from Tó Zé. We don't even know now that he came to Portugal or made it here. Surely he would have come home.'

Rebecca wanted to find out more but it didn't make sense that Tó Zé had told Carol he was going to visit home and then several weeks later, he hadn't appeared in the village. She told the others what she was thinking.

'I've an idea,' Rui announced.

'Go on,' João encouraged. 'We really could do with knowing more but I take Rebecca's point. Life may be changing here, but we don't know Tó

Zé's situation and we could be arousing suspicions or worries when there's no need.'

'I could say I was up in the area, visiting the old university, touring around this area with friends and remembered that Tó Zé had said he lived here and thought I'd look him up on the off chance,' Rui explained what he was thinking.

'But you didn't know Tó Zé, you weren't even in the same year.' Júlia was concerned.

'I'm pretty sure he would have known someone called Rui, but I might say I'm João. It's one of my names and he must have known a João. I'll see.'

'OK, then, but I think it would be better if we stayed here. It will be easier to keep it simple if you go alone and if you say friends are waiting and we really must get on, it gives you a quick way out. You know what it's like, you could end up with a lunch invite.' João went and sat back down outside the café. 'Come on, I'll get us another drink while we wait.'

With that, Rui set off in the direction of Tó Zé's family home. He wasn't away long and as soon as he got back, he seemed to want to get on.

'Have you paid for the coffees?' he asked João.

'Yes, we're all straight,' João replied.

'Come on then, we'll get back on the road and decide where we're going next.' Rui also wanted now to put some distance between himself and the village.

'What did you find out?' Rebecca was keen to know but Rui said little, 'Not a lot, I'll tell you in the car.'

They set off, beginning to retrace their route and once they were away from the village, Rui described the meeting with Tó Zé's mother.

'Tó Zé's mother was surprised that someone would call at the village. She said she hadn't met any of Tó Zé's university friends before. I thought she was rather nervous of speaking with me or rather, a bit cautious.'

'I'm not surprised,' Júlia interrupted, 'We are rather out in the middle of nowhere and to say that you were passing was a bit of a stretch.'

Rui continued without replying. 'The fact is, like the man in the café said, the family haven't heard from Tó Zé in quite some time and it was clear that it distressed his mother. She was questioning me. Had I heard from him? Did I know how he was? I felt so sorry for her. I couldn't help.'

'Do you think that Carol had been to see her?' João asked the question that was in Rebecca's mind.

'I didn't ask, I thought better of it, but thinking about the conversation, I'm sure she would have said,' Rui replied, going over it again in his mind.

For a while, everyone fell silent, deep in their own thoughts. Rui continued driving, retracing their route, heading back through Pampilhosa da Serra and beyond. After some little while, he turned off the road and brought the car to a halt.

'There's a viewpoint here, just off the road. Let's have a look.' And with that, he turned off the ignition and got out of the car. The others followed him. From the high point where he had stopped, they could see the mountains of the Serra da Lousã. The conversation about Tó Zé seemed to be halted too. None of them had much idea what to suggest that might help Rebecca find Carol. They allowed themselves to be distracted by the view and enjoyed the fresh air.

It was Rebecca who spoke first. 'I'll ring Tom this evening, see what he thinks and then take it from there.'

'Ok, then, what shall we do with the rest of the day?' Rui asked.

'Do you want to get back?' Rebecca was concerned now that she was dragging her friends half way across the country and for nothing. They were doing a lot of travelling about.

'No, I don't. What about everyone else?' Rui asked.

'I feel I'm messing up the weekend for everyone with this daft chase across the country.' Rebecca thought it better that she let them know how she was feeling.

'All the more reason to make more of our day out, I would say. Stop worrying about it. We're fine.' João spoke for the rest of the group.

Rui meanwhile had been looking at the map and said, 'I would suggest that we have a look at a couple of places on the way back, take it slowly, find somewhere to go for a walk. We can stop off at Góis, maybe pick up a few things for a picnic and then head up towards Arganil. It's a bit of a detour but not much. I think that a few kilometres outside Arganil, there's a sanctuary we can visit at Nossa Senhora de Monte Alto.' The group was happy to go along with Rui's suggestions.

'Let's get on the way, then,' João said getting into the car and the others joined him.

That evening before dinner, Rebecca went to find a phone booth to call Tom, knowing that she didn't want to put off ringing him any longer. She heard Tom's voice reciting the phone number and saying hello.

'Hi, Tom. It's Rebecca.'

'Hi, good to hear from you, Rebecca. Have you got any news for us?' Rebecca could hear the anxiousness in his voice and felt tense.

'I have news but it's not conclusive. What I mean is, I haven't yet been able to speak with either Tó Zé or Carol.'

Rebecca thought it best to begin with the idea that she knew at least one of them was in Portugal and then to go from there. She explained what had happened over the weekend and what she'd found out. She wasn't at all sure what to suggest next to help.

'Carol must be in the area, so I could stay here for a while longer, see if I could find out anything about the taxi firms she used. Perhaps she booked in advance, gave a telephone number. It's a start. Someone might know where she's been staying.'

Rebecca hadn't made any decision about staying on in the area before she picked up the phone. It came out only because she wanted to help as much as she could.

'I think I need to be there, Rebecca. There must be a flight I can get. Where's the nearest airport?'

'I would say it's Oporto further north. It's a lot closer than Lisbon and there's a train to Coimbra. I know there are flights from Heathrow with TAP, but I'm not sure about the flights from France.' Rebecca said unhelpfully. She wasn't sure about Tom coming out for a number of reasons.

'Are you sure you need to? It seems that Carol is here. I know it's strange that she hasn't been in touch with you all but...'

Tom cut across her. 'Carol's not great when things go wrong. She's had some difficult times before and if there is a problem, I would be worried about how she might react. On holiday with Tó Zé and being thoughtless about letting my parents know is one thing, this is another. I need to come.'

It was decided, then. Rebecca gave him the name of the hotel she was staying at and said that if she wasn't able to extend her stay, she would leave details of where she was staying with reception at the hotel. She tried to cover all eventualities by suggesting that he keep his parents in touch with what he was up to. They could both contact them if for any reason they missed each other. Tom said his mother had gone back home. There was nothing more she could do in Paris. Rebecca said she would ring again later in the morning to see if he had managed to get a flight.

Rebecca walked back very slowly to the hotel. Despite the situation with Carol, she was having a great time with her friends, speaking Portuguese, feeling almost as though she belonged. She was seeing places she wouldn't get to see on her own. She was submerged in what felt like the real Portugal and then, there was João. She didn't really know what he felt. There had been that wonderful moment gazing together at the night time city scape. He had been so attentive and close, but was she misunderstanding the way people were. Relationships felt much closer there. She felt as though she might never find out what he really felt. Events seemed to be working against her chances of knowing João better and she wasn't sure he was interested in her. She was feeling quite low and tried to convince herself that it would be great to see Tom again.

Rebecca waited until they had finished dinner and were sitting finishing the wine before making her announcement.

'I've spoken with Tom. I'm going to stay on here in Coimbra for a while to see if I can find out anymore. Tom's coming over from France as soon as he can get a flight. I'm really grateful to you all for coming with me. I couldn't have found out so much without your help,' Rebecca said.

'You don't need to thank us. We've had a great time and we wouldn't have had the excuse to come away without you.' Rui spoke for the three of them and Júlia added her agreement. However, she was concerned.

'Rui and I need to get back. I've only a few days at home before I have to be in Lisbon, otherwise we'd stay on with you.'

'Don't worry about me. I'll be fine and it won't be long before Tom gets here. I should know tomorrow if he can get a flight.' Rebecca was now resigned to staying and although she didn't feel great about it, she didn't want to show it.

Meanwhile, Rui was exchanging glances with João, wondering what his reaction would be. And he was a little surprised when João said,

'I need to get back home. I'll get the train to Oporto tomorrow morning.'

'I thought you'd planned to stay in Vila Real until next Friday.' This was a change of plan, Rui thought and wondered why João had changed his mind so suddenly.

'It's time I got back and I'm a good part of the way there now. There's a lot going on at home.' João also was feeling very determined in his decision.

Rebecca was feeling down. Everything seemed to have gone rather flat. She felt that she had messed up everyone's plans. Although she couldn't think of a reason why João might have suggested he would stay with her in Coimbra a little while longer, part of her had hoped he would want to. It didn't seem to be a thought that had crossed his mind.

The next morning, they ate breakfast in a quiet, subdued mood, then Rui, João and Júlia got their bags and checked out. Rui and Júlia, it turned out, were giving João a lift to the station. Rebecca didn't get a chance to speak with João on his own. She had imagined that she could walk with him to the station, have a little more time, at least. Rebecca agreed to keep in touch with Júlia and to call in and see her in Lisbon if she had time on her way back to the south once Rebecca had resolved the issue with Carol. The goodbyes were said with the usual promises to keep in touch but João's comments were not specific. Whilst the parting was warm enough, he seemed distant. Rebecca watched them drive away. She felt sad and alone.

# XV

**Paris, Friday 2nd June, 1974**

Even on the rare occasions when they had been apart, Tó Zé and Carol had spoken each day, if only briefly. They were close. Everyone who knew them said so. Now there was silence and Carol was afraid. She missed him so much and didn't know what to think. She hadn't understood his decision to visit Portugal. It had happened so quickly and her reaction hadn't helped. She had felt so irritated that she hardly spoke to him. He tried to explain. It had been so very long since he had been home and on this first visit in so many years, he felt he should go alone. Not being in touch at all was so out of character. As the days went by, it only confirmed her fear that something awful must have happened to him, but she had relied on him to ring. She didn't know where to start. She thought she would go to the Portuguese embassy, but didn't know whether anyone there could help. She tried to rationalise her thoughts. If he had been in an accident, he had all his documents with him, surely he did, and someone would have been in touch. The evening of the preview played on in her mind. She began to feel more uncomfortable about the conversation so obviously diverted as she joined the group. Claudette was quite sure that they were Tó Zé's friends. Carol was adamant they were not. Why had they been at the preview? One of them was Marie's boyfriend, of course, so there was nothing unusual in that. They were Marie's friends. Why was it, then, that she felt they had been talking about Tó Zé? It was silly. She was trying to make sense of his silence. She was anxious.

Carol was on her way home from work when she bumped into Marie by chance. She almost walked by with a quick 'hello'. Marie seemed in a hurry. Then almost as she had lost the moment, Carol had to speak. She needed to find out what Marie knew about the friendship her new boyfriend was supposed to have with Tó Zé. There wasn't an easy way to get to the point. She was thinking quickly as she spoke.

'It was really nice to see you at the preview,' Carol offered as an opening.

'Yes, you too. I really enjoyed it and I love your work. Have you sold much?' Marie asked, genuinely interested, happy enough to stay and talk now that Carol had stopped her.

'A couple of paintings, actually. I'm really pleased and whether or not I manage to sell anything, it was such good exposure,' Carol replied, but her mind was working to find a way around to the three men who were with Marie that evening. She had to mention Tó Zé.

'I was disappointed that Tó Zé wasn't able to make it, but he had to make a visit home.' Carol had to know more. There was nothing else she could do except be fairly direct, although she wasn't happy pointing out that Tó Zé had missed such an important event.

'Claudette said that your boyfriend and his friends know Tó Zé. I actually hadn't met two of them before that evening,' Carol continued, not really sure if she should have admitted she didn't know them.

'Hadn't you?' Marie sounded surprised. 'I thought they all met up fairly often.'

'Really?' Carol was now trying to think when they all might have met up. She felt uncomfortable. Marie would know how close Carol and Tó Zé were. Carol didn't like anyone questioning that.

'It's all fairly new to me. My boyfriend and I have only been together for about two months, but from what I can tell, they're all very keen to support the cause back in Portugal and when the revolution came, it came quickly,' Marie continued.

Carol was confused and was beginning to feel more anxious. She didn't know what Marie was talking about.

'Are you going to join Tó Zé out there?' Marie asked and without waiting for a reply added, 'I got the impression they expected to be able to stay now that the old regime has fallen and there's so much to do.'

Now Carol didn't know what to say. Tó Zé had said he would be away for a week, ten days at the most. What did she mean by 'they'?

'I'm waiting to hear from him,' was the best she could offer, 'then I'll see what we decide to do. It might be a consideration in the future.'

'Yes, that's possibly for the best. I don't think they're sure quite how safe the situation will be for them yet,' Marie added.

Carol was now feeling very panicked. She didn't want Marie to know that she had no idea what she was talking about. She needed to know more. There didn't seem to be a way of asking anything else without giving too much away. Now all she wanted to do was get home. It couldn't be Tó Zé that Marie was talking about. It didn't make sense.

Marie changed the subject a little. 'If you're at a loose end with Tó Zé away, Claudette and I are going out for a meal tomorrow, why don't you come too?'

'That would be nice, thank you.' Carol answered, but she wasn't really concentrating.

'See you tomorrow, then?' Marie asked to confirm, thinking Carol was looking rather distracted.

'Yes, I should be free,' Carol said vacantly and with that they said goodbye and each went on their way.

Carol walked back to the apartment in a daze. What did it mean? Once back at home, she got changed out of her work clothes and started to prepare something to eat. She wasn't hungry and having quickly cooked an omelette, she couldn't eat it. She threw it in the bin. For most of the evening, she sat in silence. She tried to make sense of how Tó Zé could have had friends that she didn't know about. How he could have been meeting them without her knowing? Why would he keep it from her? She began to feel very tired. She got ready for bed and tried to sleep. The night had closed in and as the hours and minutes passed by, Carol felt that she was suffocating. The darkness increased her feelings of panic. They had planned to stay. He wasn't coming back. She really couldn't understand it. It didn't make sense when she thought of their last conversation. There was no suggestion that he was going there to stay for longer. He had been quite clear that it was a short trip. If he had wanted to go for longer, he wouldn't have gone without her. Marie must have misunderstood what her boyfriend had said, but Carol felt so frightened. Eventually, a kind of exhaustion took over her and she slept for a couple of hours before waking with the morning light. For a tiny moment, as she became conscious, she had forgotten he wasn't there, then suddenly, everything came flooding back to her. She felt sick.

She would go and see Marie to confirm that she would join them for dinner. She hadn't asked what time and where exactly, so she had an excuse to catch up with her. She was almost too scared to find out more now, but the only person who seemed to be able to help out was Marie. There was nobody else to ask, although she wasn't sure that she knew much more. She knew where Marie worked. It wasn't too far out of her way, so she called before she went to the shop. Marie hadn't arrived for work, so Carol left a message. She would have to wait until later to speak with her again.

That evening, Carol hoped that she could bring the conversation around to Marie's boyfriend and that way glean a bit more. She didn't want to alert Marie or Claudette in any way as to suggest that she didn't know where Tó Zé was. As it happened, it was fairly easy. Marie was more than happy to be talking about her boyfriend and he too was planning a trip to Portugal. She was going to miss him, she said, because he would be away for at least a month. He was going to meet up with the group of friends who had already gone back. As she talked, Carol was trying to make sense of what could have happened. Tó Zé had got caught up in something that he had not expected or intended. She was sure that his intentions were for a short trip, whatever else he might have concealed from her. She tried not to make assumptions. She tried to believe that there was a better explanation. She said very little. She asked as many questions as she felt she could. She didn't want to seem too interested. When she had heard as much as she could stand to hear, she made an excuse about having to get into work very early the next morning to go through some new stock and left her two friends to the rest of the evening.

As she walked along, her steps getting quicker and quicker, she felt more and more upset. If Marie's innocent explanation was correct, she didn't know Tó Zé. She had never known him. He had left telling her lies. He had lied from the beginning. She tried to counter her negative thoughts, but there was an overwhelming feeling that he did not intend to return to France. She went straight home and packed a bag. She would go to Portugal. Carol didn't sleep at all that night, at least that's how it seemed to her.

The next morning, she had lost her nerve. She couldn't go. It was the realisation with the clarity of a new day that she had no idea how she could follow him. She didn't know where he was. The next days were spent in a daze, hoping each day would be the day he returned. To everyone else, she appeared to carry on as usual. She went to work. She didn't avoid friends, but kept any meeting brief, not wanting to be asked any questions. She didn't want them to know that Tó Zé had let her down, had lied to her. She wanted to be proved wrong. Then one evening, her distress increasing, unable to stay calm, feeling there was no one she could talk to, she started to look through his things. They shared everything – wardrobe, drawers, didn't keep anything separate. There couldn't be anything in the apartment that she hadn't already seen, but she needed to find something, an address book, perhaps, why wasn't there an address book? Why weren't there any clues if he had been keeping things from her? She moved from room to room, opening and closing cupboards and drawers, slamming them closed as her distress turned to anger and frustration. Nothing. She sat down on the bed, her head in her hands, frustration turning now to tears. She was right. The search had only confirmed that there was nothing in the apartment. She sat for what seemed like a long time, then began to feel tired, fed up with herself, no longer with any energy to stay angry. She got up and went over to one of the drawers which hadn't closed properly and opened it again. She began to tidy the drawer, taking clothes out and folding them. One of Tó Zé's tee-shirts had got crushed, pushed to the back of the drawer. She took it out to straighten it and as she did, something fell out onto the floor. She bent down to pick it up and looked at it more closely. It was a bank book. She had never seen it before, but there was his name. She opened it, couldn't resist. A small piece of paper floated out and fell on the bed. She picked it up and read it, an address in Portugal. She looked more closely at the bank book, turning each page slowly, carefully. Listed one after another, were transfers of money, international transfers, one each month. She stared at the page for a while, not moving, then put the piece of paper back inside, placed the bank book on the bed and began to take everything out of the drawer. When it was empty, tripping over the pile of clothes she had made, cursing, she went to get a bag and started to fill it, folding each piece of clothing carefully as she did.

Days went by. Each evening she was busy in the apartment. She carried on tidying, clearing, until she was satisfied that everything was done. Each night was a sleepless night. Each morning the same. Then one morning she got up, had a shower, got dressed and made herself a cup of coffee. As she drank her coffee, sitting on the floor in front of the sofa, she started to thumb through one of the newspapers which was waiting to be thrown out. One particular article struck her for the first time. She didn't remember seeing it before. It was about the fall of the dictatorship in Portugal. She couldn't bring herself to read all of it. She put the empty cup down onto the coffee table on a plate she had left there the night before and got up. She went back into her bedroom to get her coat and the bag which she had packed the night before. She made a final check of her bag to make sure that she had everything she needed. Yes, all of her jewellery, everything that was valuable. She removed a red jumper from the bag and threw it over the arm of the sofa. She paused with her hand on the handle of the door, wondering if there was anything else she needed, then she left the apartment, locking the door behind her. She headed towards the train station.

# XVI

**Coimbra, 10<sup>th</sup> June, 1974**

Rebecca went back to her room for a while, wondering what she should do with the morning. A new day in the city was underway. The streets outside were busy and even inside the room, the distant hum of activity could be heard clearly. Despite that, Rebecca felt a silence, the emptiness left when one has grown used to company and then suddenly it has gone. There was no point ringing Tom, not yet. She had to give him time to contact a travel agent to see if he could make arrangements before ringing him. He would need the morning at least. She felt the weekend had ended abruptly and she had lost something which she could not retrieve. She wasn't sure why she felt that way. They hadn't intended to stay more than three nights and she had made the decision to stay on, but João had been so distant when he left. She tried to drag herself away from thoughts which were only making her unhappy. It was silly to feel down after what had been such a good weekend in so many ways. Her decision to stay to help Tom was the right decision. She was in a beautiful city with so much still to see. On the first night, João had pointed out several places which she could visit. She began to feel the need to see those places now. It made a connection with him, even though he had gone. She went out and bought a guide to the city at a newsagents near to the hotel and worked out a route which she thought would be manageable in the morning. She set out in the direction of the old cathedral, walking more slowly than would have been her customary pace. She wasn't really in the mood for sightseeing that morning. The guidebook said the cathedral was twelfth century. It wasn't one of the most attractive buildings in the city, Romanesque, it was more like a fortress than a church. She went inside and was drawn towards the altar piece, gilded and ornately carved. She sat down in the calm quietness of the cathedral, contemplating the different scenes in front of her, trying to work out the meaning and allowing her thoughts to wander for a while. She checked the time. It was only half past ten. She took out the guidebook. The new cathedral, as it was called, built four hundred years later, wasn't far away, so she headed in that direction. It was much more elaborate, a real contrast to the old cathedral. It deserved much more attention, but she noticed now that she was close again to the university. She felt the need to return, to retrace the steps of the first evening. She walked again up through steep alleyways towards the top of the hill, winding through the streets lined with houses, until she came again to the repúblicas. There they were again, student lodgings since medieval times. She paused outside the one which João had pointed out to her as the place where he had lived as a student. She missed him. She wandered into the open square of the university with its magnificent buildings and views across the whole of the city. In the calmness of the morning, she wondered what it must have been like during the student protests. In the sunshine and under clear blue skies, any sense of conflict and unrest seemed impossible. Time for lunch. Rebecca had begun to feel hungry. She had picked at breakfast and apart from feeling the need to eat, lunch would pass a little more time before she rang Tom. She made her way to the upper town's main square, the Praça da República. She bought a newspaper, so that she would have something to read while she ate and then found a café, ordering a coffee and a toasted sandwich.

Rebecca checked her watch, half past one, Tom would have had time to make the phone calls by now. She walked across the square to a phone booth and dialled Tom's number.

'Hi, Tom, it's Rebecca. Have you managed to organise anything?'

'Yes, everything's arranged. I have a flight tomorrow to Oporto and I've hired a car. I thought it would be easier. You seemed to have to do quite a bit of travelling around and this way we can be flexible,' Tom said.

'Good idea,' Rebecca said. She hadn't thought to suggest it, but it would be much easier with a car.

'I've got the name of your hotel, I don't know what time I'll get to you but it'll be later on in the day. Let reception know where you're going and I'll come and find you when I get there, or I'll hang around until you're back. I've rung the hotel and booked a room.'

He had certainly got it all sorted out from his point of view, so that didn't leave Rebecca anything to organise.

'I don't know what I can do in the meantime. I could ring the café in the first village. The guy wasn't very helpful, but he may remember the name of the taxi firm that Carol used to get there,' Rebecca suggested.

'That would be a start. I know it's difficult, but there isn't much to go on at the moment, so if you can find out anything else, that would be great. See you tomorrow, then,' Tom said.

With that, Rebecca put down the receiver. 'Right then,' she thought, 'let's see what I can do before Tom gets here.' It was good to have the distraction.

Rebecca wondered why she hadn't asked the first time. The café owner did remember. It was a taxi firm based in Coimbra. She decided to go back to the hotel. Surely they would know the firm and if they had an office, it would be better to go and speak with them than to try to make herself understood on the phone, or more importantly to be sure she understood. However, when she explained to the receptionist at the hotel, he was happy to ring. As he was speaking, Rebecca was thinking that it was a bit of a longshot, but it turned out that the taxi firm kept a log of taxis booked. One of the drivers who was in the office thought he had remembered Carol, certainly an English woman of a similar description. The receptionist said he thought it was worth following up. He took out a map of the city, marked the hotel where the woman had been picked up and showed Rebecca on the map how she could get there.

'Thanks ever so much,' Rebecca said to the receptionist. 'At least I can try.'

'I'll ring ahead and let them know you're coming. It'll give them chance to look at their records,' he offered.

'That would be great. Oh, thank you. I really appreciate your help,' Rebecca said as she was heading out.

The hotel was about a fifteen minute walk away. When Rebecca got there, the receptionist was expecting her.

'We have to be careful with guest information, but I can tell you that your friend did stay here,' the receptionist explained. 'She was here for several days.'

'I know it's unlikely you would know, but did she mention where she was going? Would anyone here have remembered?' Rebecca asked.

'I wasn't on reception on the day she checked out but I'll give my colleague a ring at home, if you've time to wait,' the receptionist suggested.

'That would be great, thank you.' Rebecca was pleased that she was getting some information. At least she would have a little bit more to go on when Tom arrived. Carol had definitely been in Coimbra. She knew now.

The receptionist went into the office to make the call and it wasn't long before he came back out to speak with Rebecca.

'My colleague did remember your friend, maybe because she was a woman travelling alone which was a bit unusual and he said that she seemed rather down. He helped her make some travel arrangements. She didn't speak any Portuguese and was finding it difficult. She was heading for a town quite some distance south east of here, Pampilhosa da Serra, he seems to remember.'

'That would make sense.' Rebecca spoke her first thought aloud. 'You've been incredibly helpful, I really do appreciate it.'

She thanked the receptionist and headed back to her hotel, feeling much better to have another lead for Tom. Hopefully, Carol would still be there or they might have the same luck in tracing her next step. Carol was probably thinking that Tó Zé would turn up at home at some point. She might even have decided it was time to talk to his family. Rebecca had no idea really, she knew that and it still didn't make a lot of sense. Her thoughts turned to Pampilhosa. They had travelled through the town the day before, but she couldn't remember much about it. She wondered where Carol might have stayed. She wasn't even sure if there was a hotel there.

There was really nothing she could do except wait until tomorrow. Rebecca was in a strange city with no reason to stay there, other than to help Tom find Carol. She became aware of a growing low mood and seemed now to have far less conviction about her reasons for being in the country. She ought to think seriously about whether or not she should continue with her plan to stay there. She had lost nothing so far and had seen quite a lot of the country in the short time she'd been in Portugal. João had felt the pull of home and now she was feeling it too.

It was late afternoon the next day by the time Tom arrived in Coimbra and Rebecca found she was really pleased to see him. There was nothing they could do that evening, so it was a time to catch up. Tom spoke about his mother's continued distress. He had mixed feelings. He found Carol's behaviour and lack of consideration for her parents completely irresponsible, but he was conscious of her vulnerability and fearful of what might have happened to her.

As Tom and Rebecca sat talking, finishing a bottle of red wine after dinner, Rebecca talked to Tom about living in France.

'Are you settled in France, now, then?' Rebecca asked.

'I've rented a small apartment for sixth months. Calling it an apartment probably elevates it rather beyond its status. It's more like a bedsit, but it's convenient for where I want to be and it'll do for now until I see how things work out,' Tom said.

'What are you going to do? Have you managed to get any work? I suppose you can manage for a while.' Rebecca was interested in what he was going to do, because she felt in a similar position. She hadn't worked out where to live and what she might do if she stayed.

'I'm not qualified to apply for anything in schools over there, but I thought that I might be able to teach English. There's a language school in a town nearby and I've heard that they're always looking for people. I don't know how many hours I can get,' Tom said.

'How long could you manage out there if it doesn't work out?' Rebecca asked.

'Only about six months which is why I haven't looked for anything other than the little apartment, but I have to sort it out and get work if I want a chance with Ana,' Tom said.

Rebecca teased Tom. 'So you've given up a perfectly good job in England and you really have no idea what you're going to do. All in pursuit of a woman? What does she think about it?'

'I'm really not sure.' Tom sounded a little down too.

'As women, we're all for the grand romantic gestures, you know, Tom, but there's a bit of a balance to be struck with all of us. In my experience, it rarely works if one person is doing all the chasing, all the giving,' Rebecca said.

'Are you talking about me now or yourself?' Tom threw back at her and Rebecca, knowing she wasn't on very firm ground decided to change the subject. She started to talk about arrangements for the next day.

Rebecca and Tom had agreed to a fairly early start. They had breakfast together and were off on their way by half past eight. Rebecca was beginning to feel she knew this area well, as they drove south towards Góis. She found too that with the morning sunshine and a renewed sense of purpose, her mood was beginning to lift from the low point of the last couple of days. She knew that this would have been far harder for Tom without her. He didn't know the country. He didn't speak Portuguese. Hopefully, they would soon find out what had happened to Carol and then she could return to the south and her own plans. She was feeling much more positive again about staying in Portugal. Like Tom, she also had the idea of teaching English, although, if she were honest, she didn't want to be speaking English all day. That hadn't been her idea of truly getting to know another country. She wanted to be part of it. She wanted to understand more about the culture and to be immersed in the language.

They parked in the middle of the town. Rebecca, seeing a local policeman, decided to ask him about places to stay in the town. It struck her that it was a very English thing to do to ask a policeman. He was rather sterner and much more standoffish than she was used to. Not to worry, he had the information they needed and pointed them in the direction of a hotel which he felt would be the most likely for a visitor to have chosen to stay.

Rebecca and Tom approached the reception desk and Rebecca spoke for both of them.

'My friend and I are here looking for his sister, Carol. I wonder if you would be able to tell me if she's staying here.'

'You speak Portuguese.' For a few brief moments, the conversation was distracted as the receptionist asked Rebecca how she came to learn. It was something that she was asked frequently and almost forgetting why they were there, she was drawn into conversation.

'Yes, she was here, but I'm afraid she's not here now,' the receptionist told her. Rebecca was a little surprised. She wasn't sure why. Of course, it had always been a distinct possibility that she hadn't stayed.

Tom saw the look on Rebecca's face. 'What did he say?' he asked.

Rebecca turned to Tom and repeated, 'He says she's checked out. Let me see what else I can find out.'

'Your friend's sister is a fairly popular young woman. While she was here, two other people came to see her. I don't know how helpful it is to mention it, but you probably should know. She was fairly distressed on the last day she was here,' the receptionist said.

Rebecca wasn't sure that she should mention that last piece of information to Tom, not at that moment. She could explain later. The receptionist had obviously been quite interested in Carol because he knew more than Rebecca expected. He was fairly sure that the visitors were from a village not too far away. When Rebecca mentioned the name, he seemed to recognise it. One of the visitors was a woman, the other a priest, he told her. Rebecca spoke to Tom.

'It appears that Carol didn't say where she was going but the people who came looking for her, I'm pretty sure came from the village where Tó Zé is from, the one I visited the other day. It's about all we've got to go on,' Rebecca said.

Rebecca thanked the receptionist and the two of them left the hotel.

'Let's go and get some lunch,' Rebecca suggested. 'We need to think what to do next and before we leave, we need to make sure that we've found out as much as we can.'

After lunch, Rebecca went back to have a longer chat with the receptionist at the hotel, then she met up again with Tom.

'There's not a lot more that he could tell me. He has no idea where she went. It seems to me fairly likely that it was a relative of Tó Zé who came looking for her. Why the priest was with her, I've no idea. As I said, I've been to the village where he's from and it's not too far from here, so we could drive there. It will probably be a bit awkward. Rui said that Tó Zé's mother was rather unnerved by his visit, but I think the time has passed for us to tiptoe around this one. We need to see what the family know.'

'Did you get any idea of how Carol was?' Tom asked, as he was thinking it all through.

Rebecca was pleased that he'd asked. She knew he needed to know.

'I don't think she was very happy. He said that whatever had happened when she met the woman for coffee, she came back fairly upset and then didn't want to stay any longer.'

'This is what we're all so worried about. She shouldn't be on her own. I don't know what she'll do if something bad has happened,' Tom said.

Rebecca felt frustrated with Carol and saw things differently in a way that those close to her couldn't.

'Carol is making choices here and I feel annoyed with her that she's being so inconsiderate as far as her family is concerned. She must know that everyone is worried. She's out of contact, but we can't say she's missing. You mother reported it to the police in Paris, but I'm sure they can't help now we know she's here.'

'I need to go and see the village where Tó Zé lived before he left for France. He's bound to be in touch with his family at some point. At least I can let his family know how worried we are, that she's missing. We can try to be as subtle as we can, read the situation carefully. I don't want his family to be distressed. One family being upset is enough,' Tom said.

Rebecca understood. She wasn't sure what it would achieve or what exactly she would say when they got there because of course it would be down to her. They drove to the village. Rebecca had the address of the family home from Rui. They parked in the centre of the village and walked first towards the café, so that she could get her bearings again. Tom was quite surprised to see the village. He hadn't given it much thought as he drove there, but it was far more remote and far poorer than he had expected, leaving lots of questions in his mind about Tó Zé. Rebecca decided that she would ask at the café for directions, it would be far easier. They took the same route as Rui had a couple of days before, through the narrow alleys in between the tightly packed houses.

When they arrived, Rebecca paused for a short while, looking at Tom. He urged her on and she knocked on the door. It wasn't long before it was opened by an older woman who she assumed must be Tó Zé's mother.

'I'm really sorry to bother you but my name is Rebecca and this is my friend, Tom, Carol's brother.'

The woman looked at her quizzically, 'Carol's brother?'

The name Carol didn't seem to mean anything to her, so Rebecca clarified, 'Tó Zé's friend, Carol.'

The clarification didn't seem to bring any sense of recognition of the name and the woman replied simply,

'Tó Zé isn't here. I haven't seen him for a long time.'

Rebecca wasn't getting very far, so she decided that probably all she could do was to give her the message which Tom was keen to leave.

'Tom's sister Carol has been missing for quite some time now and her family is very worried. We know that she's been in this area and that she has visited the village. We're all very concerned about her. I'm living in Portugal at the moment. If I left you a contact number and address, please could you let me know if you hear from her or ask her to get in touch with me? Tom has travelled all the way to Portugal to try to find her and her family is distraught.'

His mother seemed genuinely concerned to her about the family's worries and promised that she would do what she could to help. As they left, Rebecca went over the conversation with Tom, reassuring him.

'She was concerned. I'm sure she'll be in touch as soon as she knows anything.' But what Rebecca didn't tell Tom, as there seemed no point, was that she was as sure as she could be that Tó Zé's mother had never heard of Carol.

Tom agreed that they probably couldn't do any more and so they made the long drive back to Coimbra. This time Rebecca was not in the mood for any sightseeing and assuming Tom would feel exactly the same, she didn't make any suggestion other than to get back. They made their way to Coimbra retracing their route and for most of the journey, they didn't speak.

That evening, over a meal, Rebecca and Tom reflected on the day. Tom's greatest concern now was what he might say to his mother having said he would ring her as soon as he knew anything. Rebecca didn't think there was anything to do except tell her what they had found out, but she also encouraged Tom to consider getting back home. She would continue to do what she could and let him know as soon as she had news.

# XVII

**Oporto, 10th June, 1974**

On the train heading north, João felt annoyed and disappointed. With a little distance, he didn't know why he had been so convinced that there was something more than friendship between Rebecca and Tom, but he wasn't prepared to stay and find out. It seemed to him there was. He tried to convince himself that he had made the right decision. It was time he went home. This holiday was his opportunity to convince his parents that his future was in London. Of that, he had been clear when he made the journey home. Now, it was less well-defined in his thinking. He had wanted a resolution, too much had hung over him for too long, but being away from home wasn't going to help anymore and there was Ana Rita to consider too. He was regretting the way he had behaved with her, continuing as though nothing had happened. It was unfair to her and it didn't show much strength of character on his part. He didn't know why he had never been able to explain that it wasn't about her, that he couldn't have contemplated asking her to go with him. All he had known was that he wanted to start again somewhere different and he had never expected to feel so settled in another country.

On that journey to Oporto, João had time to think, but it only made him more confused than ever. Instead of strengthening his resolve to stay in London and making it easier to hold his position, he was finding more to lure him back home. Yet, had anything really changed at all? He wasn't a coward. No one would ever have said that of him. He was fearless at times and he had certainly proved his character in those years at university. Fundamentally and with huge conviction, he disagreed with the conflict in the colonies. Only negotiation, not war, would have any effect and when nothing could be done to make the government change its thinking, he had felt that his country had nothing more to offer. However, here he was, connecting again through someone else's eyes. He was missing Rebecca already. Her love of the country had made an impression in an unexpected way. Her enthusiasm was infectious. She had made him feel proud again of his country and its people. He had felt it so strongly whilst he had been with her. He had realised how much he had missed his friends too, people who had known him for ever. He had really enjoyed the last few days with them. He was thinking about Ana Rita too. Despite his annoyance with the way he had handled seeing her again, it hadn't been as difficult as he had imagined and it could be put right, he felt sure. Instinctively, he had felt defensive about his family and the business, knowing now how insecure it might be. The idea that the business was irrelevant to him which he had been so determined to strengthen in the past, was fading with each day. The estate had been with his ancestors since the eighteenth century. He couldn't stay in London and leave his family struggling with a threat of such significance. His brother and his wife were expecting their first child. So many people depended on the estate for their livelihood and didn't know any other way of life. The fall of the regime should bring change in a good way, not destroy a way of life that had existed for centuries.

When he arrived in Oporto, his brother was waiting for him again, in the usual place, under the clock, but this time, the car was parked nearby.

'I could have got the train, you know,' he said to Pedro as he walked up to him.

'Yes, I know you could, but mother was anxious to have you back again and this way you can't change your mind and head off somewhere else on a tour of the country. Did you have a good time in Coimbra?' Pedro asked.

'Yes, it was good to go back and see some of the old haunts. We were helping out Júlia's English friend. The sister of a good friend of hers has gone missing and she said she would try to help find out what had happened to her,' João said.

Pedro's comments hadn't gone unnoticed and João was thinking that his visit to Coimbra might be better received by his parents if they knew that he had been helping someone out rather than having a good time with friends away from the family when they hadn't seen him for so long.

'She's gone missing in Portugal? That's worrying.' Pedro was surprised. He had only expected to hear about João's visit.

'She went missing from Paris actually,' João clarified.

'So, why does your English friend think she's here?' Pedro asked.

'Her boyfriend of several years is from a village near Pampilhosa da Serra and we think she came here to look for him. We were fairly sure that she had been in the area. The rest of us had to get back but Rebecca, that's her name, by the way, has stayed in Coimbra to see if she can get any closer to where she might be now,' João explained.

'It shouldn't be that hard to find the boyfriend if she knows where he's from,' Pedro commented.

'I agree, but the family didn't know where he was, hadn't seen him since he'd left for Paris years ago and others we spoke to were a little closed about him, not wanting to give much away.'

'That seems a bit strange. It would make me wonder what the boyfriend is up to and why he went to Paris,' Pedro said.

João agreed. 'I thought the same, but it didn't seem helpful to dwell on it and Rebecca said the family was convinced that he had moved to Paris to follow some course at university there.'

'Are you going to try and help out any more?' Pedro asked.

'I'm not sure what I can do. Rebecca has my contacts,' João replied, knowing he hadn't given any indication to Rebecca that he would help further. He wanted to talk to Pedro about Rebecca, but thought better of it and tried to sound as detached and matter of fact as he could.

The two brothers spent much of the journey comfortable in each other's company, sometimes chatting, sometimes quiet, João's eyes fixed firmly on the landscape. Strangely, by the time they drew up in front of the house, João was feeling much more determined and clearer in his own mind, although he had no idea how he could work it out and so he hadn't shared any of his thoughts with his brother.

That evening, João was confronted with a big family meal. His mother had announced it as soon as he walked through the door. She didn't know how he would feel about it, so she thought it was better to tell him straight away. João felt irritated. It seemed to him that family and friends had been convened en masse probably to persuade him subtly, or not so subtly, that his place was on the estate. They'd probably even asked the local priest, he thought. For a brief second, he was tempted to express his annoyance, but he stopped himself and made no comment other than to announce that he was going upstairs for a shower. He didn't know why he reacted that way. He had become entrenched into thinking that his family always wanted to organise his life.

After his shower, João stayed in his room, lying on the bed. He slept for a while and woke up having dreamt that he was still in Coimbra. He thought about Rebecca being there on her own. Apart from anything else, it hadn't been very chivalrous leaving her. Rui and Júlia hadn't said anything, hadn't encouraged him to stay, but he wondered what they thought.

By the time he made his way down for dinner, his grandparents, Pedro and his wife, Céu, and yes, the local priest were already in the sitting room. His father followed him in with some of his friends. Their wives were chatting with Maria João. It was a larger gathering than João had imagined when his mother had announced it. It was quite a formal affair and he was pleased that he had dressed for dinner.

Drinks were served, chilled white port, poured over ice into tall glasses. João went over to speak with his sister-in-law to see how she was feeling, escaping from any other conversation. They got on. He could always rely on her to distract him at these kinds of gatherings, but it wasn't too long before they all moved through to the dining room for dinner. In Portugal, there is a well-known saying that there is always room for soup, no meal being really complete without soup and this was no exception. The first course was a rich 'Sopa de Castanhas Piladas', a soup made with dried chestnuts which gave the dish a sweetness and a chewy texture. There were cheeses and Broa, a maize bread, thick and crusty, to accompany the soup. The conversation and wine flowed, but still João felt tense, speaking only with Pedro and Céu, avoiding eye contact with others at the table. The main course arrived, a magnificent 'Cabrito Assado', roast kid, served with new potatoes, oven rice cooked with sausages and offal and sautéed vegetables.

'I know we should be celebrating Saint Anthony today but I'm getting in a little early with our Saint John celebrations, because I know how much you love roast kid,' Maria João said turning to Joaquim, one of her husband's best friends.

'Superb,' he said, and then couldn't resist a quote from his favourite author.

"Horace would have dedicated an ode to that roast kid. And the trout, and Melchoir's wine, and the cabidela – and the sweetness of that June night, showing its dark velvet mantle through the open window. I felt so comfortably lazy and contented that, as the coffee awaited us in the sitting room, I just collapsed in one of the wicker chairs – the largest, with the best cushions – and shouted in pure delight." Eça de Queiros, 'A Cidade e as Serras', (The City and the Mountains),' he declared, as he finished, smiling and pleased with himself.

João caught Pedro's eye and they both had to work hard not to laugh. They had known Joaquim for years and it was the same at every gathering, much to their amusement. Joaquim loved literature. It was amazing how much he could remember and quote, even if a little tiresome at times. João, not always interested in Joaquim's in-depth knowledge of the great Portuguese writers, found, nevertheless, that he had missed his eccentricity and this time was pleased when the conversation turned to literature and everyone's favourite classic books.

Sweet was 'Pudim do Abade de Priscos', a dessert flavoured with Port wine, spices and lemon, named after a parish priest from the small town of Priscos who was said to have created the dish.

'A great choice too,' Joaquim said complimenting Maria João again.' The padre who invented this pudding was a man of wide ranging culture. He knew theatre, photography, was a master of embroidery and his culinary skills were so renowned that his services were called upon for many great banquets. I think he was made honorary chaplain to the royal household, they were so impressed with him.'

'It puts me to shame,' Father Lucas said, as they tucked into dessert. 'I have no such talents.'

All through the meal, João kept wondering when the subject would turn again to his plans, but the conversations continued without any reference to him; work on the estate, the expected birth, news from the local area, Father Lucas' work. As the meal came to a close, João was feeling annoyed with himself that he had presumed that he would be under pressure again with friends and family gathered together. The only pressure there was, he was creating, but he began to wonder whether, indeed, they had all been briefed to stay away from the subject. João admonished himself. He determined to relax and to enjoy the rest of the evening.

Maria João led the women through to the sitting room, saying that it was time for them to be somewhere more comfortable. João's father was proud of the many distinguished vintage port wines which his estate produced, and rightly so, and he had chosen carefully for his guests. Walnuts, rich blue-veined cheese, dried figs and apricots were brought to the table to accompany the port wine and now the conversation turned to estate business and to the political situation. João was interested to hear, both his father's views and those of his friends. They spoke of uncertainty. They were concerned. His father, without giving away too much of his own thoughts, seemed keen to know how the others felt and whether or not they had made any decisions themselves. There was some talk of moving away, mostly referenced to others they knew. For most of them, it seemed that it was business as usual or at least that was all they were prepared to disclose. Talk of other countries brought, though, the inevitable reference.

'You've been in London for quite a while, João,' Joaquim said.

João felt his body stiffen as he wondered how to reply, how to deflect the conversation as quickly as possible away from him, then his father answered for him.

'Yes, quite a while. It's a great experience for him and a help for me to have someone over there. The British market has changed so much in recent times and hasn't been as strong as we would like, but we've made changes to our products and the way we are marketing. It's good to have someone on the ground over there to give a different perspective and he always makes a strong impression, whenever he's representing the firm, a great ambassador for the business. He met with some of our contacts in the Algarve recently and did us proud.'

João was a little stunned and surprised to hear his father embellishing the facts. He certainly knew that the dinner in Vila Real had been a success, but he hadn't done anything while he had been in London to promote the business, apart from meeting friends of the family for dinner in Knightsbridge very occasionally. He had purposely avoided any opportunities that the business had presented, determined to make his own way and had stuck to casual work which he had arranged himself. He didn't know what to say but his father continued.

'It's an important market. I have kept thinking that I need to get across myself for a while but João is more than capable and I'm sure he'd rather I wasn't there getting in his way.'

And then they were all talking details and practicalities, as though João had been working for the business for quite some time.

'You know, Carlos, if it's a project that requires some office and meeting space, I can help out,' Joaquim was saying to his father.

In the past, João would have been furious with the assumptions, hearing his father planning out his life and certainly not afraid to express his views. His father had taken quite a risk, João reflected, but he knew him far better than he had ever realised. He had picked up on his indecision and as João continued to listen, he realised that his father was giving him an option which might be an answer.

'João loves London and I'd prefer to stay here. He'll be much happier travelling backwards and forwards,' his father was saying, and João found himself joining in with the conversation about arrangements. His father smiled at him.

It was getting late. The port wine began to make them feel sleepy. The conversation came to a natural conclusion and the guests, one by one, made a move to go. Maria João and the others joined them. She was thanked appreciatively for a wonderful meal and the hospitality. Carlos was thanked for the delicious port. When everyone had left and his father had retired for the night, João went to look for his mother who had gone back to the sitting room to read for a while.

'I've had some time to think while I've been away,' João said.

'I think we know how much you're enjoying it over there. You have to do what is right for you.'

His mother sounded resigned. He hadn't expected it at all.

'I'm going to go back to London,' he started to say.

'I thought as much,' his mother interrupted him.

'What I was going to say, is that father has some work that he needs doing over there and would prefer not to go himself. The contract I had in London has finished and so I can help out for a while. I'll go back to London to sort a few things out too. I've decided that it's time that I gave the business a chance to see how things go. If it doesn't work out, I hope you and my father will understand.'

João had been surprised by his own decision. In the past, he would have resisted, almost for the sake of resisting. He still didn't understand quite where this change of mind was coming from. It seemed to be a solution to his problem, at least for the time being. His mother was really pleased. He had the strongest impression that his father hadn't said anything to her before. It was quite a surprise to her too. It seemed that his father hadn't planned it either but now it felt like the right thing to do.

He went to bed still unclear in his own mind as to how it would work out practically and how much time he would need to spend in London. Then his thoughts turned again to Rebecca and as he tried to get to sleep, the strongest feeling of longing, 'saudade', overwhelmed him.

# XVIII

**Paris to Lisbon, 26th -10th June, 1974**

João and Tó Zé had never met and they had little in common, apart from the fact that they had both been students at Coimbra University at a similar time, and both of them had strong views about the conflict in Africa, certain they didn't want any part of it. Life hadn't been easy for Tó Zé, but it had built a resilience and a resourcefulness in him which many would admire. Others would accuse him of being something of an opportunist and might question his motives and his integrity with regard to the openings he had been given. He was bright, able and he had always adapted cleverly, making the best of even the most difficult circumstance.

April 25th was a day which Tó Zé, and many other of his compatriots, would never forget and for him, the 26th also would stay forever fixed in his mind. He walked into the railway station and checked the station clock against the time on his watch. It was just after half past one. Anyone observing him would not have noticed anything particularly unusual. He didn't go to the ticket office. He checked the arrivals and departures and then went back to wait by the main entrance. It would have appeared to anyone watching him, as though he was waiting to meet someone. However, no one arrived and minutes later, Tó Zé checked his watch again and then left the station, taking up another position to one side of the station building, waiting again. He was now a little more agitated, looking around, checking his watch frequently. Less than ten minutes later, a car pulled up alongside him. There were three men in the car. He barely acknowledged them as he walked to the boot of the car, pushed his small rucksack alongside other bags, in what was a rather full boot, closed the door on the second attempt and then got into the car beside the driver. As the car pulled away, he could be seen turning around and chatting with the two men sitting on the back seat. The car made its way out of Paris and headed towards the south of France and the Spanish border.

In the same way as the four comrades had left Portugal years before, with forged papers, passports and other documents, their return was covert and cautious. As they approached the border, they took an indirect route, making sure to avoid any road which might take them to a known check point. Less than forty eight hours since the troops had effected their coup, news was vague. They had no idea who was in charge of the country, nor if the resistance had continued to be strong. They did know the cruel capability of the PIDE, the feared secret police, the way they patrolled the borders, ever suspicious, methodically searching cars, hands dressed in white gloves. If they were there and under pressure, their power draining as the revolution took hold, they would be ruthless. The four men shared the driving. They slept en route, sometimes finding a remote safe place, sometimes sleeping while one of the others continued to drive, and so they travelled cautiously, making sure they didn't draw any attention.

Two days later, the small car could be seen driving towards the centre of Lisbon. They tried to press through into the city, but crowds, police and tanks blocked their way. They abandoned the car and continued on foot, reaching the centre in time to join the huge crowds who had gathered at Santa Apolónia Station to see the return of Mário Soares and many other political exiles who were arriving from Paris on the Southern Express. The four men had not considered the south bound train, afraid they might be turned back. They preferred that the authorities did not know about their return, but clearly others had been given leave to travel across the borders. Tó Zé found himself swept along by the emotion and movement of the crowds, as everyone jostled for a view of the returning heroes as they left the train. He recognised some of the communist party officials amongst them and heard someone in the crowd pointing out two well-known actresses, Maria Barroso and Maria Coelho. So many of these were his heroes too. They were citizens who had worked so hard for freedom. With unstirring courage, they had faced torture, imprisonment and banishment in order to free Portugal from oppression. Tó Zé, like so many others in the crowd, watched the scene with tears in his eyes.

The crowd poured out from the station onto the streets. The noise of the throng, their voices shouting and chanting, was deafening. Soon they were joined by the piercing sound of car horns, as drivers, halted by the crowd, lent on their horns in shared celebration. Reporters and television crews jostled with the crowd trying to catch each moment. Later that day, Tó Zé and his comrades were to see these euphoric displays replayed on every news bulletin. Similar scenes and celebrations were repeated in the streets of many other towns and cities across the country – in Oporto in the north, in Beja further south and across the southern region of the Alentejo. Hundreds and thousands of people came out into the streets celebrating their freedom.

In all the confusion, it wasn't easy to find his friends again. As he was scanning the crowd, one of them called over to him. Two of his comrades had family in the area and so they split up for the night arranging to meet back in the city the next day. Tó Zé went to Mira Sintra, some way out of the city. The intention was to stay with his comrade's family for a couple of nights, no more. As Tó Zé made his way there, still excited by the day, he had no real understanding of who was in charge of the country. He didn't know how the situation might play out, especially now that other leaders were returning from exile, but he knew he had made the right decision. He had to be part of it. It wasn't that Carol was out of his mind. This was far more important to him.

The next day, the four met again in the city as arranged. It seemed at first glance that life was carrying on as usual. The day before, the newspaper, 'República', had called in its headline for 'Normalidade em Todo', 'Everything as Normal'. The schools were opening. The banks were still closed. It was soon obvious to them that nothing was normal. Work across the city was almost at a standstill. Tanks and soldiers flooded the streets. Huge crowds had gathered in search of information. They wanted to understand what was happening. They needed to know who was in charge. People were handing out flowers to the soldiers – red carnations which some of them placed into the barrels of the soldiers' guns. Mercifully, this had been a peaceful revolution and everybody wanted to be part of it. Those not in work organised impromptu marches; the crowd watched as the hotel workers marched around Rossio Square. More and more people joined them as they headed on through the city.

'Looks like there's nobody looking after the hotels. We could sneak in and get a room, provided we don't mind looking after ourselves, I don't think anyone would notice,' Tó Zé joked with his friends.

'We do need to get organised. Apparently, some of the parties have started to occupy empty buildings. We need to see what we can find out and what we can do to help.'

Through the day, they managed to connect with old comrades, friends, students and party organisers. They were occupying buildings which had once been the realm of the old regime. As returning exiles, they were welcomed with reverence and great pleasure. The communist party had been the only real force of resistance throughout the forty eight years of the old regime. Tó Zé was keen to make contact with members of the party, joining them at their temporary headquarters, offering support for the cause. The situation was confused. Still no one was sure of what was happening. The military junta was in charge but now everyone wanted to be involved. They knew they had to capitalise on the situation and secure freedom from the old regime. Comrades were already working on their message, scrambling for power and change. Leaflets were being prepared and distributed. Tó Zé and his friends joined them. They worked through the night spurred on by the news that their leader, Álvaro Cunhal was returning the following day from exile in Russia.

News came fast, but nothing was clear. They listened to the radio. They watched television. One of the government ministers had been arrested. He had been caught trying to withdraw a large amount of money from his bank account. No one was surprised. In times of crisis, money flowed out of the banks, taken away by those who had the wealth and means to get out. Someone commented that millions of escudos had already left the country after the first unsuccessful revolt only a month ago. It was no surprise either that members of the old government would try to flee the country. The crowds wanted justice.

The communist party had been the only source of real information for many years. It had been the only voice brave enough to oppose the dictatorship, but that night on the television, they watched as other political groups started to emerge. They were free for the first time in more than a generation to express what they really felt, what they really believed in. They began to broadcast manifestos hurriedly put together. Tó Zé smiled as he watched students from Lisbon, Coimbra and Oporto making speeches; they had never given up the fight.

The next day, Tó Zé was there in the middle of the crowds at the airport who greeted Cunhal. It was the mass welcome of a returning hero. He had been away for over twenty years, arrested and imprisoned, he had escaped two years later and like many others, he had settled in Russia. He had led from afar. Now he was back. The sense of urgency increased and Tó Zé went back to the headquarters. There was much to do that evening. Some of the group were out in the city painting walls with brightly coloured party slogans. There was hardly space left, as each group vied to get their message out. Others worked through the night preparing banners to be carried and displayed the next day. The junta had announced that the traditional May 1$^{st}$ workers' day celebrations could go ahead but there was concern that there would be trouble. The authorities called for calm. It was a strong message hailed regularly in radio broadcasts. Tó Zé had no concern about the vast majority of people in the city. It would be a day of celebration, he was sure, but there were still many members of the PIDE out there. They were the feared right and they could certainly try to cause trouble. The streets flooded again with people. It seemed the whole of Lisbon was out celebrating and now everyone wanted to carry red carnations. The only way of getting into the city, other than walking, was on the metro. The carriages were crammed with people. Others arrived from further afield by the lorry load, waving, cheering, smiling and happy, free at last to express themselves. Some buses driving through the streets were still displaying their destinations but not travelling any of the declared routes. They had been commandeered by workers. Banners and flags were billowing in the wind, people hanging out of each window. The noise in the city was louder than ever.

There was a big rally planned. Tó Zé made his way with thousands of others to the stadium. It had been renamed in the last few days; the First of May Stadium. They arrived to hear those they most admired, those they hoped would lead them to a new, free, equal Portugal. The workers' trade unions were there in force with their leaders. So, of course, were Soares and Cunhal. A sea of red flags, with hammer and sickle emblems filled the stadium as Cunhal rose to speak. Tó Zé was captivated and excited. He listened, watching the crowds as each person stood up to speak. Soares had a great following too, he noticed. He wasn't sure that either leader really understood the mood of the people gathered in the huge crowd. The workers were eager for change. They were animated, confident now that they could run their own factories. Talk was of how that might work. This was real change, not words, not gesturing politics. Tó Zé felt proud.

The day continued as it had started. There was almost nowhere to move in the streets. Military bands were playing, people were dancing. Soldiers and police were joining in with the celebrations, people climbing up onto the tanks, travelling along with them. Groups formed, unrehearsed, to sing songs which they had first heard again in the early hours of that late April day, and to join in other songs which for so many years had been banned. Tó Zé loved to sing. His voice sounded out strong and distinct amongst the group. Songs he hadn't sung or heard for years, words which he thought he had forgotten, all came rushing back effortlessly. Music, dancing, singing, laughing, embracing, the celebration stretched into the early hours. No one wanted to go home. No one wanted the celebrations to end, but as the hours wore on, exhaustion took over. Tó Zé made his way back to the headquarters with his friends who wanted to try to get some rest.

There was no rest for Tó Zé, though. He was consumed by the cause. He thought of almost nothing else and when thoughts of elsewhere did nudge into his mind, he dismissed them. He had work to do. It was far more important. Everything was happening so quickly, he had little time to think. In the next days, urged on by the excitement of the 1st May, strike after strike broke out across the country – miners in the Alentejo, the fishermen of Matosinhos, train conductors in Cascais, strikes at the docks, at the Timex watch factory in Lisbon. Workers called for more money, more holidays, more say in running their factories. It seemed everyone was interested in politics, not only in the factories, but in cafés and in the streets. It wasn't just talk. People were organising. They were taking action. To Tó Zé's disappointment, the communists seemed to be far too cautious. Worried about the economy, they tried to persuade workers not to strike. He tried to make sense of it. The biggest fear seemed to be that the strikes would allow the old regime to take power again, but that wouldn't happen, it couldn't.

Tó Zé worked hard to support the party, getting involved wherever he was needed, but as days became weeks, he began to feel irritated and frustrated. There was little change. His hopes and those of others he heard expressed each day on the streets were ignored. Strikes, chaos, confusion. This was a chance to make real change and no one with any influence seemed to have the heart to respond. Yes, they were calling for the end to the colonial wars, amnesty for deserters and draft dodgers. No one would argue with that, least of all Tó Zé. The socialist party seemed more aware, more able to understand, but he wasn't sure that he trusted their leader. Tó Zé's opposition to the regime, all those years before, had been quite specific; he was against the war like so many students and young people. He hated the oppression, the restrictions, the poverty, the hopelessness. He had aligned himself with the communist party because it was the only real voice of resistance. He had huge respect for the returning exiles, but he felt they were out of touch, long years of exile in Russia, influenced by ideas that didn't seem relevant or to be what his country needed now. Some of them had begun to sound almost like the politicians of the old dictatorship.

It was the day after the celebrations, when Tó Zé was feeling tired and a little deflated that he heard that people who had lived in the city's shanty district for years, were occupying buildings in the suburbs. They were squatting in empty apartment blocks but they were meeting serious resistance from the police and the army. The student movement that had been so important to him was involved. News came that some families were going to try to occupy some unfinished housing blocks in Boavista. Some of the women who worked at the Santa Maria Hospital near the university campus, close by the Faculty of Medicine were involved. They had seen many student meetings over the years. They had watched the protests and clashes with the authorities and now they had begun to talk to university students to find out how they might organise squats. This was the cause for Tó Zé, a real revolution. The country was in confusion. All the people knew was that change was now possible and they were going to make it happen. People needed decent homes. Tó Zé could help.

Tó Zé, like so many others, continued to work hard for the cause, as the politicians jostled for power. Life had to go on. People needed to work, to feed their families, live their lives, but now many of them knew what they wanted and they were becoming difficult to control. The newspapers backed them and the politicians tried to meet their demands. Small business people were anxious. They didn't have the same means and couldn't ride the situation like the big companies. Those with power weren't ready to let go. By the middle of May, everyone watched as a new government was formed. It was a coalition of many colours – communists, socialists, the military, and seven ministers of unknown affiliation. Palma Carlos, a corporation lawyer, became the first Prime Minister. For so many years, there had been no choice, only one political party. Now there was so much, and no one knew who would emerge the strongest.

Tó Zé was absorbed. Although, every now and then, he was reminded of home, he didn't think that his family would be missing him. They had no idea where he was but as more and more emigrants returned, he knew they would be expecting news. He thought of Carol and pushed the thought away. He had become involved with people who needed him. It was too important, his two lives on hold and so he continued.

Tó Zé and his friends still looked to the communists for a lead, for support. As the days wore on, neither the communists nor the socialists seemed easy with the coalition. Cunhal called for elections, the only way to bring reform to the country, he said, but the strikes continued and the communists urged them to stop. The press became more careful, the media no longer so open. Still the resistance built. On the national day, June 10th, people burst out onto the streets again, as they had at the beginning of May. Hundreds of thousands wearing red carnations. Artists oppressed through the old regime had planned a festival. They organised a community painting in the Mercado do Povo, one artist for each year of the old regime. Musicians joined too and the television company was to broadcast the event. This time, though, the authorities were not so keen to see the celebrations go ahead. The military intervened. Then just before midnight, the message came that the broadcasts must stop. Those who had moved indoors to watch the festival on television became aware of a problem only when an American film suddenly appeared on screen.

At a time when it seemed there was every need for Tó Zé to stay in Lisbon and every excuse not to face his personal responsibilities, a member of the party came to find him to tell him that someone had some important information for him. He thought it would be wise to meet. There was little he could tell Tó Zé, but it was enough to make him feel concerned and so Tó Zé asked him to set up the contact as soon as he could.

# XIX

**Janeiro de Cima, 2ⁿᵈ-3ʳᵈ June, 1974**

Jacinta hadn't mentioned to anyone that she knew a woman had been to the village looking for Tó Zé. It troubled her. She needed to know who the woman was. She wasn't sure who else knew, but as her daughter, Conceição, hadn't mentioned it, she thought that maybe Tino had been a little more careful who he had spoken to than would be usual. He liked Conceição. He was being protective.

Fatima wasn't expecting her mother and was in the middle of preparing dinner. Jacinta was pleased to find her on her own and as soon as she walked through the door, she announced that she had something important to talk about, but didn't have long.

'Sit down, mother, what is it?' Fatima asked, concerned that her mother seemed quite flustered.

She told her everything she knew, which wasn't much. Fatima had been wondering if Tó Zé would return. He didn't have to stay in Paris. Surely the revolution had changed that for him. She hadn't mentioned anything to Conceição. She didn't think it would help.

'I'm really worried about Conceição. She has had so much to deal with on her own. It's been hard for her and if there's a problem, the more we know, the more we can help. I have been thinking. Tino has the address of the hotel where this English woman is staying but I can't go, Conceição would ask too many questions, I hardly ever go to Pampilhosa. Will you go and see her, please, Fatima? I don't know what else to do.'

'What, to Pampilhosa? What would I say to her?' Fatima was taken aback and didn't think it was a good idea.

'I don't know what you'd say. It would be more a case of trying to find out why she's here and if possible, discouraging her from coming to the village again.'

Then it occurred to Fatima. 'Does she speak Portuguese?'

'Not very much at all, only a couple of words Tino said.'

'What can I do, then? I don't speak English. Even if I was able to see her, I couldn't speak to her.' Fatima was reluctant to go.

It hadn't occurred to her mother until that moment and for once, she was lost for words. There was a long pause and then she had an idea.

'Padre Francisco speaks English. Surely he'll help when we tell him our concerns.'

'Your concerns, mother. I'm not sure that we need to interfere or that it's a good idea at all. It might be nothing. She's probably back in England by now.' Fatima wasn't convinced at all.

'She lives in Paris,' her mother clarified.

Fatima wasn't quite sure why that made a difference but now she felt unsettled. 'Don't you think we should have a word first with Conceição?' She asked.

'No, I don't. If there's nothing to worry about, it's one less problem to deal with. Please will you go and see the Padre, explain and see if he'll help. The sooner you can go the better.' Her mother was getting upset.

'Ok, I'm not promising anything but I'll go after dinner when the children are settled.' Fatima knew that once her mother got something into her head, she wouldn't let go.

Padre Francisco was a kind, measured man, always able to see his way calmly through any problem. He was used to dealing with his community's crises, big and small. Fatima thought that maybe once the Padre knew, he would be able to make some sense of it and talk with her mother. After dinner, Fatima told her husband that she needed to speak with Padre Francisco. He was interested to know more, but she dismissed it as one of her mother's silly worries. She didn't think that it was important and would talk to him later, but wanted to see the Padre that evening so she could reassure her mother. Her husband knew her mother well and he didn't need to ask more. It was probably something and nothing.

Fatima headed to the little house by the church in the middle of the village. She knocked on the door and the Padre's house keeper greeted her. Padre Francisco was at the church and so Fatima went to look for him. She was pleased to find him on his own. He was used to visitors at all times of the day and night and was always welcoming and cheerful.

'Nice to see you, Fatima,' he said.

'Good evening, Padre Francisco. I need to talk to you, if you have time,' Fatima said, checking around the church again to make sure that they were alone.

Padre Francisco noticed her nervousness.

'Let's go next door. It will be more comfortable and warmer now the evening has set in.'

Fatima followed him and as he walked through the door he said, 'Come in and sit down. Would you like something to drink?'

Padre Francisco never made any assumptions. When his parishioners called to see him, it was rarely a courtesy call, but he found it best to be patient and listen.

'How are you?'

'I'm fine, thank you. We've just had dinner and I haven't got too long before I need to be back.'

However, when Fatima didn't seem to know where to begin, he asked gently, 'What can I help you with?'

'It's not me, it's my mother.'

'Is she well?' he asked.

'Very well, thank you. No, it's not that.'

Fatima then relayed the conversation she had had earlier that evening, her mother's request and her own worry that the English woman didn't speak Portuguese. Padre Francisco had heard about the visit to the village. Tino had been to see him. He had wondered himself about Tó Zé and if he would return.

'I know it's a lot to ask and I would understand if you weren't able to help.' As Fatima explained to him, she was becoming more convinced that she should go to Pampilhosa and see what she could find out, but now that she was talking with the Padre, it seemed like a huge imposition. She felt embarrassed that she had asked and as she drew to a close, she was apologetic.

'I'm sorry. Now I feel really awkward asking you. I don't suppose it's something you would want to be involved in, but I do feel I have to see what I can do. There will be someone at the hotel who speaks English, or someone there will be able to give me a better idea of who she is and satisfy my mother that there's nothing to be concerned about.'

Padre Francisco was quiet for what seemed like a long time, only making Fatima feel more embarrassed that she had asked him for help. He always wanted to help, but he was careful not to interfere. This needed a little thought. He could see Fatima's dilemma. He knew how insistent her mother could be and that it wasn't an easy trip to make on her own. He needed to go to Pampilhosa sometime in the next few days and there was no reason why he couldn't go the following day. It would at least be company for Fatima, and for him. They could talk further about it on the way. It might make more sense to her with a bit of distance from the village. He noticed Fatima's tension at his silence.

'I find that whenever there's a problem and we're not sure what to do, it's good to give ourselves a little time to consider, to think it through and not to dash at it and make it worse.' Padre Francisco thought he would explain his silence, but Fatima continued,

'I know Padre, but this is one of those situations where, if I'm going to find anything out, I don't have much time. I need to go. I'm sorry I asked.' Fatima was feeling anxious. She had made her decision and thought it better to get back home. She would worry about exactly what she would do when she got to town. She would go in the morning and take it from there. It didn't commit her to anything.

'I have a suggestion. I have to go to Pampilhosa soon on a church matter and there's no reason why I can't go tomorrow. It would be good to have some company. You could have a look around the town or help me if you wanted and the journey would be a chance to think a little more about what you might want to do.' Padre Francisco didn't want Fatima to do anything rash.

Fatima was relieved. It was a good solution. It would satisfy her mother's immediate concerns and she would be able to think it through on the way, as he had suggested, and share some thoughts with the Padre. She thanked him, agreed to return first thing in the morning and headed home. It was better, she thought, to let her mother know. She would be waiting for news, so she made a detour on her way back home.

Her mother and father were sitting at the kitchen table with Nuno, who was tucking hungrily into some bread and cheese. Seeing Nuno still at the house, she was careful what she said.

'Hi, everyone. Had a good day, Nuno?' she said smiling at her nephew. He was a bright, cheerful child and eager to talk about his day.

'Yes, aunt, really good. I've been playing out with my friends this evening. We've been playing in the square.'

'Sounds good,' Fatima said, a little distracted, as she wondered what to say to her mother with everyone else around.

'I think he's pretty tired after his long day. It won't be long before he needs to get to bed.' His grandfather had noticed Nuno looking sleepy, but Nuno was never one to give in easily.

'I'm ok, I'm not tired at all,' Nuno protested.

Then Fatima turned to her mother and said, 'I thought I'd call in to let you know that I'm going to Pampilhosa tomorrow with Padre Francisco. I'm going to help out with some arrangements that he has to make for next week's celebrations. Can you look after the children for me?'

'Isn't there anyone else who can help the Padre, I would have thought you have plenty to get on with here,' her father commented.

His wife shot him a look and turned back to Fatima. 'No problem, I'm always happy to have the children. It'll be a help to the Padre and a change for you. I think it's a great idea.'

'Thank you. I don't know when I'll be back, but I'll call in on my way home to pick up the children and catch up with you. I'd better get back now. I haven't told Paulo yet but I don't think he'll mind as long as the children are being looked after,' Fatima said.

'See you tomorrow, then, and thank you.' Her mother was certain now that it was essential that someone in the family found out what was going on. She was relieved to hear that Fatima was going to try to help out.

The next morning, having finished breakfast, Fatima took the children to her mother's house. She didn't know what the day would bring or when she would be back. Her mother had already been to see Tino for the details of the hotel. Fatima was pleased about that. She really hadn't wanted to get into a conversation with him. She knew she could trust the Padre but she was never sure about Tino. Her mother had obviously been giving Fatima's trip to Pampilhosa a lot of thought and was full of suggestions as to how she might handle the meeting. Fatima really had no idea what she was going to do and wasn't even sure that she would be able to see the English woman. Carol, apparently, was her name. Her mother was pressing her for a plan and it really wasn't helping.

'Mother, I've said I'll go. Let me handle it,' Fatima protested.

Her mother conceded, realising that her daughter was not particularly keen to go at all and knowing when to stop pushing.

'I'm pleased you're going with the Padre. He'll be a support at least and someone you can talk to.'

With that, Fatima said her good-byes and went to meet Padre Francisco.

The Padre's car had seen better days, but it served him for the journeys he needed to make. The town was about thirty kilometres from the village. They wound their way along twisting roads, crossing the River Zêzere a little before Cambas. For the first part of the journey, the Padre kept the conversation flowing, asking questions about the family. Fatima began to relax, almost forgetting the reason she was heading to Pampilhosa and began to enjoy the day. It was good to be getting out and about, doing something different. She decided that she would get the best out of the day whatever happened. As they got closer to the town, Padre Francisco started to talk about what he needed to do and how that could fit in with whatever Fatima wanted to do. He had avoided asking her directly, waiting for her to broach the subject, but as she hadn't mentioned it, he thought he had better make a suggestion.

'When we get there, I'll park in the town square not far from the church. I need first to go and see Padre José. I won't be long. You can come with me if you like or I can drop you off somewhere and then we could meet up again for a coffee at the café in the square?' He checked his watch and suggested eleven o'clock.

Fatima was now feeling that this was a daft idea. Her nerve was failing her.

'I haven't worked out what to do but now I'm here, I need to do something. I can't go back and tell my mother I didn't try. I won't hear the last of it. I'll go and ask at the hotel.'

'That sounds like a start and then over coffee, you can tell me what you know and if you have any more thoughts. I'll drop you off near the hotel before I go and park the car, then, if that's what you're going to do.'

Fatima walked into the reception of the small hotel and took a deep breath. The receptionist seeing her enter, got up from his paperwork and leaned forward over the large polished wooden reception desk.

'Good Morning. Can I help you?'

Nothing now to do but to ask, Fatima thought.

'I'm looking for an English woman named Carol who is staying with you at this hotel and left her contact details for me.' It was stretching the point a little, but she had left this forwarding address at the café in the village, so clearly she was open to someone looking for her at the hotel.

'Yes, Carol is staying with us and she did mention that she had been looking for a friend and had left the hotel as a contact. She went out after breakfast, though.'

Fatima felt quite relieved, she couldn't do anything if she wasn't there, but then she wasn't sure what to do next. She didn't want to leave her name.

'Have you any idea when she might be back?' she asked. 'I'm going to be in town for a while today.'

'She sometimes comes back before going out for lunch. I'll tell her you've been looking for her. What name shall I give?' he asked, naturally.

Fatima felt flustered. She didn't know why she didn't want to leave a name. 'I've got to dash, I'm meeting someone at the café in the square. I'll call back at lunchtime. What time do you thing would be good?'

The receptionist didn't ask her name again, noting her reluctance. 'Around mid-day is a possibility, but I couldn't be sure.'

'That's fine, I'll call back later,' Fatima said and then went for a little wander around the small town, as it wasn't yet eleven o'clock.

When she arrived at the café, Padre Francisco was already sitting outside, enjoying the late morning sunshine and reading a newspaper. He looked up sensing her approach and asked,

'Did you find her, then?'

'No, she went out after breakfast apparently, but sometimes she calls at the hotel before lunch, so I said I would go back later,' Fatima explained.

Padre Francisco then talked about what he needed to do for the rest of the day and how Fatima might help if she wanted.

'It's up to you. Relax and enjoy the day looking around the town if you want. I can manage,' he said.

'No, I'm really grateful for the lift and the company, I'll come with you, if that's alright.' Fatima didn't want to hang about and she had seen most of the town while she waited for him.

'Certainly. Now have a coffee, you must be ready after the journey, and I'll have another one too when the waitress appears.'

It wasn't much later when Carol walked back into reception and asked for the key to her room. The receptionist was quite surprised having been talking about her.

'I didn't expect you back so soon and actually, someone has very recently been asking for you,' he told her.

Carol's Portuguese was almost non-existent, but the receptionist knew some French and they were usually able to get by.

'Who was it? Did he leave a name?' she asked.

'She said she would call back around mid-day, but she didn't leave a name,' the receptionist said.

Carol heard 'she'. All this time, she had been hoping for Tó Zé. She felt unnerved, but didn't ask anymore. She took the key from the receptionist and went to collect the cardigan that she had forgotten earlier. There was nothing she could do other than come back at mid-day and see what she could find out.

In her room, she found herself pacing up and down, wondering who it might be. She sat on the bed and told herself to calm down. When she couldn't, she decided it would be best to go for a walk. She could go up to the high point above the town, she had been there before and found it a good place to sit and think, out of the way. She went back downstairs and handed the key to the receptionist.

'I've remembered,' he said. 'She was heading to have a coffee at the café in the square. You might still catch her there.' Then realising that Carol might not know who to look for, he added, 'She was wearing a dark blue dress and a grey cardigan.' He picked up a town map and showed her which café he meant. 'It's close by. You must have noticed it.'

Carol thanked him and walked out of the hotel. Pausing outside the door, she wondered what to do. There was no guarantee that this woman, whoever she was, would return at mid-day. She had to try to see her. She hadn't found out anything else that could help her know what had happened to Tó Zé. She took a deep breath and made her way to the café. As she approached, she noticed a woman dressed as the receptionist had described. As she continued to walk towards the café, she looked around to check if there was anyone dressed in a similar way. No, there was nobody else there. It must be her. It was then that she noticed the woman was sitting having coffee with a priest. It hit her like a bolt. Why would she be with a priest? There were many reasons, of course, but only one thought in Carol's mind. This couldn't be good. Something must have happened to Tó Zé. That's why she hadn't heard from him. As she approached, Padre Francisco noticed her and spoke to Fatima.

'I think this may be Carol,' he said.

There was no time for Fatima to think. Carol, conscious of the probable language problem spoke her only Portuguese phrase, as best she could in a heavy English accent.

'I'm sorry, I don't speak Portuguese and I don't understand it.' It wasn't the best greeting, but it was all she could manage.

Padre Francisco hadn't planned to be involved. He hadn't thought much further than giving support to Fatima in deciding what to do, but Carol was here now.

'I speak English. Are you Carol?' he asked.

'Yes, were you looking for me?' Carol decided that she had to be as circumspect as possible. Fatima also wanted to give away as little as she could, so she remained silent, letting Padre Francisco do the talking. She understood little of the conversation.

'Would you like a coffee?' Padre Francisco invited Carol to join them.

Carol didn't really want one, but she wanted to be polite, so she accepted the invitation and sat down, feeling uncomfortable and letting the priest continue to talk.

'We heard that you had been asking for Tó Zé in the village and as we were in Pampilhosa, we thought we would see if you were still here,' he explained.

'Yes, I didn't manage to see him when I was there. Apparently he hadn't been home,' Carol said.

Padre Francisco noticed her reticence and continued.

'He hasn't been back to the village, although we have been expecting him since the revolution. He's been away from home for a long time and may not yet have been able to get away from his commitments in France. Fatima, who is with me here, is part of the family.'

Carol was beginning to think that this must be one of Tó Zé's sisters, in town and curious.

He then turned to Fatima and introduced her to Carol. 'This is Fatima, Conceição's sister. I don't know if Tó Zé has mentioned her to you.'

Carol and Fatima greeted each other politely and Carol managed a 'muito prazer', a pleasure to meet you, which raised a smile from Fatima. Carol tried to remember the names of his sisters. She had never heard the name Conceição, she was sure. At first, she had felt quite relieved that she had managed to make contact with someone from his family, but now she was feeling confused. She didn't know what to say next.

'Do you know Tó Zé well?' Padre Francisco asked.

'Yes, quite well.' It was said with an irony that she felt would be lost. It was an understatement of course, and then as she continued something made her avoid saying 'we', as would have been natural to her. 'I live in Paris and have done for a number of years, though of course, I'm English,' Carol said.

Padre Francisco excused himself for speaking Portuguese for a moment and turned to Fatima to translate and to ask her if there was anything she would like him to ask Carol. He explained that he assumed that Carol was a friend. It was very hard to find out more without asking direct questions. Fatima wasn't sure what to suggest and so Padre Francisco continued to talk with Carol about her time in Portugal, trying to keep the conversation flowing. He thought he would find out more while they finished their drinks. As he began to think that it was probably time to be getting on, he returned to speak about Tó Zé.

'I assume that Tó Zé has your contacts and when he does return, we'll tell him we've seen you. Are you expecting to be here long? The family hasn't heard from him yet, but is sure he'll be wanting to see Conceição and Nuno. It's such a long time since they have seen each other. Nuno was only a baby when he left for Paris.'

Who was Nuno? There was a child. Carol felt panicked. She wanted to know who he was. She knew what she feared straight away, but couldn't bring herself to ask. She didn't want them to know that she had never heard of Nuno. She needed to think. Now she wanted to get away.

'I'm not sure of my plans.' She began to get up. 'I must get on. It was lovely to meet you both.'

As she left, Fatima turned to the Padre and asked what he thought.

'I'm not sure, Fatima, but she is close to him. How long has it been? It must be more than five years. It's not a surprise that he made a new life over there. He may have hoped to return, but he wouldn't have been sure he could come back here.' Padre Francisco thought it was better for Fatima to know what he thought.

'She wasn't just a friend,' Fatima said as they headed back towards the church.

'No, I don't think so, but I couldn't be sure, so be careful what you say to your mother,' Padre Francisco advised.

Carol didn't go straight back to the hotel. She started to walk, without any sense of where she was heading. She had to walk, to put one foot in front of the other. She headed up hill and out of the town. Now, she felt angry. She had never met anyone connected with Tó Zé's past. She had spent years with him, accepting him as an individual, accepting his reasons for living in Paris and not being able to go home. She had never doubted him. It had all seemed so plausible, but now, she knew. It confirmed everything she had felt before she had set off for Portugal. She didn't know him at all. Tears began to brim in her eyes. She fought them back, aware that people might notice her. She doubled back and headed for the hotel. As she dashed into reception and asked again for the key to her room, she had almost lost the battle with her tears.

'Are you ok?' the receptionist asked her, concerned.

'Fine, thank you.' She didn't want to speak. She ran up the stairs. She couldn't bear to wait for the lift. She unlocked the door of her room, went straight over to the wardrobe, grabbed her bag and began to pack.

Jacinta had tried to keep busy all day but she couldn't stop thinking about Fatima, wondering if she would be able to find out anything about Carol.

As the afternoon wore on, doubts set in and she started to consider what else she could do. She didn't like not knowing. The fact was, she usually knew everything that was going on in the village, it was well known. Her relationship with Tó Zé's family had been strained ever since he had left. They rarely spoke but she was convinced his mother must have some idea. Unable to wait any longer, once her husband returned, she left him with the children, saying she wouldn't be long and headed to Teresa's house.

'I thought it was time we had a chat,' she said as the door opened and Teresa greeted her, surprised to see her there.

'Come in.' Teresa knew better than to resist.

They sat down at the table and Jacinta said that Tino had told her about the woman who had been asking for Tó Zé. She assumed that his mother knew already.

'I'm sure there's more to it. That English woman seems to be keen to get hold of him. I'm really quite concerned. Have you tried to contact her?' she asked.

Teresa was a little taken aback and didn't know what to say to her.

'I don't know where Tó Zé is. As far as I'm concerned, he's still in Paris and as for an English woman, I really don't know what you're talking about.'

She was naturally protective of her son. She knew that some of his actions were hard to defend, but she had never appreciated Jacinta's interference, not in her family's business nor in anyone else's in the village.

Jacinta didn't believe her. 'You must have heard from him by now and if that woman is looking for him here, then he must be in Portugal.'

'He's not here, is he?' Teresa was beginning to feel upset. She had expected him to return after the revolution. She felt sure that he wouldn't want to stay away once he could return, but she had heard nothing.

'I can't imagine for one minute he'll still be in France. He was too involved to stay away. I don't know what was wrong with him. He had the opportunity of a great future, something not offered to many people around here. If he had got his head down and studied, they could have had a good life.'

Jacinta had expressed this view many times before. Teresa's mother didn't appreciate the criticism and had to work to control a growing temper.

'He wasn't doing anything more than many of the students. They were all a target because of their views and if he had stayed he would have been sent to Africa, and what then? I haven't seen him for five years, but I might never have seen him again. I'm not sure I want him to come back if he has to face conscription.'

Jacinta wasn't going to change her view of Tó Zé. 'That may be, but he has responsibilities here.' There was nothing more to say she thought and with that, she left.

Tó Zé's mother was confused and worried. She didn't know what to think but she had no intention of speaking with anyone about it. If there was a problem, it was better that she didn't interfere, that she kept quiet. She had learned that. When only a week later, one of his university friends and then soon afterwards, two English people came looking for Tó Zé, she began to fear that something awful might have happened to her son. She told them as little as possible.

# XX

**16ᵗʰ June, 1974**

People present themselves in different ways. Individuals are subject to the perceptions and attitudes, and, at times, the imagination, of others. What one person feels inside is often not what others see of them. This can be a frustration for some who feel misunderstood or misrepresented in life, but people's perceptions were not something that troubled Clara. Indeed, she was more than content to be misunderstood and over the years, it had served her very well. When Júlia got back from her stay in Vila Real and told Clara about the trip to Coimbra, she was able to give her more information about Tó Zé and Rebecca's search for Carol. This time, Júlia knew his full name, where he was from, the fact that he was probably back but hadn't returned home. Clara recognised the name and although it was quite possible that he wasn't the only António José Gonçalves da Silva in the country, she was sure that it was the Tó Zé she had heard about. She knew also that he and some of the others were back and although Rebecca hadn't managed to track him down as yet, Clara was sure that he was in Lisbon. She thought it best to try to get in touch with him. There might be a problem and he might not know that people were looking for him. She thought it was better that he was forewarned. She didn't know what his circumstances were, whether he had returned legitimately. He might not want to be found. It was much safer now in Portugal. Members of the old regime had been marginalised, but there were still many reasons why someone might not want to be found.

Over the years, Clara's close colleagues had been aware of her views. She had shared some of them, but they were gently expressed and without any conviction or hint of being radical. She had good reason to keep her strongest views quiet and despite the changes in recent weeks, she wasn't yet prepared to be open. Colleagues didn't know that she had been a member of the Communist Party for many years. From an early age, she had been fascinated by the stories of those opposed to the dictatorship, struggling against a harsh, oppressive regime. She knew many had been imprisoned for their views, held in the notorious dungeons at the prison in Peniche and tortured by the PIDE. Others had been forced to leave Portugal to escape punishment. Clara's family were thinking people who privately never accepted Salazar's dictatorship and as long as she remembered, longed for change. As a young person, clandestine radio broadcasts had been the only source of information in a country heavily controlled by censorship. In the evenings, the family would close the doors and windows and listen to Radio Free Portugal to hear the views of the free world and to have news of resistance to the regime. Her parents were fearful and discouraged involvement, but Clara felt she had to do something to help and so she became involved. At first, it was in little ways. She kept her activities very much a secret, even from her family, helping where she felt she could, connecting with activists operating clandestinely, making sure that any activity appeared as innocent as possible. If they needed to meet, they met in the street, on a park bench, arranged to go for a walk, giving the impression that it was nothing more than the meeting of friends. If they met in a café, it would be a place where they could be sure that any member of the PIDE could be easily recognised.

As it happened, that evening, after Júlia had spoken about Tó Zé, Clara had arranged to see her old friend and mentor. They got together once a month, a meeting which Clara looked forward to. The Party's work was changing and there were fewer reasons to be quiet. In days gone by, it was these meetings which had kept her informed about the activities of the resistance and importantly, the problems the dictatorship was experiencing. Hearing about the struggles had always raised her hopes that one day she would see the government's demise and here it was. It was in these meetings that she heard about the continued activities of the students and their teachers in the universities of Lisbon, Oporto and Coimbra. Clara supported them whenever she was asked. In those days, her mentor insisted on secrecy. It was the best way to make sure that Clara and those with whom she associated were kept as safe as possible, working on behalf of the party. It was through her mentor too that she had access to important books and the Communist Party's publication, Avante, which was banned by the government. He taught her how to hide those materials from any unannounced searches by the PIDE, constructing a false shelf at the bottom of the bookcase in her apartment. Clara devoured the books she received and looked forward to each issue of Avante, another way of getting information about the resistance and the activities, legal and illegal, of comrades across the country and abroad. As a recruit, Clara would listen carefully to her mentor. He did the talking. Both of them knew how important it was to know as little as possible, whatever part each comrade played in the struggle. If there was something to be done, the task was given and it was carried out without question and without any more intelligence than was necessary. Knowing more would only increase the risk to everyone involved. They had to trust each other.

That evening, her mentor was speaking about the activities of returning nationals and the work of the party since the revolution. He was working at the headquarters in Lisbon. Clara felt sure that he would have come across Tó Zé and having confirmed that he had met him, she told him that she knew he had been followed to Portugal. She was fairly convinced that Rebecca's only reason for trying to find him was to locate Carol and that Carol had no other association with Tó Zé than that of being his long-term girlfriend, but if he was in the country without papers, was taking any risks and didn't want to be found, she thought it important he knew. Her work for the party with student activists had brought her into contact with people who knew Tó Zé. It had been a long while since she had heard anything about him. She didn't know what he had been doing in Paris. Her mentor agreed that it might be helpful to talk with Tó Zé and said that he would try to speak with him in the morning. They agreed to meet again the following evening. Clara suggested that they meet in Prince Edward Park. It was a detour on her way home from work and although it wasn't necessary to be too cautious now, she didn't want her colleagues to know about her past. She didn't want any complication and felt it was more useful to keep her job at the radio station until she understood more of the future. All she had ever wanted was freedom and change. She had no political ambition, but as different groups jostled and struggled for power, for a louder voice in the new government, her distrust remained.

The next evening, Clara and her mentor met as arranged, a casual meeting in the evening sunshine.

'I managed to catch up with Tó Zé. He was interested to know more, so I've arranged for you to meet him. I think it's better that you tell him first-hand. He wanted to know more than I could tell him.'

'When do you want me to meet him?' Clara asked.

'Tomorrow at lunchtime, if that's possible.'

Clara agreed. The time and place her mentor had suggested to Tó Zé suited her. She could go out in her lunch hour. She had no real idea if the information she had would be a concern to Tó Zé. Part of her wondered if she was straying into someone's personal life when it wasn't really her business and might be seen as interfering, but years of being careful encouraged her that it was right to speak with him. She made no mention of the meeting to anyone and certainly not to Júlia.

The next day over coffee, Clara told Tó Zé about her friends and the search for Carol. He listened and made little comment as she recounted the visits to the two villages and how they found out that someone matching Carol's description had been there before them. When she had finished, he asked one or two questions, wanting to know exactly how long ago they had been to Janeiro de Cima. There were so many questions that Clara would have liked to have asked, especially about Carol. He hadn't given much away and had shown little emotion when she had explained that

Carol was missing and her family was concerned. She couldn't read him at all. Tó Zé thanked her for letting him know and with that, they both left the café.

As Clara walked back to work, she was feeling a little concerned about how Rebecca might feel if she knew that she had found Tó Zé. However, he had no knowledge of Carol's whereabouts and so she wouldn't be helping Rebecca, even if she told her. She did ask Tó Zé to let her know if he found out where Carol was. He promised her that he would.

## Janeiro de Cima, 20th June, 1974

Tó Zé knew that he had to go home, but it was a few days before he could get away. He managed to arrange a lift with a friend who was going to Covilhã to support workers in the textile factories in the town. Tó Zé had been in Portugal nearly two months for the most part feeling unconcerned, because he assumed that his family didn't know he had returned. He had been busy. He would go home when he was a bit more settled. He thought about Carol, with a kind of strained tension. He pushed her out of his mind. She would have to wait too. It had been nearly six years since he had seen any of his family. Any news or direct communication had been rare. Almost completely in his mind, he had left his life behind. The circumstances in which he went away had allowed him to keep the door closed on his old life and over the years, he had almost convinced himself of his own reinvention. Now it was different. He needed to get home.

He asked to be dropped off about a mile outside the village. He needed time. He wanted to take in the landscape again and prepare his thinking for his return. He walked along the narrow road with fields either side until the small village nestled on the bank of the River Zêzere came into sight. Tó Zé stopped and looked for a place to sit. He was still some distance away, but he wasn't ready to carry on yet.

The most familiar of places can seem strange and unfamiliar given time and distance and that was how his village and the surrounding area now seemed to Tó Zé. After years in Paris, he had forgotten how small it was and also how remote and somehow dark to him. It was a hard but simple life which he hadn't missed. It offered him so little.

Tó Zé was the eldest of five children. He had a brother and three sisters. All of them would still be living in the village or in the surrounding area as far as he knew. He thought that at least one of his sisters would be living in the family home with his parents. He wanted to arrive around dinner time. The house would be busy. The meal would be a distraction and he had no concern that his mother would not have prepared enough for an extra mouth. There was always plenty to eat. He checked his watch, making sure to delay the last mile of his walk home until the last minute. Finally, he got back up on his feet and took a determined pace towards the village. He still had no idea what he would say. He had to let his return take its own course. He increased his pace as he entered the village. He was bound to see people he knew, but he didn't want to get delayed or to have to speak to anyone else before he had been home. Luckily, most of the villagers were already settled in their own houses ready for the evening meal or taking a drink in the café before going home for dinner. Tó Zé made one last detour to avoid the café. Finally, at the door of the house, he paused for the last time. He considered knocking, thought better of it, turned the handle and walked in, as though he had simply been out for the day. For a second or two, everything carried on as normal. His father was sitting down, looking tired after his working day. His mother and sister were deep in conversation. Then there was recognition, a few stunned moments and for a while, nothing more than hugs, smiles and greetings. Having given him the longest hug of all, his mother was the first to speak.

'What a surprise! Why didn't you tell us you were coming? I'd hoped it wouldn't be too long now that the borders have been opened and there was really nothing to keep you away. Your father wasn't sure, but I knew you'd be back as soon as you felt you could get here.'

'I couldn't have given you much notice, I didn't want a fuss. I thought it would be good to surprise you,' Tó Zé said.

It had not been that simple in his thinking, he knew that. The decision to return had not been an easy one. It had been rather forced upon him. As he stood in the kitchen of his old family home, part of him still wondered if it would have been better to have remained in Paris. He should have moved away for good, lost himself there. He was proud of his country, though, and not to return would have meant to live in his own forced exile. He didn't want that. He wanted to be part of a better future for his country. The time had come to understand what that future had to offer him. He also had to face up to everything he had left behind in such a hurry. For now, though, he wanted to be distracted into the ordinary, into the routine, for a short while, at least for the evening of his return. He didn't want to face any of the heavy questions which he knew were to come.

'What a fantastic smell! You can't imagine how much I've missed your cooking, mother. I'm starving,' was his opening attempt to focus on the simple, on dinner. It could have been that everyone was hungry, ready for a meal at the end of a long day. Maybe it was the element of surprise. The missing years were ignored, as if nothing had changed, no time had intervened. They sat down at the table, enjoyed the meal and the company. Tó Zé worked hard to keep the conversation focussed, asking questions about his family and life in the village.

The evening went by quickly. His father was characteristically the quietest of everyone, preferring to listen. It wasn't long before he decided it was time for bed. His sister followed, making what felt to Tó Zé like a tactful withdrawal, recognising that her mother would want some time with her newly returned son.

'It's an early start for work tomorrow, so I'll get to bed,' his sister said. For a few more moments, his mother carried on, clearing away the remains of the dinner and starting to wash up. Then she turned and spoke to Tó Zé,

'I take it you've already been to see Conceição.'

Tó Zé had wondered how long it would be before his mother asked him. He was surprised that she hadn't spoken about it over dinner, but she had thought better of it.

'No, I came straight here. Conceição doesn't know I'm back, so she won't miss me,' Tó Zé said.

'She'll know by tomorrow morning, that's for sure. You know how quickly news gets around the village. You need to see her.' His mother was insistent.

'Tomorrow morning, I'll go tomorrow morning. That will be soon enough. Is it alright if I stay here tonight?' he asked.

'I suppose it'll have to be.' His mother was far from happy, but she knew him and she knew how far she could encourage him before he closed off from her. She changed the subject.

'How long have you been travelling? Did you get the train most of the way?' she asked.

'No, we came by car. I've been in Lisbon.' His mother would find out soon enough, so he decided it was best to be open with her.

'Who do you mean by 'we'? She began to feel concerned. 'And what were you doing in Lisbon? I thought you'd want to get back here as soon as you could. It's been six years for goodness sake.'

'I came back with Alvaro, Fernando and Brito. We needed to check things out in Lisbon. There's still so much to do if we are to capitalise on the recent victory.'

'Oh, Tó Zé, did you not have the chance of a new start in Paris? Why do you have to persist with all this? It's still not safe. The old regime is over and there will be a better future for all of us, I'm sure. Let the new government have a chance, see how it goes.' His mother was getting upset.

While his family had every sympathy with Tó Zé's politics, his mother had seen his views take him away, at the time not knowing whether he could ever return. Now that he was back, she didn't want to lose him again and she wasn't sure that there was any need for the struggle to continue as before.

'We'll see. So many people lost so much for the cause and for a better future for this country. It's not finished yet. You can't assume it will all be alright. I don't think it will.' Tó Zé saw the tension in his mother's face and realised it wasn't the time to try to convince her, so he tried to ease things a little.

'I'm here now and there are things that I need to sort out. I need to see Conceição,' he said.

'You certainly do.' His mother couldn't resist one more dig.

'I'm going in the morning after breakfast. OK?'

'OK. There's a bed made up in your old room.'

With that, Tó Zé went to bed. The significance of his mother keeping a bed ready made for him in his old room did not escape him.

Tó Zé found it difficult to sleep. The conversation with his mother playing like a soundtrack on a loop against the deep silence and the pitch black darkness of the village outside. He had grown used to city life. He slept very little and as soon as it became light, he got up, went into the kitchen and made a sandwich. He left a note for his mother and went out for a walk to clear his head. It was far too early, but he would have to see Conceição. His mother was right. If she hadn't heard he was back, she soon would. Better to get there first. He checked his watch. Conceição wouldn't be up and about for at least an hour, he thought, then realised a lot of things might have changed in six years. It suited him, though, to go for a walk and have time away from the house to think about what he might say. Deep in thought, he walked back out of the village into the surrounding countryside and for a while, he lost track of time. When he checked his watch again, it was after eight o'clock and then he realised how far he had walked. Time to get back. Everyone would have been up and about for a while by now. He set off back to the village. When he arrived, he found that Conceição wasn't at home, so he began to walk back in the direction of his parents' house, then annoyed with his stalling, he turned around and headed to Conceição's parents' house. Surely they would know where she was.

Seven o'clock in the morning on what promised to be a bright, sunny day and Conceição was preparing breakfast. She called out,

'Nuno, are you dressed yet? Your breakfast is nearly ready.'

No reply, so Conceição went into his room to see if he was out of bed and there he was sitting on the floor slowly pulling on his socks.

'Didn't you hear me, Nuno? I called to you. You need to have breakfast before we go and we don't have a lot of time,' Conceição said, a little irritated, but trying not to show her impatience.

Nuno was only six years old, but already fiercely independent. He liked to do things his own way and when it came to getting ready, it was always a fairly slow process. However, he wouldn't have his mother help him and she knew that gentle persuasion was always better.

'I have to put my socks on and then I'm coming. Am I staying with my grandparents today?' Nuno asked.

'Yes, of course. I have to go to work,' Conceição said as she was leaving to go back to the kitchen.

The small wooden table in the kitchen was laid out for a very simple breakfast with the warm bread that Conceição had bought from the bakery a few doors from the house while Nuno was getting ready. There was some cheese, honey, milk and fresh fruit too. Nuno wasn't long before he joined her. He pulled out a chair and arranged the cushion so that he could reach the table and then he grabbed a roll and made a sandwich with the cheese. Conceição came over and joined him at the table, pouring him a glass of milk, both of them saying little. They ate mostly in silence.

It hadn't been easy at all for Conceição over the last six years as a single parent in a small village, but she had managed. Many there knew her story and tried to help out as they could. She wasn't completely on her own. All of her close family lived in the village. They worried that she seemed lonely. She longed for a different life. Nuno was a quiet, thoughtful little boy. He was loving and very protective of his mother. He was a joy to her. He kept her busy and was great company, but she had little time to spend with him. She felt guilty that she had to leave him so often with the family, but it was being able to work that had kept her sane. Still, Nuno seemed happy. He loved to help out his grandfather and he had his cousins to play with when he wasn't at school. Noticing that Nuno had finished, Conceição got up from the table.

'Have you had enough to eat, son?'

'Yes, mother, thank you.' Nuno always remembered his manners.

'Go and get your coat and bag then, and anything you might want for the day.' Conceição said as she washed the few dishes they had used for breakfast and continued, 'I'll be ready in five minutes, so let's get on.'

Conceição and Nuno walked the short distance to her parents' house, through the narrow streets, bathed in gentle morning sunshine. The house wasn't far away and they were soon at the front door. Nuno ran ahead of his mother and greeted his grandmother and grandfather enthusiastically, giving them both a kiss, as they were sitting at the kitchen table finishing their breakfast. Both his grandparents gave him a big hug. Nuno loved them both, but he loved his grandfather especially. He looked up to him and hung on his every word. He was the father figure that he didn't have. He loved trying to help out and so he was keen to know what there was to do that day. He was asking his grandfather as soon as he had said hello. Conceição was struck by the difference. The quiet boy who had sat in silence with her at breakfast was now very animated. He didn't want to sit down and was quickly deep in conversation with his grandfather.

'Your grandfather has something to show you outside, Nuno. Go along with him.' His grandmother looked at her husband, encouraging him with a 'go on' look.

'What's that? What do you want me to show him?' her husband asked feeling confused. He wasn't sure what she meant.

'You know' his wife replied with a sterner look exasperated that he hadn't worked out that she needed to talk to Conceição on her own.

This time, he understood the look. Unsure what he would show Nuno when they got outside, he got up, hoping something would come to him. As young as he was, Nuno was very quick at picking up any sign of a problem and his grandfather would need to come up with something convincing.

'Here, you've time for a quick drink before you go and there's something I wanted to mention to you,' Conceição's mother said as soon as her husband and Nuno were out of the door.

Her mother seemed concerned. Conceição felt unsettled.

'What's wrong? Is something wrong with one of the family?' Conceição asked. She needed to get to work and time was short but this sounded serious.

'No, actually, it's about you,' her mother replied.

For a second or two, Conceição tried to think what she could have done that would be concerning her mother so much. She had time for little, other than work and looking after Nuno, but she didn't share everything with her mother. It was easier that way.

'What do you mean, 'It's about me'?' She asked, still confused.

'Tino from the café called by last night. He's seen Tó Zé.' This was her mother's news and it was unexpected.

'What are you saying, he's seen Tó Zé, where?' Conceição was now very unnerved.

'He says he's sure he saw him walking through the village towards his parents' house last night around dinner time,' she replied.

'But do you know that he's sure?' Conceição wasn't sure that she believed it. 'We would have heard, wouldn't we? His mother would have told me if she had heard he was coming back.'

'Perhaps it was a surprise for her too,' her mother suggested.

'Why hasn't he come to see us, if he's here? It doesn't make sense.' Conceição asked, trying to work it out.

'Try not to read too much into it, he always was his own person, likes to do things his way. You can expect him if he's here, I'm sure.' Her mother could see that Conceição was unhappy and tried to reassure her.

'Whether he's here or not, I've got to get to work, so it will have to be this evening,' Conceição said suddenly feeling annoyed.

With that she said a quick good-bye to her mother, almost rushing towards the door. She now had one thing in her mind and that was to make sure that she didn't bump into Tó Zé in the street. That really wouldn't do.

'Say goodbye to Nuno and father for me. Tell them I had to dash, oh, and please can you make sure that Nuno is out of the way?' She said, pausing with her hand on the door handle.

'I'll do my best, but it's a small village. I'll have a word with your father, see what he can do. Try not to worry about it...' Her words trailed off as her daughter closed the door with somewhat more force than usual.

About fifteen minutes later, there was a knock at the door. Conceição's mother was still in the kitchen. Her husband and grandson must have found things to do because they hadn't been back since Conceição had left. Hearing the knock, her heart leapt. Instinctively she felt sure it was Tó Zé and she was worried that Nuno and her husband might return. There was nothing she could do. She walked to the door and opened it slowly. Sure enough, there was Tó Zé standing waiting. The years hadn't changed him much at all and for a second, it seemed to her too that no time at all had passed since he had last walked through the door.

'Hello, Jacinta,' he said and kissed her. 'I've been looking for Conceição, she's not at home.'

'You've missed her, she's gone to work,' she told him.

Tó Zé seemed surprised. 'Gone to work? I thought she would be alright for money.'

She felt her annoyance rising. Six years, so little contact. He knew almost nothing about how life had been for them all.

'It's been hard, Tó Zé, a real struggle in so many ways. You have no idea. She's needed to work to keep busy and to get out of the house. It's not easy on your own with a small child.' She stopped herself short. It wasn't the time for this. She knew she would only make the situation more difficult by saying what she really felt. She wanted him out of the way, so she continued.

'She'll be back this evening. Leave it with me. I'll get a message to you to let you know when she's at home and you can go and see her,' she suggested.

'Where's Nuno?' Tó Zé then asked, which was exactly what she was hoping to avoid. Of course, she knew he was close by. Having told Conceição that she would do her best, she was now very much on edge that he would come back in at any moment.

'He's out for the day with his grandfather. You'll have to catch up later.'

'I didn't know she was working.' Tó Zé was disappointed but he knew it would be wrong to insist on seeing Nuno, so he left and headed back towards his parents' house.

Jacinta waited long enough for him to be out of sight and then went to find her husband to urge him to try and avoid any chance meetings. As she continued with the day's work, thoughts of the English woman came back to her and began to play on her mind.

Tó Zé wasn't sure what to do with the day and was wondering who of his old friends were still living in the village. He was tempted to head to the café and catch up with some of the villagers. He also wanted to have a word with Tino to find out what he knew about the visitors from Coimbra, but he thought better of it. His mother would be wondering where he was and would probably have some breakfast waiting for him.

'You've been a while. Did you manage to see Conceição?' his mother asked as soon as he walked through the door.

'No, I missed her. Her mother is going to get a message to me once she has spoken with her, so that I can see her this evening.'

'What have you been doing? You needed to speak to her this morning. It will be all around the village soon that you're back.' His mother was concerned.

'I made a sandwich before I left this morning, but I'm still hungry and I see there's some breakfast left.'

Tó Zé tried to steer the conversation away from Conceição. He was genuinely hungry after his morning walk and after taking such a long detour. He made no mention of that to his mother.

'I thought I would go and see who was at the café a little later, catch up with Tino,' he said, changing his mind again about going there.

'No, no, don't do that,' his mother said without thinking.

Tó Zé didn't expect her to object. 'What's wrong?'

'There was something else that I wanted to mention to you,' she said.

'What was that?' he asked. His mother looked serious now.

She made a drink for Tó Zé and put some bread, cheese and butter back onto the table before sitting down to join him while he ate.

'A little while ago now, I had a visit from an old university friend of yours. He said that he was touring with friends and was in the area and thought he would look you up on the off chance you were back.'

'Who was it?' Tó Zé asked, knowing, but acting as though he didn't.

'He said his name was Rui. He could have been younger than you, so he might not have been in the same year,' his mother replied.

'Didn't he give you any other names? There were several students called Rui at university.' Tó Zé was curious. He hadn't asked Clara too many questions and she hadn't explained exactly who was with Rebecca. He began to wonder if Rui did know him. It was a fairly common name, but without a surname, he couldn't think who it might have been. There hadn't been anyone called Rui amongst his close friends at university.

'No, he didn't say anymore and he was in a rush because he'd left his friends at the café and they were wanting to get on and visit some other places.'

'Oh, I see. Shame I missed him.' Tó Zé was wanting to sound as matter of fact as he could. He didn't want his mother to know that he was aware that someone was looking for him. It would only lead to questions he didn't want to answer. His mother continued.

'I thought it was strange that someone who knew you might think you were back, when we hadn't heard, so I asked Tino what he knew about the group. There were four of them, two men and two women. They had appeared to be friends on a tour around the area, as that young man had said to me. Tino had seen them looking at a map and discussing what they might do. I know something else, though,' his mother said.

'What's that?' Tó Zé was fairly sure what she would say next. He had hoped that his mother didn't know anymore, but it was obvious that she did.

'Some days before that, there had been a woman on her own asking about you.'

'Who was it? What did she look like?' Tó Zé asked, but his mother didn't seem to know much more, except that she was English. He knew it was Carol, of course. Clara had told him that when he met her in Lisbon, but he hadn't intended to bring it up. It was all too complicated and difficult as it was.

'That's not anyone I knew at university.' Tó Zé didn't want to lie to his mother. He had often kept things from her, but he made a point of not lying to her.

'I think I'd better catch up with Tino and find out what he knows. I'll go over now,' he said, getting up from the table and washing the dishes he had been using.

'Are you sure that's a good idea? I really wish you'd see Conceição before getting out and seeing others. It's only fair. She's not likely to be too happy hearing all about you from everyone else in the village.'

'I know, but she's at work and I can't sit around here all day. It might turn out to be something important. I want to know more.'

With that, he set out in the direction of the café. Tino wasn't on his own when he arrived at the café. One of the villagers, a friend of his father, had called in for a quick bica, a shot of espresso coffee.

'I bumped into your father this morning and he said you were back. It's been a long time. How are you?' His father's friend asked him.

The questions turned to Paris and Tó Zé was pleased that they were able to keep the conversation fairly general. They chatted for a while before he decided that it was time he was on his way. Once they were alone, Tó Zé got straight to the point, not knowing how long they would have before someone else called in.

'I hear I had some visitors recently. What do you know about them?' he asked.

'Not much more than I'm sure you know already. I'm assuming you've spoken with Jacinta and that's how you know,' Tino replied.

So others knew too. It wasn't how he had found out, of course, but he didn't want Tino to know any more than he needed to know or already knew. Tó Zé wondered how he could find out what Tino knew without sounding too curious. He needn't have worried. Tino was interested in Carol, more so even than he might have imagined.

'Her name is Carol and she was staying in a hotel in Pampilhosa da Serra. I have the name, address and phone number of the hotel if you want. She didn't say how long she was staying and it was some time ago, but I got the impression that she was hanging around for a while. What does she want, do you know?' he asked.

Tó Zé didn't want to answer the question. 'I think I should contact her. Have you got the address?' he asked.

Tino went back behind the counter and copied out the information he had onto another piece of paper. He wanted to keep a copy.

'Here you go,' he said, handing the piece of paper over to Tó Zé. 'She shouldn't be too difficult to find if she's still there.'

Tó Zé thanked him and as he walked towards the door, he added,

'It would be good if you didn't mention to anyone else that I've been asking until I know more.'

'Ok,' Tino said, but Tó Zé wasn't sure that he wouldn't say anything. He knew he had to make the journey into Pampilhosa as soon as possible. He walked back to the house wondering if he had time that day. He didn't and also, he didn't want to draw more attention to his interest in Carol. He didn't want any more questions.

When Tó Zé got back to the house, his mother was on her own. As soon as he walked through the door, he could tell that something was wrong and she didn't wait to tell him how annoyed she was feeling.

'I suppose it's to be expected. There's so little going on in this village and everybody thinks they can get involved in other people's business,' she blurted out, without even mentioning who had called.

'Who's been to see you?' he asked her.

'Conceição's mother, of course, interfering again.'

'Did she stay long?' He really didn't want to get into the conversation.

'I mentioned to you that she was going to let me know when Conceição would be back this evening. I didn't expect her so soon. I'm sorry I wasn't here. I know the two of you don't get on very well.'

'Huh, don't get on very well! She didn't stay long, thankfully. She was full of it. I don't know how she's kept it to herself all this time. Apparently, after the English woman had been to the village – Carol, that's her name, isn't it? – Fatima went to see her with Padre Francisco. That was nearly two weeks ago. She still doesn't know who she is and was insisting I told her. Who is she, Tó Zé?'

Tó Zé now felt unnerved. Did Conceição know too, then? 'She's a friend.' He told his mother. 'I told her I was coming back to Portugal. She's obviously decided to look me up.'

His mother wanted to know more, but all he would say was, 'She's a friend, mother, that's all.'

# XXI

That evening, Conceição's mother made a point of meeting her on her way back from work. She wanted to make sure that she wasn't overheard by Nuno, so she made an excuse that she was visiting a neighbour. When Conceição saw her mother, she knew what it was about.

'Is he here?' she asked.

'No, he came this morning, a little while after you had left. I said that he wouldn't be able to see you until this evening and that I would get a message to him to let him know when you were at home,' her mother explained.

'I want to see him alone.' Conceição was insistent.

'Of course. If you go straight home now, Nuno can stay with us for dinner. I'll tell him you've been delayed, he doesn't need to know why. You can come and collect him when you're ready,' her mother suggested.

'That sounds a good idea. I'll go straight home.'

'Right then, I'll go and let Tó Zé know you're at home. I'll be thinking about you.'

'Thank you,' Conceição said and they both went quickly on their way.

When Conceição's mother knocked on the door, it was Tó Zé's mother who answered. That shouldn't have been a surprise but she was hoping she wouldn't have to speak to her again that day and thought Tó Zé would be expecting her. Suddenly, she felt a little awkward and hoped she wouldn't be asked inside.

'I'm in the middle of preparing dinner, so I must dash, but I said I would get a message to Tó Zé to tell him when Conceição was at home. She's there now. Must go. Bye.' And off she went, not leaving any time for a reply, but feeling sure that Tó Zé would get the message. He was sitting at the kitchen table and heard her, so when his mother came back in and closed the door, he said straight away.

'Ok, I'm going,' and went towards the door.

'Will you be back for dinner?' his mother asked.

'I don't know when I'll be back, but don't wait for me. Save me something, I'll eat later,' he said.

'Yes, of course, there will be plenty. Behave yourself,' she said.

It was a long time since he had heard his mother say that to him, but he always knew what she meant. It was her way of cautioning him to get it right, whatever that might be.

When Conceição's mother got back home, she began to feel concerned. There was so much she hadn't told Conceição and now that Tó Zé was on his way to see her, she was wondering if she had done the right thing. She hadn't known what to do, she hadn't wanted to worry Conceição unnecessarily or give her any reason to be more unsettled about Tó Zé's return than she would be already. She didn't know who the English woman was and that bothered her. When Nuno and his grandfather returned to the house, she sent Nuno out into the quintal on a little errand and then spoke quickly with her husband.

'I haven't told Conceição everything that Tino said to me. I didn't mention the woman who has been asking about Tó Zé in the village or the others and I'm fairly sure she doesn't know. I don't know what it's about really and I didn't want her to worry. What do you think?'

'I think you've done the right thing. This is Conceição's issue.'

'It's been so hard for her, though, and if there's anything I can do to make it easier I will. I'll see if Tino knows anything more about that woman. I'll have a word with Fatima this evening and see if she thinks there's anything else we can do.'

'I'm really not sure that Conceição will thank the family for getting so involved. If she knew what you've done already, I think she would be fairly upset with you.' Conceição's father hadn't been happy when he found out why Fatima had gone to Pampilhosa with Padre Francisco but over the years, he knew better than to try to persuade his wife when she was in that mood. It was not in her nature to leave things alone. Nuno came dashing back into the kitchen and the conversation turned quickly away from Conceição, his grandmother asking him about his day.

'Can I go and see if my friends are playing in the square?' Nuno asked.

His grandmother saw the opportunity to go and have a word with Fatima and there was a little time before dinner. The preparation was on its way and nothing would spoil. Tó Zé would already be with Conceição.

'Only for half an hour, then. We're having dinner here this evening. Your grandfather will come and get you when it's ready.'

Nuno hadn't asked about his mother, which pleased his grandmother. The fewer explanations she had to make at the moment the better. She turned then to her husband.

'Dinner is on its way. It should be alright to be left. You don't need to do anything except keep an eye on it to make sure nothing burns. I'm going to have a word with Fatima, I'll be back in time for you to go and call Nuno in for dinner.'

'Ok, then.' Her husband didn't put up any further protest. There was still a chance that Fatima would talk some sense into her.

Fatima understood her mother's concern for Conceição, but she was astonished when she asked her if she would go again to Pampilhosa and see if Carol was still there. She had told her that she thought Carol was a friend, nothing more. She was sure that even if Carol had stayed in the area for a while, she would have gone by now and from her reaction that day, she didn't think she would have stayed.

'Mother, I'm sure she's long gone. We've done enough, probably too much already. Tó Zé is back now. Let them sort it out themselves.'

Conceição hadn't been in the house more than half an hour when there was a knock on the door. She knew at once that it was Tó Zé and went to greet him. She hadn't known what to expect, how she would feel, but now that he was here, she felt quite ill. She wondered why she hadn't prepared herself better and paused at the door, taking a deep breath and hoping that she would know what to do, what to say. She thought it would be better to keep this first meeting as brief as possible. She was anxious now to go and collect Nuno. It was getting late and she didn't want him to worry where she was. She opened the door and Tó Zé greeted her cheerfully. The familiarity jarred with her and made her more determined to keep the conversation brief.

'I don't have very long, Tó Zé. I've been out all day and Nuno will be wondering where I am.'

'How is he?' Tó Zé asked. 'I wanted to see him, but your mother preferred for me to speak with you first.'

'He's fine, absolutely fine, thank you for asking. As I was saying, I don't have much time this evening, so I've a suggestion. How about tomorrow? We could all go to the river, take a picnic. It will give us a chance to talk and spend some time with Nuno.'

She wasn't sure that it was a good idea as soon as she had said it, but she wasn't ready to talk to him either. She wanted him to go.

Tó Zé wanted to stay and talk. It hadn't been easy to come over to see Conceição and now that he was there, he was ready to talk, but he didn't feel there was any point trying to change Conceição's mind. She was already moving towards the door, encouraging him to leave.

'Ok, then. What time should I call for you?' he asked. They agreed a time and he left without another word.

The meeting had been a little awkward, but what had he really expected? As Tó Zé made his way slowly back to his parents' house, he wondered how the next day would go. He hoped that it would be easier to talk with the distraction of a day out, a chance to relax and enjoy the countryside. They needed to talk and it would be good to spend the day together, to spend time with Nuno.

As Tó Zé passed the little café, he felt suddenly tense. Even though it was a while since Carol had been to the village, Tino had seemed convinced that she would have stayed in the area. If she turned up again, it would be awkward. He needed to see her. He hadn't said anything at home, but he hadn't intended to stay longer than the weekend, not this time. He needed to get back to Lisbon and his friend Brito had said he would call back for him on Monday morning. Tó Zé was sure that Brito wouldn't mind making a short detour. They could go to Pampilhosa on their way back and if Carol was still there, he would have to face up to her and explain. After tomorrow, he would be clearer about a lot of things and he would know what to say. He paused and checked the time. His mother would be waiting to see how his meeting with Conceição had gone. He would be as positive as he could. She would be pleased that he and Conceição were spending the day together. He would ask her to prepare a picnic for them. His mother was indeed pleased to hear his news and he managed to avoid any more awkward questions that evening.

It was quite late by the time that Conceição went to collect Nuno. It wasn't that Tó Zé had stayed a long time, of course, but no one was to know that. She had needed some time on her own once he had left. She needed to think about the following day and what she would say. She also had someone she wanted to see. Her mother had told Nuno that she would be late. He was tired after his long day and a big dinner and was asleep in his grandparents' bedroom when Conceição arrived. She went to check on him and sure enough, he was fast asleep. She needn't have worried about him. Her mother was keen to hear all about her evening, but she wanted to get back, so she explained that they were spending the day together. It seemed to satisfy her mother. Her father went to get Nuno while they were talking, taking him in his arms. Nuno was in a deep, relaxed sleep, the kind of undisturbed sleep that only children can achieve. Her father walked her home, carrying Nuno in his arms and tucking him into bed before he left without him waking. He didn't ask Conceição anything about Tó Zé. He didn't want to know.

# XXII

**Castro Marim, 15ᵗʰ June, 1974**

Back in Vila Real de Santo António after her journey to Coimbra, Rebecca had decided that it was time to do a little exploring of the town and the surrounding area. She couldn't do anything more until she heard from Júlia and whilst she remained concerned about Carol, she felt she had been distracted from her own plans for too long. She wanted to find somewhere more permanent to stay and to start investigating if there was any possibility of work, even if only casual. She was heading for the nearby town of Castro Marim. She had found out that there was a market that day and she wanted to have a look at the town. She searched through the notebook she had brought with her to find the address of the family she knew there. She wasn't sure whether she would feel confident enough to call unannounced after so many years, but she wanted to have the address just in case.

Rebecca had seen the town in the distance, its ruined castle and fort dominating the small settlement, high on the hill overlooking countryside. It had been an important town once, vital in protecting the border. Now, at least in that way, it was redundant. She had looked across at the town from the railway station. It didn't seem far. Stretches of low-lying land and salt plains separated the two towns. She had intended to walk but when she mentioned it, Júlia's mother had looked rather uneasy. She was concerned that the pathways were unclear and the route rather remote.

She persuaded her that it was safer to get the bus. Rebecca took her advice and headed to the bus stop. As she didn't know the town at all, she asked the driver if he would show her the bus stop which was nearest the centre of the town. She needn't have worried. There were others who, like her, were heading to the market.

'This is the stop you want,' the driver called back to her.

She thanked him as she stepped off the bus and into the sunshine. She took her sunglasses, a silk shawl and a hat from her bag. She didn't like wearing hats and in this sunshine, a hat only made her feel warmer, but the sun seemed quite intense and there wasn't much shade. She walked along, draping the fine silk shawl over her shoulders. Hanging back a little, she followed the other passengers, assuming they were heading to the market. It would have been easy to ask but it seemed quite straightforward. She was walking along what seemed to be the main street and the closer she got to the market, the busier the town became.

She noticed a café opposite and as she looked further down the street, another on the same side of the road. Both seemed quite busy, but she was hungry and thirsty now, having skipped breakfast to get an early start. It was better to have something to eat, she thought, before she explored the market and town. She intended to walk up to the castle to see how far she could see from that vantage point. As she walked towards the nearest café, she felt self-conscious for a moment and hesitated. Groups of friends were sitting outside the café, talking, laughing together, and enjoying the freedom of the weekend. Most people preferred to sit outside which gave the impression that the café was busier than it actually was. Rebecca removed her hat and smiled, not at anyone in particular. She wanted to be friendly. She went inside the café to take advantage of the shade, finding that there were plenty of free tables. She chose one which had only two seats, not wanting to commandeer a larger space, and was pleased to see that the television was on in the corner of the room. She could at least watch television as she ate and have something to distract her. There were two people, a man and a woman, working behind the counter. Watching the way they were interacting, she assumed that they were man and wife, the owners of the café. It was a fair guess. There were many such small establishments run by husband and wife teams, working long hours, the café their life. The man came over to her, smiled and took her order for a coffee and a 'tosta mista', a ham and cheese toastie. The toastie arrived, smothered in butter. It was delicious and as she tucked in, she realised how hungry she was. She stayed only as long as it took her to eat and finish her coffee, then leaving the café, she made her way to the market, soon walking amongst market stalls.

Rebecca loved the markets. Somehow everything seemed so much fresher than at home. Fruit and vegetable stalls overflowed with the season's very best produce. There were large sacks teeming with dried beans and nuts. There were stalls piled high with homemade breads of all sizes – rye bread, the small 'papo seco' bread rolls which seemed to be served with every meal – and some breads that were a meal in themselves, filled with sausage. Other stalls sold nothing but cheese. Rebecca had never seen such a variety, some made from ewe's milk, others from goat's milk. There was a huge variety of cured meats and sausages – Chouriço; Salpicão, made with pork loin; Farinheira, a pork sausage cooked in wine and the flour which gave it its name; Morcela a seasoned blood sausage – and the little chicken pies, called empadas. There was a stall selling dried salt cod, huge pieces which were being chopped to size as requested. There were other stalls selling cakes of all kinds, delicious, moist cakes made with oranges, honey, carob, yoghurt or almonds. There were tiny marzipan fruits, figs studded with almonds, olive oil, huge tubs of olives, jars of honey, spices and teas. Another seller displayed the local liquors such as amarguinha, the strong bitter liquor made from almonds, and medronheira, made from the fruit of the strawberry tree and sweetened with honey. Of course, there was a stall selling little hessian bags of the sea salt drawn from the salt plains outside the town, but it wasn't only a food market. There were traders selling brightly coloured wares – pottery, metal and leather work, handmade textiles and wicker baskets. It occurred to her that it was a shame she hadn't waited to eat, rather than calling in at the café. There was so much delicious food to try. Not to worry, she could have something later after she had walked up to the castle.

As she was making her way out of the market, her gaze fixed on the castle, wondering where she might find the pathway to the top, she heard a man's voice calling her name. At first she dismissed it, thinking that she must be mistaken. She had misheard in the cacophony of the market's noise she thought and so she continued to walk, looking for the route up to the castle. There it was again, and again, closer now.

'Rebecca...Rebecca, is it you?'

In our minds, when we try to remember people who have faded from our lives, their images are faded and blurred too. We may try to remember features, details, the colour and wave of the hair, the intensity of the eyes, but after a while, we're not sure if we would recognise even those faces which had once seemed so familiar. Rebecca looked again in the direction of the voice. There he was, and there was no doubt about recognition or familiarity. He was a little taller, yes certainly, and a fuller figure. It was the stature of a man and not of a boy, but he had the same huge, kind smile and shining eyes, unmistakable.

'What are you doing here?' he asked. 'I mean it's great to see you, but what a surprise.' He spoke English to her.

'Visiting the market. I'd heard so much about the town that I wanted to see it for myself,' Rebecca replied, determined to speak Portuguese.

'You didn't forget, then?' He said, moving naturally back into his own language. 'It's been so long since we have heard from you.'

'No I didn't forget. Never. How could I?' Rebecca said.

The 'we' rather than 'I' hadn't escaped her, but it had been so long, so much had changed, she was sure. The hopelessly romantic part of her had hoped it hadn't.

They continued to look at each other, wide smiles on their faces. For a moment, Rebecca felt as if she were part of a film, a brightly coloured, noisy, moving scene, the backdrop of the market, the white painted houses and brilliant blue sky; seconds suspended in time.

'Prof,' Rebecca said, bringing herself back to the real moment. She used the nickname she had given him all those years before. He laughed, remembering the name.

'So, then. I must have been successful. You're speaking Portuguese and you're fluent.'

'Not fluent, but you're the reason that I speak it. That was when I developed my interest and with a bit more time and determination, I will be fluent. I'm determined. That's why I'm here in Portugal.'

Now she had said it, she felt a little silly, but Ricardo was the reason. Yes, she had loved the sound of the language when she heard it for the first time. Yes, she loved to learn, but her interest had started because of him. She had often wanted to tell him, to let him know how that chance meeting had enriched her life. She wanted to explain more, to sound less naïve than her opening statement made her seem and to say thank you. It was so great to see him. Then in the crowd, she became aware of someone else. He turned to the woman who had joined them, now standing a little behind him to his left.

'This is Rebecca. Do you remember the English family that I told you about, all those years ago that we met when we were on holiday in Cornwall? Here she is, my little pen pal and she speaks Portuguese,' Ricardo explained, obviously delighted.

'It's a pleasure to meet you,' she said, as she kissed Rebecca on each check, beaming a bright smile.

'My mother and father are here too. We're meeting up with them later. Are you here for the day? Who are you here with?' The questions came quickly. 'Can you join us? You must join us.'

Rebecca opened her mouth to respond and before she could, he continued,

'I'm completely forgetting my manners. This is Maria Eduarda, my wife.' And then looking down towards two small boys who Rebecca hadn't noticed, but who were now looking up at her with bright eyes and big smiles, two little doubles of Ricardo, only a year between them, 'And here are my sons.'

Again, a pause, and the film rolled on around her, slightly slowed, but as bright and noisy. Seconds of hesitation. She wondered if anyone else had noticed, as she tried to take everything in.

'Pleased to meet you all,' Rebecca said. She had the address, but it hadn't occurred to her that she might meet Ricardo or one of the family by chance. Even in the same town, you can go for weeks and months without seeing someone you know. Ricardo's father was a businessman. The family might not have stayed in the area or Ricardo either. He could have moved away.

The longest pause, it seemed to her, which Ricardo broke into quite naturally.

'Can you join us? We'd love to have you along, wouldn't we?' He turned to his wife and children. They agreed enthusiastically, no edge, open, warm and welcoming.

Rebecca checked her watch to see how much time there was before the last bus back.

'Yes, of course, but only for a while. I came on the bus from Vila Real. I was going to walk, but I was advised not to. I think it's a bit too far to walk on my own, so I need to keep an eye on time.'

'Don't worry about that. Is there anything you need to get back for?' Ricardo asked.

'No,' she said, trying to think. 'Nothing.' In fact, Rebecca didn't really want to go back. She felt at a loose end back at Júlia's parents' house.

'Then it's decided. One of us will give you a lift back whenever you're ready or you can stay with us. Whichever you prefer, you don't need to decide now. We're going to get some lunch. Are you hungry? Come on everyone.' Ricardo started to move away from the market.

He led the way through the busy streets to a little restaurant, a regular haunt for the family. The restaurant owner shook his hand and kissed his wife and then Rebecca was introduced before they all sat down. The menus came, drinks were ordered and in the midst of all the activity, Rebecca was quiet. He was married. People's lives moved on at such a pace and at times, she felt that hers went by, yes, as quickly, but somehow out of sync. Others got on with their lives, made sensible, natural decisions. It seemed she had waited, and for what she wasn't sure, as life went by.

'What would you like, Rebecca?' She was brought back from her thoughts.

'I'm not sure,' Rebecca said continuing to look through the menu.

'How about we order an 'Arroz de Marisco' to share?' Ricardo suggested.

'I'm happy with that. What do you think, Rebecca?' Maria Eduarda asked.

Rebecca was thinking that it wasn't long since the toastie, which she was too polite to admit. The idea of sharing seemed a good one, so she agreed that it was fine with her.

Ricardo poured her a glass of wine. It seemed early to have a drink, but that was how it was over there and she needed to relax a little. The wine might help. The awkwardness faded, conversation was easy and soon they began to catch up with the missing years.

'So, you're on your own now, Rebecca. It can't be easy and making this journey too. I really admire your independence. There do seem to be so many more opportunities for women in Britain than here, but I think things may change now,' Maria Eduarda commented.

'I have to admit that I was fairly ignorant of the situation here before I came, but as far as I see it, this country has many more advantages than disadvantages and such potential now.' As Rebecca was speaking, she had a sense, for the first time, of how insignificant her own problems seemed. She didn't want her old relationship back. She felt happy. There was only a brief wave of a feeling of missing João intruding on her good mood, which she quickly dismissed.

Rebecca explained that she had been heading for the castle when Ricardo had called over to her. Seconds later and she wouldn't have been at the market. A walk up to the castle seemed like a good idea to everyone. They had a couple of hours before they had arranged to meet Ricardo's parents for afternoon coffee and cake, so they agreed that after a pause to allow lunch to settle, they would take Rebecca and the boys up to the castle.

The view from the castle was marvellous, miles of countryside, small settlements and farms dotted across the landscape and to the south, views back to Vila Real and the river and sea beyond. The boys enjoyed playing in the castle grounds, lost in their own imagination of days gone by, stories of knights and jousting. The three adults found a shady place to sit and chatted, watching as the boys played happily together. Time seemed to pass too quickly and it wasn't long before they needed to make their way back down into the town. When they arrived at the café, Ricardo's parents were already sitting outside. Rebecca recognised them straight away and as they approached, could see them noticing, wondering who was coming along with the family, until finally the look of recognition and surprise. Both of them got up and greeted her warmly. Rebecca's day was getting better and better, as the years fell away and it seemed that no time at all had passed.

That day, Rebecca told the family about her plans for a year in the country and they were really keen to help her to get settled. Júlia's family had been lovely too, but she didn't want to impose on their hospitality much longer. Meeting up with old friends made her feel so much closer to the place she had chosen for her year away. Of course, in the background of her thinking, Ricardo had been the draw, but she hadn't expected it to be so easy again with the family. A couple of days after she had met them in the market, Ricardo was in touch again to offer help finding an apartment. His wife, he said, loved looking around houses and knew quite a few of the agents in the town. It should be easy to find something with a little bit of local knowledge. So the following day, Rebecca met Maria Eduarda for coffee at the café on the corner of the square in Vila Real so that they could discuss what Rebecca was looking for before they went to see an estate agent.

'I would really like to be in the centre of town. It's so lovely and there's everything I'd need here. It can be somewhere small, but it would be great to have a couple of bedrooms, so that family and friends can come and stay with me. They're keen to come over as soon as I'm settled,' Rebecca explained.

'It shouldn't be too hard to find. There are quite a few apartments over the shops and cafés in the centre of town, but we need to remember the cafés can be busy into the evenings, so there would be some noise, if you were right in the centre. I'm sure there will be places available not too far from the square.'

Rebecca didn't see the busy town as a disadvantage, especially living on her own. She liked the idea of being able to walk everywhere. As for the neighbourhood, she was only renting and could move again if she changed her mind. They finished their coffee and Maria Eduarda took her along to see a good friend of hers, Edite, who was one of the local agents. They decided to have a look at three different places which Edite said would give an idea of what was available. The first was on the main street leading up to the market, a two bedroomed apartment over an ironmonger's shop. It had a small kitchen, a living room that looked out onto the main street, one bedroom and a bathroom. It was fairly compact and there was no outside space. When Rebecca mentioned that, Edite said she wouldn't miss having her own space outside – people spent so much time outdoors. Rebecca wasn't convinced, but the apartment was tempting because the rent was reasonable. Without a job, she would need to keep to a tight budget, so it wasn't dismissed. The next place they looked at was a little house in the old part of town, a short walk from the town square. The front door opened straight into the living room and there were stairs up to a roof space that was big enough for a large second bedroom. Downstairs there was a kitchen, a little bathroom and the main bedroom. The kitchen, which was big enough to sit down and eat in, had a door leading to a little quintal. It was an outside space at the back of the house, with room for a table and chairs to eat outside on warm days. To one side, there was a flower bed, well-tended with pretty flowering plants. Rebecca loved the house as soon as she walked in. It seemed so Portuguese. Once inside the first apartment, she could have been almost anywhere, but not here in this little house. Edite led them both up the stairs to have a look at the room above and to Rebecca's surprise, through another little door to a small roof terrace. Rebecca was so taken with the house she didn't need to look any further, but was afraid to ask how much the rent was. It might be too expensive. Edite was keen to show them the last apartment before Rebecca made up her mind. They walked back into the town square and up the street running parallel to the one where they had seen the first apartment. The front door was down a side street. It led into a hallway, beautifully tiled with a stone staircase leading up to two apartments on the next floor. They walked into a long, thin hallway, three main rooms, side by side, one a living room and the other two bedrooms leading off. Edite took them first to see the small bathroom and kitchen at the far end of the corridor. There was a small terrace leading off the kitchen. There at the back of the apartment and even outside, it seemed a little dark and enclosed. It would have had the sunshine at some point in the day, but at that time, it seemed rather cool. In every other way, it was a lovely apartment. The main rooms were the same size, square and large. Each of them had French windows leading out on to small balconies overlooking the busy street below with its cafés and shops. Light and sunshine were flooding into the rooms and as Edite opened the doors out onto the balcony from the living room, a gentle breeze was moving sheer, white curtains. There was something romantic about the apartment. It appealed to Rebecca, to her sense of place and history, to the past, all those people who must have lived there over the two hundred years the town had been in existence. As she stood on the balcony looking down on to the café opposite, she wondered how the townsfolk might view this English woman, sitting out on her balcony, watching the world go by.

'You did want to be in the centre of it all and you certainly have that here,' Maria Eduarda said. 'What do you think?'

'I really like this apartment. I could see myself sitting on the balcony, although it's a little public for my liking, but if I can afford it, I loved the little house as soon as I set foot in it,' Rebecca said.

'The rent is actually the same as the first apartment you saw. This one is more expensive because of the proportions of the main rooms and its position. We have an apartment that has a river view if you would like to have a look, but it would be more expensive because of the view,' Edite explained.

Edite offered to take them to see it and as both Maria and Rebecca were curious, they went along. Rebecca knew before she went that it was out of her budget, but they were enjoying looking around and seeing what the town had to offer. The view was fantastic over the wide expanse of the River Guadiana looking across to Spain and to the right, to the mouth of the river and the Atlantic Ocean beyond, but it was too expensive and a little further away from the centre of town than she had wanted.

Rebecca had decided on the little house, but Maria Eduarda said they would get back to Edite, probably the next day, either with a decision or to see what else was available.

'What are you doing for the rest of the day, Rebecca? If you've nothing on, come back with me. We'll pick up the boys, go down to the beach for an hour or so and then you must come back to ours for dinner. Ricardo's parents are coming over too and we can talk about your plans and where you're going to live.'

Rebecca had no plans. She needed to look for work and it was time to make a start, but another day wouldn't hurt. Maria Eduarda drove them back to her house and Rebecca waited while she went in quickly to pick up towels and the boys' swimming things. They collected the boys from Maria Eduarda's parents' house and Rebecca was introduced. They seemed lovely and insisted that Rebecca went over one day soon for dinner. The four of them then drove to Monte Gordo and parked the car in front of the beach. The boys were excited to be at the beach and played very happily together again. They got on so well. Rebecca and Maria Eduarda sat chatting. Rebecca was struck by how comfortable she felt in Maria Eduarda's company. It could have been awkward, at least in Rebecca's mind. Memories had drawn her to the south of Portugal. Part of her had hoped that time had stayed still, but it was years ago. It had no significance for Maria Eduarda and there was not a trace of awkwardness. As the boys paddled at the edge of the sea watched over carefully by both of them, the conversation turned to Rebecca being on her own and her decision to come to a different country. Rebecca began to talk about Andy for the first time in quite some months. Somehow, it was easy to talk to

Maria Eduarda who was understanding and not knowing Andy, had no preconceptions.

'You must have been very hurt,' Maria Eduarda concluded. 'I can see why you needed to get away.'

Rebecca hadn't wanted or been able to talk about him for so long but talking with Maria Eduarda, she was quite certain it was past. It had been so very upsetting. It had seemed like the end of the world. Now her old relationship, which had been so important to her, began to feel distant. It was as though she were looking the wrong way through a telescope. It didn't matter anymore and she said as much to Maria Eduarda,

'Do you know, I think I've finally left it behind,' Rebecca reflected, coming to the end of the story.

'And what's his name?' Maria Eduarda asked.

Rebecca looked confused, as she had been referring to him by name. 'Andy? His name's Andy.'

'No, the new guy. It often takes someone else to finally get us to move away from the past, so who is he?'

Rebecca laughed, 'There isn't anyone... There's João, but I don't think he qualifies at all.'

Rebecca then began to talk about João, how they had met, meeting up again in Vila Real, the trip to Coimbra. She talked about how affectionate he had been and then how his affection seemed to fade. He had left for home. Now she didn't expect to hear from him again.

'If I go with your theory, he must have been the guy I needed to help me break away from obsessing about the past,' Rebecca suggested.

'From what you're telling me, I wouldn't be giving up on him yet. He seemed pretty keen,' Maria Eduarda said.

'Not that keen, obviously.' Rebecca was really disappointed, not understanding why he had gone quiet on her. 'I kind of assumed that there must be someone at home and I was a temporary distraction. Reality kicked in when he realised that he needed to get back home. He had a lot to say about London, but nothing about his life here in Portugal. I'm beginning to think that maybe Portuguese men play by different rules.'

Rebecca had mentioned Carol when she had told Maria Eduarda why they had all gone to Coimbra. Now she explained more of what she knew about Carol's situation. Whilst Maria Eduarda stood up for the qualities of most men she knew, she was highly suspicious of Tó Zé.

'I think of the two men you've spoken about, the one most likely to have a past is Tó Zé. What do you know about João? What's his full name? You say he has connections here. It's a small town, I might know of him or someone in the family might.' She was very curious about João.

Rebecca mentioned his full name and told her as much about him as she knew, as the boys continued to play together on the beach. It wasn't long before the sun began to sink low on the horizon.

'Gosh, we'd better get back. There's not much left to do for dinner, but I need to get on with it before the in-laws arrive,' Maria Eduarda said.

She called to the boys who were reluctant at first to leave the beach. Finally encouraged by Maria Eduarda and the thought of dinner, they ran back. They wrapped themselves in large beach towels before climbing into the back of the car. Everything packed away, they made the short drive back home.

Over dinner, the conversation turned first of all to the morning's search for an apartment. Rebecca was now quite sure about renting the little house and there was general agreement that it was a good choice. Ricardo's parents knew the family who owned the house and said they would be good landlords and so it was decided that Maria Eduarda would get back to Edite first thing in the morning. Rebecca mentioned where she had been staying and how kind Júlia's parents had been. They were happy for her to stay longer but Rebecca was keen to get established. It wasn't long before Maria Eduarda found a way to mention João. She was very mindful of Rebecca's feelings and careful not to break her confidence. Rebecca appreciated her sensitivity. When Maria Eduarda mentioned the name, Ricardo's father seemed to know of the family and once it was established that they were good friends of Rui's family who owned the yellow house on the river front, he was sure.

'You've hardly set foot in the country and you're mixing with some very interesting people.' He seemed impressed, but as Rebecca knew so little about João she couldn't imagine what he meant. She was really pleased when Maria Eduarda asked,

'How well do you know the family?'

'I don't know them personally but I know of them. They own one of the large estates in the Douro region. They make port wine and have done for centuries.'

Now, there was general recognition of the name. Rebecca was stunned and although she didn't say it, thought it was certainly the last she would ever see of João. She was pleased when the conversation eventually moved on.

'Have you thought about what you might do whilst you're out here? You said that you were looking for work,' Ricardo's father asked Rebecca.

'I don't think it will be easy to get something, but staying out for longer does depend on getting something. I have saved up, but the funds will only last so long,' Rebecca explained.

'I've got a proposal for you. I don't know if it will appeal, as the work would be as it comes in rather than full time and we would have to see how it went, so it wouldn't necessarily be permanent,' Ricardo's father started to explain.

'I'd be prepared to try anything. I don't mind what I do, well, within reason, that is.' Rebecca didn't know what he was about to say, so thought she had better not commit herself blindly.

'My construction firm is now focussing on the tourist market. It's fairly lucrative and we are beginning to tap into the British market. The Dutch are also buying and their English is far better than their Portuguese. It would be great to have a native English speaker to show them around and someone like you with such a love of the country would be a great natural salesperson. What do you think? It might only be a day or two each week – until we see how useful you are.'

He was a shrewd business man. Rebecca remembered her father saying that all those years ago when the two families had first met in

England. She didn't think he would offer her something to take pity on her but didn't want to impose. 'It sounds great, certainly something I could do and I would genuinely be able to promote the country, but are you sure? You don't know if I can do it.'

'I think you probably can and as I say, the offer is for piecemeal work, so I wouldn't be taking much of a risk at all,' he said.

'That would be great, then, thank you.' Rebecca was really pleased and couldn't believe her luck.

'Very good. You can start tomorrow. We have a client looking at apartments in Tavira. Have you driven over here? It would be easier for you if you could take one of the firm's cars.'

Rebecca was surprised he wanted her to start so soon but was feeling really enthusiastic about the prospect of some work. It was something so different from anything she had done before. 'Yes, I've driven here. I quite like driving on the right hand side.'

'Just as well. Keep it that way! Come to the office in Vila Real tomorrow at nine o'clock.' And he explained where the office was. With that it was decided. Everyone seemed really pleased.

'Who would have thought all those years ago when I gave you your first Portuguese lesson on the beach in Cornwall that one day we'd both be working for my father,' Ricardo said.

It was getting late. Maria Eduarda said that she would give Rebecca a lift home. On the way back, Rebecca checked with her, still a little concerned that she was imposing on the family.

'I hope he isn't offering me a job to be kind. I'm determined to show him what I can do,' Rebecca said.

'Believe me, he wouldn't have offered if he hadn't been sure that it was something that would work for the business. He's a kind man, but he'd help out in other ways. He's fond of you, you know. I remember the family talking about their holiday in Cornwall and the friends they made. Ricardo often talked about his little student. He was very fond of you too, you know. What about your Portuguese boyfriend, then? You certainly know how to choose them.'

'He's not my boyfriend and come to think about it, I didn't choose him. He attached himself to me, twice, as I remember. I had come to the conclusion before that there wasn't any future in that one and now I learn more about him, I'm certain. No wonder he wanted to keep things quiet. My money is on a long-term girlfriend. I think I was a flirtation, nothing more,' Rebecca replied with mixed feelings.

'We'll see and if not, there are plenty of nice men I can introduce you to. I think you would like my brother.'

As Rebecca got out of the car, she thanked Maria Eduarda for the lift and then she remembered,

'Oh, heck, Maria. I haven't brought anything with me that is suitable to wear to meet clients. I travelled with a really small bag and the only clothes I've bought so far are quite casual. I was going to do some more shopping, but I hadn't got around to it. I got distracted in Coimbra.'

'That's certainly what I've heard,' Maria Eduarda joked.

'No seriously, what time do the shops open?' Rebecca was now really concerned.

'Ten o'clock, but don't worry. It doesn't have to be a suit. I'll give Ricardo a few of my dresses for you to try. We're a similar size. He can call on his way to the office,' she suggested.

Rebecca was really grateful. Maria Eduarda seemed quite amused and happy to help. She suggested that Rebecca call to see her after she had seen the first English clients so that she could tell her all about it and also so that they could go back to the estate agent and get the paperwork underway to rent the little house. She would speak with Edite first thing. As Rebecca was getting ready for bed, she wondered if Maria Eduarda had any concerns that Rebecca might still have feelings for Ricardo. She didn't know how much he had said to his wife about their friendship. She was very fond of Ricardo but it was now a very different feeling. More than anything, she was happy to feel so connected and so welcomed again by the family. There was no wish to go back.

# XXIII

The next morning Ricardo called at the house with six dresses. 'If you're quick, I'll give you a lift to the office,' he said.

Rebecca shot upstairs and tried on the dresses as quickly as she could. The first two didn't work, but she was reasonably happy with the third and didn't want to keep Ricardo waiting.

'Looks good,' he said as she dashed down the stairs, 'you're not going to show us up.'

Ricardo's father was insistent that she take great care of the clients, an English couple. Rebecca had to drive to their hotel and take them to the development. There was still some time before the appointment. The head of sales briefed her on the development and then they drove out to Tavira to see the apartments. It wasn't going to be difficult. They had been finished to a very high specification and were in a great position overlooking the sea. Rebecca was conscious of the contrast between these luxury apartments and the lifestyle so many Portuguese still had, especially in the rural areas where most of the population lived. Places like the villages she had visited recently. There were many homes without electricity or running water and here were luxury bathrooms, all with bidets, apparently on the insistence of the old dictator, Salazar, who had a thing about bidets, her new boss told her.

Rebecca's first meeting was successful. The clients were impressed and although they already loved the country, Rebecca's enthusiasm and her recommendation did seem to influence them. They asked her if they could go straight over to the office in Vila Real to make arrangements to buy. As they were sitting with the head of sales, Ricardo went over to Rebecca. 'Impressive.' he said.

'Beginner's luck. I think they were already sold. It didn't take much persuasion.' Rebecca was modest.

'Don't do yourself down. They certainly hadn't decided before you met with them. It was only one of their options,' he told her.

Her work for the day over, Rebecca went to see Maria Eduarda and then they both called in at the estate agent's to make arrangements to rent the house. Although Rebecca's Portuguese was improving by the day, she was really pleased to have Maria Eduarda with her to give her the confidence not to get anything wrong.

A couple of days later, Rebecca had picked up the keys to the house. Júlia's parents had been really good and said that they would be happy for her to stay, but she had imposed on their hospitality long enough. Also, she wanted her independence, to have a place where she could come and go without worrying about disturbing anyone, to have her own space. Júlia's mother insisted on giving her some old crockery and cutlery, to get started. The house was partly furnished and certainly sparsely enough to suit Rebecca's taste. She didn't need much and between Júlia's mother and Ricardo's family, soon had everything she wanted for the time being.

Ricardo's father was really pleased with her work and soon offered her two days a week with the firm. Things were working out and as she sat one afternoon on her little terrace with a drink, eating a pastel de nata, her favourite little custard tart, Rebecca reflected that her plan to spend a year in the country was coming together. It now seemed possible, not simply a wild idea. She was happy, no hankering for the past, only an overwhelming feeling of contentment. Andy came back into her mind. Nothing. Yes, it felt closed, and as for João, she had become fond of him very quickly, but it obviously wasn't to be. She felt pleased that she hadn't got so far into it as to feel lost again. As Maria Eduarda said, there were other guys and for once in her life, she was happy on her own.

Maria Eduarda wasn't convinced at all. It was a theme which she often returned to over coffee, pointing out eligible men as they passed, making suggestions as to who she thought would be a great match for Rebecca. Rebecca was sure that it was out of a genuine concern for her being alone, rather than any worry that Rebecca might still have feelings for Ricardo. Some women seem very alert to the possibility that their men would stray. Rebecca had always wanted to be able to trust, to be sure of a relationship. It shouldn't be hard work. It should be easy, natural. Perhaps she was being naïve. Her attitude was different from many women she knew. Her mother had insisted that relationships needed work. Perhaps if she had tried harder with Andy, they would still be together. Still, she was pleased they weren't. It had turned out for the best. As for Ricardo, Rebecca was sure that he was completely devoted to his wife and that Maria Eduarda had no need to worry. Rebecca felt fortunate to have both of them as good friends.

Maria Eduarda had invited Rebecca over for dinner, which was becoming quite a regular event and something which Rebecca really enjoyed. Maria was a marvellous cook and Rebecca would often go over earlier to help out with the preparation and to learn as much as she could about Portuguese home cooked food. Food was such an important part of the culture and it was something else that she wanted to master while she was in Portugal.

'You're a good cook,' Maria Eduarda said to her, 'You'll make someone a good wife.'

'There you go again. I'm happy on my own at the moment. Actually, I don't think I've ever felt quite as content and certainly not in a long while,' Rebecca told her.

'I ought to confess, then, that I've asked someone to join us for dinner.' Maria Eduarda had thought about not saying anything, but she wasn't sure how Rebecca would react when he arrived, so thought it better to broach the subject.

'Maria.' Rebecca couldn't hide her irritation. 'Who is it? Does he know I'm going to be here? It's going to be so embarrassing.'

'Don't worry. He's a good friend of Ricardo. He often comes over. I've told Ricardo to let him know that you'll be here, but I knew how you would feel so I've told him to play it down and not to suggest it's a date,' Maria Eduarda explained.

'That makes it a bit better, but don't be making any hints,' Rebecca pleaded.

'Don't worry, I'll make sure there aren't any awkward moments,' she assured her and Rebecca reminded herself of how careful she had always been, mindful of her feelings.

It was about an hour before Ricardo and Manuel arrived and by that time Rebecca had managed to get worked up, feeling embarrassed about the evening to come. She knew that Maria Eduarda had every good intention in inviting Manuel and so, although it was a thought, dismissed the idea of trying to find a reason why she needed to get back. She had to relax and not to take everything so seriously. Maria Eduarda was true to her word. Rebecca needn't have worried. The evening didn't feel at all like a date. It felt like a group of friends enjoying an evening together and as ever, the focus was on good food and wine. Maria Eduarda had cooked 'Atum à Algarvia', fresh tuna steak with onions in a rich tomato sauce topped with sautéed potatoes. It was accompanied by a mixed salad of lettuce and beef tomatoes with a light olive oil and vinegar dressing. As always, warm fresh bread and butter were on the table, along with olives and cheese. Ricardo opened a bottle of red wine from the Alentejo, commenting that Manuel was from the Alentejo, a little village called Semblana, and he couldn't resist a joke about alentejanos. For some reason which Rebecca didn't understand, people from that region seemed to be the target of jokes. Rebecca nibbled away at the bread and cheese, as she sampled the wine. She didn't want to spoil her enjoyment of the main course, but had a good appetite and hadn't had much to eat during the day. Maria Eduarda had excelled herself with a pudim flan, a version of a crème caramel which she had prepared in a large mould, rather than the small puddings Rebecca had seen before.

The boys ate with them, but as soon as the meal was over, Maria Eduardo took them up to bed. They were tired. There was a little protest that they wanted to stay up longer, which was ignored. The conversation turned to the business. Manuel, as it happened, was also an employee of Ricardo's father, although Rebecca hadn't come across him. He worked on the construction side of the business, a young architect, clearly passionate about his work. He was keen to make sure his designs stayed as true as possible to traditional architecture, even though he was aware of the economic pressures to cut corners. Rebecca was pleased to hear how important it was to him to make the designs sympathetic to the landscape and the beauty of the Algarve. As the conversation about work continued, Manuel became aware that Maria Eduarda might be feeling a little out of it. She knew enough about the business, but wasn't involved day to day, being busy with the house and the two boys. Rebecca noticed his deliberate change of conversation and warmed to his sensitivity. It was the start of many happy evenings together, trips to the theatre and cinema. Manuel was easy company and Rebecca liked him. With the help of Maria Eduarda and Ricardo, she was meeting new people and began to feel settled in Vila Real.

# XXIV

**London**

If João were honest with himself, whilst he had loved living in London, work had not been as satisfying as he had imagined it could be. Although he had had every intention of staying and of trying to find something worthwhile to do, he had not been successful by the time he returned home in the spring of 1974. Work had been casual, short contracts. He had been able to take the trip over to Portugal because his contract came to an end. He knew also that, as much as he might delude himself that he was independent, there was no way he could have afforded the apartment in London without his family's help. It might not have bothered others. His background brought him privilege. Many wouldn't have given it any thought, but he wanted to be his own person. He wanted to achieve in his own right, to be recognised for himself and not for his background. His thinking had been clear. Now it wasn't, but he had a solution, at least for a while. He blamed Rebecca for unsettling his thinking, but how could that be? She knew almost nothing about him. She had a love for his country, an appreciation of the land, the culture and the people. Listening to her had given him a fresh perspective. Somehow, it had connected him again with an innate pride, it was a deep bond. João hadn't run away from his country. His life had felt wrong and he had to change it. He hadn't considered all the consequences at the time. He had left a situation, rejected the restrictions imposed by a dictatorship which had no relevance to him.

He had spurned a life which had seemed planned out for him by what he perceived to be the expectations of his parents, of his family and the will and demand of an oppressive regime. He had made mistakes, many; his impulse in asking Ana Rita to marry him was one. Looking back, he didn't know what had prompted him to leave so suddenly. He had enjoyed university. Being with other students, each with their own experience of life had opened his mind to other possibilities. His opinions and actions at university had brought him close to danger. Neither he nor any other young man could ignore the inevitability of being drafted into a hopeless conflict. Now, not by being away, but strangely in returning, he had begun to question his thinking and all the assumptions he had made. Had his parents ever had any other wish for him than that he had a happy and successful life? Perhaps they were more concerned that he didn't seem to know what to do than that he didn't want to work for the estate. Perhaps they had been more concerned with the crass way he had conducted his personal life than anything else, even though his mother hadn't supported his decision to marry Ana Rita. They had never really talked through the important issues. His decisions were based on supposition.

He took a TAP flight back to London from Oporto. As the plane prepared for take-off, he listened to the safety information in both Portuguese and English and then settled down to read for a while, as the air hostesses brought around the drinks. He managed only a couple of pages before his mind wandered. He felt a draw to Britain, not as defined or as intense as that which Rebecca had described about Portugal, but it was there and inexplicable. Home had begun to take a strong hold again. He felt confused, not really understanding why he was so unsettled, trying to justify his feelings. The estate was part of his heritage. He had made the decision to work for the firm. He had said that he would give it a year. That was what he announced before travelling back to London. Rebecca had inspired the time frame of twelve months. She came back into his mind again. He could still be flexible. Life in his country was uncertain. He had to think carefully; he didn't want to lose the freedoms he had become so used to in London. As he sat with his book in front of him, abandoned, open on his lap, wondering about his decision, he took out a note pad and a pen from a small travel bag. He started to write a list of the pros and cons, London versus home. No matter which list turned out to be the longer, he might learn something simply in writing. He put his friends in London at the top of the list. They were a great group of people. Their way of living and thinking seemed so much more open, so much less confined than he had been used to at home. He felt freer there to be himself. He had great friends at home too, friends who had been there for ever and who knew him so well. He wrote their names at the top of his second list. He was sitting next to an older woman and as the in-flight meal was served, they spoke for the first time, except that was for the polite exchange as they had taken their seats.

'You look busy. Are you going to London on business or for a visit, a holiday?' she asked.

'I've been working over there and have been home for a visit.' João didn't explain any further.

The conversation then turned to London and they shared observations and opinions. They discussed favourite places. She had, for many years, she said, been making the journey between the two countries. Each had something special to offer her. Hearing that comment, João became more interested. Here again was someone who shared his draw to another place. For quite a while, he let her talk and listened carefully. Becoming aware of his quietness and wondering if she was talking too much, she paused and said,

'You seem deep in thought. What was it you were working on earlier?' and quickly realising her question might seem an intrusion, added, 'If you don't mind me asking.'

'I'm writing a list of pros and cons of staying in Britain, 'João replied.

As soon as he'd said it, he felt stupid. How must he be coming across? She had thought he was a business man, now he was exposed. However, it didn't faze her at all.

'I sometimes find the best way of making a decision is to take a large book with lots of pages in it. I choose a page and let the book fall open.

If the book opens before the page I've chosen, then it's a 'yes'. If it's after, then it's a 'no'. If I find I don't like the decision the book has made for me, I still have my answer. I know where my instinct is and what my preference really is.'

'I might have to try it when I get to London,' João said and then started to tell her about his dilemma. As Rebecca had found, he was often only too happy to talk, but to give away his inner thoughts and anything that was really personal to him, was unusual. There are times when we feel comfortable with a stranger, when we make a connection or maybe it is simply that believing we won't meet again, it doesn't matter what they know of us. His travel companion listened attentively as he talked, making only brief comments to show her interest. She encouraged him gently with questions, mindful not to ask too much or to appear too intrusive. She understood his need to talk. Once he seemed to have nothing more to say, she made only one comment.

'One of the most compelling needs we have is to belong, to know that we are part of something. We can find it in place and in people and in ourselves, but when we do find it, we know that's where we need to be.'

The comment struck him. It meant something to him and it was to stay with him, pervading his thinking. The announcement came from the captain to let everyone know that London was twenty minutes away and to prepare for landing. João had genuinely enjoyed the company and said so when they said goodbye. As they walked down the steps of the plane, it was raining.

João took a bus into the centre of the city and made his way back to his apartment. He opened the door to the lobby and took the stairs to his third floor apartment. Once inside, it might have been more usual after a journey to unpack but he left his bag to one side of his front door. He went into his bedroom to look for the suitcase which he had brought with him the very first time he came to London. He put it on the bed and then started to take some of his clothes out of the drawers and the wardrobe. He placed them on the bed at the side of the suitcase. Once that was done, he went into the kitchen, found an unopened carton of orange juice, poured himself a glass and went to sit down on the sofa. He hadn't booked a return flight when he set off from home. He didn't know how long he would need to be in London and despite what he had said at home, he hadn't been completely settled in his own mind. As he was sitting, slowly sipping the orange juice, he noticed a large book on the shelf. He went over to the bookshelf, picked up the book which had caught his attention and chose a page number before closing the book. He took it back to the coffee table and once he was sitting on the sofa again, he balanced the book on its spine, allowing it to fall open. Stay in London was the decision the book made for him. He felt disappointed. His decision was right. The book had got it wrong. He felt cold, got up and went into the kitchen. He put the glass down at the side of the sink and walked over to the window. It was still raining, quite heavily now. The sky was a deep grey and looked as though it were darkening. There was more rain to come. He went to get a coat and then made a phone call to one of his friends, arranging to meet up later.

He had been working in a restaurant not far from his apartment and headed there first of all, walking quickly as though he wouldn't get as wet that way. The main street was quite busy, people walking by with umbrellas, hoods up, heads bowed against the rain. He walked past a row of small shops, a grocery shop, a florist, a wine shop and a small delicatessen, before arriving at the restaurant. It was larger than it appeared from the outside. The owner had expanded in good times, renovating the space upstairs which had once been an apartment. He had doubled the number of covers in the restaurant. Now he was thinking that in these strained times, it would have been better to have had the rent from the apartment.

When João arrived, the owner and a couple of the staff were sitting at one of the tables having a drink and talking together. The mood seemed somewhat subdued, as he walked in smiling, pleased to see them. No greeting was returned from the owner. He looked up at him and said grumpily,

'I hope you're not looking for any shifts, João. Business is pretty poor. It was fortunate that you wanted to get away for a while or I would have had to have laid off one of these two.'

The others looked at João, raising their eyes in a gesture which he translated as 'you know what he's like'. Whilst he hadn't been going there to ask for work, it wasn't quite the reception he was expecting and so he was pleased to be able to put him straight. He had understood his contract had finished.

'No, I'm not available for work. I'm working for a firm back home. I'm over here for a little while, not sure how long, but I'll be going back and forwards. I'm trying it out to see how it goes.'

'Good for you,' one of the others said to him. 'I really hope it works out for you.' Mário was Portuguese also, from Beja in the Alentejo region. 'I'd love to go back but there's no work. It's not great over here, but at least I have work and can send money back to the family.'

The owner ignored his news and turned his comments to the state of the country, the strikes, unemployment and people who were not, in his opinion, prepared to spend money on eating out. The others had heard it many times and let him bluster on. The conversation slowed and when no one seemed to have anything more to say, João took the opportunity to leave, feeling now that he wanted to get away. He said he would keep in touch with Mário and send him news from home, but even as he said it, he wasn't sure he would. Then the owner said to him,

'If you're ever back here, come and see me. I'm sure I can give you some shifts. Business is bound to improve.' He was strangely more optimistic, a twinge in his ego. He hadn't expected João not to be interested in working there.

It had never bothered João before, but the wet, grey London day was beginning to invade his mood. He wished, after he had walked out of the restaurant, that he hadn't told them that his work was temporary, but the lack of permanency had helped him to feel more settled about his decision. He thought his friends and colleagues would be pleased it was temporary. It is strange how the smallest episode can change views or strengthen thinking. He walked away feeling annoyed for not having had more ambition whilst he had been in London. It had been an easy lifestyle, possible because he knew that he had a different life to fall back on. He found himself thinking again about Rebecca. She had the determination to change, to take a chance. He had been so undecided, but maybe his situation was far more complicated than hers, he thought and then he realised that he didn't know. She hadn't talked much about it and he hadn't asked.

He looked at his watch. Being in the restaurant had made him feel hungry, so he headed for a café to get something to eat. He knew the woman who ran it well. She was pleased to see him and asked him about his holiday. When he said he was going back, she seemed pleased for him. Again, not quite the reaction that he had been expecting. By the time he arrived at the Red Lion, a couple of his friends were already there. He got a pint of lager at the bar and asked the others if they wanted another drink, then took his lager and two pints of beer over to join them. It wasn't long before others arrived and soon the group of friends were together again, keen to catch up with João and hear about his holiday in Portugal. João held back on mentioning his plans. Not seeing as much of this group of friends was the hardest part of his decision. He didn't know why, but he was soon talking about his chance meeting with Rebecca and his visit to Vila Real and their weekend in Coimbra. He might have expected the teasing.

'Sounds like you're fairly smitten,' his friend Sue said to him.

He hadn't expected that observation.

'No, not at all.' He tried to deny it. 'She's with somebody, though, so no point pursuing that one.'

'Are you sure? Just because she had a friend who was a guy, it doesn't mean they were together. I think you've made some assumptions there. I'm a good friend of yours and there's nothing romantic between us. When you talked about your female friends, I don't think that Rebecca would have made the same assumption. Can't you have women as friends in Portugal?' Now she was really teasing him but soon changed the subject. 'I've got some news, that is, we've got some news.'

She turned to John who was sitting next to her. They beamed at each other. 'You tell them,' she said, and with that prompting, he announced to the group that he had proposed. They were getting married. More than that, they were in the process of buying a house in Surrey, because they wanted a family and didn't want to bring the children up in the city. There were congratulations, talk of when, the venue, everyone looking forward to a party, a celebration. It was an evening for news. Another one of his friends announced that they had taken a job in the north, in York, which had been home before university. João had to be given a little geography lesson, not sure exactly where it was but he was interested because he remembered that was Rebecca's home city. He hadn't expected so many changes in such a short space of time. Everyone seemed so positive, not at all concerned that friends were moving on with their lives. He began to think they wouldn't be as disappointed with his news as he had thought and he was right. As soon as he told them, they were already planning a trip over to Portugal the following summer.

As he walked back to his apartment on his own, he thought again about the conversation on the plane. Nothing stayed as it was and if he thought it could, he would only get left behind. Probably given time, all of his friends in London would move out but they were great friends. He was part of this group now. He felt he belonged and that wouldn't change. Back in the apartment, he packed his large suitcase so that he could take most of his clothes back with him. He would leave only a few things. He didn't expect to be spending a lot of time in London over the next months, only a week or so at a time, he thought. He didn't need to pack, indeed, he might be needing some of the clothes that he had put away, but he wasn't thinking sensibly. It was a gesture. He was tired, so he got ready for bed. As he lay in bed, beginning to fall asleep, he decided that the next morning, he would work out how long his business in London would take him this time and then, he would go to a travel agent. He would fix the date for his return home.

The next morning, he went into the office and rang the contacts his father had given him. He was able to set up the meetings he needed across the next two weeks. Later in the afternoon, he called into a travel agent and booked his return flight. He was feeling much more settled and now that he knew when he was going back, he was looking forward to the next two weeks. His father was trusting him with some important clients. He was keen to do a good job. He hadn't completely changed his mind about London but this way he didn't need to. Anyway, there were some more compelling reasons for him to be spending more time in Portugal at the moment.

The next two weeks went by quickly. He had a tight schedule and was kept busy meeting clients and working with new business contacts. He kept in touch with his father who was extremely pleased with his work. It was certainly more satisfying than he had been used to in London. It was giving him a sense of achievement for the first time in many months. He hadn't had much time to see his friends while he was over, but he caught up with them the evening before he was due to fly back. They were a little surprised that he was leaving for home so soon but as he was planning to be back, there were no big farewells.

# XXV

Over the next months, João was to make several visits over to London and divided his time happily between the two places. It was on one of his return journeys when he hadn't been specific about when exactly he would be travelling home that he thought of making a surprise visit to see his favourite aunt who lived in Oporto. He hadn't seen her since he had been back at home.

As João waited for his suitcase to come around on the baggage carousel, he was thinking about the practicalities of a visit. He had more luggage with him this time and having a larger suitcase was a bit of a nuisance for getting around the city. He had packed a small overnight bag in case he decided to stay over and remembered that he could leave the suitcase at left luggage at the train station. He made his way there first. João's aunt was his father's youngest sister. As he placed his suitcase in one of the lockers, he felt pleased with himself that he had had the idea to call on her. He knew she would love the surprise and it would give him the chance to talk a few things over with her. She had been one of the few people in the family who he felt had supported his move to London wholeheartedly. She had certainly helped to smooth things over with his parents at the time, especially with regard to Ana Rita, which despite their misgivings, his parents had been embarrassed about. He picked up his bag and headed for the exit, glancing towards the clock on his way and remembering the last time his brother had met him there. To his surprise, he saw Ana Rita waiting in the same place beneath the clock at the side of the newsstand. She was clearly looking out for someone. He wondered if she had seen him. For a moment, he thought it might be better not to intrude, then he changed his mind and walked over to her.

'Ana Rita, I didn't expect to see you here,' he said.

Ana Rita looked a little startled rather than surprised. She glanced behind him towards the other passengers who were coming out of the station before she gave him her full attention. 'Gosh, João, I didn't know you were back today. I don't think anyone is expecting you for at least a couple of days.'

'I'd done everything I needed to, so there wasn't any reason to stay on. Are you heading back home?' He didn't think so, but it seemed a better question than to ask her what she was doing.

'No, I've friends in Oporto. I often come over for the weekend. I'm waiting for a friend.' Ana Rita made another quick scan of the station.

Things had been much better between them since João's return. He was fond of her and felt very protective of her. He still felt guilty. A certain regret made him wonder what he should do, especially as he still hadn't spoken to her properly. It felt unfinished.

'Careful, you could get used to city life and then you'll be leaving us,' João teased her knowing how she had always been so adamant that she would never leave. He was quite surprised to hear that she was spending so much time in Oporto.

'No, I don't think so.' Ana Rita was distracted. João could sense it.

'I'm going to see my aunt. I thought I'd have a day or so here before heading back home. They're not expecting me yet, as you say. I can see you're busy. How about we meet for a drink this evening and then go for something to eat?' João suggested.

Ana Rita had plans of her own and they hadn't included spending an evening with João, but at that moment, she wanted him out of the way. She agreed a time and place and was relieved to see him walking out of the station. Another minute and she would have had an awkward introduction to make.

João's aunt was really surprised to see him, but pleased that he had decided to call. She had heard what he was up to from his father and knew that he had been back to London again.

'João, how lovely to see you, but what are you doing here?' she asked him as she led him into the sitting room.

'I'm on my way home, but they're not expecting me back today and I had this urge to come and see you. It's been so long.'

His aunt knew him well. 'I heard you're back working for the business. Still it's a big decision, you were happy in London. What has changed your mind?'

'I really don't know. It was all very clear until I came back for the holiday, but I met someone who gave me a different perspective. Try as hard as I might to ignore it and move on, I made a mess of things before I left and it did seem like running away. I didn't like myself for it, although I did a good job of ignoring it while I was living in London. I knew it was time I sorted it out.'

Everything seemed to come out at once. João could always be open with his aunt. He knew she would be honest with him.

'You weren't very brave at the time and you were thoughtless when it came to Ana Rita. She was so hurt. You'd always tried to do what was expected of you. You wanted to please everybody, even when you knew it was wrong for you. You should have been more honest.' His aunt was always direct with him.

'It's time I sorted things out properly with Ana Rita. I bumped into her on the way out of the train station. She's here for the weekend visiting friends. I've arranged to see her this evening for dinner. I am fond of her and so sorry I left her the way I did. She's such a good friend, I shouldn't have given up on her.'

His aunt felt concerned. 'João, you're not considering rekindling that relationship are you?'

'I got it wrong. I owe it to her, if that's what she wants,' João said. It was something that had been bothering his conscience.

'I'd like to say that you know your own mind, but the best advice I can give you is to start thinking about what you really want. You know, there's a little café that I like to go to when I'm in Lisbon. On the wall, there is a clock which is rather unusual. Its hands move backwards in time and not forwards. Sometimes it seems to me that we are a nation of people who look backward. We continue to celebrate our discoveries, our past glory, now centuries ago. Some people are still waiting for Dom Sebastião to return. We have spent decades suspended in the past under Salazar and not all of those attitudes are helpful to our present or to our future. You know how patriotic I am. Our country is glorious and we should be proud of it and of our past achievements. You should be proud of your family's history. Nostalgia is an innate quality. Some people say that it's never good to go back. I disagree. We look to the past; it defines us and we should learn from it, good and bad, then move forward. His aunt was digressing, she knew and came back to the point. You've missed being here, I can tell, but coming back doesn't mean returning to everything how it was. We have to take the best from our past, not feel tied to it.'

João seemed distracted. He was certainly pensive, but he was listening. 'I'll see how it goes when I meet her this evening. It is alright if I stay a couple of nights?'

'Of course it is, stay as long as you like,' his aunt was happy to have his company.

As João was getting ready, he was rehearsing what he might say to Ana Rita. The only thing he was certain about was that this time, he wanted to apologise. It had seemed so difficult back at the estate, too public somehow to have the conversation.

He was late to meet Ana Rita, something which annoyed her. She felt on edge because she had her own evening to get on with and she had to find a way to tell João that she wouldn't be joining him for dinner. She preferred not to give too much away if possible, especially as her family had no idea about her relationship. She wondered why she was being so cautious about telling João. Surely he would be pleased to think she had moved on. There was nothing to do but to tell him straight away that she couldn't stay.

'João, I should have mentioned earlier, but I already have an arrangement for dinner this evening.'

'Oh.' João hadn't expected that.

'I've got half an hour or so. We can have a drink and catch up with your trip to London,' Ana Rita said trying to soften the blow. João didn't seem too pleased. At one time, it might have made her concerned and left her trying to retrieve the situation, but on this occasion, she was irritated. A strong feeling came over her that she didn't care anymore. Yes, she liked him. She felt a fondness towards him, but he did not figure in her life now in any significant way. She started to ask him questions about London and for a while he obliged her with replies until finally, he interrupted her questioning,

'There's something I wanted to say to you.' He seemed very serious now.

'I got it wrong when I left you. I wanted to tell you that and also that I'm very sorry. I ran away. It was cowardly. You didn't deserve that. Above all, you were my best friend. I want to try to make it up to you.'

Feelings came to Ana Rita in quick succession. First of all surprise that he had returned to the subject, then pleasure. Somehow the apology did help. Then a concern as to what he might say next. She felt she needed to interrupt.

'That's the second apology I've had since you've been back. Your mother had a similar conversation with me and I do appreciate it. You did get it wrong. There were better ways you could have handled it. So, thank you. But, João, I've moved on too.'

'I wanted you to know that I'm here for you if you want me,' João said.

Ana Rita didn't know exactly what he meant but she was more concerned now. She needed to stop him saying anything else and felt she had no choice but to trust him. It was the only way she could be clear with him.

'João, I'd rather you kept what I'm about to tell you to yourself. I'm asking you as a very good friend to keep my confidence. I'm seeing someone here in Oporto. We've been together now for almost a year. I haven't told anyone in the family. I don't want the interference and if they did know that it wasn't only friends I visited, it's very likely they would stop me coming over at the weekends and that would make things very difficult for me. This way, I get some independence. This way I get a private life.'

João didn't know why he had assumed she was on her own. She had kept the secret. Suddenly, he was feeling jealous and acting more like her father than a friend.

'Who is this guy? What do you know about him? I hope he's behaving properly. You haven't got the protection you would have at home. You should be careful. He may not be as serious about the relationship as you are,' João blurted out without thinking.

Ana Rita couldn't believe what she was hearing. She said as much to him, but there was a part of her that was pleased to know it bothered him. This wasn't about her safety. He was jealous and even now, there was something satisfying about that.

'And what does he do, can he support you?' João continued to throw questions at her.

'João, stop it. I'm happier than I've been in a long time and I do believe I have a future with him. I haven't thought about how it all might work out but it's really great and I do trust him. I'll tell the family when I'm ready, when there's something they need to know, but until then I hope you'll do me this one favour of keeping what I've told you to yourself. You did say that you were here for me.'

Ana Rita thought it important to appeal to his good word.

João said he wouldn't say anything, so long as she promised that she would tell him if there were any problems. She agreed and then checking her watch, she told him that she really did need to dash. She would catch up with him when they were both back at home. Then João was on his own again, with his thoughts, staring into his cold beer. He finished his drink slowly and then he walked away, his ego feeling bruised. It was strange. Deep down he knew that he didn't want to rekindle a relationship with Ana Rita. He had begun to feel so guilty. He was genuinely very sorry and wanted to make amends.

'You're back early. I thought you were out for dinner. Have you eaten?' His aunt asked as she answered the door.

'No, we only had a drink,' João replied, still distracted and a little troubled.

'Let's have something to eat then and you can tell me all about it. The meal will be about half an hour. We can open a bottle of wine while we wait,' his aunt suggested, noticing his unusually low mood and passing him a bottle of red wine, two large glasses and a corkscrew.

His aunt always put on a marvellous spread but the meal was far too much to have been prepared for one person. It appeared she had expected him back for dinner. He couldn't imagine why. He had been clear he was going out for dinner, but her intuition was so good. It was frightening at times. He felt comforted, like a little boy again. When he commented on her having so much prepared, she dismissed it, saying that he had said he would stay for a couple of days and she was getting ahead while he was out. He wasn't convinced but was hungry and when the food arrived he tucked in without much more thought. There was a really substantial soup for the starter, 'Sopa de Camarão e Mexilhões', a prawn and mussel chowder. As his aunt served the soup she looked at him, smiled and said,

'Of soup and love, the first is best.' João smiled back remembering the old saying and his aunt continued. 'You'll feel better when you've had something to eat.'

'The soup's delicious,' he said.

For the main course, she had prepared a 'Frango na Púcara', chicken cooked in a deep earthenware pot, served with chips, salad and plenty of chunks of fresh bread to dip in the gravy. His aunt was famous for her puddings and had made a 'Doce Dourado de Chila'. She reminded him, though he hadn't forgotten, that it was a dessert first made by nuns at a convent in Oporto, a very sweet pudding, made on a base of sponge cake drenched with a syrup made from oranges and then covered with a mixture of jam made from spaghetti squash, candied lemon peel and ground almonds, finally topped with a custard made from egg yolks and sprinkled with cinnamon. It was delicious.

As they sat finishing the wine, João started to open up and describe the meeting with Ana Rita. He forgot all together that he had given his word to Ana Rita that he wouldn't tell anyone about her relationship.

'Oh, heck, I wasn't supposed to tell you that bit. I gave my word to Ana Rita.' He was annoyed with himself.

'You know me, João, I don't gossip. I won't mention it to anyone else,' his aunt reassured him.

João knew that she wouldn't. He admired his aunt. She was an independent woman who had not been concerned with most of the expectations people had of her as a woman. She was her own person who answered to no one else. That was the way she liked it. Some may have argued that she had given up a lot to keep her independence. She wasn't on her own in that, but she had always felt it was a compromise worth making and her huge extended family made up for any lack on her part. She was particularly fond of João and wanted the best for him, whatever that was.

'You were bound to feel a little jealous. There had only been you as far as Ana Rita was concerned. Perhaps part of you thought that would always be the case.'

'I'm not jealous.' João was indignant.

His aunt looked at him quizzically.

'Perhaps a bit,' he said.

'Given a day or two, you'll realise that this is the best thing that could have happened. I was worried when you went out this evening that you were about to make another mistake,' his aunt said.

Whether or not it was a need to put a bit of distance between him and Ana Rita, he didn't know. He couldn't get her out of his mind. She was there in Oporto for the weekend with her new boyfriend. João woke up the next morning ready to go home. He packed his bag before going downstairs. He was conscious that his aunt would be expecting him to stay at least another night, as he had suggested when he arrived, but he needed now to tell her that he wanted to catch the afternoon train. Over breakfast he spoke with her. She didn't mind. In fact, she didn't seem at all surprised and said that, as coincidence would happen, she had planned to spend the following weekend with the family. It had been so long since she had been home, so would see him again soon.

When João arrived at the station, he collected his suitcase from left luggage and with minutes to spare caught the train to Pinhão. Each time he made this journey now, he did so with an awakened perspective, impressed by the beauty and drama of the landscape, his homeland. By the time the train pulled into the station, he felt quite content. He had forgotten to ring ahead from Oporto to arrange a lift but even that couldn't lower his mood. There was no rush. He rang from the station. His mother answered the phone. She was surprised and delighted and said that someone would be there shortly to pick him up. She needed to see who was available.

João sat down to wait outside the station. After about half an hour, he began to wonder where they had got to. Perhaps everyone was busy. He hadn't given them any notice that he was on his way back. After about an hour, he thought about setting off to walk and asking the station master if he could leave his suitcase there. He had only just stood up and was walking back into the building when a vehicle came hurtling down the road towards the station. His brother was driving and as he pulled up sharply beside him, he yelled through the open window,

'Quickly, get in the car.'

João was a bit taken aback, but did as asked, throwing his suitcase in the back and then getting in, slamming the door in his haste.

'What's going on, has something happened?' João was worried. It was so unlike his brother.

Pedro didn't answer his question directly. 'I've got to pick up Doctor Guilherme. He should have been at the house by now but there's something wrong with his car.'

João was really worried. 'Who is it? What's wrong? Is it father?'

'No, it's Céu, her waters have broken, she's in labour,' Pedro explained.

João didn't know how he could have forgotten. 'But I didn't think she was due yet.'

'It's a couple of weeks early according to what we'd worked out, but we've got to get the doctor to her.' Pedro was clearly very anxious.

The doctor was waiting outside his house, carrying his black bag as he climbed into the back, pushing João's suitcase along the seat to give him enough room to get in. João apologised,

'I'm sorry, Doctor, I didn't know we were picking you up when I got into the car or I'd have made room.' Then he turned to his brother and said, 'Let me drive, you're not really fit.'

He thought that Pedro would insist on driving but he didn't, saying, 'Quickly then, swap places with me.'

They were soon back, no time for welcoming João this time. His mother was upstairs with Céu and the doctor made his way to join them. As he was walking up the stairs, he turned to Pedro and said, 'It could be quite a while. You probably don't want to be far away, but you might want to find something to do.'

João started to follow him up the stairs and said to Pedro, 'I'll put my bags in my room, then I could do with a snack, so let's go to the kitchen and see what we can scrounge.'

'I'm really not very hungry,' Pedro said.

'Yes, I get that. But you need to give Doctor Guilherme time to assess the situation,' João suggested.

Again, Pedro seemed happy to be guided by his brother.

Paula, the family's cook, was in the kitchen baking bread. She had been with the family since the children were very small. João had known her all of his life. She was a happy character, a fantastic cook. She had a kind and generous nature. As children, the boys would often gravitate towards the kitchen when hungry and also at times when they needed to talk, when something was bothering them. Paula would cheer them up with her stories. She was a great story teller and knew all the gossip, past and present. As soon as the brothers walked into the kitchen, she gave them both a big hug, João for his return and Pedro in the excitement of the expected birth.

'Not long now and I'll see the first of the next generation of the family, your turn next, João,' she said.

'Steady on there, Paula, I think there are a couple of steps missing. It could be some time, so don't hold your breath.' João was used to her ways.

'I still have hopes that you and Ana Rita will get back together. You always made such a lovely couple and she's good for you,' she said, not knowing how awkward it was to hear that.

João had to stop himself saying that it didn't seem at all possible now that Ana Rita was in another relationship and had to remind himself that he had promised Ana Rita.

'She'll always be a good friend. It's ok between us now. Time for both of us to move on. I don't think my mother ever shared your enthusiasm, Paula,' he said.

'I'm certain that no girl will be good enough for you in your mother's eyes,' Paula replied and João knew she was right.

Paula made some sandwiches with ham and cheese, enough for both the brothers, but as she set the plate down on the kitchen table, Pedro who had been very quiet said he wasn't hungry and would go and see if he could have a word with Doctor Guilherme.

'You'll need to keep up your strength,' Paula said as he was leaving.

'It's not my strength I'm worried about,' he called back to Paula.

'Don't you worry,' Paula called. 'She's a strong woman.'

It was almost midnight when Céu gave birth to a baby boy, mother and baby absolutely fine. João was now an uncle. If he hadn't felt grown up before, he felt different now. He was overwhelmed with pride and overjoyed to have been at home for the birth of his nephew and the family's celebration. It was a great night.

The next day, bursting with the need to tell someone, he rang Rui at work.

'That's fantastic news, give my love to everyone, but you're still at home. I thought you were heading back to London.'

João explained what he had been doing over the past weeks and why he was back at home. Rui was quite surprised.

'You seemed so happy in London. What changed your mind?' He asked.

'It wasn't one thing. It's complicated and quite hard to explain. I'm not sure I understand myself,' João said.

'I'm in Oporto at the end of the week. I could stay on for the weekend and we could meet up,' Rui suggested, thinking João might appreciate having someone to talk to. 'I wasn't in touch because I thought you would be in London. You went rather quiet after Coimbra.'

'Yes, sorry about that. I had a lot on my mind. Why don't you come out here for the weekend? My aunt's coming over on Friday evening. You could get a lift with her.'

João didn't want to be away in Oporto with everything so busy at home. He knew that Ana Rita would be in Oporto at the weekend and it was something he still wanted to avoid. Not only that, after his short stay with his aunt, he didn't want to be away again.

'That's a great idea. It's ages since I've been. How many years must it be? Are you sure it will be alright? You're all going to be fairly busy and family over too.' Rui didn't want to get in the way but he was really pleased that João had suggested the idea.

'You know my mother. She loves to have the house full of people and you can see my new nephew. I'll get in touch with my aunt and then you can arrange a time with her once you're in Oporto. She'll be pleased to see you too,' João said.

So it was decided. The house would be full of visitors the following weekend, everyone wanting to see the new baby and congratulating the couple on the birth of their first child.

The next day, once the excitement of the birth had calmed down a little, João went to have a word with his father to brief him on his most recent trip to London. His father was reading in his study. João knocked and entered when his father answered, inviting him to sit down in the armchair opposite. His father was really pleased with his work. The meetings João had set up were opening new possibilities for the market in Britain. He explained that he would need to go back but not for a few weeks. João was keen to know what his father had in mind for him on the estate, as he wanted to make the best of his time at home.

'I know you've a good idea of the workings of the estate and you need to keep in touch with clients, but you can spend the time while you're here helping out wherever it's needed. There's still a lot you can learn from the staff here.' João's father hadn't thought his suggestion would go down very well. He thought that João would probably prefer to focus on his own interests within the business. To his surprise, he was happy with the suggestion.

'Sounds like a good plan. Where do I start?' João asked.

That week, João got back to work on the estate, spending most of his time with the taster. It was such a change from his work in London. He saw Ana Rita most days and she seemed happy. He didn't mention their conversation, nor did she. The week passed surprisingly quickly. In no time the weekend was upon them and his aunt and Rui were coming up the driveway to the house. That evening the whole family got together for dinner, the first formal celebration after the birth. Paula excelled herself. She had made a partridge soup, with homemade bread, warm, straight from the oven. His father had chosen a suitably mature Dão, a rich, red wine. The main course was bacalhau, salt cod. As was fitting for the occasion, of the hundreds of ways there were to prepare salt-cod, Paula had chosen the most elaborate, 'Bacalhau à Gomes de Sá', named after the salt-cod merchant from Oporto who first created it. The cod had been soaked for a day in water and then boiled. Paula had carefully flaked the flesh into a huge, deep dish, covering it with hot milk and leaving it to soak again. She added onions and garlic fried in oil and sliced potatoes once she had drained the milk away and then placed the huge earthenware dish into the oven for the final bake. When it was ready, she garnished it with boiled eggs, olives and parsley and served it with dishes of fresh vegetables from the garden. There was a huge chocolate mousse for those who still had room or fruit for anyone who wanted to freshen their palate and a short rest for everyone before a very special vintage port was opened.

Long after the others had gone to bed, João and Rui were in the sitting room chatting and finishing the port wine. Rui was in good spirits. He said that since the trip to Coimbra, he and Júlia had become much closer again. He was planning to transfer to his father's office in Lisbon to give the relationship a proper chance this time. The distance between them had been the cause of them drifting apart more than anything else. Júlia wanted to be able to work and loved the job at the radio station. Rui was too fond of her to want anything other than what she wanted.

'The revolution will open more opportunities for people, I'm sure and why not for women? I think spending time with Rebecca, appreciating the freedoms she has, convinced Júlia more than ever that she wants her own career.'

'Rebecca seems to have had an effect on more than one person,' João said reflecting on his own actions recently.

'What do you mean?' Rui was curious. 'Are you talking about yourself now and is there something I'm missing?'

'She had such enthusiasm and such a refreshing perspective on the country and I think it helped me take a different view. It certainly was a factor in making the decision to work again for my father and spend more time over here to see how things go,' João explained.

'But you haven't seen her or been in touch since you left Coimbra and you left fairly quickly for home as soon as Júlia and I set off back, which must have felt a bit sudden for Rebecca. What was all that about? I thought the two of you were getting on well and if I'm not wrong, there seemed something fairly special going on. I don't think I've ever seen you so relaxed and happy.' Rui had heard from Júlia that Rebecca didn't understand why he left without saying a word to her after they'd seemed close.

'That English boyfriend of hers was on his way and I didn't want to hang about.' João was honest with Rui.

'What made you think he was a boyfriend? He's an old school friend. There's nothing between them. Júlia asked her about him. Tom has a girlfriend in France.' Rui could hardly believe that's what he thought. 'She didn't give me the impression either that there was anything going on. I don't know why you would think that.'

'Is she back in Vila Real, then?' João hadn't stopped thinking about Rebecca, even though he had done his best to put it behind him and focus on work.

'Yes, she was a few more days in Coimbra. As far as I know, they didn't find Carol. Rebecca's friend Tom stayed on for a while in the area, hoping he could find her. I don't know how much you know about Rebecca and why she was heading for the Algarve but she had some old family friends in the area, although I think they'd lost touch. She met up with them again. She's working a couple of days a week for the family firm and really enjoying it. You've probably heard of the family. My father knows them. They own the big construction business that's currently working on holiday villas and apartments in Tavira, mostly for the tourist trade. It's big business. There's a lot of money in it and reports are that the business is doing well. It can only get better now, I'm sure. Júlia also said that she's moved out from her parents' house and rented a little house in the centre of town not too far from the town square. She seems to be getting settled.' Rui had seen Rebecca a couple of times in town, but he hadn't spoken to her about João.

João sat for a minute or two without speaking. Clearly something was bothering him, and then he said, 'I think I might have got it wrong.'

'I think you might have,' Rui said, smiling at him.

The next morning, after breakfast, Rui said that he was keen to have a look around the estate again. It had been so long since he had visited. Paula made them a packed lunch, as they intended to explore on foot as far as time would allow. They spent the best part of the day out and about, resting only to have lunch. As they ate, João confided in Rui about Ana Rita. He trusted him. He told him the whole story, conscious that Ana Rita might not be impressed if she knew that now both Rui and his aunt knew about her relationship but there was no reason for Rui to say anything to anyone. He wouldn't break João's confidence. He was pleased to hear that Ana Rita had moved on. As much as he liked her, he didn't think it would have been good for João to have gone back. He knew his reasons for leaving had been complicated but if the relationship had been really strong, nothing would have dragged him away.

The next day, João took Rui to the railway station. João's aunt had decided to stay on for a few more days and although she offered to take Rui back, it was a long drive and he didn't want to abuse her kindness. Rui insisted that he was more than happy to take the train. It was such a beautiful route and he was looking forward to travelling it again. He said that he would let João know his address in Lisbon as soon as he had sorted out where he would be living.

'You're not planning to stay with Júlia, then?' João asked.

'I don't think that either my parents or hers would like that and I'm keen that the relationship goes well this time, so I'm trying to do everything properly,' Rui said.

'You do sound very serious about it.' It occurred to João that Rui wouldn't be in Vila Real for much longer and that he wouldn't have any reason to visit fairly soon.

'How long will you be before you move to Lisbon then do you think?' He asked and was quite surprised at Rui's answer.

'I hope not much longer than a couple of weeks. I'm going to stop off in Lisbon on my way home. I can look at a few apartments and once that's done, I'm set up and I can start work.'

João waited at the railway station with Rui to see him safely on his way. As he drove away, his thoughts went back to Vila Real de Santo António. It rather seemed as though circumstances were playing against him meeting up with Rebecca again and the more he thought about not being able to go, the more he wanted to go. He'd been travelling around the country enough recently and now that he was working on the estate, he could hardly ask for a few days off. That would really give the wrong message to his family. He wanted to show his commitment to getting up-to-date with the business and making a proper contribution. He needed to get Rebecca out of his mind. She was probably no longer very impressed with him and Rui seemed to think she was happy. It couldn't be any more difficult if they were in two different countries. It was hardly a distance that would work for a relationship; Rui had realised that and Lisbon was far closer to Vila Real.

That evening after dinner, his aunt said she would like to have a stroll. It would help her dinner to settle. She asked João if he would accompany her.

'It's not that I'm afraid to walk around after dark, but the company would be nice.' She had noticed that he had been rather quiet over dinner and wondered if there was something wrong. She hoped he wasn't still upset about Ana Rita. She couldn't think that was the reason. He had become used to life in a big city and this was such a contrast. She knew that if he was feeling unhappy, he wouldn't want to talk about it at home.

For a while, they talked about Pedro, Céu and the new baby. João let her do most of the talking, his continued quietness finally giving her a way in to ask him a more direct question.

'How's the work going, then?' she asked.

'Really good. My father's pleased with the business I've been handling across in London and until I need to go back again, he suggested that I spend a little time in all the different areas of the business. I spent last week with the taster and really enjoyed it.'

For the first time all evening, João was quite animated and enthusiastic and as his aunt listened to him, she was sure there must be another reason why he had seemed down and quieter than usual.

'So you're going to stay?' He was enjoying the work but she wondered how settled he was.

'Yes, I've committed to the year in my own mind. I think it's only fair and I've done enough casual work over the last couple of years. Even though I love the life in London, the work was beginning to bore me. It might seem like selling out, especially when I was so determined to do something else, but I've come to the conclusion that I won't know, if I don't give it a chance. If it doesn't work out, then this time, I will have to think seriously about another career, if I'm to convince the family that I'm not wasting my life. I haven't left London for good and at least being back here, I have time to reflect. I'm keen to see what happens now that the new government is in place. My father seems quite concerned about what it might mean for the business; it's the wrong time to be away.'

'Your father isn't the only one to be concerned. The communists seem quite a strong force and they would have very different ideas about businesses like ours if they had overall power, but it isn't clear how it will be. It's all rather a mess at the moment. I'm losing track of the number of strikes there have been. It's hard to know what might happen next but your father loves this estate. He'll do everything he can to keep it with the family, I'm sure.'

His aunt paused for a while, still thinking there was more to João's mood, as they continued walking.

'So tell me then, if you're truly happy with what you are doing at the moment, why have you been so quiet today? I can tell there's something bothering you. You're not still upset about Ana Rita are you?' There was no point skirting around it, she thought.

'No, not at all. I see her most days and I think both of us are keen to stay good friends. It would be such a shame to lose that, but she seems really happy, so I hope it works out for her. If it does, she may move away. I never thought she would or at least she was always adamant that she wouldn't but when you meet someone, all the ideas and plans you thought you had can change.'

'Oh, so that's it. I see. What's her name, this young woman who's making you reassess your plans?'

'I wasn't talking about me. I'm talking about Ana Rita.' João pushed back, but here she was again, so intuitive. She didn't miss anything and she wouldn't be at all convinced. She was quiet. He looked at her and saw that quizzical expression. She was waiting for him to tell her all about it.

João gave in. 'Her name is Rebecca. She's from the north of England and I met her on the train when we were both on our way to Paris.' He then outlined the rest of the story, including Coimbra and what seemed now to have been a wrong assumption about Rebecca's friend Tom. 'This is another one where I need to say, don't tell anyone, least of all my parents. She's miles away and I know they will immediately think I'll be off again.'

'As I reminded you only recently, you know me. I won't say a word. What are you going to do about it now?' she asked.

'I've no idea. I think I've come to the conclusion that it wasn't meant to be. Yet again, I didn't handle it properly. She's probably forgotten all about me and as far as I understand, she has old friends down there. She's lovely, so she'll soon find someone else,' João said sounding disheartened.

'I may be wrong, João, but you're not really acting like someone who has moved on and I know you, it will eat away at you. I understand that you don't have a reason to visit. Rui will soon be living in Lisbon and I agree with you that it's far too soon to be suggesting you need to go away again. Why don't you write? Start up a correspondence with her. That way you can explain as much as you want to and hopefully start to get to know her again. You'll soon find out if she's keen to continue to be in touch,' his aunt suggested.

João was quiet for a few minutes and his aunt only spoke to suggest that it was time to get back to the house. As they got closer, he was liking the suggestion.

'It might be an idea and at least I will be doing something about it rather than dwelling on it all the time. If you've noticed my mood, it won't be too long before my mother is asking me what's wrong.'

'Sometimes I find it helps to write it down, then you can decide whether or not you want to send it,' his aunt said, as she opened the door. He thanked her for the advice.

João went up to his room thinking that there was no time like the present. He didn't have any writing paper with him, but did have some other paper that would do for the draft and so he started on what turned out to be the first of several drafts. The opening was the hardest part. The rest he felt would be easy, as he had plenty of news.

*Dear Rebecca,*

*I've been meaning to write for ages (ever since I got home/since Coimbra?)*

No, he couldn't write that. If he was going to write, he had to be honest. He hadn't intended to write at all and it hadn't been his own idea.

*Dear Rebecca,*

*I wanted to write to you because I felt I needed to apologise for leaving Coimbra so quickly. Once I knew that your friend Tom was coming over to join you, I thought I would be in the way.*

Not entirely honest, he was jealous and he wasn't going to hang around feeling as he did.

*Dear Rebecca,*

*I'm sorry I left Coimbra so abruptly. I really enjoyed our time together but I didn't think it would be appropriate to stay once I knew that Tom was on his way.*

That wouldn't work either. He knew now that Tom was a friend and as Rebecca had made that clear to Júlia, she would probably not be convinced. This was going to be harder than he thought and he was beginning to feel tired. It was already after one o'clock in the morning. He had to be up early and looking half asleep wasn't going to help him keep this one to himself. Even though he hadn't made much of a an attempt at the letter, he was feeling better already and promised himself that he would try again after work the next day.

After breakfast, he found a moment to speak with his aunt before he set out to the office.

'I started the letter last night.'

'How did you get on?' she asked.

'Not great really. I couldn't get beyond the opening sentence.' He told her what he had written.

'No, that won't work, João, you're trying too hard. There'll be time for apologies later if you feel it's appropriate. The letter is just to get in touch with her again, simply that. Let her know you want to continue your friendship. Tell her what you've been doing. Let her know that she helped you to your decision and ask after her. The opening is never easy but you'll be able to write it once you've sketched out the rest of the letter,' she suggested.

'Sounds like a good idea. I'll have another go at it this evening.' João said as he was leaving.

# XXVI

One day when Rebecca got back in, she was surprised to see a letter on the doormat, a letter written in a hand she didn't recognise. So far she had only received bills and letters from home. This one wasn't from England. She looked at the post-mark but didn't recognise the place. That was something she could do with, she thought, a map of the country. She opened the envelope and then scanned the letter to the bottom for the signature. It was from João, the last person she had expected. She had thought it was unlikely that she would hear from him again, hear about him, as Júlia knew him, but not hear directly from him. She made herself a drink and a sandwich and then went outside on the terrace into the sunshine to eat her lunch and to read the letter properly. Having read it, twice, she wasn't sure what to make of it. She knew that Maria Eduarda would be at home, so after she had finished eating and had washed up, she went to see her, taking the letter with her. She found Maria Eduarda busy in the kitchen and went straight to the reason she had called around to see her.

'I wanted to ask you, what do you think about this letter?' Rebecca said handing Maria the letter to read.

'What is it about? Who is it from?' Maria Eduarda asked.

'It's a letter from João, you know, as in Coimbra.' Rebecca was sure that Maria Eduarda would know who she was talking about. She hadn't talked about any other João.

Maria took the letter, looked at the post-mark, opened it and began to read.

*Dear Rebecca,*

*I've been wondering how you've been getting on ever since we were all in Coimbra. Rui came to visit me at home this weekend and it was good to catch up with him. He told me that you were settling into life in Vila Real de Santo António. I was really pleased to hear because I know how important it was for you. I suppose you've probably heard from Júlia that Rui is moving to Lisbon to work. From time to time, he has business too in Oporto so I'm hoping that I might get to see him a little more than I have been able to in the last few years. Spending time with my old friends really did make me realise how much I've missed them whilst I've been away.*

*I also wanted to tell you my news. I've decided to spend more time over here and I've been back over to London, working for the family business. I'm not sure how it will work out long term but I'm going to be spending time in both countries. Back here, I'm trying to get my affairs in order and I've started what you might call an apprenticeship. I thought I knew the business thoroughly growing up with it, but I've been out of it for too long so I feel I've a lot to catch up with and some things that I need to learn. I think it's fair to say that I have surprised myself and my family, with the decision. I was convinced that I wanted to follow a different career and be more independent. It was a combination of several different factors. Perhaps most importantly, there was a lot going on at home. I had been rather cut off from all the politics hiding away in London and hadn't realised how much it was affecting people. We're uncertain about what the future might hold and the changes it might bring. Obviously, I would want to be optimistic. This country has suffered too long and hopefully, it will be a better place to live for everyone. I suppose I realised too that as much as I was enjoying being away, I was missing out on a lot too. My brother's wife was expecting a baby and I was lucky enough to be back on the day my nephew was born and to be part of all the family celebrations. I'm now a very proud uncle to a lovely little boy, named João. I like to think it's after me but it is one of my father's names too.*

*I'm thinking that you also might be quite surprised to hear I'm back in Portugal. I must have seemed a true anglophile. Before I came down to Vila Real de Santo António and we all went to Coimbra for the weekend, I had continued to feel the pressure of being away and the weight of expectation that my place was at home. As I say, being back with friends began to make me realise what I was missing too but I really enjoyed the time we had together in Coimbra and our excursion into the countryside and wanted you to know that the time I spent with you had helped me make up my mind. You have such a love of the country and such a fresh perspective, I found I was looking at everything in a different way. As it happened, they were thoughts that were reinforced by another of those chance meetings on a journey – I must stop doing that! I met a woman on the plane going back to London; she has a place in England but still has strong ties with Portugal and lives between the two places. I came to the conclusion that I didn't need to make a choice.*

*It has occurred to me that I'm now probably further away from you than I would have been if we had both been back in Britain, although I know that your plans hadn't been to be back for quite a while. I wanted to say that it would be good to stay in touch and that I would like to hear from you if you have time for letter writing, in and amongst all the excitement of your new life.*

*Abraços e beijos,*

*João*

Maria read the letter carefully and then read it again, keen to have a good understanding of its contents. She wasn't surprised to hear that he had resurfaced from everything that Rebecca had said. She had been sure Rebecca would hear from him again.

'It's a friendly enough letter,' was Maria Eduarda's opening comment. 'And, obviously he seems keen to stay in touch.'

'I'm not sure why and there's that comment about being so far away. I think he has a bit of a guilty conscience. He doesn't mention it but it wasn't great the way he left. If I reply, it may make him feel a bit better but I'm not sure what he really wants from me other than that.' Rebecca wasn't convinced and the letter was beginning to annoy her.

Maria Eduarda was off now on a different tack. 'He doesn't give much away, does he? Rather holding back on the family business and being part of such an empire.'

'I don't suppose he would be bothered about me knowing much about him if the letter is only a way of appeasing his guilt,' Rebecca said.

'I might have another interpretation, more than one, actually. He might, as most people do, want you to know him for himself and not for his family. He was trying his best to break away from all that when he went to London, so it wouldn't surprise me and it could put some people off. I remember you making a comment that he was out of your league, when you heard about his background, so that could be in his thinking.'

Rebecca was listening, but making her own interpretation. 'It seems to me that there's another woman on the scene and if she has two places, one in England and one here at home, then she's probably much more his kind of woman.'

'Are you going to write? I think you should. It wouldn't be very polite to ignore it. You're reading a lot into it that might not be there.' Despite everything that Rebecca had said, Maria Eduarda still had a good feeling and didn't want Rebecca to give up on it yet.

'What about all your matchmaking with Manuel? I thought you'd got your sights on someone else for me at the moment,' Rebecca said.

'It never hurts to keep your options open,' Maria Eduarda joked with her.

'Go on, write to him and then see what the next letter says. It should be clear by then if your interpretation is right.'

'I'll think about it. I have to see a client this afternoon, so I'd better get on. I'll let you know what I decide,' Rebecca said on her way out.

'Just keep it to your news, that's what he's asking about, if you don't read anything further into it. And don't forget that we're going to the cinema this evening with Ricardo and Manuel,' Maria Eduarda called after her.

Rebecca went away determined to put the letter out of her mind, at least for a while. That way, she thought, it might become clearer what she really wanted to do. How many times had friends told her not to be so keen? A little waiting wouldn't hurt. He might be wanting to continue the friendship but she wasn't sure that it was good to be distracted by someone at the other end of the country. Her plans were working out here and she didn't want anything to spoil them. She noticed the time, still having a couple of hours before she had to meet her next clients. It was a lovely afternoon and it seemed a waste not to do something with it. As she had the car, she could explore the coastline on the way to Tavira. Maria Eduarda had mentioned a place called Cacela Velha which was meant to be beautiful, a little settlement right on the coast – well worth a look. Rebecca went back to the house to get her camera, thinking it might be a good opportunity for photographs. She had wanted to keep a photo record of the year and although she had taken some pictures, it had almost gone out of her mind. Time to start in earnest then. She took the main road out of Vila Real de Santo António towards Tavira, looking out for the road signs, not sure exactly where the turning was and remembering it as being closer. As she got nearer to Tavira, sure she had gone too far, she spotted the road sign. She turned onto a long country road, skirted by fields planted with olive trees. Never having complete confidence in her own sense of direction, as the road stretched in front of her, she began to wonder if it was the right road and started to pay close attention, thinking that she might have to retrace her steps. Sure enough, it wasn't too much further and there was the small hamlet in front of her. She parked the car and walked up towards the church, imagining it must be the centre of the village and a good place to start to explore. This must be one of the prettiest little places on the coast, she thought. The sun was shining brightly on the whitewashed houses with their brilliant blue borders and bright red tiled roofs. Fishermen's houses, she assumed. There was a pride in how carefully presented these little houses were. She walked around the church alongside a solid stone wall and was met by the most magnificent view out across the sea. Now she could see that Cacela Velha was perched on a cliff, a tiny presence at first sight, but nevertheless imposing itself on the landscape. It dominated the coastline, a fortress, a spectacular vantage point. Rebecca felt the closeness of centuries of history. As she looked out to the west, she could see that the vast Atlantic was held back by a wide area of lagoons. A little strip of sandy beach could be seen close to the land, but as the tide was further out, it revealed long stretches of wet, dark sand and what looked like little crabs scurrying across the sand and disappearing again at the sight of any danger. Inlets and channels and lines of small sandy islands sheltered this part of the coastline from the open sea. Boats of different sizes and colours, some with sails, others small rowing boats were dotted across the water. Hardly anyone around she noticed and then wondered if there was a way down to the beach. There must be, of course, but it seemed such a long way down. She walked back along the side of the stone wall and there it was, a deep set of stone steps, leading down to the beach. She checked again. There was no one around. It seemed quite out of the way, but she felt safe and so started to make her way down the steps. As she continued down and down, the sides of the path became more overgrown with large cactus plants, small trees and scrubs until the steps eventually levelled out, giving way to loose sand under foot and she emerged onto the beach. She took off her shoes and stepped out on the little area of dry sand which the sea reached more rarely, being careful not to tread on the shells, the driftwood, and the pieces of cord and net which gave away the main activity on this beach. The brightly coloured rowing boats moored on the wet sand were drawing Rebecca's attention. She took out her camera and began to take pictures of peeling paint and years of wear, wandering as far along the beach towards the east as she dared, feet sinking into the deep muddy sand, before turning back and making her way to where she had emerged from the steps. She sat down on the dry sand.

Afterwards, she wasn't sure how long she had sat there on that tiny parcel of dry sand, sheltered by the dense shrubbery behind her with the warm breeze from the sea gently calming and lifting her spirits. A stillness brought a deep sensation of connection, of being part of something beyond her. She had a sense of the past not being past at all, but of being present. Its sting had gone and in its place a kind of acceptance and peace. The sound of someone calling out brought her back from deep thoughts, noticing two small boats. Although quite far apart, fishermen were speaking across the water, talking about the catch, old friends calling to each other, the words disappearing on the breeze across the lagoon. Checking the camera, she noticed had taken almost all of the film and hoped for some good shots. She continued to gaze out across the lagoon and for a while remained lost again in her thoughts, wandering, random, nothing in particular, a warm feeling of contentment. This was a place where she could stay for ever. The church bell sounded, a second awakening from her thoughts. She looked at her watch. Time to go, she didn't know quite how long it was going to take her now that she had made this detour off the main road and needed to get on. Being late would not give a good impression. She hadn't factored in the long drag back to the village, either. She dashed up the steps and reaching the top, felt quite exhausted and pretty hot. It was not the way to arrive to see a client. She would need to find somewhere to freshen up if there was time.

As she drove away, she thought about all the building work along the coast and hoped that this little place would not succumb to the huge villas, towering apartments and overly grand hotels she had seen elsewhere. There had to be progress, everyone was saying that, but it must not be at the cost of the rare beauty of the coastline. The beach was small and the surrounding lagoons would restrict building, protecting this little hamlet from development. Perhaps it would be alright.

# XVII

**Monday 24th June, 1974**

By the time that Tó Zé reached Pampilhosa, Carol had left. In fact, she had left quite some time before. He had got it wrong, many would say. He knew that now. The strong resolve which had always been there driving him on in everything he did had taken him back to Portugal, without considering the consequences. He had needed to be part of the revolution. He had never left the struggle behind, but he had hidden his loyalties from Carol, convinced that it was necessary. His resolve had shaped all his decisions, but the belief that he was doing the right thing was now fading in and out of his determination as each day he was confronted with the effect of his decisions. There was nothing he could do. His friend, Brito, was waiting for him at the café in the square in Pampilhosa and although Tó Zé hadn't said how long he would be, Brito was quite surprised to see him back so soon. Tó Zé said nothing about what he had been doing, what he had found out, how everything was now changed for him and only spoke to say that they could carry on the journey back to Lisbon.

Throughout his life, Tó Zé had got on well with people. He had a certain charisma, a kind of charm, an attractiveness about him which had meant he was always surrounded by friends. He was often the loudest voice, more the dominant presence than simply one of the group. For as long as he could remember, he had possessed a single-mindedness. If he wanted to do something, he would do it. He rarely thought through the consequences, because they didn't occur to him. His motivations were distinct, obvious to him, but not always understood by others. Sometimes his errors would shape his next decision, but not always. As a boy, some of his actions, which could have been described as reckless, were often dismissed as 'boys being boys', but he took risks without much thought and for the most part, his friends admired him for it. The girls admired him too. He had quite a following of loyal supporters, who despite his actions seemed very taken by him and could see only good in him, He was driven even as a child, there was no doubt about that, wanting to learn, wanting better for himself, to have something different than the life his village could give him. In this determination, his parents supported him. He was bright. He seemed instinctively drawn to people who could help him and was soon learning as much as he could, soaking up knowledge and instruction wherever he could find it. His mother was convinced that he would become a priest. She had no reason to doubt. It was an intention expressed by Tó Zé from an early age. He appeared devout, committed and thoughtful in his understanding of his faith. His father, whilst he had always kept his thoughts to himself, was not convinced. He recognised the drive of self-interest, but if it meant that his son had more opportunities than might otherwise have been afforded to him, he was prepared to overlook any selfishness. It was a means to an end. He wouldn't restrict his son's ambition.

Tó Zé was educated by the local priest, a kind, well-respected man who recognised his ability from very early years and who was keen to encourage him into the priesthood and as time progressed and Tó Zé demonstrated his devotion, to find a way to support him through university. Tó Zé became the first in his village to study in Coimbra. He knew that he was hugely privileged to continue his studies, and at a university with such history, such distinction. As a boy, he had read about the university with its magnificent library, a temple of learning, built with the proceeds of Brazilian gold. He had seen pictures of its gilt ceilings and painted scenes. He had imagined himself there. He had had every good intention when he began his studies to make his mentor and his family proud, but was soon enjoying the freedoms of university life. He found his voice and an exquisite tenor voice too, joining one of the fado groups and spending evenings singing the beautiful, sad, mournful songs which so pulled at the heart strings of those who heard them. He loved his country. In his remote village, poverty was a way of life and few had questioned it, too busy making a living, an out of touch government seeming almost irrelevant in the toil of each day. It was different in the city. By the time that Tó Zé arrived in Coimbra, student unrest and resistance to the dictatorship had developed from minor skirmishes and disturbances to much more violent protests. Young people felt completely estranged from the ideology of those in charge. Tó Zé was soon captivated by the views of the most radical student activists. The university was an obvious place for revolutionaries to recruit, particularly as the government continued to conscript so many students into the army training corps in preparation for military service. The situation in the colonies worsened, violent outbursts, massacres of settlers, people determined to retrieve what was theirs, to rule themselves again. The reasons to resist were compelling and soon Tó Zé had joined in opposition, not at all deterred by the numbers of students who were being imprisoned for their views. The secret police tried their best to infiltrate student groups, but with little success, so strong was the defiance. Tó Zé joined in with the protests, the demonstrations, political debates, academic strikes and true to his character, was not prepared simply to follow others. His profile quickly drew attention, as he took more risks, showed little fear, until one day, he found himself far too close to arrest. He had taken a lead in the demonstration of hundreds of students at the opening of the new mathematics building, an important event, attended by the President of the Republic, Américo Tomás. In the days that followed, the police increased their determination to break the student leadership. Tó Zé had gone too far and he had no wish to be imprisoned or to be forcefully drafted into the army and into the conflict in Africa. He had to leave and he left suddenly, with only a brief word to his family, supported by people who had helped so many others across the border.

In many ways, the events in Coimbra and Tó Zé's escape to Paris played neatly into his hands. He was sure now that his ambitions were no longer for the priesthood. His aspirations were political and his hopes were for a free Portugal. For the time being, he had little choice other than to get away. He wasn't on his own. Several student leaders left that day. Across the years, others, for less critical reasons, had journeyed to Paris, looking for work or choosing to continue their studies abroad, taking a chance for a better life. In Paris, he was able to reinvent himself, something which appealed and whilst secretly he continued the fight, it was not only for his safety that he was quite prepared to embrace a different way of life. Like many others, he left responsibilities at home which in his case, he chose to keep distant. It was a waiting game, years to plan and to hope, ambitions undisclosed other than to a few trusted comrades. From afar, Tó Zé and others in exile supported the cause. They pushed and prepared, convinced that change was only a matter of time, determined to be ready to return when the time eventually came. So he led two lives, very successfully. He had fled with few possessions and very little money. The first months were hard, but he was helped by others who had arrived before him. His French was good. It wasn't long before he found work. By the time he met Carol, his new life was established.

All those who were part of his life with Carol could not have missed his apparent devotion to her. He loved her. He knew that to be the case, as soon as he saw her, but more importantly, he believed it. They met by chance. He was on his way home from work one evening and called in at a local shop to get something for dinner. It began with a conversation, standing in a queue, waiting to pay for a few groceries. The person who was being served was deep in conversation with the proprietor and Tó Zé was feeling impatient, not because he had anywhere that he needed to be, but because he didn't like waiting for the incidentals in life. He looked around and found a similar expression of frustration on the face of the young woman behind him and in the first exchange of words noted an accent which he found immediately appealing.

'You're not from Paris,' Tó Zé said, with a bright smile.

'Nor are you,' Carol replied. He liked the way that even though she was friendly enough, she wasn't drawn in and he had to work a little harder to continue to keep her in conversation. It was usually much easier for him and so he was attracted by the challenge. No further opening was given and he paid for his groceries. He didn't look back as he left the shop, but felt determined that he would be calling there more frequently for a while. It took more than one visit, but sure enough, a week later, on the same day, there she was, a person of habit, he noted. This time, he wasn't walking out without being sure that they would meet again.

It was easy with Carol. They had much in common and where there were differences, Tó Zé's seemingly easy-going nature adapted. It suited him to find that they were both on their own in Paris and although in different circumstances, at some distance from family. He chose to talk little about his, hinted occasionally at the problems, but never said much. Carol had the impression from the beginning that he wanted to return one day, but believed him when he said that it wasn't safe for young men his age and that he was settled and happy with his life in Paris. Carol accepted what he said, because it suited her to do so and because it seemed plausible. There were many Portuguese living in the city. It seemed quite natural that he would choose France. She was happy and didn't want anything to get in the way. Their life together in Paris was quickly intense and intimate. They were soon inseparable. Carol had her own reasons for keeping her life with Tó Zé apart from her previous life at home. Perhaps she wanted to avoid the obvious questions she was sure her parents would ask. Tó Zé was happy to stay at some distance. He never asked to join her on the infrequent visits home.

Knowing what they felt for each other and how they lived their life together, it was hard for many people to understand that when Tó Zé left Carol at the café, he knew there was a possibility that he would not see her again. Everything had changed. He had waited patiently for that change. He had stayed true to the cause and now his determination returned. He knew that he had to go back. If he had been asked, would he have said that he had fallen suddenly out of love with Carol? Not at all, he was reacting to the circumstances without much thought for anyone else, and as had always been the case, he rarely saw the need to work out all the detail. He would deal with each issue as it arose. That was the way it had always been for him. He had expected Carol to try to get in touch with him, but not for a while. Despite her move to Paris away from friends and family, she was not given to adventures and had come to rely on him more and more. She had good friends. They would help. He hadn't expected her to be confident enough to follow him to a country that she didn't know and whose language was alien to her, especially at a time of unrest and fear. He was sure she would perceive it as a huge risk to go there. It seemed to him out of character. Here she was in Portugal. She had been to his village. The woman he had believed he had loved had been so close to him, but he had missed her. He didn't know what to do. Nothing any longer was as it had seemed. For the first time in his life, he felt lost. He had loved her. He still loved her. This time, he left a contact and a letter for her should she return to the hotel. He wanted to see her, he said. He needed to explain. If she chose to go back to the village to look for him, it didn't matter anymore. He knew that but for now, at least, Lisbon called him back.

# XXVIII

**25th June, 1974**

Everything that Carol knew to be of her life in Paris, how it had been these past years, all of it was a lie. It was as though an enormous hole had opened up and she had fallen far, far down into its depths. She couldn't get out. There was nothing left for her. She had no idea what to do, no idea where to go. She hadn't been able to face the family, had pushed them out of her mind, too intent in her search. Now there was a growing feeling that she needed to hear her mother's voice, needed to know that something was constant in her life. She rang from the telephone exchange in the town. She would tell her mother that this had to be a short call. She would be in touch again. It was important not to break down in tears on the phone. Carol heard the familiar dialling tone, only three rings and her mother answered the phone in her familiar way, reciting the number, so that any caller would know straight away if they had dialled correctly.

'Mum, it's me,' she said quietly.

'Carol? Oh, thank goodness. Where are you? What on earth is wrong?' Carol's mother stopped herself. She didn't want to push, to take the chance that Carol would put the phone down.

'I'm alright.' It wasn't true. Her mother wouldn't believe her. She was trying to convince herself as much as anyone else. She didn't want her mother asking her lots of questions that she wasn't ready to answer or didn't know the answer to and so quickly continued.

'Things are not great between Tó Zé and me. I've been trying to sort it out, but I don't think it's possible. I'm not sure what I'm going to do, but I can't go back to Paris.'

'Come home, Carol. Whatever it is, we can sort it out,' her mother urged her gently.

'No, I've still got things to do here.' Carol insisted she needed to stay.

'Carol, I know you don't like us to interfere, but we were all so worried… your brother is in Portugal. We thought that was where you might be when we found out that Tó Zé went back.'

Carol felt a huge sense of relief. It was true. She had always hated the family's interference. She didn't know how on earth she was going to face everyone, feeling so stupid and used. However, for once it felt good that her brother was near. She didn't want to stay on the phone, making excuses about having to go and meet someone, but did give her mother the name and address of her hotel before hanging up.

'I don't know exactly where your brother is at the moment and I have to wait for him to contact me, so it could be a few days, but hang on in there. Nothing can be so bad that it can't be sorted out.'

'Not this one,' Carol thought, but didn't say it and hung up having promised to wait for her brother before doing anything else.

After her conversation with the Padre, Carol had to get away. She didn't know where, only that she couldn't stay. She packed her bag, checked out of the hotel and took the first bus out of the town without checking its destination. Madness, she thought, as the bus twisted its way, edging along the bottom of the mountains of the Serra da Lousã. When it reached Góis, she got off the bus, suddenly concerned that she needed to find somewhere else to stay for the night. It was there that she waited, for days and days, not knowing what to do, lost and unaware that Tom and Rebecca were so close by. Finally, she had given in and rung home. Now she waited again until she received the message that her brother had contacted her and left a number for his hotel in Coimbra.

Tom had stayed much longer than he could afford. His attempts and Rebecca's to find out more had come to nothing. He was ready to go back, knowing he would have to go home to see his parents, so they could decide what to do next. He was so relieved when he heard from his mother. When Carol rang, she said very little, only that she would come the next day to Coimbra. There was no point staying where she was.

## 28th June, 1974

Carol sat on a chair in Tom's hotel room staring straight ahead of her. She made no sound, but tears were running slowly down each cheek.

'What the hell has been going on, Carol? Why weren't you in touch with us? It's been weeks. Mum and Dad have been worried sick. I can't believe how inconsiderate you've been.' Tom's first reaction had been relief, but now he was with Carol, he was angry.

'I couldn't tell anyone. I had to know,' Carol said quietly, still staring into the space in front of her.

'We've always been able to talk. You could have been in touch. You could have asked me for help. When did running away solve anything?' Tom couldn't hide his exasperation.

'I didn't run away. I went to find out for myself,' she said.

'You came to a foreign country which you knew nothing about. You couldn't speak the language. You didn't tell anyone where you were going. You knew there were problems in the country. You didn't know what you were going to find.' Tom couldn't help himself, he continued to vent his frustration. 'What did you find out? Where is Tó Zé? The best I can find out is that he's not at home. He's probably in Lisbon and it's a big city. Without more information, you'll never find him. All you can do is wait to hear from him. It's so unlike him from what you've told us of him. There must be an explanation.' Tom didn't know what to say. Now he was speaking to fill the silence and distract his thoughts from Carol's tears.

'I don't know what I'm going to do. I only know that I'm not going back to Paris.' Carol ignored the mention of Tó Zé.

Carol was his elder sister and whilst others wouldn't have had him down as the most sensible of characters, this wasn't the first time that he felt much older and more responsible than Carol. It had irritated him how much grief she had caused over the years, always doing what she wanted to do, without thinking things through properly.

'I think it's about time you told me what is going on?' He snapped at her.

It was going to be much easier to tell her brother than her parents and so she started to tell him what she had found out.

'The fact is, I have been living with someone who I thought I knew, but I didn't. He had another life that I knew absolutely nothing about,' Carol began to explain, tears continuing to roll down her cheeks and finding it hard to get the words out.

'What do you mean? How could that be?' Tom didn't understand.

'He didn't come to Paris because he wanted to study.' Carol's explanation came slowly.

'He was at university in Paris, wasn't he?' Tom was trying to remember what he knew of Tó Zé.

'I don't know. I'm not sure now and if he had been at university, he had finished by the time I met him. As far as I was concerned, we had a great life together, I thought he loved me. He lied to me, he lied about everything.' She was sobbing now.

Tom didn't like to see his sister so distressed and tried to console her.

'He's not the first person to lie about his education. I know quite a few people who embellished their CV's.' Tom tried and failed to lighten the mood.

'It's not that, although I can't stand lies. If only it had been so simple. I found out before I came here that all the time I'd known him, he had secretly been part of a group in Paris, political activists, doing their best, from a distance, to support the resistance and all those who were working against the dictatorship here. I knew nothing about it. How could that have been?'

'I don't know much about the situation in Portugal, other than hearing reports about the revolution in April. I think it was fairly peaceful. I can't imagine he's been involved in anything you should be too worried about, but from what I can tell, there's a fair amount of confusion and unrest now.'

'But why didn't he tell me?' Carol wasn't interested in the revolution.

'I don't know what to say, Carol. I'd only be guessing, but don't you think he might have thought it safer not to involve you? I don't really know the guy but from everything you've said, I'm sure he loved you.' He tried to reassure her.

'So why hasn't he been in touch? He must know now that I've been looking for him,' she sobbed.

'I don't know, perhaps he needed to sort it out before he spoke to you. Maybe it was all more difficult than he'd imagined when he left.'

'Maybe he doesn't want to tell me that he's married and has a family and a whole different life in Portugal waiting for him to return.' She blurted it out.

'What do you mean, he's married?' It was the last thing that Tom expected to hear. 'How do you know that? Are you sure?'

'Yes, I'm sure, as sure as I need to be. I was staying in Pampilhosa, after I'd been to see if Tó Zé had returned home and I'd left my contact at a little café. A woman, his sister or someone's sister and the local priest came looking for me. The priest was able to speak English and he talked about a woman and a child. He assumed that I knew, as I was a friend of Tó Zé.'

'Did he refer to the woman as Tó Zé's wife?' Tom wasn't convinced. He was beginning to think that he needed to have a word with Rebecca to see if Clara knew anything about his past. Surely she would have said.

'I can't remember. I'm not sure whether he used the word, but it was so obvious, Tom.' Carol was now absolutely distraught. 'I can't go on, Tom. There's nothing left for me. What am I going to do? How can I ever believe anything about anyone again? I had no idea. I've been so stupid.'

'I think you're jumping to conclusions.' Tom wasn't at all convinced, but his priority now was to calm his sister down. He was beginning to think that the best thing he could do was to convince her that she needed to go home. He wasn't prepared to leave her in Portugal or in Paris for that matter, although she was adamant that she wasn't going back. He needed her to see sense. He couldn't stay any longer, either. He needed to get back.

'Let's get out for a while. The evening air will do you good and it's about time we had something to eat. I haven't had anything all day and I don't suppose you've been eating much. I'll speak with Rebecca while we're out and see what she can find out for us,' he suggested.

Speaking to Rebecca wasn't quite as easy as Tom had imagined, as she was no longer with Júlia's parents, the only telephone contact he had and of course, his Portuguese was non-existent. He hadn't wanted to worry Rebecca, but he thought it best to use the word urgent when he said he was trying to get in touch with her. Ring again in an hour was the instruction at the other end of the phone in broken English and so he hung up. He assumed he had been speaking with Júlia's mother. He had left Carol at the café and in her current state, he was pleased to see her still sitting there when he returned. Straight away, she wanted to know what Rebecca had to say and seeing her disappointment, he tried hard to reassure her that he would be able to speak with her that evening, something he wasn't convinced about himself. However, an hour later when he rang, Rebecca was waiting at the house and Júlia's mother handed her the phone as soon as she had confirmed that it was the Englishman who so urgently needed Rebecca.

It had been almost eight o'clock at night when Júlia's mother had knocked loudly and insistently on the door. She was very worried, but all she could tell her was that it was a man, he was English and it was urgent. That opened up several possibilities for Rebecca and her first thoughts were not for Tom, but for her family. She dashed back to the house with Júlia's mother and then the wait for the phone call seemed endless.

'What's wrong? Has something happened to Carol?' Rebecca asked with some relief that it was Tom who needed her urgently, then immediately was annoyed with herself for feeling relief. This might still be serious. 'Have you found her?'

'Yes, she's here with me in Coimbra, but I'm afraid she's really distressed and at the moment, I can't persuade her to come back with me. I'm sorry I had to worry you but I don't know what to do. We think Tó Zé is most likely to be in Lisbon, but Carol has no idea where or how to find him. It's a big city. She seems convinced that he's some kind of political activist. Would it be worth getting back to any of your friends at the radio station to see if they can look into it again? The thing is, I really need to get back. I can't spend the next, however many weeks, trying to find Carol's boyfriend. I've been here long enough, but I can't leave her either.'

Tom clearly was in a bit of a state himself and Rebecca wasn't sure how much help she could be. 'I can speak to Júlia again when she's at work tomorrow and see what she has to suggest but it could take some time.'

'I don't know what to do. Maybe if you were here, you could talk some sense into her,' Tom said.

Sometimes Rebecca said things and then wondered afterwards what had possessed her. The next suggestion she made was one of those occasions. 'I told your parents I would help all I can and I meant it. Carol can't do anything at the moment if she goes to Lisbon and, as I say, I'm not likely to find out anything more, even if I can, for a few days. Is she there with you now?'

Tom explained that she was waiting for him at the café and Rebecca asked him to go and get her and then ring back. She would wait for his call. When Tom put Carol on the phone, Rebecca knew that she would have difficulty in persuading her, but she had the advantage of not being one of the family and being able to be straight with her in a way that Tom couldn't be. It's strange how at times, we can be more inclined to listen to someone we hardly know rather than be persuaded by someone close. Somehow Rebecca managed to convince Carol that the best thing to do was not to go to Lisbon, paying for yet another hotel room which very soon she wouldn't be able to afford, but to come down to Vila Real de Santo António for a few days. It would give Rebecca's friends long enough to see what they could find out about where Tó Zé might be. Rebecca like Tom felt that Carol needed either to go back to Paris or if that were really impossible for her, then to go home to England, but Carol clearly needed some time to come to terms with everything she had found out.

'I know you might not feel like doing much, Carol, and this town is some way from Lisbon, but you could get back there in a day if you had to and there's some stunning scenery here. You could take some time out to think and even do some sketching. At least you'd be making good use of your time while you decide what to do next.' Carol was quiet at the end of the phone, so Rebecca continued to talk, saying how good it would be to have a visitor at her new house, describing the town. She paused and prompted Carol to speak, finally persuading her of the idea.

'Ok, thank you. It's kind of you. I'll come,' Carol said quietly, sounding resigned, but not completely convinced that it was the right thing to do.

'Put Tom back on the phone, then. I'll speak to him about how to get here. You don't sound as though you could take it all in at the moment. I'll give him a work phone number so that he can let me know your travel arrangements as soon as they are confirmed,' Rebecca suggested.

Tom hadn't expected Rebecca to help out in the way she did, but he was grateful.

'Are you sure?' he asked now feeling a little guilty.

'I'm sure,' Rebecca said, but had a moment of wondering what she had done. She stayed a little while to speak with Júlia's mother, feeling that she owed her an explanation. She was concerned to hear Carol's story, but she didn't seem too surprised, commenting that many people in Portugal had had to live their lives in ways which elsewhere, we might not fully understand.

Rebecca went back to the house and whilst it was fairly tidy, because that was the way she kept it, she fussed around for a while making sure everything was clean and in its place, anticipating that Carol could possibly arrive later the next day.

The next morning, Rebecca rang Júlia. As she had expected, Júlia said the best she could do was to ask around and have another word with Clara. As Clara hadn't come back with much last time, she was unsure there would be anything new. There were many people who were returning from exile, but unless they were well-known, it would be hard to track them down. His wasn't a name she knew, but Clara had recognised it, so there was still a chance she could find out more. Rebecca told her not to worry, because she was only ringing to be seen to be doing something. The best thing for Carol to do was to get back to some kind of normality. It had happened. It was dreadful. Rebecca, like everyone else, was angry with Tó Zé, but she felt the only option Carol had was to get on with her life as best she could. If she really couldn't go back to Paris, then she had to go home or start again somewhere. When she had spoken to Tom to make the arrangements, she had made it clear that her intention in getting Carol out of Coimbra and away from Lisbon was just that. She suggested that as soon as he got back, he had a word with the family and they gave some thought as to what Carol would do next. Rebecca was hoping to get her into a more receptive frame of mind. She said that she could stay for a week and Tom agreed that, even though his place wasn't big enough for guests, Carol would then go to him if she couldn't go back to Paris. A good plan, Rebecca had thought. As it turned out, Carol didn't arrive the next day, giving her a little more time. Tom had wanted Carol to stay with him in Coimbra until he had everything in place, including his own journey back to the south of France.

For the first few days, all that Carol wanted to do was talk. She was heartbroken. Her conversation was confused, emotional and repetitive. As Rebecca listened, she was struck by how little Carol had found out and how much she was assuming and imagining. Whatever the real story was, Tó Zé had lied. He had not been in touch for many weeks. It was unforgiveable. The days passed. Carol seemed to become calmer and more willing to get out and do things. Rebecca loved walking and it was good to have a companion. It allowed her to explore some of the longer, more remote routes which she hadn't been prepared to explore on her own. One day, they walked across the countryside behind the town, picking their way through the salt plains to Castro Marim. Another, they went further along the beach and back through the woods nearby. They walked in the early morning or into the late afternoon and evening to avoid the full heat of the sun and to take advantage of the changing light. Rebecca took her camera and Carol her sketch book. Rebecca was pleased when Carol began to talk enthusiastically about her work again and to talk about the possibility of another exhibition. Surely she could move on, Rebecca thought. It would take time, but she was so talented and whilst Carol wouldn't be able to see it for a long time, there would be someone else. By the end of the week, she was still adamant that she was not going back to Paris. She had left the apartment and the city for good. Rebecca knew that. She had seen the apartment, the way Carol had left it and now she understood. She had known then it was over. Carol couldn't be persuaded by her friends in Paris to return. The job wasn't a draw at all, although she was sorry that she had left without an explanation. However, Rebecca did convince her to stay with Tom for a while. She booked the tickets for her at the train station and travelled as far as Faro with her, still a little concerned that it would be far too tempting for her to break her journey in Lisbon.

# XXIX

**September, 1974**

João hadn't expected an immediate reply, but as the days wore on, he thought it unlikely that he would hear again from Rebecca, so when a letter appeared for him with a Vila Real de Santo António postmark, he was very pleased. His mother was, as ever, curious.

'You have a letter. I don't recognise the handwriting.'

He feigned lack of interest. 'I'll have a look at it after dinner.'

So his mother tried a little harder. 'Who's it from?'

'I'm not sure.' Though his statement was true, he didn't know who it was from, it was unlikely to be anyone else. 'It can't be anything important or they would have telephoned. I'll look at it later.' He resisted the temptation to take it from the hall table and went upstairs to get ready for dinner.

It was late that evening, therefore, when he got to open the letter and he went straight to the signature. Yes, it was from Rebecca and for a second or two, he hesitated in reading it, because he wanted it to be encouraging and he wasn't sure it would be.

Rebecca had given her reply some thought and had taken her time, but when she did sit down to write, she was a lot more relaxed about it than when she had first spoken with Maria Eduarda. Events had taken over. Carol's experience had put hers into perspective. She hardly knew João, she reminded herself, and then resisted the voice which was telling her she had known him forever. She chastised herself, determined now not to over think either his reasons for writing or her reply.

*Dear João,*

*Thank you for your letter. I'm sorry that it's taken me a while to reply, but I've been pretty busy since I got back to Vila Real.*

The letter continued in similar chatty style. She made no assumptions that he would know any of her news. She told him about meeting up with her old friends, smiled to herself as she mentioned Ricardo and left out the detail that he was now married and his wife had become a good friend. She told him about the house, the job and how much she was enjoying it. She then told him about Carol and was strong in her opinion of Tó Zé's betrayal, whatever his reasons. Then, finally, she wrote about what a good social life she was developing, dinners out, the cinema, concerts with friends and how happy she was. João read to the end and wondered what to make of it. She gave nothing away either as she ended in the letter.

*It sounds as though you're enjoying your time between England and here and that you still feel you have made the right decision.*

*Lovely to hear from you.*

*Love, Rebecca.*

That was it. A newsy letter. It was all he had and at least she had replied. He picked up a pen and started to write without any thought this time about why he was writing or whether it was a good idea. He wanted to write. He replied in the same friendly way, talking about his work and his new nephew. He didn't care that he was replying quickly. Now that he had heard from her, he had to pursue it. Rebecca, in her turn, although careful not to be too keen in her replies, was happy to be in touch and so began their correspondence, and it continued in the same friendly way. For João, the letters and the time that he spent writing them began to have more and more significance. It was his way of being with Rebecca. His feelings for her grew the more he felt the distance and the more he felt the distance the more he missed her, feeling it as an almost insurmountable problem. They were too far away from each other and she was happy without him. The regret of leaving so abruptly grew, along with the feeling that he had missed his chance. He began to feel jealous, sure that she must be involved with someone else but was choosing not to tell him. He could ask her to visit. He considered the possibility, but he had no privacy at home and to invite a young woman home would have real significance for the family. He needed to think of another way for her to visit or he had to go and see her. For a mad moment, he considered asking her to pretend she was interested in some aspect of the port trade. He thought about suggesting that they have another weekend away, but he didn't imagine that she would agree. She was an independent woman but nothing about her suggested that she would risk her reputation and he wouldn't want that either. He wondered if Rui could organise a weekend in Lisbon and invite Rebecca, but the harvest was approaching and it was not the time to be away from the estate.

João wrote often, not waiting for replies, telling himself that she was probably busier than he was. There was little to do in the evening on the estate. He missed city life. He missed the company, but above all, he missed Rebecca, missed everything about her and couldn't get her out of his mind.

As his aunt had cautioned him, it wasn't long before his mother was worried. He couldn't hide the letters, at least the replies. He was dismissive when she asked, saying he was keeping in touch with friends. She was concerned that he was lonely and was afraid to ask, not wanting to hear that he couldn't settle at home. She wanted to help and was unsure how to until one evening, unable to concentrate on the book she was reading, an idea came to her. It wouldn't just be for João either, they all needed something to look forward to. The next morning, when everyone was having breakfast, she made a suggestion.

'I've been thinking. I know things are uncertain. We're not sure the harvest this year will bring the best vintage, so even more reason to give everyone on the estate a lift. Let's invite some friends to celebrate the harvest, organise a festival for everyone.'

Her husband wasn't convinced, but once his wife was fixed on an idea, there was no stopping her. 'I'm far too busy to think about it, Maria João. It will be a lot of pressure on you and you can't expect much help from Céu this year.'

'I'll help out as much as I can.' João was quick to see it as a possible answer to his problem. 'I assume it's alright if I invite a few friends.'

'Of course,' his mother said, smiling at him and feeling pleased now with her suggestion.

That evening, he rang Rui and after a couple of phone calls, established that Rui, Júlia and importantly in João's thinking, a good friend, Paulo were all able to come. João was open with Rui.

'I really want Rebecca to come, but I don't want my mother getting any ideas. I'm going to write to her this evening, but can you ask Júlia to help out if Rebecca needs persuading?' João asked.

'I knew you were taken with Rebecca.' Rui was amused and said he would help if he could.

Rebecca was enjoying João's letters, even though she was determined not to seem too keen in her replies. When the letter arrived, the invitation was a surprise. Despite his newsy letters, he had always been rather circumspect about home. João enthused about the celebration. He said that harvest time was the best time of year to visit, an event which a self-confessed lusophile couldn't miss and had to add to her experiences of her year in Portugal. He invited her for the weekend, acknowledged that it was a long journey, but said that Rui and Júlia were going and she could travel with them from Lisbon.

'It's harvest time. A great time of year up there.' Maria Eduarda had commented when she mentioned the invite to her. 'I think you should go. It's not an experience that everyone can say they've had and it seems that they're organising quite a celebration. It is significant that he's asked you there, too. I wonder what he's said to the family.'

Rebecca didn't take much persuading, but tried to convince Maria Eduarda that she was going because there might not be such a good opportunity again to visit the north while she was over and it would be great to see the harvest celebrations. She got in touch with Júlia who was really pleased she was going and arranged to stay over with her to break up the journey. When the weekend came, she took the early morning train to have plenty of time in Lisbon. On the way to the station, she called at the bakery, which was open early as usual. She bought some food for the journey, a 'Pão de Deus', 'Bread of God', a soft white roll with a delicious custard and coconut filling and a bottle of orange juice which she intended to have for breakfast as soon as the train was on its way north. She also bought a 'merenda', her favourite soft bready pastry with layers of ham and cheese, a kind of ready-made sandwich. She had developed a taste for them in Lisbon, and of course, she had to get one of her favourite custard tarts too, fresh from the morning oven and still warm. She smiled at herself walking out of the bakery. How easily she was pleased these days. She felt very happy. This time, there was only a short wait in Faro for the connection to Lisbon. She sat down, carefully choosing a window seat. She unpacked her breakfast and took out the book which she had brought for the journey, but was content with her thoughts and the scenery as it steamed past the window. She never tired of it. As she ate her breakfast roll, the book remained unopened on the table in front of her.

The next morning, Júlia and Rebecca met Rui, and to Rebecca's surprise, his friend, Paulo at the station for the journey to Oporto. Júlia had assumed that Rebecca knew Paulo was coming too. The introductions over, they caught the train north. The journey passed quickly, as they chatted about work and life in Lisbon and in Vila Real and of course, the visit to the estate. Everyone else had been before and was excited to be returning to such a beautiful place. Rebecca was going to love it, they were sure.

As they alighted the train and walked down the platform, Rebecca was the first to hear João calling to them, struck, for an instance, by how familiar his voice was. When she saw his beaming smile, she felt a wave of happiness seeing him again, the lingering irritation at his behaviour the last time they were together dissolving into the warm early afternoon air. João greeted everyone before turning to her, a kiss on each cheek. She would never tire of the greeting, but somehow, it troubled her that he hadn't turned to her first of all.

'Come on, give me your bag, we need to get our connection,' he said to Rebecca and hurried everyone along.

Rebecca hadn't thought about the final leg of her journey that day, other than to reflect that it would be a route she hadn't journeyed before. The others hadn't mentioned it, as they were sure she would be impressed and wanted it to be a surprise. As the train made its way along the river, beginning to cut through the hills, Rebecca, like so many travellers before her, was struck by the beauty of the landscape. The scene kept her in silence for much of the journey, as the others continued to chat. João didn't disturb her. He sat opposite her in the carriage and as he talked with his friends, he watched her, sitting quietly looking at the scenery. He knew it was making its impression on her. He was happy she was there and he felt proud seeing her gentle reaction. For Rebecca, each mile of the journey was to make the strongest impression and she was no less captivated when they arrived at the little station, decorated with its beautiful tiles. She hadn't known what to expect of the estate and João's home. She thought that it might be considerable, but wasn't prepared for its grandeur and the extent of the quinta. João pointed out the estate's land to her as they made their way on the final part of the journey that day, the sun setting and darkness drawing in. This time her silence hid a concern that this was all too overwhelming. She felt a little anxious and wasn't sure why.

Paulo was a good friend and had been briefed. Aside from anything else, João knew he would be busy hosting the celebrations and there was a lot to do on the estate that weekend. He wanted to be sure that Rebecca enjoyed her visit and would feel welcome. Paulo was to be her escort and João had planned the weekend carefully. The grapes were picked by hand on the estate, the work beginning each year in mid-September and now this year's harvest was coming to a close. The following morning, the friends travelled up onto the terraces to see the last of the fruit being picked. The grapes were being loaded into huge wicker baskets carried down the steep hillsides, balanced on the shoulders of strong, wiry men and held firm by leather straps secured across the forehead. It was heavy work made lighter by it being the final day and the promise of a party.

João had told them that he was going to be busy elsewhere for most of the day and it was early afternoon before Rebecca saw him again. He came walking up the steep terraces towards them. He wasn't alone. He was with a young woman, the same age, Rebecca thought. They were chatting as they walked and were happy and relaxed. Everyone else seemed to know her and Júlia, realising that Rebecca didn't know Ana Rita, introduced them to each other. João said he was keen that Rebecca saw all of the process and suggested it was time to go back. He and Ana Rita led them down through the terraces to the winery to see the grapes being placed in wide, deep granite tanks where they were being trodden by foot. As they approached, Rebecca could hear the sounds of chanting and singing, music and the aroma of grape juice, mixing in the air. Those treading the wine – all men, she noted – had linked arms and were walking in a tight line, moving very slowly, shoulder pressed to shoulder, as they paced across the tank, thigh-high in grapes. João explained that this was the first stage of the treading, releasing the juice and the pulp from the grape skins. When that was done, she would see them break the line and start to move freely around the tank, making sure that the grape skins stayed under the surface. He showed her the long wooden plungers that they used to push the skins down into the wine. Fermentation would take several hours. It was hard, laborious work, but so important to the quality of the port wine. He introduced her to the wine maker who he said would give the signal for the fermentation process to start. He was quite the tour guide now.

'When he signals, the treading will stop and then the skins are allowed to rise back to the surface. They'll form a solid layer and then afterwards, the fermenting wine gets drawn off into vats. That's when we add the brandy, very good quality brandy.'

Rebecca was enjoying the atmosphere and was happy to be with him. Paulo was great company, but it was João's attention that she really wanted. 'What happens next to the wine?' she asked.

'This wine will stay here until the spring and then it'll be transported to our lodge down river on the coast. That's where we mature the wine and bottle it.'

'Do you still use the boats? They look so beautiful on the river.' Rebecca had seen them as they had left Oporto.

'No. The rebelos were used until around the middle of this century, but the last ones finished sailing about ten years ago. I remember them as a child. Nowadays we transport all the wine overland by road,' João explained.

The group of friends made their way back to the house to get ready for the evening. Once Rebecca was alone with Júlia, she asked her, 'Who is Ana Rita?'

'She was João's girlfriend for many years, from being very young. In fact, she was his only girlfriend. They were going to get married before he went to London and then João backed out suddenly. Ana Rita was very hurt at the time, but they seem to be fine now. Has João never mentioned her?'

'No, never,' Rebecca said feeling uneasy.

As they got ready, Júlia told her what she knew about Ana Rita. Rebecca began to wonder if she had never really understood João's attentions.

The last load of grapes had arrived in the trailer by early evening. The family and their guests gathered at the house for drinks and to relax for a while. It was to be a long evening for everyone. Grapes were now being trodden in three of the large tanks; the work couldn't stop, even though the celebrations were underway around them.

The evening wore on, happy, good fun, busy and noisy. João's aunt was watching from a distance, enjoying the music, the chanting and the laughter. She was people watching. She felt a little tired now. She had been dancing too, but the wine and food were beginning to slow her down. In her usual quiet and understated way, she had circulated amongst the guests, keen to search out Rebecca and know more about her. Now, she was sitting quietly. She didn't need to join in, happy to watch.

Seeing João on his own, she waved to him and he joined her.

'So that's the young woman,' she said, nodding over in her direction. Rebecca was standing by one of the tanks watching the treading with Paulo. 'I like her, João. You haven't spent much time with her today.'

'I've been fairly busy and I made sure my guests were entertained. Paulo has been great with Rebecca. They've had a good day,' João replied, watching Rebecca.

'What are you worried about, João?' His aunt knew that he always complicated things and it rarely helped him.

'I'm not worried. It's not straight forward. I don't know what I'll be doing. We're so far away from each other. She seems happy and though she doesn't speak much about the past, there's some sadness there. I've hurt enough people. She deserves more than the complications I would bring. I don't have enough to offer her.' João was thinking aloud, trying to understand himself. 'I needed to see her, but I didn't want my mother to get any ideas when I don't know what I can do or what Rebecca might want.'

'You shouldn't worry about your mother. That's an easy one to resolve, but don't let Rebecca get away too easily. Go and talk to her.'

After a little while, João walked over to Rebecca, taking her another drink.

'Thank you. I think I've probably had enough. I could do with cooling down, though,' Rebecca said. João suggested they went for a walk.

They wandered away from the celebrations, the music and laughter fading.

'I'm sorry I haven't been able to spend much time with you all, but I'm really pleased you came, Rebecca. I wanted you to see this place.'

Out there in those remote hills, the night was as dark as any Rebecca had seen and the night sky was flooded with stars. She remembered as a child how her father had taught her about the different constellations. 'It's beautiful.' Rebecca said. 'You're very lucky. Such a fantastic landscape and sense of history, centuries of belonging. I envy you.'

'It's a bit of a contrast from London,' João said lightly, mismatching her mood.

'There's no comparison. I don't share your fondness for London. For me, it's a dangerous place. I wouldn't be able to go there without worrying that someone has planted another bomb. I know it's silly. Yes, there's lots to do and see, museums, theatre, but it's not for me,' Rebecca said seriously.

'I didn't see it that way. There was fear here too, a different fear. In London, I felt I could escape and think differently,' João explained.

Rebecca tried to understand. 'I suppose it's different for me. I'm a visitor and can return anytime. I don't fully understand the situation over here and the pressures and constraints. Will you have to join the army if you stay?'

'Very likely. It will be a while before that situation in Africa is resolved and none of us are exempt from conscription. You'll still write to me if I have to go?' João asked.

'Of course.'

João took Rebecca by the hand and they walked slowly back to the winery. As they began to emerge into the light, João gently dropped her hand and they joined the others.

The next day, as the friends needed to get back for work, they packed their bags after breakfast and João gave them a lift to the station. This time, he didn't travel to Oporto with them, explaining that he had work to do that day.

As he said good-bye to Rebecca, kissing her on each cheek, he smiled and said quietly, 'I'll write soon.'

# XXX

**March, 1975**

One day, there was a different letter from Vila Real de Santo António, but this time, it was addressed to the whole family. João's mother had opened it when the post arrived late morning and could hardly wait to tell everyone when they came back to the house at the end of the day. João and his father walked in together and hearing them in the hallway, she went to speak with them straight away.

'We've had a letter from the Costa family. I had no idea. I knew there was a possibility, but he didn't say anything when he was here in September. Did you know, João?' It was her opening statement and João and his father looked at each other, a little confused as to what she might be talking about. They were used to her beginning a story part way through.

'You're going to have to help us out a little with this one, mother,' João said. 'Who are you talking about?'

Then she explained that they had all been invited to Rui and Júlia's wedding. 'I love a wedding,' she said.

João wondered why Rui hadn't mentioned it to him, but it had been a while since they had spoken and Rui liked surprises. He knew how strongly he felt about Júlia. He had moved to Lisbon to be with her all those months ago. They had to get married if they wanted to live together. Neither family would have wanted it any other way, but João knew that wasn't a problem. They wouldn't have felt pressured. It was the right thing to do and it would work out for them, he felt sure. They were good together. As he was pondering Rui and Júlia's relationship and thinking about the wedding, he realised that it was very likely to be in Vila Real de Santo António, their home town. He wouldn't have missed it wherever it was, but now he was feeling as enthusiastic about the prospect of a wedding as his mother had been.

'Where is it being held? I'm assuming it must be in Vila Real. What's the date?' he asked, trying not to sound too eager.

'Yes, it's in Vila Real de Santo António, in about a month's time, so quite soon,' his mother said, opening the envelope and checking the invitation again.

'That doesn't give us much time to make arrangements. I wonder why it's happening so quickly,' his father said.

'I don't know, but I'm sure there's nothing more in it. I know them well and they wouldn't want to wait once they had decided. They want to be together,' João explained. 'Rui has moved to Lisbon to be with Júlia, but they've been living apart and where's the sense in having two apartments? They love each other, always have. I don't know about the rest of you, but I'm certainly going.'

João's father approved that Rui had been mindful of the family's reputation and said so. 'Of course we'll all go. The estate can do without us for a few days, we're not too busy at this time of year. We'll make a little holiday of it. We could do with a break. What do you think, Maria João? I haven't been able to get to the Algarve for quite some time. It will be good to be there again and catch up with the Costas.'

'Great, it's decided then. I'll speak with your brother and sister. I'm sure they'll want to come,' his mother said, as she headed towards the kitchen. 'I'll see if dinner is ready. I don't know about the rest of you, but I'm hungry and we can talk about arrangements over dinner.'

João went upstairs to get changed. He was happy. He was thinking about Rebecca. She was sure to be invited. He began to wish that he was going on his own. Being with the family would make it awkward and he would need time to talk to her. He didn't know how she felt about him.

They had stayed in touch since her visit in September and the friendly, frequent letters gave him some hope. His feelings for Rebecca hadn't changed. In fact, they had only grown stronger as the weeks had passed by. He missed her. He imagined what his aunt would say to him. She hadn't been able to understand when he tried to explain back in September, but Rebecca had seemed so happy and settled in the south. He was committed to the estate and the future was uncertain. He hadn't been able to see a solution, so he had said nothing, done nothing. Now, at least, he had a reason to see her again and soon. As the thoughts went round in his mind, João, as he always did, was focussing on the complications. He hadn't talked to the family about Rebecca. He had deliberately presented her as one of his friends in September and had kept what he thought was an appropriate distance. He hadn't wanted them to interfere and he wasn't ready to tell them now. How stupid would it seem when he then had to explain that Rebecca probably had no idea how he felt? Add to that the fact that she was English and his mother was likely to conclude that he would want to return to England permanently. Even if he could convince them that Rebecca might be interested in settling in Portugal, her work was hundreds of miles away in the Algarve. No, he wanted her to be happy. It was all too complicated.

For some reason, he decided that he wouldn't tell Rebecca that he was going to the wedding, unless she asked. He didn't know exactly why, perhaps he liked the idea of a surprise, but he wasn't sure how much time he would be able to spend with her. The family was having a few days away together and that would bring certain expectations. He didn't want to make arrangements which would be difficult to keep. He needed to think it through before he said anything, see what happened in Vila Real. He had been too evasive every time he had seen Rebecca. This time he was determined to be different when he was with her. He just wasn't sure how.

Rebecca was at home, having finished work at lunchtime. Maria Eduarda was in town and had called to see her.

'I have an invite to Rui and Júlia's wedding. It will be my first Portuguese wedding and it occurred to me that in all the months I've been here, I haven't seen a wedding at the church in the town square. I'm really looking forward to it, but I could do with some help choosing what to wear and knowing what to expect,' Rebecca said to Maria Eduarda, as she was bringing them both a drink up on to her little terrace.

'I don't think you'll find them much different from weddings in England. I thought you didn't like weddings. So, what's the attraction of this one?' Maria Eduarda said and then offered a possible answer to her own question. 'Ah, you're thinking that João might be invited too.'

'That has nothing to do with it. It's another experience of the life and culture that I'm here this year to enjoy, and do you know? Being here has changed my attitude to a lot of things. I love this little house and I've started to think about how wonderful it would be if I could own one like it, my own little part of Portugal.'

'Why not?' Maria Eduarda said, wondering where this was taking her. Rebecca continued,

'I love it here and I feel so different. I'm coming to realise that I have spent a lifetime with views and opinions that have only got in the way of my happiness and in the way of simply enjoying life for what it is. I don't know what it's about really, some kind of an attempt to protect myself from disappointment or some bizarre form of self-sabotage. It would probably take years of therapy to untangle it,' she joked, laughing at the thought, 'but here, I feel I can leave that all behind.'

'Goodness me, quite the revelation... but I still say it probably has more to do with João than anything else,' Maria Eduarda teased her.

'It's been lovely getting letters from him. I had wondered what on earth was going on with him when he left Coimbra and I was still no clearer when I went in September. Now I feel that I have a good friend, albeit at a distance. It's great to keep in touch with him. We're not likely to see that much of each other, because we're so far away and long distance relationships have never worked for me. I end up feeling hurt and abandoned. I'm pretty sure that he's with someone. He still seemed close to Ana Rita.'

'Why would he bother writing if that were the case?' Maria Eduarda genuinely couldn't imagine any other reason for him to stay in touch other than because he was very fond of her and still held out some hope. 'No girlfriend would be happy with him writing to someone else and certainly not as often as he writes to you, sometimes two or three times a week.'

'I'm English and he's wanting to keep all his connections. I don't think he knows what he wants to do. He still might go back there permanently,' was Rebecca's explanation.

'He'd been in London quite a while. Didn't you say he had lots of friends over there?' Maria Eduarda tried a different approach. 'You should follow your new found philosophy and take it for what it is?'

'Sounds like a good idea,' Rebecca concluded and then suggested that when they had finished their drinks, they could go into town and see what the shops had to offer in the way of a suitable dress for the wedding.

Rebecca did want to look really nice for the wedding. She had even gone to the unusual extent of having her hair done at the hairdressers, which was a bit of a risk in her thinking. Other women seemed to love having their hair cut, but not Rebecca. There were so many things she would rather do than go to the hairdressers. In fact, she would avoid going until she had to. She put it down to two disastrous haircuts when she was a teenager. Those digs and comments from so-called school friends left deep impressions. However, today, she felt good. She had had to travel to Faro in the end to find a dress that suited her. It was a deep, bright blue of course, her favourite colour, a simple dress but not her usual style of a shift dress. This one was fitted into the waist and had a flared skirt, a little Audrey Hepburn, 'Breakfast at Tiffany's' thing going on. For once in her life, as she walked down the street towards the town square, she was feeling elegant. She was looking forward to the day and was determined that nothing was going to spoil her good mood and enjoyment. On that early April day, the sun was without its intense summer heat, but it still seemed very warm, like late spring or early summer in England, she thought. She walked into the square and found that it was already busy with people. She assumed they must be guests, as they were in what her grandmother would have described as their 'Sunday Best' and they were standing in groups near the church. As she looked around, she saw others were sitting in the cafés around the edge of the square. Even today they needed that little sugary hit of caffeine. As she approached the church, she could see a group of men talking together by the doorway, all looking very smart and elegant in their suits. She recognised only Rui amongst them, couldn't see anyone else she knew and hesitated before she approached the 'men only' gathering. She smiled. Rebecca could never resist pushing at any convention, and so went over to join them, to say hello to Rui and see how he was feeling. He was in a great mood, so obviously happy. He introduced her to his friends, though she was sure she wouldn't remember their names later. Most people were still outside the church, enjoying the sunshine. Rebecca took her leave of the group. She wanted to get a seat in the church before it was too full, feeling a little self-conscious on her own, the only one, as far as she could tell. She looked around for a good position where she could see the other guests, anyone she knew and to have the best view of the ceremony. This was a nuptial mass and she'd never been to one before, not even in England.

João didn't mention the wedding in his letters and for some reason, she hadn't either. She had been sure that he would have been invited and that he would want to be there. When she heard nothing, she wondered if he was busy on the estate and it was too far to come. Rui and Júlia had arrived late the night before from Lisbon. Even if Rebecca had been able to see them, they had promised João they wouldn't tell her he was coming, wanting to be in on his surprise. Rebecca took a seat near the back of the church, slightly to one side, a good place to see everything. She was surprised to find so few people inside and checked the time, only five minutes to go, but it wasn't long before the church began to fill up. She watched as the guests entered, interested particularly to see how everyone was dressed and how like a British wedding it was, reassuring herself that she was suitably dressed within the convention. Her choice was fine. If anything, it was much less flamboyant than some of the other outfits, but that suited her. She looked around for people she might know. It wasn't easy being there on her own when everyone else seemed to be with family and friends. It was going to take a little effort to push through her natural shyness and the awkwardness she felt. She knew Júlia's family, of course, but they were busy attending to all their guests. This was certainly a grand affair. All the town's well known figures were there. Deep in her own thoughts, trying to remember the name of the town's deputy as he passed by with his wife, Rebecca almost missed him. It was a brief moment of recognition, disturbing her contemplation. Had she glimpsed João? She looked again. It could be someone similar. No, sure enough, it was João. She felt a rush of emotion which she hadn't expected at all and steadied herself, wondering why he hadn't told her. Who was he with? – His mother and father, his brother, Pedro and his wife, Céu carrying the baby. João was following them with another young woman. For a second, Rebecca felt tense, then realised it was his sister. As they moved to sit down, she noticed how attentive he was to her, his hand gently held in the small of her back, guiding her into the row of seats, following the rest of the family. As she watched, there was a feeling which cut deep. João was like that with everyone; he was courteous, he was considerate. She had misunderstood him, she thought. At least she would be able to tell Maria Eduarda that she had been wrong.

The ceremony was long and formal. She followed it carefully and noticed with a smile that it didn't seem to be customary for some of the male guests to stay throughout. They wandered in and out of the back door of the church close to where she was sitting, checking how much longer there was before the reception. It's always such a cliché to say that every bride looks beautiful on her wedding day, but Rebecca thought that Júlia looked particularly stunning in an ivory gown, a long train and flowing veil. As the bride and groom began to move down the aisle, leaving the church at the end of the service, some of the guests moved outside, so they could be there to see the couple leave the church or in the case of some of the men, to go and get another beer, Rebecca thought. She wasn't ready to speak to João, so she quickly joined those who were leaving ahead of the couple and melded into the crowd outside. She emerged into bright sunshine to see an open topped carriage, pulled by a grey horse and attended by a driver in traditional costume. Quite a crowd had gathered now to see the couple leaving the church. As photographs were being taken, Rebecca managed to have a quick word with Júlia's parents who were really pleased to see her and she began to feel a little more a part of the day. Everyone seemed happy and the mood was infectious.

The photographs over and the bride and groom on their way, the wedding party began to walk slowly towards the reception venue, which wasn't far from the town square. Rebecca stayed with Júlia's family and as they moved inside, Júlia's mother spoke to her,

'I don't suppose you know many people here, Rebecca, but don't worry.'

She guided her towards one of the tables and Rebecca felt a rush of embarrassment for a moment. It was a large table, set for twelve people, most of whom were already seated. As Júlia's mother approached the table, she announced,

'I'd like to introduce our good friend Rebecca to all of you, as she's here on her own. I thought this would be a good group for her to join, as she has already met some of you and I know that you'll all make her very welcome. João, you'll be happy to take care of Rebecca, of course, won't you?' Júlia's mother directed Rebecca to the seat next to João. They now had to speak. João stood up quickly and as if there was nothing more natural to him, he greeted her and then moved the chair out so that she could sit down.

'Lovely to see you, Rebecca,' he said, and really meant it. He didn't miss the look on his mother's face, nor would have anyone else, and so João was pleased that at that moment, everyone was looking towards Rebecca. As he sat down again, his mother shot him an enquiring look, which he ignored. Yes, she had met Rebecca in the party of friends who João invited for the harvest, but what was Júlia's mother inferring? She watched him carefully. She knew her son. She knew that look. He was very much taken with Rebecca, she thought and noticed how attentive he was to her as the meal was underway. She was pleased, then, when her daughter asked the question which was on her own mind. She hadn't felt she could ask it, not wanting to irritate her son. It was a question better coming from Inês. João wouldn't mind so much.

'It's a pleasure to see you again, Rebecca. We didn't get a lot of chance to speak properly when you visited. It was such a busy time for us. How did you and João meet?'

Rebecca felt all eyes on her. She had also noticed his mother's look when she had been introduced and realised, with some irritation, but with a certain resignation that João couldn't have talked much about her. As she was collecting herself and wondering where to start and how much to say, João intervened.

'We're forgetting our manners. Rebecca doesn't know everyone here, I don't think it's fair to interrogate her. Take no notice of my sister, Rebecca. She's not usually so direct.' And then he continued, purposely addressing his comments to the whole table rather than to the family. 'Rebecca is one of my English friends, from the north of England. We met on a train journey and we have kept in touch ever since. It's a bit of a long story and quite a coincidence, but it then turned out that Rebecca was also a friend of Júlia. Neither of us had any idea at the time we met that we had a mutual friend. It's strange how things work out.'

He felt that he had said enough for the time being and changed the subject, conscious also that Rebecca was looking a little tense with all the attention.

His mother was quiet for a while, now connecting the letter writing with Rebecca. Not liking surprises where her son was concerned, she was annoyed with herself for not having been more curious about the letters. Her greatest concern was that Rebecca was English and it wasn't long before she couldn't hold back any longer, despite João's attempts to keep the conversation away from Rebecca.

'Your Portuguese is very good, Rebecca. Have you spent much time in Portugal?'

Rebecca was feeling more relaxed. João had stepped in and helped her with the difficult question. This was a subject she loved to talk about, her natural enthusiasm for Portugal and the language taking over as she explained. João was happy that his mother's question had, perhaps, inadvertently, taken the conversation away from his relationship with Rebecca. As Rebecca talked with her usual ease when asked those kinds of questions, he noticed that his mother was becoming as enchanted by Rebecca's passion as he had been when he had first met her. He began to feel more relaxed. Since the invitation had arrived, he had been thinking a great deal about how this day might be and how he would manage to spend time with Rebecca. He needn't have worried. For now at least, he was with her and she was charming his mother, even better.

João couldn't take his eyes off Rebecca, even though he tried his best to show interest in all the conversations around the table. While Rebecca was speaking with his mother, Céu took the opportunity to speak to João and her comments disarmed him.

'She's lovely, João. Why didn't you say anything when she visited and why haven't you spoken to us about her?'

He spoke quietly, not wanting to be overheard and surprised himself with how open he was in his reply. 'I've liked her from our very first meeting. I don't think she has any idea how I feel about her, but it's my fault. I never handle these situations very well. I've been so unsure about the future and I made some wrong assumptions about her. I've been looking for a way back in ever since.'

'It looks to me as though you might have an opportunity this weekend to put things right. You need to speak to her,' she suggested.

'I don't know what she's up to now. She may be with someone.' He lowered his voice further, wanting to talk, but conscious now that his brother had become interested in his wife's comments.

'He would be here with her. Júlia would have suggested she bring someone with her. You know how family centred weddings are. She wouldn't be on her own, I'm sure, if there was someone else. I thought she was seeing Paulo.'

João thought that Céu was probably right and decided it was better not to try to explain about Paulo. He didn't reply.

As the meal came to an end, the guests started to get up from the tables, gradually at first, beginning to circulate, catching up with friends and family. Not wanting to be the last one to move and feeling she needed a break, Rebecca decided to go to the ladies. As she moved away, João thought to follow her, not knowing where she was going and a little concerned that she might be leaving, though he didn't know why. He smiled at her and then for a minute or two remained at the table talking to his brother, not wanting to make it too obvious. He had one or two brief exchanges with some of Rui's friends as he moved across the room, keeping his eye on the exit where he assumed he would be able to catch Rebecca. He was trying to think what to say, but nothing that was coming into his head seemed quite right. Then there was Rebecca coming towards him, making her way back towards the table. As she noticed him, she smiled.

'Do you want to get some fresh air? I thought I'd have a walk and try to wake up a little. I'm feeling a bit lethargic with all that food and drink.' He wanted to get out of the way of any interested eyes.

'Yes, that would be good. I could do with a break. It's hard work keeping conversations going when you don't know many people.'

They walked out and back towards the town square, then crossed over towards the river, heading down to the river mouth and the wide open expanse of the Atlantic beyond, calm and deep blue. João was in a good mood and did most of the talking, reminiscing about the times he had spent in the town as a child and telling her about some of the antics that he and Rui had got up to. They walked past the riverside taverns and he pointed out his favourite and said he would take her there one day soon. When they could walk no further, they stopped to watch the fishermen preparing their small boats for a night's fishing and to observe others on the riverside casting their fishing lines far into the river and waiting patiently. João motioned towards a small bench and they went to sit down where they could continue to look out beyond the river mouth to the sea. The sun was beginning to go down, casting a deep orange glow across the sky. Rebecca would often come and sit there, thinking and watching, taking photographs. Each time she came it was different, she explained enthusiastically to João. She loved that spot she told him and the town. It was such an elegant town with its well-ordered buildings in their distinctive white and grey colours. She loved her little house. She wanted to own one like it one day, she said. João listened intently. He loved being with her. As he listened, slowly but with an increasing strong hold, he became overwhelmed by a feeling that if he didn't act, he might lose his chance.

'Rebecca,' he said interrupting her, 'I've something I have to say to you.'

Rebecca, woken from her own musings, felt unnerved. She had been so comfortable with him, as they had walked along. This sounded important. Now she wondered if he was about to say something which would spoil everything. She never knew what to expect of him. She looked at him and frowned.

For a second or two, he was unsettled by her obvious irritation, but he was committed now.

'Rebecca. I got it wrong in Coimbra and I'm so sorry. Ever since, I've been annoyed about it and I should have mentioned it before. I should have told you when you came for the harvest. I don't know what's wrong with me. I can't stop thinking about you. I know we've hardly spent any time together and I can't explain it, but I miss you so much.'

Rebecca was stunned. Everything she had told herself, all the times that she had denied her feelings for João to herself and to friends, all of that drained away in a flood of emotion and her guard melted away. 'I've missed you too and I'm not sure how that can be because, as you say, we hardly know each other, but somehow I feel like I've always known you.'

'I feel that too. I wish I wasn't so far away.'

João turned towards her and kissed her gently on the forehead. She recognised the gesture of respect and affection, feeling its strength more than any other gesture could have suggested. He put his arm around her and drew her in close beside him and for a while they sat close to each other, saying nothing, simply feeling the warmth of their bodies next to each other and watching the glow of the evening sun across the river.

Rebecca could have stayed there for ever, bathed in sunshine and contentment. It was João who drew away. He didn't speak. He got up and held out his hand towards her and they began to walk back along the riverside hand in hand. It was significant, she knew. He would not have made such a public display of his affection lightly. Rebecca felt as if she were holding her breath. She didn't want to spoil the moment. She felt only his hand holding hers. They had reached the row of small taverns and cafés looking out across the river to Spain beyond before João spoke again.

'Shall we get back? It was probably fairly obvious earlier that I haven't spoken much at home. Things haven't been straightforward with me and the family for a while and I've got used to keeping my feelings to myself.' He kept hold tightly of her hand as they crossed the road and walked back across the square. Some of the townsfolk had come out to sit on the benches under the orange trees, as they often did in the evenings when the weather allowed. The trees were in full blossom. A sweet smell hung in the air. There was a group of men in one corner sitting around a table playing a game together. Small groups of men and women were chatting, catching up with the day, and a group of small children were playing around the obelisk in the centre of the square. There were people there who Rebecca knew by sight and she saw them notice her, aware that her affection was public. She felt safe with João.

The room was busy, noisy and animated. Live music was playing. Rebecca recognised the folk song which some of the guests were dancing to. Others were singing along, joining in with the song, sure of every word. The rest were still sitting at their tables, deep in conversation. Rebecca noticed that João's brother and his wife were at their table, the baby asleep despite the noise. João led Rebecca over to join them again. However, not one of the family missed their entrance or the fact that João was hand in hand with Rebecca.

João's mother managed to draw his father away from a conversation. 'Have you seen João? I don't understand why he hasn't spoken to us about this girl. He's clearly besotted. I've never seen him like this and certainly not with Ana Rita, even though they were such good friends. I knew that relationship wasn't right and perhaps he never would have gone away. I think Rebecca may be the one and I have to say, I really like her.'

João's father was feeling relaxed. 'They say that life has a funny way of working itself out. At least she seems taken with Portugal. She might be very good for him. João will talk to us when he's ready. You know what he's like, he keeps everything very close. He'll tell us soon enough, but I think it's fairly obvious what he's saying to us today.'

The evening was drawing to a close and guests beginning to leave. Rebecca went over to see Rui and Júlia who had noticed that João and Rebecca were together and were delighted. She then went over to thank Júlia's parents. Júlia's mother was particularly pleased that her plan of sitting Rebecca at the same table had worked out.

'Perhaps it will be you next, Rebecca,' she said. Not expecting the comment, Rebecca didn't know what to answer. She laughed nervously.

Whilst Rebecca was away, Pedro took the opportunity to quiz his brother.

'You kept Rebecca fairly quiet. Mother is beside herself that she didn't know, as she can see how you feel. Was it wise not to tell her? You know how much she worries.'

'I didn't really know until I saw her again how things would work out. I only knew what I felt about her. There was no point saying anything.'

'Are you moving to Vila Real then now?' Pedro teased him.

'I haven't thought it through, but no. I've committed to the business this year and that's what I must do. I haven't spoken to Rebecca about it, I've only told her what I feel and all I know is, that if I can help it, I'm not going to let her go.' And he added, 'She seems to be ready to leave, I'm going to walk her home. I'll have a quick word with Rui and Júlia before

I leave. I might be a while. I need to talk to Rebecca and with everything that mother has planned for this weekend, I'm not sure I can see much of her tomorrow. Will you cover for me, Pedro?'

'Of course, it won't be the first time.' João went over to speak with Rui and Júlia and Rebecca joined them again before they made a quiet exit.

When they got outside, João asked, 'It is alright if I walk you home, isn't it?' He didn't want to be presumptuous, even though it had been his intention.

'Of course, but it's safe enough and not very far, so if you need to stay, I'm fine.'

'No, I'm not sure what I'll be doing tomorrow and I don't want to go back without having had a chance to talk to you.'

Rebecca was feeling quite tired now and wasn't particularly happy to hear that although he would be in the town, he wasn't sure he would be able to see her tomorrow. She fought back her usual reaction to such disappointment and reminded herself that she was determined to think differently. It had been a lovely day, her time with João so unexpected and she wasn't going to spoil it by wanting more. The family was here together. Negative thoughts got in the way.

The street was in darkness and there was no one in sight which made it easier to invite João inside. It was beginning to feel a little cool and she was too tired for a conversation in the street or even to sit on the bench in the little square nearby. She opened the door and he followed her in.

'This is a lovely little house, Rebecca,' he said looking around, 'and you've made it feel very homely.'

'I love living here,' she said, as she began to make a drink for them both in the kitchen. João wondered if there was a message in her statement for him. She was settled there.

Rebecca led him back into the little front room and sat down on the sofa. João sat down beside her and now in the privacy of her little house, couldn't resist taking her in his arms and kissing her. Rebecca didn't resist. Many people go a lifetime without experiencing a deep, genuine love for another person. Many fool themselves into thinking that they have found that love when they haven't. As soon as she kissed him, she was lost in a feeling like no other which was so strong that she was almost overcome. They looked at each other and without speaking, Rebecca knew he felt it too.

'It's mad, Rebecca, we live miles apart, but I so much want to be with you.'

He wrapped his arms around her and they held each other until both of them fell asleep. Rebecca didn't know how long they had been asleep, but she was the first to wake. Feeling her move, he woke too. Neither of them moved out of their embrace. Rebecca waited for João to speak.

'I meant what I said, Rebecca. I want to be with you. I haven't wanted anything else as much in my whole life or been so sure. It's only that, after committing to a year at home, I feel I must see it through. I know it's no easier than if I were in England. It's so far. What do you think?'

Rebecca didn't know what to think and that was all she could say. 'You need to get back before you're missed, João. As much as we might know what we've been doing, it's not going to do my reputation much good if you're seen leaving in the morning. I don't think my neighbours quite understand me as it is. They don't really get the independent woman on her own here.'

'OK, I'll get back. My mother has the whole day planned tomorrow and I'm expected to be there.'

'I understand,' Rebecca said, 'You go ahead with your day.' She didn't really understand. She was trying to understand, to think differently.

'No, I'll be back to see you after breakfast, if that's alright with you.' João gave her a big hug, kissed her again and then left to go back to the hotel.

When João got back, it seemed that only the night receptionist was awake, but as he saw João come in, he told him that his brother was still in the bar and had asked him to mention that he was there.

'What are you doing still up?' João had asked him to cover for him. He didn't expect him to wait up.

'Little João Pedro woke up and wouldn't settle, so I let Céu get to bed and then I went a walk along the river side until he was asleep. He's asleep now, I'm trying not to disturb him.' Sure enough, he was in his pram fast asleep.

'How did it go?' Pedro was curious.

'I couldn't really say. She didn't say much, but I am sure that she feels as strongly as I do.'

'What do you know about her, about her family, her background?'

'You sound like mother now.' João was surprised at his younger brother and felt defensive. 'Hardly anything actually, but it doesn't matter to me.'

'I'm only anticipating your conversation with mother over breakfast later. If you're happy, João, you're right, what does it matter? She's charming and she's clearly very well educated. Mother couldn't help liking her, although she was a bit surprised. No one will ever be good enough for you, you know that. The bit I'm struggling with and I'm sure it's the same for both mother and father, is why you didn't mention it before. You're so unpredictable and when it seemed to them that you were settling down a bit, you hit them with a mysterious English woman. We have many connections with Britain, you know that, but it's another reason for you to leave again.'

'Rebecca loves Portugal. She's not drawing me away. It was Rebecca who made me think differently again. I think she brought me back.' João then told his brother all about how they had met, his time in Vila Real and in Coimbra. He admitted that his attraction had been immediate. The need to see her and to be with her had worn away at him, even as he had left the train in Paris, and his feelings for her strengthened more and more each time he saw her. He had spoken with his aunt and she had suggested that he write to Rebecca.

Pedro listened carefully and when he had finished he said, 'Wow, you've convinced me. I've never heard you talk about anyone else like that. Go and tell mother what you've told me. I'm sure it will make it all a lot easier, but speak to her before breakfast, so we can all get on with the day without any more histrionics. I suggest you leave out the bit about Aunt Emília knowing and giving you the advice to write. There's always a bit of jealousy where mother is concerned with Aunt Emília, but only because you've always told her things.'

'I never want to worry my mother, which is ironic, because I always seem to cause her great concern. You're right, though. What time did everyone say they were having breakfast? I'll go and speak with both of them before we eat. It's not a conversation to have in the restaurant.'

João Pedro was still sleeping soundly when they went up to their rooms. João thanked his brother for his good advice and for staying up to speak to him, as he knew his nephew was only an excuse. He didn't sleep much at all. He was anxious both about how Rebecca might be feeling, having had time to take in everything he had said to her and also, how his mother would react. He was annoyed for suggesting to Rebecca that his family might have to be a priority. Why had he said that? He had been thinking aloud. There was no way that he would spend the day there without Rebecca.

# XXXI

Before breakfast, João went to his parents' room and was met by his mother looking a little perplexed. He ignored the expression, asked them to sit down, as he needed to speak with them. Taking Pedro's advice, he simply repeated what he had said the night before. As his brother had anticipated, the part about Rebecca and Portugal and the influence she had on him pleased his mother. She didn't need to be convinced, as she had heard Rebecca speaking the day before and knew her enthusiasm was quite genuine. It wasn't long though before she was back on track, pointing out how little João actually knew about Rebecca. His father intervened, gently closing down the conversation and nudged them in the direction of the dining room for breakfast.

Rebecca didn't sleep much either. She was too excited and wanted to be ready when João called, so after a few hours tossing and turning, she decided to get up and went to sit on the terrace and take in the cool morning sunshine. When there was a knock on the door not long after 9 o'clock, she dashed downstairs to answer it.

'Oh, Maria Eduarda, it's you.'

'I take it I'm not the person you were expecting,' Maria Eduarda said, as she saw Rebecca's expression change. 'We were on our way to Mass. Ricardo has taken the boys to the café on the square and I wondered if you wanted to join us for breakfast, but now I see you're expecting someone, I'm even more curious than I was before to hear about yesterday, so come on, let's catch up over breakfast. Ricardo can look after the boys and we can have a chat.'

'I'm expecting João, who I think is going to be busy with the family today. He said he would call after breakfast. I'm hoping we can spend some time together before he goes back.'

'First of all, I'm pleased that it seems I could have been proved right about João, but you are talking about the João who was so attentive in Coimbra and then walked off without hardly a word, are you? And what is this about having to spend time with the family? I do get family expectations, but does he want to see you or not? Also, did he give you a time this morning? He could call any time. You can't hang around on the possibility that he'll call in the next hour or so. There's time for a coffee and some of that toast that you love so much.'

Rebecca was a little bit stunned, 'You were the one who was encouraging me.'

'Encouragement is one thing, letting you get hurt is another. He's Portuguese, you may have to adjust some of your compromising ways.'

Rebecca knew she was right, but still protested. 'I don't want to miss him this morning if it's the only opportunity to see him.'

'It had better not be the only chance. That really wouldn't do. Look, I assume they're staying at the Hotel Guadiana. Write a quick note saying where you'll be and we'll drop it off in reception on our way. I don't think it will do any harm to show him that you're not waiting in for him and that you have a life and friends here. Come on.'

Rebecca quickly wrote the note and they took a short detour on their way to the square. Maria Eduarda spoke with the receptionist who assured her that João would get the note. So by the time he turned up at the café about half an hour later, Maria Eduarda had managed to hear about Rebecca's day and was giving her some very sensible advice.

'Portuguese men are not like British men. I'm sure that's a good thing in many ways, but you need to know how to handle them. I do hope he's changed his mind about today. If not, you need to be as cool with him as you can when he arrives.'

'If he arrives,' Rebecca said, now feeling very nervous about the whole situation.

'I don't know him, but I think you'll find he's walking across the square towards us now,' Maria Eduarda observed and Rebecca looked up to see João striding quickly in their direction, with a huge smile on his face.

'*Very* nice, Rebecca. I approve so far,' Maria Eduarda joked with Rebecca before João was close enough to hear. She was trying to lift her out of her tense mood. Rebecca couldn't help smiling.

Rebecca introduced João, first to Maria Eduarda, who called over to Ricardo and the boys. They pulled up some chairs and sat down. João ordered another coffee and asked the others if they would join him. Rebecca asked for another galão, her favourite milky coffee. Anything else was too strong, but the others declined. The church bells were now ringing for Mass and Maria Eduarda gathered the family together to walk over to the church. They said their good-byes and Maria Eduarda turned to Rebecca as she was walking away and said, 'I'll be at Mass, then.' Which Rebecca knew to be shorthand for, you know where I am if you need me. 'See you soon.'

'Are you doing something with Maria Eduarda and the family today?' João hoped not, but was wondering, seeing them together.

'I've nothing definite planned. They're great friends and I often spend time with them, so there's an open invitation most of the time. They've been really good to me. They're the reason I've settled in so easily.' She hadn't any plans and as always, had to be honest, but she wanted to give the impression that as he had said he was busy, she had other options too.

'I'd like to spend the day with you, Rebecca. What do you think?'

'I thought you said you had to be with the family today.' Rebecca hadn't been impressed and despite all her best intentions to be different, couldn't let it go unmentioned.

'I need to stop voicing my thoughts. It only confuses others. The family has all been invited over to Rui's parents. It's a kind of post wedding event, but also it's such a long time since their last visit. It's an opportunity to spend time with them and do a bit of reminiscing. My father has said I can have the car. I agreed that we would be back to have dinner with everyone. I hope that's alright with you. Have you ever travelled up the river?'

316

Rebecca had braced herself for a short conversation about the day before and to feel annoyed with him, so his suggestion was unexpected. She wasn't quite taking it all in, but responded to his question. 'No, I've been meaning to, but haven't had the opportunity.'

'Great, it's decided then. You go and get whatever you need from the house for a day out. I'll go and get the car and pick you up outside your house in fifteen minutes. Does that give you enough time?'

'Yes, I'm sure.' They finished their coffees and headed off to get ready.

Rebecca dashed back to the house, not wanting to waste a minute. She still wasn't sure of him. Against her new found philosophy of enjoying life for what it was without overthinking it, she slipped back into wondering if even now, he might change his mind, but sure enough, there he was less than fifteen minutes later, waiting in the car outside her house.

'Of all the rivers in Portugal, the Douro is the greatest in my opinion, but I love the Guadiana too, so today you can sit back and play the tourist with your own private tour guide,' João said, as he turned the key in the ignition.

'I suppose you're bound to be biased, as you're from the Douro. There are a few people in Lisbon who might disagree with you,' Rebecca teased him, but on this one, he was really serious.

João drove out of Vila Real towards Castro Marim, past the salinas, the salt plains and the stretch of flat marsh land where the people of the town had produced salt for centuries. As the castle and fort came into view, João started his commentary. 'This is a really important area for wildlife as well as for salt. There are a huge number of different birds here. When we were little, my father used to drive us up into this area to see the flamingos. I hear that they are talking about designating it as a nature reserve, so it can be protected into the future, which would be really good.'

It wasn't the day that Rebecca had expected at all, but now that she was on her way, she relaxed into the passenger seat. She reminded herself that she needed to enjoy the day for what it was without any expectations. It wasn't long before João took a detour, driving towards a little place called Beliche and explaining that he wanted to show her the view across the Barragem de Beliche, a large area of dammed water along one of the tributaries of the Guadiana. Rebecca was struck by the contrast. They had quickly left behind the flat lands of the coastline, and deep amongst the rolling hills there was an expanse of aqua blue water. Rebecca was pleased she had remembered to bring her camera and plenty of film along with her. She would make a picture record of the day. João came over to her as she was lining up her picture in the view finder, trying to find the very best aspect to capture the scene. He was interested. She explained to him how she was trying to frame her picture. He had a look too and approved, standing behind her as she took the photograph. He put his arms around her, drawing her in close to him, as they both stood quietly admiring the view. Rebecca was taken back to Coimbra. This was how he had held her when he had wanted to show her the view over the city that night. She had missed this so much. A cool breeze began to blow gently across the hills. Rebecca shivered, a natural prompt for them to go back to the car. João explained that he was heading first for Alcoutim. He wanted to follow the river as much as possible, so would head towards a little place right on the river bank where they could have their first view of the river upstream. It was a pretty little hamlet of houses amongst fields and orange groves, right by the river bank, exactly as João had described. They stayed long enough for Rebecca to take another photograph and then drove on keeping the river close by along a fairly rough and winding road to Alcoutim. Rebecca didn't need to talk. She was happy simply to contemplate the beautiful countryside, fascinated by the closeness of Spain on the opposite bank, little houses nestled amongst the hills. The wild flowers were in full bloom, scattering the hills in a myriad of colours. João parked a little distance outside the town centre, leaving the car sheltered from the sunshine and took Rebecca's hand as they walked across a bridge and into the town. He was talking non-stop, telling her about how important this little place had been centuries ago, giving her a history lesson about King Fernando I and explaining that by the seventeenth century this little place was made infamous by smugglers. He wanted Rebecca to see the view from the town across the river. From there, they climbed up to the ruined castle to get the most spectacular view of Alcoutim and its Spanish twin, Sanlúcar de Guadiana sitting on the opposite bank. It was sheltered on all other sides by a high range of hills rising steeply from the river and was dominated by its own hill fort. Spain seemed now so close to Portugal, almost as though Rebecca could reach out and touch it, the river much narrower.

'I thought we'd go a little further for lunch,' João said, as he watched Rebecca taking more photographs from the high point of the castle. 'How do you fancy lunch in the Alentejo?'

Travelling to a different region for lunch appealed to her and it was somewhere else Rebecca had never been. She was loving her day, so happy to be with João. He was delighted with her enthusiasm and her fascination with everything he was showing her. They walked back to the car and took the narrow road north which quickly began to wind away from the river.

'Where are we going then for lunch?' Rebecca was beginning to feel hungry now, the buttered toast and coffee seeming a long time ago. She could feel her stomach grumbling.

'Mértola. It's another riverside town, as stunning as Alcoutim, if not more so and as steeped in history, though, like Alcoutim, you wouldn't know now how important it had been. It was a river port for centuries. I think it goes back to the time of the Phoenicians and certainly was really important to the Romans and the Moors. The church used to be a mosque, but at some point, it was taken over by the Christians. It looks the same as it did when it was a mosque. It's impressive. There's another castle that we can have a look at too.'

'And what about the cafés?' Rebecca, even though she was as interested as ever, was now less focussed on history and more on food. 'There's more to a country's culture than spectacular scenery and impressive ancient buildings,' she joked with him.

'You don't have to tell me that, I'm Portuguese, and I'm beginning to think that you must have been in a past life.'

'I'm sure, although I can't decide whether I was Philippa of Lancaster and came here from England or Catherine of Braganza and introduced afternoon tea to England. What do you think?'

João was impressed, but not surprised with her knowledge of Portuguese history. He followed her line of thought. 'I'm not sure, but I'd like to think that your past life was much closer to mine, so perhaps you were the daughter of one of the great port dynasties.'

He spoke so little about the family business that she was surprised at the reference. This time, when they arrived, they parked in the centre of the town and instead of more sightseeing, they headed straight to a modest little restaurant on the Avenida Aureliano Mira Fernandes. João suggested that as they were now in the Alentejo, Rebecca should try something which was a speciality from that region and admitting that she knew very little, she let him choose for her. He ordered a soup to begin, 'Sopa Alentejana', made with bread and laced with garlic, olive oil and coriander, Rebecca's favourite herb, and topped with a poached egg. It was a little oily for Rebecca's taste, but she didn't want to disappoint, so she ate it all. She was pleased that she had asked for a half portion of the main course, Borrego Ensopado, a lamb stew. It came with more bread to mop up the delicious gravy and when she had finished, she couldn't manage dessert. They took their time over lunch and then wandered slowly uphill to have a look at the church and the castle beyond and the views high over the River Guadiana before heading back again to the car.

As they were about to get into the car, João paused, 'I've been meaning to ask you about Carol.' He knew some of the story from Rebecca's letters. 'Have you heard how she has been since she went back?'

'She hasn't heard at all from Tó Zé, as far as I know. I still don't think she has any idea where he is, other than that he's probably in Lisbon. She's given up looking for him. People here have tried to explain his actions, even excuse them. It doesn't seem to be a surprise to some I talk to. So many others have chosen to live abroad, escaping persecution, looking for a better life. I understand the context, but I can't see what he did to Carol as anything other than wrong. It was deceitful, cruel. He abandoned her. To think he was married with a child all that time.' Rebecca felt angry every time she thought about him and she hadn't forgotten that João had left someone too.

'Did she ever know that for certain?' João asked. 'People's lives can get complicated. He may never have intended to hurt her.' He too was thinking about his own actions and not feeling great. Rebecca had strong views.

'Tom said the evidence was fairly compelling and whilst both of them thought about confronting Tó Zé and exposing him to his family, Carol couldn't do anything that might hurt the child. She knew the family would probably see things very differently and be pleased to have him back.'

'He's probably in Lisbon, as you say. I can't see him staying in the village, not someone with his political ambitions. Did Carol go back to Paris?'

'No. Tom said he had to deal with the apartment. She was so distressed, when she left Paris for Portugal. Tó Zé had lied from the beginning and she had no idea. It was devastating. When I saw it, the apartment looked lived in at first glance, but Carol had removed everything of his. She cleared the place out and turned all the pictures to the wall. It troubled me seeing the apartment like that, but then, I could relate to it. I suppose the pictures were about their life together. Before she left, she couldn't get rid of them, but she couldn't bear to look at them, either. She told Tom to destroy them. He couldn't do it, so much was Carol's own work and her photographs. She's given up her life in Paris. She went back home, terrible really, as she was beginning to get some recognition for her work as an artist over there. She's having to start again in every way. Last time Tom wrote, he said she had moved to Cornwall. His mother has a friend who has opened a gallery down there. Carol is working for the gallery and there's the space and time for her to do her own work. I hope it works out for her.'

'How is Tom? I thought you two were an item,' João confessed.

'Oh, I see. That makes sense. Once maybe I thought I would like that, a long time ago, but now we're good friends. Tom is Tom, I'm not sure he'll ever settle down.'

They got back into the car and at first retraced their route out of Mértola towards Alcoutim, after a short while turning onto narrow roads again. Rebecca had been completely lost in her day, forgetting all her earlier concerns, but as the hours wore on, with lunch behind them and now clearly heading south and back to Vila Real, she became aware of the time. She didn't want her day alone with João to end. They began to weave their way, climbing and descending through a high range of hills. Rebecca had only seen them before from a distance. Narrow twisting roads passed through woodland in lower areas and scrubland as the route took them higher, roads which made Rebecca feel a little nervous. She trusted João's driving, but she would have preferred to have been driving. She remembered that João had invited her for dinner with the family. Now she was pleased that, at least, her day wouldn't end when they got back to Vila Real, but it wouldn't be the same amongst all of the family. João, as he had promised, had been the perfect tour guide. He had introduced her to a beautiful part of Portugal, right on her doorstep, which she had heard about, but had never been able to visit. Last night, he had said that he needed to talk to her. Today, it didn't seem to be crossing his mind. She wondered if that was significant. The road straightened out as they reached a high point and João turned the car off the road, bringing it to a halt and switching off the engine.

'Come on. One more view,' he said, as he got out of the car, taking a blanket from the back seat and waiting for Rebecca to join him. Taking her by the hand, he walked a few yards further on. 'There,' he said.

The view was even more spectacular because Rebecca hadn't expected it. She had often looked towards this high range of hills as she travelled along the road close to the coast, but she had never imagined the view back to the coast. The mountains plunged down to the sea and Rebecca could see the vast expanse of ocean below, the deepest bright blue, edged by a line of golden sand. Single houses and small settlements dotted their way down the hillside and Rebecca could see a much larger settlement beyond.

'That's Tavira,' João explained. Rebecca hadn't realised that they had travelled so far west on their way back from Mértola. 'We'll join the main road back to Vila Real just outside Tavira.'

'It's beautiful,' Rebecca said. 'An amazing view. I could stay here for ever.'

'Let's stay a while,' João suggested, as he spread the car blanket on the ground in a spot where they could continue to admire the view. João sat down and waited. Rebecca spent a while taking photographs, moving around to try to get the best position. The view was so expansive that any photograph she took could only be a reminder, the lens quite inadequate for the scene. She explained as much to João as she was taking the photographs.

He watched her for a while and then said, 'Come and sit down.' Rebecca sat down by his side and he put his arm around her, kissing her on her cheek, as they continued to look towards the sea. He moved her close into him and sat with her wrapped fully in his arms.

'This is my second favourite view in Portugal. The first is the one I can see from my family home.' He began to talk about home, the family business, their history, and the problems they faced. Rebecca felt happy to hear him talking with such affection after so long of seeming unsure.

'At times, the estate hasn't seemed as though it has had any relevance to me, Rebecca. It might sound a strange thing to say, but the only thing that has made any sense to me in the last few months is you. I've made a commitment to my family, though. It's a difficult time for the business. We don't know what's going to happen and how it will affect us. Some of our neighbours, Portuguese families who have owned and worked the land for many years, have felt forced to leave and have abandoned their properties. My father is determined not to give in. Every so often we hear rumours of take-overs and nationalisation. It would never be the same again. If we're not careful, we'll lose all the traditions, like the grape treading which you saw when you came last September. We've been lucky so far to keep our staff, but many people are emigrating. There's a shortage of labour already. I can't stand by and watch it all go. I need to take responsibility and help my father. I've spent enough time finding myself,' he said, trying to lift the mood, realising that he had become very serious.

Rebecca was concerned and tried to reassure him. 'You know I think it's wonderful to be part of such a long history. It is a huge responsibility, but one that many would envy. Your family must have overcome many difficulties to have survived this long. I'm sure you'll find a way through it.'

João had been so worried that he had lost Rebecca. Over the months he had been away from her, he had been concerned that she would find someone else. All he could think of was that he couldn't lose her now. The previous night, when he was unable to sleep, he had made a decision. He had thought it through carefully. This time he was not being impulsive. He would not make a mistake again. It was clear in his mind.

'Rebecca, I've something to ask you.' Rebecca couldn't imagine what it was.

'As soon as you can, I'd like you to come and visit the estate again. We didn't spend any time there together and there's so much I still want to show you.'

'I'd love to,' she said, feeling that she wanted to try and support him, understanding more, as she had listened, how difficult it had been for him.

He took her hand and kissed it. 'I have another question and if you can't answer it now – you might need some time to think about it – promise me you'll answer when you visit.'

Later, looking back, Rebecca wondered why she hadn't had any idea about what was in his mind. From the very first meeting, there had been an inexplicable connection, which she had fought unsuccessfully ever since that first day. In the last few months, through his letters, even though they hadn't been together, she had felt close to him. She didn't like long distance relationships any more than he did. The request which she might have anticipated that day was different, thinking he would ask her to move closer to him. His question was unexpected, but anyone who had known her would not have predicted her answer either. Still holding her hand, he looked straight into her eyes and held her gaze. 'Rebecca, will you marry me?'

Rebecca sat and looked at him for so long that he thought he had got it wrong. It was too much. She must think I'm mad. But Rebecca's time in Portugal had changed her. She was different. She understood better what she wanted. She knew what made her happy in a way she had never allowed herself to acknowledge before and was determined to be true to those feelings. She would no longer over think every decision. When he asked her the question, she knew straight away. There was no concern that it was too soon. Other people knew very quickly. Why shouldn't it happen to her? It was the strongest of feelings, far different from anything she had ever experienced. He was her soulmate. She knew it with a certainty that she had never had about anything else. These were the thoughts which rushed through her mind. After what seemed an almost unbearable amount of time, Rebecca replied.

'I don't need time to think. Yes, I'll marry you. You can have my answer now. I have something to ask, though. I would like to complete my year here in Vila Real and I want to work, and one day, I would still like to own a house here, exactly like the one I'm renting.'

The detail didn't matter to João. It wasn't long to wait. He smiled at her. He was so happy and for once in his life, he was sure of his decision, without any doubts or concerns.

'Trust you to issue me with conditions. It's no less than I deserve. Anything you want.'

Rebecca didn't know why, but her wide smile broke out into laughter and they rolled back onto the blanket, giggling as they held each other. Rebecca felt truly happy.

'Come on. Let's get back. We need to get ready for dinner. We need to tell the family,' João said.

'Are you sure?' Rebecca was surprised. She thought he would want some time to explain to his parents. She wasn't even sure that they would approve and she said that to him.

'I'm so happy, Rebecca. I wouldn't be able to contain it. No, as long as you're ok with it, I intend to tell them this evening.'

João dropped Rebecca off at her house and said that he would walk around to collect her in an hour's time. They were eating at the hotel, he thought. What João hadn't appreciated was that Rui's family was joining them for dinner. Pedro reminded him when he got back in. When João thought about it, he decided that it would make it easier. Rebecca got ready quickly. She needed to make a phone call and had to go out and get back before João returned. Her mother knew that Rebecca intended to stay but she was unsure for a few moments when she heard her news. She was not surprised, though. Rebecca's feelings had been much clearer to others than they had been to herself.

It was a great evening. João's father was in a good mood too, worries about the estate forgotten for a while. João waited until the port wine was being served before standing up and making his announcement. He turned to his mother. 'I'm staying, you'll be pleased to hear, but Rebecca will be with me.'

The tension he had anticipated wasn't there, only congratulations and celebration, his mother tearful and happy, hugging them both. His father shook his hand and smiled. No words were necessary.

Later, João accompanied Rebecca the short distance back to her house.

'How do you feel?' he asked as they arrived at the door. He wrapped his arms around her. 'Have you made the right decision? It won't be easy. I don't know how things will work out here. Nothing seems certain and as you know, if I stay here in Portugal, I may have to go away.'

'I know that, but somehow I think it will work out. This wonderful place must have finally made an optimist out of me,' she said with a smile.

'You will write to me,' he said, remembering another conversation under a similar starlit sky.

'Always.'

The country she had been drawn to lay in the far south west corner of Europe, a long, narrow stretch of land. It was tiny really, no more than three hundred and sixty miles in length and a hundred and forty miles wide. Surrounded on land by Spain, but not part of Spain, not one of its territories; its people disliked the inference. On two sides exposed to the Atlantic's wind and waves, a sea which for centuries had tempted its people to their own discoveries. The Portuguese left their homeland behind, understanding the true meaning of nostalgia. They lamented their absence with the poignant, expressive sadness of music and song. This feeling of longing, this deep emotion, Rebecca felt too, quite inexplicably. She had been drawn to the past and had found a place in the present where she belonged. She loved in a way others would doubt was possible. She had felt João's absence even before she knew him, their lives entwined long, long ago, an alliance of centuries. Yes, she had made the right decision. She knew that now.

# XXXII

**Janeiro de Cima, 22nd June, 1974**

For Tó Zé, an expert, some might argue, in walking away, the day that he had spent with Conceição and Nuno would be another day which would stay long in his thinking.

He remembered how his mother that morning had told him how pleased she was that he was making the effort, long overdue in her opinion. She was keen that the three of them had a good day. She wanted her family back together. Ever since he had mentioned it the night before, she had been making suggestions as to what he might do with Nuno on their day out by the river, telling him what Nuno liked to do, urging him to take care with what he said to him. It would all seem so new. She was up very early in the morning, baking and putting together a picnic for the day, making sure that it contained all of Nuno's favourite treats.

Tó Zé made the short walk to pick them up feeling nervous about spending time with Nuno and not knowing what to expect. Nuno had been a tiny baby when he left. He wouldn't know Tó Zé at all. He wasn't even sure if Conceição had spoken to Nuno about him. He was a stranger as far as that little boy was concerned. As he approached the house, he felt pleased with himself, at least in one respect. Conceição was fortunate in being able to have her own place. Others in her position lived with their parents. She had worked hard too for her and Nuno to live better, he understood, but this house was entirely down to Tó Zé. He had bought it. He had worked the extra hours, kept secrets, gradually paying off the loan his uncle had given him. It had been important to him that he had provided for them and little as it was, he sent them what he could.

They took their picnic down to the river bank and having found a sheltered spot, left everything they were carrying, placed safely under a tree. They carried on walking along the river bank. Conceição chatted with Tó Zé as they walked. She seemed relaxed enough, much of the tension of the evening before had gone. Nuno ran in front of them, inquisitive about everything around him, pointing out wild flowers, remembering the names his grandfather had taught him, collecting small white stones from the edge of the river bank. He really was a lovely little boy. His mother had been right, and bright, very bright. The people of the village had land and kept animals on both sides of the river and there was a boat moored close by. Conceição called over to one of the villagers who was working in the field and asked if they could borrow it. He smiled and nodded,

'I'll need it in an hour or so, though.'

Nuno was excited and ran to the bank. Tó Zé pulled the boat towards them and held it first for Nuno and then, Conceição to climb in. Once they were settled, he climbed in too and took the oars, rowing them further down river. As they travelled along, they appeared the perfect family. For a while, Tó Zé thought about little but the river and Nuno's delight as they glided along. Life in Paris and Lisbon seemed so distant.

Nuno was getting hungry, so they turned around, Tó Zé finding the rowing a little harder as he worked against the flow of the river. As a child, he had spent many happy hours fishing and had brought his old fishing tackle with him.

'We can see what we can catch when we've had our picnic,' he suggested. Nuno looked at him, said nothing, but smiled.

Tó Zé's mother had made a lovely picnic. They were all hungry by the time they handed the boat back to the waiting villager, so they ate straight away and as Conceição tidied up, Tó Zé and Nuno went down to the riverside and Tó Zé prepared a rod for Nuno.

Nuno sat quietly for a few minutes and then when no fish had appeared to bite at the bait, he handed the rod back to Tó Zé and seeing two of the older boys from the village coming down towards the river, he ran over to play with them.

Tó Zé went back to sit with Conceição. The sun was now at its full height and she had moved into the shade of the tree and was sitting quietly.

'I need to talk to you.' she said, as Tó Zé sat down beside her. He felt defensive, wondering what she was going to say and knowing that he would need to tell her that he was going back to Lisbon.

'I can't stay long,' he said, 'but I'll only be in Lisbon and once things have settled down, we can work out what we're going to do now I'm back and I can start to get to know Nuno properly.'

'No, Tó Zé. Enough of all this. Listen to me,' Conceição said and there was a long pause before she added. 'I can't go on.'

'What do you mean?' Tó Zé asked, confused. She had waited here for him all these years. What was wrong now?

'I have something I have to tell you,' she said, staring across to where Nuno was playing. 'He isn't your child,' she said. 'I've always known, right from the beginning.'

Tó Zé was stunned, trying to think through and make sense of the words he had just heard.

'I don't understand. You said he was mine. There was no doubt. Why are you saying this now? Are you sure?' he asked.

'Certain,' she said.

'Whose child is he?' he asked beginning to feel angry, as he realised what it meant. She refused to tell him.

'So all of this time I've been sending money, buying this house, keeping both of you, it was nothing to do with me. I said I'd marry you, I came back to make it right. I left everything I had in Paris for you. Why, Conceição?'

'Quiet, Tó Zé, please don't let Nuno see you angry. It's not his fault and I don't want him hurt.' She urged him to stay calm. 'Life was hard here. You got away, started again. You had a good life in Paris, you could afford the money and I was angry with you. You had never really cared about me.'

That was the only explanation she had to give. She knew she had used him.

'Who else knows?' he asked, beginning to feel the weight of consequence bearing down on him.

'Only Nuno's father,' she said.

That evening, Conceição walked to the little café in the middle of the village. It was dark now and though it wasn't too cold, on that late spring evening of 1974, Tino had lit a small fire in the little fireplace. There was no one else there. Conceição smiled at Tino as she entered. 'I've told him,' she said. 'It's over now.'